GIVEN
TO THE
EARTH

GIVEN
TO THE
EARTH

MINDY MCGINNIS

G. P. Putnam's Sons

G. P. PUTNAM'S SONS
an imprint of Penguin Random House LLC
375 Hudson Street
New York, NY 10014

Copyright © 2018 by Mindy McGinnis.

Library of Congress Cataloging-in-Publication Data
Names: McGinnis, Mindy, author.
Title: Given to the earth / Mindy McGinnis.
Description: New York, NY : G. P. Putnam's Sons, [2018] | Sequel to: Given to the sea.
Summary: While Khosa, whose marriage to King Vincent precludes her being sacrificed to
the sea, struggles with her longing for Donil and for the rising water, Donil's twin, Dara,
pursues vengeance against the leader of the Pietra, who destroyed the twins' people, the Indiri.
Identifiers: LCCN 2017013759 (print) | LCCN 2017043759 (ebook)
ISBN 9780399544668 (ebook) | ISBN 9780399544644 (hardcover)
Subjects: | CYAC: Fantasy. | Revenge—Fiction.
Love—Fiction. | Ocean—Fiction. | Islands—Fiction.
Classification: LCC PZ7.M4784747 (ebook)
LCC PZ7.M4784747 Gi 2018 (print) | DDC [Fic]—dc23
LC record available at https://lccn.loc.gov/2017013759

Printed in the United States of America.
ISBN 9780399544644
1 3 5 7 9 10 8 6 4 2

Text set in Granjon LT Std.

For R. C. Lewis—Reader. Writer. Friend.

CHAPTER 1

Dara

IT IS IN MY BLOOD.

It is in my bone.

It is in my being.

Before my mother became earth, she told us our names, her final thought becoming our first as my twin brother and I crawled from the pit that held our slaughtered people, our infant feet now the last on this land to carry the Indiri marks.

"Dara." I say my name now, our word for "vengeance." To the side, a tree shrinks from me. It knows my tongue, as do all things of the land. And like all things of late, it wishes me gone.

"Donil." I say my brother's name, the word for "family love." Our mother knew us well, though she would never see our faces. No matter their meaning, my words are heard only by wild things and my horse, an animal that none in the Stillean stables could lay a hand on without losing a finger.

"Famoor." One ear turns back to acknowledge that I have spoken, but otherwise the stallion ignores me, as is fitting for a proud animal named after the Indiri word for "unbroken." That I sit upon his back is a temporary arrangement, and I would that he remember it.

When I fall, I do not wish for him to return to Stille, to stables and harnesses, the civilized world shaving away his wildness until he thinks not of foraging but of the hand that will bring the next meal to his wooden box, where he is protected from the rain and the earth, sealed off from all that calls to him. It was my own mistake, years ago, and I will not have it played out by any other, be they two-legged or four.

I left that behind me when I passed from the castle's shadow, my former home. Stille will not welcome me again, not after I led the king's beloved to her near death, a foolish choice, twice over. For both Vincent and my brother care for the Given, and she had called them to her as easily as the sea drew Khosa herself.

I would see her crowned with seagrass, but now she sits enthroned beside Vincent, the boy whose heart I cannot have.

The forest moves around me, the dying rays of the sun touching briefly on my speckled skin. I cannot look at my own flesh without marveling that I carry it, a dressing on my bones that only one other wears. As falling rain sinks through the earth to feed salium and igthorn alike, my spots have burrowed within, giving life to what is both beautiful and poisonous at my core.

I am one of the last Indiri, the violent half of the whole, the prideful carrier of deep wrath, which wants only to bury itself in the Lithos of the Pietra, even if it be my last act. The love I carry for my departed people is a song made with war drums, the name my mother gave me inked deeply on my being. I close my eyes against the bright flash of fiverberries, the sun warm on my eyelids as Famoor goes on without my guidance.

The Given would laugh to see me here, at this place I recalled for her from my third-great-grandmother's memories. The ancient tree the Tangata cats use to sharpen their deadly claws stands as she saw it then, though larger now and marked with the use of many in their clowder, cats long dead.

I swear as I dismount, though I had expected to find as much. Many things can be said of the Given, but not that she is dim. Together we worked in the place she felt most comfortable and I entombed, stone walls rising to our sides and smaller walls, bound in paper, stacked beside us. That I am here now, reminded of the Given even as I banish myself from Stille in order to forget her—and how others felt for her—is both a prick to my conscience and a chink in my armor.

In her maps and books Khosa saw many things, as Donil does in the track of an animal, three days spent. These small moments she deciphered, trapped in time like a paw print in dried mud. There she saw the doom of our island, a rising sea that would never stop, the memories of the Indiri people helping to point the way.

I rest my head against the tree, and it tells me stories of cats digging deep, fibers carried away in claws, a small death each day, a dismemberment spanning lifetimes. If I were stronger, I could ask for more, push for the tree to give me the tale of Onwena, my ancestor, and how she fell in love at this place. In her time the sea was far from here; in mine I can hear it striking the beach, and carrying away the earth as it leaves.

But I am weak, and maybe the surf itself is to blame, earth taken and made infertile by salt. The tree could perhaps not part with the story, either, its lifesap leaving with the effort of telling. Underneath my hand, it shivers, and I see the tail of a Tangata above the waterleaf rue, a confident curl bending its stripes as it comes to tear bark from branch, skin from bone.

I nock an arrow and send it through the violet rue, drawing a harsh cry followed by silence. I follow where the arrow hit true and retrieve it, leaving the cat for the oderbirds. Famoor shies from me as I approach, the blood on my hands scenting the wind. I cannot blame him. I smell of death and the wild, violence and the wind.

"Famoor," I say, recalling his name and its meaning to him, so that he may stand with pride at my approach. Unbroken.

Again his ear turns to me, and I allow a smile for this one living thing that would have me near it. But my mouth is not accustomed to the shape, and the smile falls quickly as I mount, cat blood mixed with earth falling from my boot heels. I spare it a glance before spurring Famoor on, this mixture that I am bound to be a part of one day.

Blood and earth.

I'll have one, before I become the other.

CHAPTER 2

―◦◉◦―

Witt

My Lithos."

I close my eyes against Hadduk's voice saying Pravin's words, but force my mouth around the proper response.

"My Mason." I nod at him to continue, ignoring the salt that streaks down my throat as he updates me on the state of the Pietran army. My army. I taught myself to cry only inwardly at a young age, knowing my mother's deepest wish was to send me to the Cliffs of Alta, where I would train to become what I am now. The Lithos, leader of the Pietra, a man as hard as the Stone Shore he protects. Mother's wish was granted, and she knew no regrets when I put her in the boat and pushed her out to sea with no oars.

We have no need for more saltwater, and so I swallow mine, rather than let it leak from my eyes. Much and more laps at our heels, pulling away the very soil we stand on. Our rocks are crusted with its leavings, a briny reminder that time passes, and so shall we—sooner rather than later if we do not hold the entirety of this island for ourselves. Even from the cliffside where I view what remains of the once sprawling Pietran army, I imagine I can hear the tide, though we are safely inland.

"As for my own men," Hadduk concludes, "most were lost to the wave. Only a handful found the fires and returned."

I make a sound in my throat, one that he's prickly enough to interpret correctly.

"None would abandon, my Lithos," he says, dark eyebrows coming together at the inference, though his tone remains respectful. "They were trained by me and earned their armor."

"And drowned in it," I say, recalling the pull of the water at my own feet as I climbed a tree, the weight of Pravin's hand on my ankle swept away as it receded.

"That they did," Hadduk agrees. "And I'd rather have it be so than see them walking dry on the land and not in step with their commander."

"It is not in them," I concede, and know it to be true. Hadduk is a hard man, one of the soldiers who rode down the Indiri on the Dunkai plains, blood of children flinging from the tip of his sword. His men would either fear him or be like him. Either way, they would have found our campfires if they could, returning for the promise of more fighting, or to avoid his wrath. Either way, I do not care what urges their feet to return to their army, only that they come.

The army below us stands in rank and file, a mouth with more gaps than teeth. Some men are without armor or weapons, shields and swords torn from their grasp by watery fingers, their mail blown from their bodies to be dragged to the depths and then rust. Even this sight does not slow Hadduk, his eyes making quick work of the picture below.

"Fold Gahlah's men in with Fadden's. Spears are easily made, and both commanders taught them well."

"Though there is only one to lead them," I say, eyeing what's left of Gahlah's lancia, their commander no doubt swollen with the sea by now.

Hadduk only shrugs. "Fadden is the better man."

The better fighter perhaps, but I've seen Fadden's wife and children dappled with bruises, as if they stood beneath a Hadundun tree on a clear day, the shadows of the leaves marking where they would slice, should they fall. Yet to Hadduk he is still the better man.

And as Lithos I should be nodding in agreement, glad to have such a fine commander under my watch, not thinking of his wife and children at home, who would have found their lives much easier if the wave had taken him.

"Ula's spada barely stands," I say, continuing our assessment of the units.

"And swords take time to make," a voice behind me says. Hadduk and I turn to see that Ank has found his way up the cliff.

"Lithos." He nods to me, and I note that he has left off the traditional "my." The Feneen may fight beside us as part of our agreement to make them fully Pietran after Stille is defeated, but I am not their leader yet.

"Where's your pretty snake?" Hadduk asks, when he sees that Nilana is not riding in her harness on Ank's back. Though she is armless and legless, Nilana is as deadly as any of the Feneen, and many times more beautiful.

"Nilana minds our camp," Ank says, one sweep of his gaze assessing what remains of our army. "A somewhat bigger task than minding yours, I think."

Hadduk bristles, exactly as Ank intended. "I'll show her something big—"

"Enough," I say, raising my hand. Hadduk falls silent, but there is nothing I can do to wipe the smile from Ank's deceptively youthful face. Though his hands bristle with age, the caul he was born with kept him looking far younger than his actual years. Even without wrinkles, his eyes show a lifetime of wandering with the Feneen, morbid castoffs and unwanted members from other peoples.

"How many of your soldiers were born Pietran?" I ask Ank,

surprising him. His eyes go upward as he pretends to ponder, though I have no doubt the answer is easily summoned. The Stillean mother who abandoned him was foolish indeed to quail at the sight of his caul. Underneath it is the quickest mind I've seen.

"A full third," he answers. "Though they are all Pietran in the end."

Hadduk clears his throat and spits, and I know where his thoughts go. The terms of our agreement to bring the Feneen into our people as one were deftly made, Ank's offer of an entire army of blooded soldiers difficult to refuse. Pravin assured me that the most hideous of their kind—those with three heads or misplaced arms—would be bred out within a generation, Pietran blood only diluted, not overwhelmed, the Feneen rewarded with the acceptance denied them at birth. Yet now I have no doubt the Feneen stand three deep to a single Pietran, and any offspring that should come from our mingling would have more wildness in them than stone.

"In the end," I repeat, thinking of a moonlit beach and a wave that rose as high as the Lures' cliff on the Stone Shore. The Feneen were spared that sight, their attack on the front gates shielding them from the merciless sea. It was Pietra and Stillean who saw a watery death fast approaching, the strength of the depths come to crush them. And though the Feneen may be Pietran eventually, I've learned what no Lithos can know too well.

In the end, we all go to the depths.

CHAPTER 3

Khosa

"W OULD YOU HAVE THE CORAL OR THE SEAFOAM?" the girl asks, and Khosa closes her eyes against the color choices that mimic her greatest tormentor.

"Your decision," Khosa says, flipping her wrist in the dismissive way she's learned from watching Dissa, her husband's mother, a woman long acquainted with the vestiges of power.

The girl flushes with pleasure and hangs the seafoam dress back into place. The fabric falls around Khosa's ears, even the noises it makes mimicking the sounds of the tide. She grits her teeth as the girl fashions her hair, yet another style that calls to mind seashells cupping the sides of her face. Only two moons ago, the same people she now rules over would have rejoiced to see real shells against her skin, the soft, uncountable legs of sea-spines crawling upon her rotting flesh as her body tossed in the depths.

Yet she is no longer the Given, the wave that her sacrifice was supposed to prevent being not a punishment but a deliverance, as it tore the Pietran army from the sand like weeds from a wet garden. They went in her place, and now Khosa is the Redeemed, her husband the king, and all of the young girls vie for the chance to dress her in sea colors and fashion her hair after salt creatures.

"Enough," Khosa says, her voice unintentionally harsh as the girl's fingers brush against her temple. The girl pulls back as if bitten, and Khosa fights to find the appropriate smile to calm her, settling on one her own husband wears for her every night as he climbs into their bed.

"I would finish alone," Khosa says, finding the girl's eyes in the mirror.

"Do you not care for—"

"It is lovely," Khosa says, and manages to deliver the lie well. "I only wish to be alone."

"Yes, of course." The girl nods to her as she leaves, unable to conceal the disappointment as her time with the Redeemed queen is cut short. Another may not have spotted the small twitch at the corner of her eye, the slightest flicker deep in the girl's gaze, but Khosa has spent a lifetime learning to read others so that she may replicate their emotions later, her own face never naturally expressing the intricacies of emotion.

Khosa practices now, staring at her reflection in the mirror as she perfectly executes the girl's expression. Her Keepers taught her mimicry early, so that Stille would not know that the Given was not entirely whole. It was a charade meant to last only until she produced an heir, the next Given, and then all playacting could be abandoned, as the depths cared not how she reacted to death, only that she died.

The muscles in her face convulse as Khosa stares at her hair, obscenely twisted into seashells. Every part of her body remains at the mercy of the Stilleans, though now they curse her to live instead of drown. The game she was meant to play for a short while now grows long, her death as a young sacrifice now usurped by wishes of a long life for their queen. An heir is still demanded, but this one to live and to marry, produce another and another after that. How long until the

Feneen blood of her father comes to the surface? Until a wild thing emerges from her womb, tearing and spitting?

She rests her face in her hands, a heavy sigh drawing her chest tight against the lace framing it, fashioned in the shape of whitecaps. She need spend little worry on the quality of her descendants, as she cannot bring herself to make even one. Vincent is patient with her, climbing into their bed every night expecting nothing more than a quiet "good night" and her back facing him. It is not his demands that worry her, but those of Stille, and his mother.

"Stille needs a child," Dissa had said, handing her a vial of alium water, rumored to quicken the womb.

"Stille needs . . . Stille needs," Khosa says to herself, eyeing the vial that rests on her vanity. She'd choked back a retort to Dissa that a child would be short in coming if Donil were sent to Khosa's bed in place of her son, though the heir would surely bear speckled Indiri skin.

Heat rises in her even at the thought of him, a new experience for Khosa, who knew only irritation at another's touch until she brushed hands with Donil. She should have handed the alium water back to her husband's mother, asking instead for a flask of wine if she truly wanted a grandchild.

And that particular route had been attempted, at Khosa's own request. Vincent brought a bottle for each of them to their bed one evening, shamefaced with anticipation. It had ended not with their bodies twisted together under blankets, but with both of them retching over the nightbowl, emptying their bellies of a batch of bad wine.

Only Khosa was able to spot the smirk on the kitchen girl's face the next morning, buried under supposed concern for the queen's well-being. Donil had assured her that Daisy had no malevolence in her, that bad food finding its way to Khosa's plate was merely chance and not the result of him spurning his former lover. But Khosa is not the only girl who can interpret a glance, and Donil is not well trained in hiding his emotions. Every look he gives her burns.

Khosa raises her head to her reflection as the girl returns, knocking softly on the door before she enters.

"I'm sorry, milady," she says. "Your husband is waiting."

A smile twists as Khosa sets the Stillean crown on her head.

"You have no idea."

CHAPTER 4

Vincent

INCENT TAPS HIS FINGERS ON THE EDGE OF THE TABLE, the lacquered base of a massive tree whose edges roughly mirror the island kingdom.

My kingdom, he thinks to himself, not without bitterness. All his life he'd dreaded taking the throne and claiming the fate that had been determined for him the moment his older brother, Purcell, died. Peace and long Stillean lifelines had assured him a lengthy, but not unwelcome, wait. Now even that had been taken from him, and his ascension did not come with glory or shouts of joy from his people.

His failure to protect his grandfather from the Feneen in the field of battle brought him one step closer to his fate; his mother's rage and his own complicity in his father's murder sealed it. And when he walks the streets of his city, it is his wife's name the people call. Yet none of it rankles, for how can he demand respect when he knows himself to be a coward and a patricide?

He knows well why the Stilleans call for Khosa, shower her with dried alium petals, and bring her strings of sea pearls torn from dying mussels. She is their savior, not he. Even in his own mind, he has caught himself thinking of her as the Redeemed, a lie repeated so often it feels real. In one evening the Curator had sent stories throughout the people, half-truths that spoke of Khosa dancing on the beach to call the wave down on the Pietran army. She had danced, to be sure, but the wave came of its own volition, and Khosa would have never stood on the sand if not for Dara.

Dara. Vincent's hand curls into a fist as he thinks of her, whether to drive it into her face or clutch tightly to her and beg her not to leave him, he does not know. She had gone without a word, unable to watch him wed another—especially the Given, the girl she had led to the sea but failed to drown. No, Dara the prideful Indiri would never have stood by as he married Khosa the Redeemed, the wife he loves and cannot touch.

As if the thought of her were a summons, the door opens and Khosa enters, the spires of the crown preceding her as she tilts her head toward his mother. Dissa rises and dips into a small curtsy, an action that has never been required of her toward another woman. He can see resentment in the stiffness of her spine, the tightness of her mouth. And if he can see it, Khosa can too.

Yet she has never asked that his mother not pay her that respect.

"You are waiting for me?" Khosa asks, coming to him with one gloved hand outstretched. He takes it, squeezing her for a moment, which she allows before pulling away.

"Yes." Vincent nods to the table before them, the burnt etchings that mark the stony shores of the Pietra, the dead plains of Dunkai where the Indiri fell, and the sprawling Stillean lands. "The sea took many Pietra, but others will come. We must decide what action to take."

"Action?" Khosa's brow furrows as she looks at the table before her, her fingertips brushing the smooth surface. "And what do I know of battle, husband?"

"Of battle, not much," a new voice says. "But of the sea, you can speak leagues."

"Sallin." Dissa greets the Stillean military commander, who makes a quick bow to Vincent and Khosa.

"The sea," Vincent hears his wife mutter under her breath, those small words filled with more venom than an igthorn bush.

"And what is the sea, to a battle commander?" Vincent asks, raising his voice to cover his wife's tone.

"Our greatest enemy," Sallin says as he circles the table. "One that rises still and surrounds us on all sides—something I need not explain puts us at a distinct disadvantage."

"No, you need not explain," Vincent says. "Although I fail to see how we would fight an enemy that would rust our blades and flood our lungs."

"Then who do you propose we fight, young king? The Pietra?"

"Who else?" Vincent asks. "Who other than those that came to slaughter us?"

"And slaughter us they would have," Sallin says, running his finger along the edge of the table to the point on the beach where the wave had swept the Pietran army away like so many ants. "If not for the Redeemed—"

"Do you think so poorly of your own men that you lay the salvation of our kingdom entirely at my wife's feet?" Vincent interrupts.

Sallin pauses, weighing his words. "It is not courage they lack, but training. If Stillean swords had crossed with Pietran, I have no doubt the sand would have been as wet as if the wave had come, but with our blood spilled upon it."

"But you mean no disrespect, of course," Dissa says, laying a hand on her son's shoulder.

"Disrespect means little to a man bleeding out," Sallin says.

"And what battle would you have us fight against the sea?" Vincent challenges him. "With what weapons shall we stab it, and how are wounds made upon the tide?"

Sallin smiles and turns to Khosa.

"How better to fight the sea than with ships?"

CHAPTER 5

Donil

"THAN WITH SHIPS, HE SAYS . . ." I WATCH VINCENT TAKE another pull from his wine bottle, one that I made sure didn't pass through Daisy's hands, just in case.

"Ships?" I can't help the stirring in my belly at the very thought, as if I were at sea already, the sturdiness of dry land gone from beneath my feet. "Ships to take us where?"

"There is nowhere else," Vincent and I say at the same time, then drunkenly raise our bottles to each other.

"Truth." I nod. "Stillean, Pietra, Indiri, even Feneen. That is one thing we agree on."

"Which is why we all fight so boldly for what land there is to be had," Vincent says, his voice trailing off as his gaze becomes unfocused.

I don't tell him that the men of Stille had not fought so boldly when the Pietra took the beach. Some did, to be sure, but most did exactly as Dara and I had feared. Dropped their weapons or, worse, ran home with them in hand to protect their own families, instead of fighting where they stood. Discipline could not be taught within a few moonchanges, and Stille had enjoyed peace far longer than they had feared war.

"So this commander . . ." I prompt Vincent.

"Sallin," he provides, draining the last of his bottle and nearly missing his mouth in the process.

"Sallin proposes what? That you sail in hopes of finding something out there? Depths, Vincent, you wouldn't even know which way to sail."

"Or how to," my friend adds. "No, it's the most foolish thing I've ever heard. And yet . . ."

I raise an eyebrow, watching as Vincent rolls his empty bottle against the table, a hollow sound filling the silence while he searches for words. I try not to follow the curve of his fingers, or think of him going to his bed after this, to his wife. To Khosa.

I clear my throat. "And yet?"

His eyes refocus on mine, his thoughts back in the present, as I will mine to cling to this moment with my friend, and not how he passes nights with his wife.

"And yet is it so mad?" he finishes. "We know the seas rise. Even should we win every handsbreadth of land on this entire island, what do we gain? A generation to catch our breaths? And for what? So that our grandchildren fight, facing each other down with the tide touching both their heels?"

I shiver at the thought, imagining our whole world shrunk to a sliver of land where the blue edge of the sea can be seen from all sides.

"I don't know, Vin," I admit. "But there is nowhere else."

"Do you know this?" he asks, voice low. "Or do you only believe it?"

"I . . ."

"It's a strong demarcation, is it not?" Vincent's hands return to the bottle, this time to bring it to his wine-stained lips and blow a hollow note over its rim. "There were things I thought I knew, before . . . and now I've come to find I only believed them."

"Knowing is a strong thing," I tell him. "You're aware of what the Indiri call ourselves."

He nods, blows another note on his empty bottle. "Born knowing," he says. "Able to walk and talk at birth because your mother knew how."

"And fight," I add, thinking of Dara, my fierce twin.

"And love and hate, and all the other things we manage to do in our lifetimes."

"As well as those before us," I remind him. "We know everything our ancestors knew, back to the dirt in our mouths and tree roots in our eyes."

"But have you actually seen that?" Vin asks, the mouth of the bottle now pointing at me. "That's what I'm wondering. Have you followed your Indiri memories back to the beginning, to the rain that woke your people . . . or do you only believe it?"

I look past the mouth of the bottle, down the thin neck and the wider base to the eyes of my friend, a brother in so many ways, the husband of the girl I love, and now the king of Stille.

"Why do you ask these things over wine? We should be playing ridking, or watching Rook pissing on the helmets of the gate guards from the parapets."

Vincent drops the bottle to the table, where it spins aimlessly. "I ask because I've seen how the histories are written, brother," he says. "And I know that the hand that holds the quill sometimes has its own aims."

I glance around the kitchen to ensure our privacy, then drop my voice so low Vincent has to lean in to hear me.

"I know as well as you that Khosa is no more the Redeemed than you are a rankflower," I tell him. "That wave would have killed her, you, me, Dara, anyone standing on that beach. It was only chance that the Pietran army stood on the sands when it came, and Khosa no more called that wave than a baby lamb calls for a Tangata cat. But saying so can lead only to harm, and if the histories lie, then I say let them. They'll all float in the water soon enough."

"Unless we go elsewhere," Vincent says, holding up one hand to stop me from repeating that there is nowhere else. "The histories insist we stand on the only earth, but they also say I stood as tall as five sea-spines on my last Arrival Day."

"Are the bottom three crushed?" I ask, and he kicks my foot under the table.

"You take my meaning, whether you want to hear it or not," Vincent says. "The histories tell us many things, and I no longer know which are true and which I believe because that is what I have been told."

"And how do you weed out one from the other?"

My friend shakes his head, his fingers going to the indentations that the Stillean crown has formed at his temples. "I do not know, brother," he says. "I do not know."

CHAPTER 6

Khosa

T HE WEIGHT OF HER HUSBAND'S BODY HITTING THE OTHER side of the bed startles Khosa awake, and sends her hands gripping the covers and pulling them to her chin.

"Hush, it's only me," Vincent says, his breath thick with wine, no doubt the reason why he sprawled so casually on their shared bed. Sometimes in his sleep he moves as if he were still alone, and more than once he's called out Milda's name. Though the baker's daughter has long since been sent from his side and she herself is unwilling to fill the absent girl's duties, it rankles. In sleep, her husband's body acts as if she were not there, and his dreams are filled with another.

"Vincent?" She reaches for him carefully, every evening attempting to see how much contact she can bear. Tonight she manages to stroke his face, a quick swipe of the jawline before the sound of her skin brushing his sends clam chowder, burning with bile, back into her mouth.

He takes her fingers in his and presses them against her own pillow, giving her palm a chaste squeeze.

"I'm sorry I woke you," he says. "I had a drink too many with Donil."

"Or a bottle too many," she chides, aware of how slow his voice is, his movements clumsy.

"It's rather difficult being married to a woman so adept at reading others," he says, but his laugh is bitter rather than amused. She coils into herself further, managing a quiet "good night" and a halfhearted stroke of his hair before closing her eyes.

Yet she cannot sleep with such a heavy silence between them. It presses down upon her, a new disappointment she has brought to Stille after failing her Keepers in Hyllen so often. She is so aware of Vincent, even in the darkness, that she knows he does not sleep and that they both stare at the same spot of nothingness. And though he may tease her about the difficulties of being married to her, they are quite real.

"I'm sorry." His voice is a wine-soaked exhalation so quiet she is at first unsure which one of them spoke it.

"What have you to be sorry for?" she asks, moving her hand closer to him under the covers, enough for her to feel the heat radiating from his body.

"To come to bed drunk, to wake you from sleep with the crash of a body next to yours. You might have thought . . ." He lets his sentence fade out, not wanting to recall spilled milk and blood, the mildew stench of the dairy, and Cathon the Scribe's teeth scattered on the stone floor.

"He is long rotting," Khosa says, though she suppresses a shudder. "And Merryl guards our door. He'd let no one in who would do me harm."

"Some nights I doubt he'll let *me* in," Vincent says.

"I would never give such an order," Khosa says, a bit too sharply.

"I know that," her husband says, but they are quiet again, and she fears they both think the same thing: *Only because you don't have to.* No, all it takes to dissuade Vincent from touching her is his respect, her reluctance a wall between them.

She wishes she could reach for him and do what most wives find pleasurable, or bearable at the least. Every night she tries to take the wall down, stone by stone, one more breath of touch, a moment more of shared heat.

Khosa tries again, in the dark. With her eyes closed and her mind on another, she presses her palm against Vincent's bare back, her hand soft against the muscles between his shoulder blades, which flicker under her touch. They lie together silently, tense as Tangata about to pounce, each of them silently counting the other's pulse beats. She pulls away at last and wipes her hand discreetly.

Vincent rolls to face her, and her heart dips, the soft sheets around her suddenly as rough as Cathon's robes had been. Rotting or not, the Scribe still haunts her. But her husband is not that man.

"What did you think of Sallin's proposal?"

Khosa's heart slows, and she settles more deeply into the cocoon of the bed, pleased that her husband shares the running of the kingdom with her, even if its citizens so recently would have seen her drowned.

"Honestly?"

"Always."

"It is not unwise."

"A hearty endorsement," Vincent teases, and she hits him with a pillow.

"Truth now," he says, after tossing it back. "What are your thoughts?"

Khosa bites her lip in the darkness, searching for words. She wants to answer Vincent honestly, but must do so with care. The closeness of their bed this night may not be what her husband wishes for, but is more than they've shared in recent memory, their friendship weakening under the requirements of matrimony.

"You know that I still dance?" she asks quietly, her feet twitching even at the words.

"Yes, of course," he says. "Though I had hoped it might fade, in time."

"It may," Khosa agrees, but one ankle gives a sharp jerk in disagreement. Only she, the king, and Merryl know that the bars on their chamber window are not to ward off attackers, but to keep the Redeemed from the sea when her body demands it.

"You do not think it will?"

Khosa sighs, her fear sailing to the arched ceiling above them. Only another Given could understand the pull she feels—*or,* she thinks darkly, *one of the unfortunate sea creatures captured in a trapman's net, dragged to the shore to drown in air.*

"Is it . . ." Her husband's voice is hesitant again, another stone returned to the wall between them. "Is it like desire, then?"

"Somewhat," she says, rolling onto her own side to face him. "Like being near the one you want, but keeping yourself from them because you must."

"I can certainly understand that," Vincent says, his voice stiff and formal as when he addresses people in the great hall. "You speak as though you know how it feels to deny yourself."

"Yes," Khosa says slowly, dropping her eyes.

"You still feel for Donil?" he questions his wife.

"Yes," Khosa answers, raising her gaze to his without shame, for she harbors none.

Vincent sighs, closing his eyes against her. "Very well. Continue," he says.

"It is like that," she goes on. "I do not believe that I am Given to the Sea. It is life that calls me. I feel it for Donil, and I felt it too for Dara, in that moment when she led me to the water. She'd pulled life from a tree only moments before, killing it with her magic and bringing it into herself."

The silence from his side of the bed is heavy with anger now, toward her or Dara she doesn't know, but she plows on, the damaging words already out.

"Whatever is inside of me, husband, it's calling for life. Perhaps

I go not to the sea but to something beyond, to land not yet inked on maps. Our world is dying. Ank the Feneen said as much. Birds do not build nests, the Tangata do not make kits, the Indiri themselves are of the very earth and do not thrive. Where we stand fails. Why fight for soil that reeks of salt? Why not do as Sallin says and strike out for new earth?"

In her passion, she's clutched onto him, her hand linked in his, their knucklebones digging into one another. She attributes his silence to this, his bated breath held by her reckless words.

Until it is released in a long, wine-soaked snore.

CHAPTER 7

Dara

I'VE BEEN ALONE LONG ENOUGH TO KNOW WHEN I AM THAT no longer.

The weight of a glance can be felt, and this one presses upon me. I've felt it for three suns, on my lee and to the stoneward, though never on my back. No enemy circles behind an Indiri, even those we cannot see. The fire I've built burns low enough not to blind my eyes to the dark, my shoulders are pressed against a tree, my fingertips rest on the blade at my hip, my crossed swords on my knees, my bow beside me. Nothing that bleeds will come near without losing a bit of itself.

The *crack* that comes from the darkness is purposeful, a foot brought down on a branch meant for me to hear. Alongside it, I catch a whiff of Tangata, a mix of wet beast fur and the darrow root they seek out. But no cat treads on sticks.

"Come out, then," I call. "Or the next sound you hear will be the last beat of your heart."

I'm answered by a cat, a long, low purr that has me reaching for my bow only to be stopped by a voice at my ear.

"Slow then, young one," it says. "How be it that I come upon the last, and her so easily led astray by my pet?"

"If a Tangata be your pet, then you are in luck. My blade will take you down and save you the indignity of a death by its claws." Though my words are sharp, I have to squeeze them past the pressure in my throat.

"Are we not all undone by what we love, in the end?"

The blade at my skin eases, and I look down to see it is held by a hand as speckled as my own, though it is old and withered. Thoughts of violence flee, and I am left waxen, a half-melted candle bent at the middle.

I have never seen an elder Indiri, only glimpses of white hair and spotted skin drawn from my ancestor's memories. And so I memorize her as she moves into the firelight to sit across from me, that my children, should I have any, may hold the sight dear.

"I thought I was the last," I say, the Indiri language tripping from my tongue for the first time with someone other than Donil.

"Not the last, but the only one able to bring more of our kind to the world. I am long past such things."

"I am Dara."

"Faja," the woman replies, tilting her head. "Who was your mother?"

"Ingris," I say. "And her mother, Fanwe."

Faja closes her eyes for a moment, diving into her memories. "Ah, yes, Fanwe."

"And your mother?" I ask, but Faja shakes her head.

"You can search your ancestors back to the dirt we came from and not find her, child. My mother had finely pointed teeth and lovely stripes in her coat."

"You are the Indiri raised by Tangata."

I search the older woman's face, having never seen it among the memories of my ancestors. I cannot help but be prideful at the sight of her. The Given's musty scrolls and stacks of books may have held their own kind of truth, but they had proclaimed the Indiri extinct except for myself and my twin. But one had lived on. Raised among cats and wild as a Pietran Lusca, but alive.

"You are flesh and blood," I say. "Not the legend some think."

"A little too real." Faja winces as she straightens her legs. "Legends live long, retaining their youth and beauty with each generation. I am fading and not long for this world."

"The world is not long for itself. The sea—"

"I know," Faja says, unconcerned.

"How, when Stille has only just learned?"

Faja's brows draw together, dark lines meeting in the firelight. "Do you not feel it, young one? When I was small, I ran through these woods fearing nothing, knowing the branches would catch me if I stumbled, leaves would move to cover me if it rained. Now if I fall, I land on sharp rocks, and the trees watch me bleed."

I nod, having gone through memories and seen my ancestors sleeping unconcerned beneath trees that would wake them against enemies, while I spend sleepless nights in the forest.

"It is all I've ever known, this weakness," I tell her. "When I search my mother's memories, and those before her, there is a feeling of strength I have never called my own."

"It left with the Indiri," Faja says. "The day our people were culled, our magic left too, leaching out with every rain until there is hardly any left. Our earth grows smaller, and what's left of the Indiri weaker with every pull of the tide that takes a bit of the shore out to sea."

I am quiet, too aware that though the Stilleans fear my might, I am merely an echo of those who came before me.

"Are there more?" I must ask, though I know and fear the answer.

Faja shakes her head. "Yours is the only face I've seen that reflects my own, and you smell of the surf, not the woods."

"I smell like the only place that would offer my brother and me shelter," I snap. "If it be near the sea, what of it? Better to stink of salt than the rot of death."

Faja's smile is buried in wrinkles, one hand up to ward off my anger. "Ah, there's an Indiri. I see her in there now, under those nicely stitched clothes."

I come to my feet, hating the very wool of the Hyllenian sheep that swirls around me as I do. "Were you not Indiri, I'd have you on your back for that."

Faja's humor disappears. "I doubt that, young one. You're a warrior—I can see it in the lines of your body—and where you're from, I doubt any can best you. But I'm Indiri born and forest raised. Come at me, and you'll find that the Tangata taught me a thing or two."

I unclench my fists, ignoring the anger still coiled in my belly. "I've not spent my entire life searching for an Indiri only to spill her blood. Do you not have any word to give me? Rumors of others or a hint of hope?"

Faja meets my eyes over the fire, her spots darker than mine with age. "There are no others, child. As for hope—it goes out with the tide." She comes to her feet somewhat shakily, her years betraying her. "Go back to where you came from, Indiri. As for any word I can give, there is only one for all of us. Indiri. Stillean. Pietra. Feneen. We are destroyed."

CHAPTER 8

Ank

M Y MOTHER NEVER MEANT FOR ME TO LIVE, AND MORE than once, I wished it had been so. The caul I was born with kept me from seeing with my eyes, but gave me a different gift, to know a person's true nature with a brush of a hand, their skin upon mine. Though my caul fell away years ago, it hangs, curled and dry, in a pouch around my neck. I have often wanted it back upon my face, to spare me the sight of things that cannot be unseen.

Feneen floating in the river, Pietra crushed by the sea, Stilleans feeding girls to the depths, and the Indiri reduced to a dirt plain where nothing grows. Except for the two Indiri . . . I smile at the thought of them. The girl, ready to slice my throat at a cave's entrance for an imagined insult. The boy, loyal and foolish, stepping in front of the Stillean prince to protect his friend, though his own blood is rare.

The Indiri are true, the girl a whirlwind of pride and wrath, the boy a pillar of loyalty and trust. Others have proven less worthy, and it was with no little happiness that I heard of the death of King Varrick, a man of dark appetites. Yet even an aged caulbearer with the face of a youth can be surprised, as I was when I touched the young Lithos.

Of all those I have known at a touch, the Lithos is the most at odds with himself. Outwardly he must behave as the leader of the Stone Shore, a man as hard as the place his people call home. He has no family, fathers no children, and knows no friends, so that ties will never compromise his battle acumen. The Lithos sends his own people into the sea on the Culling Days, ridding the land of the old and infirm, the weak and the dying. Boats without oars go into the sea to be tipped by the Lusca, foul sea beasts that have learned the cycles of the moon and know when to come close to Pietran shores for their fill of flesh.

Witt does all these things. I have seen him send young mothers and weak babies to the monsters, slit sickened throats with bladed Hadundun leaves, order his men across a river on a human bridge, all while wearing a stony face. Yet inside he cries, so much that I believe him to have drowned long ago, although his heart has yet to hear of it.

"Let us hope the Hyllenians have shorn those sheep," Hadduk, the new Mason, mutters beside me, pulling his hood closer to his face against the rain. "I'd have a new cape out of one of them, or it'll be mutton."

"The Hyllenians know best when to shear their own sheep," the Lithos says on my other side, rain running down his own unprotected face. "I'll not tell them how to shepherd, and they'll not teach me to make war."

Hadduk grunts in response, and I nod my approval to Witt, who ignores it.

"Lithos, what are your plans for the Feneen once we reach the Stony Shore?"

It is not the first time I've asked, all other answers I've received not to my liking. The Lithos sighs. I am as persistent as the rain that's fallen on our march during the past three suns. We return home with an army more Feneen than Pietra, and many families will be lost to grief upon our arrival. I'd see my people's arrangements settled before that grief turns to anger and the Feneen are counted as enemies in their midst.

Witt spits rainwater from his mouth. "Ank, I've not thought much past getting what's left of my men back home."

I know this is untrue, as I've seen the young Lithos's eyes scanning his troops and seeing more of my own among them than faces he knows. Any commander worth his steel knows when he's outnumbered, and not only by the Feneen who march with him. Stille holds many and more. How the Pietra will lay claim to the land is hard upon the Lithos's mind. As well it should be, with the tides rising on all sides and generations of his people yet to come needing somewhere to put their feet.

"Gahlah's lancia is undone," I say, ignoring the sidelong glance from Hadduk that would slice me to spine if it were a blade. "Give us their barracks and any bedding not warmed by Pietran backs. My people can sleep easily under stars, but a layer of feathers between them and the ground would not be unwelcome."

Witt waves a hand at me as if it were already done, and I see the price I asked was too low, something to remember for later. I offered the might of my people once to the Stilleans, only to be rejected by Gammal, and then his son, Varrick, both dead now—something I had not looked for. Had I known that Vincent would ascend so soon, I might have stayed true to my mother's Stillean blood and fought against the men I now ride with.

My hand goes to the caul at my throat for reassurance. It has never led me wrong, and I know that for all his actions, the Lithos of Pietra is a good man. I keep saying this to myself.

For I cannot afford it not to be true.

CHAPTER 9

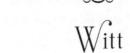

Witt

I STINK OF RAIN AND WET BEAST, MY CLOTHES SOAKED SO thoroughly they weigh more than my body. Still, I will be the last man to bed. First I must see to my horse, Cavallo, who does not know that much has changed since our leaving. He will find rest long before I do, as there are homes to be visited, homes that no soldier will be returning to. I envy my horse the luxury of ignorance.

They anticipate my coming, these houses where lights still burn. The men who survived the Stillean shore were given leave to return to their families for the night. They bed their wives in the dark, while others cling to hope, lanterns lit. I move from light to light, extinguishing them with a word.

Hadduk is with me, though the task does not suit him. Pravin knew always what to say, even when duty made for hard words. He found ways to soften blows that landed on hearts, though none would ever call him weak. I feel my throat closing at the thought of him, as another light goes out at my back and we proceed to the next, a line drawn through a name on Hadduk's list.

Choosing him as Mason was a poor choice, one made in haste on a night filled with loss. In my own grief I had looked on Hadduk, who was unmoved at the loss of so many, and thought him a good candidate. In truth *he* should be Lithos, and I no more than a lancia. If it were so, I'd be behind one of these doors, bedding my own wife.

I bite my tongue hard enough to draw blood at the thought. I've never known a woman, and never shall. The Lithos cannot be distracted. I have not strayed from this path, something again that Pravin excelled at: maintaining my focus. But with Hadduk by my side, all jests soon turn to bedding women—usually Nilana—and my mind has wandered of late.

I swallow the mouthful of blood I drew, and it joins the salt in my throat, a slick mixture that coats the words I speak to the face that comes to answer my knock. I continue to the next home, and another light goes out behind me.

I would let the darkness follow me to my chambers where I can be what I am, a crying child. But the Keeper waits for me there, a warm fire in the hearth and a drink at the bedside table.

"You'll make me soft," I warn her, but sink, exhausted, into a chair nonetheless.

"This man, I think not." She clucks her tongue as she removes my boots, something she's never done before. I see the streak of gray in her hair has widened since I left and wonder if worry for me was the cause.

We have become close, this woman who raised the Stillean Given and I. I killed her husband, but spared her so that she may teach me how she closed her heart so tightly that she can raise babes into women, knowing they go to drown. And yet this person who should be as hard as any Pietran stone shield is made of kindness and cares for me now as she did the little Givens. As if I myself were to go to the sea.

I shiver at the thought that I nearly did.

"You are cold, my Lithos?"

"No," I tell her. "Only remembering."

She takes the seat opposite me on the other side of the fire, rekindling the habit we had taken up before I marched for Stille.

"I think it did not go so well," she says drily, eyeing me over her own cup.

I do the one thing I haven't done since I left this room. I laugh. "No," I agree, taking a drink of the wine she had warmed for me. "Not so well."

"I hear Pravin was lost?"

I nod, the laughter dead.

"And many?"

"Many and more," I say. "I would guess Feneen feet outnumber Pietran in our army now."

"Is that because the Feneen outnumber us or because so many of them are three-legged?"

She's aiming for another laugh, but gets a smile only, and that not for the jest. "Us?" I repeat.

The Keeper shrugs and looks to the fire. "I was made to care for things; it is my nature. If you were a Stillean, you'd go by King, but because your blood is Pietran, the people call you Lithos. You are a leader; I am a caregiver. My allegiance is to that which I care for."

"You are a comfort to me," I say, and those very words should make me drag her by the hair and throw her from the room. The Lithos of Pietra knows no comfort, that he may be unflinching. If Pravin were alive to see this fire and warm wine, he would toss the Keeper into the stables. Hadduk will only assume the bedsheets were turned down as well, her welcoming body under them.

"I should send you away," I say. "You make the room warm and say kind things to me. You are a mother to a boy who should have no family."

"Nay," the Keeper says, poking an ember that slides from the fire with the toe of her shoe. "I'm the punishment you weren't expecting. For every kindness I give, you heap coals upon your own head. I know well that you killed my man and razed my village. So I'll make your food and unlace your boots, and the hate will rise up inside of you, higher every time, like the tide that eats the beach. But it's not the hate they taught to make a Lithos, not the rage of sword and slice of blade. It's the slow, rotting death of self-hate I'm treating you to, boy."

She reaches for me, covering the distance between us so that her hand rests on my arm, the weight of it more than my salt-crusted armor.

"It'll make you harder than any lesson they taught you on the clifftops," she says. "I'll do it with love and mean every kind word."

"You'd see me dead," I say, the only thing I can understand.

"No." She shakes her head. "I'd see you live a long life and fully know what you've done."

We stare at the fire in silence until a knot pops, a spark flying to catch among her skirts. She reaches down and pinches it out, smoke trailing from her singed fingertips as she rises from her chair as she leaves the room.

"Tomorrow is a Culling Day, my Lithos," she reminds me, and my head sinks farther at the thought of all the darkened houses, the wives and children who may bring boats to the shore in their grief and ask to be given to the Lusca so that it may end.

"Depths," I say, alone in my warm chambers with good wine in my belly. "Depths."

CHAPTER 10

Dara

To travel with an Indiri not my brother, Donil, is an odd feeling indeed. And though Vincent was a decent woodsman and we knew each other's movements from child-hood, his blood remained Stillean; his toes would catch in roots, his hair snag in branches. Faja is like me; her feet make no noise, and the trees part for her as we pass, something I've never seen.

"They know me," Faja says in Indiri, when she catches me glancing behind us to see the canopy closing again. "You, they fear. There's a bit of stolen lifesap in you."

"I pulled down a tree," I admit, something I am not proud of, though it gave me the strength to kill many Feneen on the battlefield. And Tangata, too, I recall, eyeing the cat who walks beside us, tail haughtily curled in the air. Faja calls her companion Kakis, though I would sooner call her gone.

"A tree," Faja says, slightly out of breath as she tries to keep pace with my mount, Famoor. Her hand brushes my ankle purposefully. "More than one, I think. That was badly done. None wanted to go."

I think of the tree I took down the night I drew Khosa to the water. Too much wine had found my tongue that night, and the life I pulled was not taken on purpose. Still I must have been forgiven, for it was the same tree's branches that saved me from being pulled under with the wave, tangling me in an embrace even as it died, salt-crusted and weary.

"Nothing ever wants to go," I say to Faja, who laughs.

"Live to my age and see if you say the same."

Beside us, Kakis sneezes, a sound suspiciously laced with amusement. I give her a dark glance, but the cat only stares at me, wide-eyed and innocent.

"I don't think I will live to your age."

"You march for death," Faja says. "Maybe not your own, but some will die at your hand. I see it in your walk, the firmness of your mouth. Tell me, Indiri girl, who is it you would kill?"

"The Lithos of Pietra," I say. "I saw him on the beach before the wave came, and though he had become a man, I know well the face of the boy my mother looked on before she died. He leads the people who killed my own, and neither of us children now."

Faja is quiet, all teasing gone from the air between us. Even the curl is out of Kakis's tail; it hangs low behind her, gray and black rings nearly dirtied as we go.

"The Pietra." Faja spits after speaking, the words foul in her mouth. "I was not there on the plains of Dunkai, but I have been, after, and seen the earth where nothing grows."

"You were not there because you chose the Tangata over your people," I remind her, and see Kakis's ear turn to me as if she were listening.

"Good that I wasn't, or who would you speak with now?" Faja shoots back.

"No one and nothing," I tell her. "And maybe the better for it."

Kakis stalks past us and crouches in front of Famoor to relieve herself. He halts and snorts, appalled. Faja hides a smile in her hand, but I catch it.

"Does the cat understand me?" I ask Faja.

"You're not terribly complicated."

"You know what I say." I drop my voice, the tone used for an Indiri challenge, no matter what words are spoken.

"Peace, young one." Faja raises her hands in the air. "I've spent my life in the woods, and none who pass know my tongue. I only like to make words with another who can answer—forgive me if I treat you lightly."

"Forgiven." I say, my voice lightening. "Now, explain that." I nod toward the pile Kakis has made directly in Famoor's path.

"A lifetime among the cats found them as my speaking companions, and Kakis is one of the kits who nursed beside me. Indiri I may be, but the Tangata lead a harsher life yet, and without her as my companion, I would have gone to the earth long before now. Kakis taught me to live as a cat, and I taught her to think as an Indiri, learning our words."

"They can live so long?" I ask, urging Famoor forward and favoring Kakis with a swing of my boot, meant to warn but not connect. She raises her lip, showing teeth that I'd do better to avoid.

"The cats can live long, though Kakis and I perhaps have outstripped our usefulness with our years. We're wild things, the both of us, and not meant to age."

"Nor am I."

We walk in silence a bit longer, Kakis brushing beside me close enough that her tail touches my hand.

"What is this wish to die that you carry?" Faja finally asks. "I have seen the young Lithos a time or two, in my wanderings. Even in my youth, I would not have faced him assured of my victory."

My hands find Famoor's mane, and he soon sports a row of braids as my tongue searches for words.

"You see that I walk a path of death," I tell Faja. "And being Indiri, you know that we are all fierce in both loving and fighting, but each has their own inclination."

She nods. "Yours is clear."

"Knowing that I cannot find a mate, I will make bodies instead of babies. There will be no Indiri from me; the least I can do for my people is avenge them."

"I would not turn you from it, even if I thought I could," Faja says. "I would ask, though, that you let the beast go."

"Famoor?"

"Unbroken," Faja repeats, smiling. "He is well named, but the fact that you name him at all undermines the meaning, yes?"

"And what does Kakis mean?"

"Ask your ancestors," Faja says. "Yet my Tangata wears no bridle, and I do not sit upon her back. That Famoor carries an Indiri is a compliment to him, that he is asked to bear a rider, an insult."

"My horse is my concern," I say, not sharing that I agree.

"To the edge of the forest, young one," Faja says. "And then I leave you."

"Then I shall spur my horse," I say.

But I don't.

CHAPTER 11

Donil

I GO TO MEET HER, THOUGH I KNOW I SHOULD NOT.

I love my friend's wife, and she me. Yet because we both love Vincent in our own ways, we must remain chaste. We speak without touching, both of us vividly remembering the one time we gave ourselves freedom with our bodies, nearly fulfilling the act. I would have damned her with my touch, had we made a child together. Her destiny of providing a new Given would have been fulfilled, and Stille would have pointed her to her final destination—the sea, a place no Indiri can follow.

That danger is gone, replaced by another. If a speckled child were born to her, we would both be killed as traitors and the babe drowned as a bastard. And though I fear no executioner's blade, I would go to my death knowing it was well deserved, for betraying my friend.

Yet when I am with Khosa, everything fades, even Vincent. It would be easy to forget him and dare all of Stille to deny me what I want. It seems almost understandable, easily explained if we were seen together, our happiness so evident none would deprive us of it.

If Dara were here, these meetings would never happen. She'd shade my steps, give me the sharp edge of her tongue, and her blade after that if I persisted in this madness. But my sister left me, what little of her that was made for love shattered. I have never seen Dara shrink from pain, but to see Vincent beside Khosa she could not bear. My rage with her for harming Khosa would have faded with time, but not so her feelings for Vincent. So she left, as I would if I were half sensible. Instead, I persist in a folly that will lead to nowhere good. I go eagerly.

Khosa has arrived in the clearing beforehand, and I take a moment to watch as she waits for me upon a rock. She is wise, wearing the crown of Stille at all times, not as a gesture of power but to remind herself—and me—of who she is now. No longer does she choose her own mate, and I do not ask how she spends her nights with Vincent.

The crown sits heavily. As a child, I placed the one Vincent now wears on my head in jest, and all of us laughed at the idea of an Indiri ruling Stille—although Dara laughed last, and somewhat bitterly. I remember how it pinched, and how my neck ached for days afterward, as if I'd slept with a tree root in the wrong place.

No, Khosa wears the crown not in victory, but as punishment.

I go toward her, breaking a branch beneath my foot to warn her of my approach, an old Indiri courtesy. But she is lost to me, staring beachward with the blank look of a baby oderbird. Alarmed, I break into a run.

"Khosa," I call, and am on my knees in front of her in a moment, ready to pull the very feet out from under her if she heads for the sea.

"No fears," she says to me, her voice calm, the brush of her hand through my hair. "I am myself."

I rise and walk to the edge of the clearing to put a safe distance between us, urging the swell of panic in my throat to cease.

"How fares Vincent?"

I always ask these words first when we meet, acknowledging the third who stands between us.

"Unwell, I fear," she says, her voice carrying to me. "He drinks wine too easily these days."

"I am partially to blame," I admit. "We should seek a better way to pass our time."

"He needs the release of being with you," she says, waving away my apology. I can't help but wonder if he finds any release in her bed, then shake my head clear of the thought.

"He has much to think about of late," I say. "I fear he has taken Sallin's proposal of building ships into consideration."

"Is it so mad?" Khosa asks, and my heart dips into the dirt.

She would go and Vincent with her. Dara has left me, and now the two others in this world I care for would sail into nothingness. I cannot bring myself to the thought of standing on the bones of trees killed so that people may go upon the water, an unnatural action, even if there were a destination.

"Filthy fathoms, yes, it is mad," I say. "What is the Pietran saying? *Boats are for the dead.* The Lusca may haunt their shores and eat their flesh, but the creatures are not the only thing to fear. Would you risk going to the depths based on a misbegotten whim?"

I have said too much and spoken too harshly. Khosa gathers her skirts to rise, her face betraying nothing, as usual.

"I suppose I am a madwoman, then," she says. "For I would go, and take any who wish to leave with me. The tides rise, land slips beneath the sea—"

"You need not tell me that," I snap, the Indiri temper Dara wears so close to her skin flaring in me as well. "I am of the earth. Do you think I do not feel keenly how much more powerful the sea is than—"

"Then why will you not *listen*?" Khosa yells, crossing the distance between us, anger finally forcing her stone face into an emotion. "There is something else out there, Donil, I feel it. I am drawn to it even as I am drawn to you."

"There is nothing else." I repeat the words I said to Vincent the other night, though my voice is weak after her frank admission.

"There *is*," she insists, and pokes a finger into my chest. "And I go to it still. Whether I go with a boat beneath my feet or not, it will have me eventually."

"We can fight it," I say, breaking our vow not to touch as I take her hand in mine. "I'll lash you to a tree—"

"And watch me go mad?" All anger is gone from her voice, her eyes trained on our intertwined fingers. "I would tear my own limbs off to reach it."

I sigh, bringing our clasped hands to my face, where they rest against my lips, for a moment only. I have never touched her without desire. I keep it at bay, and see the same feeling pulsing within her. Yet today there is something stronger running through my love. There is a vibration that runs throughout her body, like a note already played yet still hanging in the air. It pushes against her very skin to be near mine, and I know it pulls with equal strength in the opposite direction— toward the sea. She would indeed be driven insane denying this call, and anything Vincent or I would do to keep her from it will only end in harm.

I release her hand.

"What would you have me do?"

CHAPTER 12

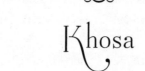

Khosa

"WHAT DO YOU KNOW OF BUILDING SHIPS?" KHOSA ASKS. "Less and little," Donil tells her, his eyes unnaturally bright in the wake of his outburst. "The Indiri have nothing to do with the sea."

"Has it always been so?" she presses, but lightly, aware that his patience has already been tested this day.

Donil runs a hand over his face and squeezes his temples. "You'd have me ask my ancestors?"

"I mean no harm, or offense." Khosa's hand flutters toward him, but she resists the impulse, and it falls, twitching by her side, a butterfly with a broken wing.

"There is no offense in asking," Donil says gently. "I am not my sister, enjoying anger so much that I seek out chances to feel it."

Khosa drops her eyes, as she always does whenever Dara is mentioned.

"I will search my memories, but it may take time," he warns. "I've never come across a ship in them."

"You've not looked," Khosa says, shading her eyes against the sun as it sets. "Dara did not see many things until I asked her to find them.

Your memories run deep and long, and are like a library where books sit unused until someone takes them up."

"Some of my memories are less like a library and more like a pleasure house," Donil says, and Khosa smiles to see his lighter side return.

"Perhaps, as in a library, the hand returns to the ones it likes best?" she teases, and Donil has the grace to blush at her implication.

"No," he says, "the best memories I have are my own." His eyes hold hers, and the waves come and go twice while they take each other in, his body as unreachable as the land Khosa feels pulling at her from across the sea.

"The histories . . ." Khosa's voice fails her as she tries to break the silence, so heavy with want that words fall short. She clears her throat and tries again. "I believe we may find assistance in the histories."

"How so?" Donil allows himself the luxury of taking her hand as they turn from the beach in the dying light, still hidden from view by trees brave enough to grow seaside.

"When I was a girl in Hyllen, my Keepers tried to occupy me indoors, so that I would not stray toward the sea. They had a book that told tales of a Stillean who wandered far, never wanting to tend sheep or bend metal to a sword. All he wished for was discovery, and his steps covered all the land, from the Stone Shore to Dunkai and the outposts of Sawhen.

"I believed he was only a myth until I came here, but then I used many of his maps while I studied the tide. The man saw much and drew well. Once he knew all the land like a Seer knows a familiar palm, he became restless. His only trade was in mapmaking, and he'd inked every known place. So, legend says, he took to the sea."

"Don't tell me." Donil holds up his free hand to stop her. "Never to return?"

She raises an eyebrow and matches his dramatic tone. "Never to return."

"Poor bastard," Donil says, easing a stray hair behind her ear.

Khosa presses her face against his palm for a moment, then separates from him, reclaiming her hand as well when they clear the trees and approach the castle. "I will search the histories," she goes on. "For him to take to the sea, he would have had to build a boat. There may be plans for it somewhere. Even a single line may give us what we need."

"And teach you to sail?" Donil asks. "An impressive line."

Khosa sighs again, but is too weary to feel anger and too happy in Donil's company to darken their time together. "I know well enough that it may be useless. But what can one do in the face of futility?"

Donil falls behind as Khosa takes a side entrance, both of them knowing better than to return together. But she hears his response as the sand beneath her feet gives way to cobbled stone.

"What indeed?"

CHAPTER 13

Vincent

VINCENT CLIMBS THE WINDING STAIRS TO MADDA'S TOWER, the stones to either side growing darker with accumulated years of incense as he goes. He can't smell nilflower without thinking of his Seer; every fine silver strand of hair and each fold of her clothing exudes the fragrance of the seaside plant. He enters her chamber to see fresh bunches hanging from the ceiling to dry, their petals falling to be crushed underfoot or trapped in her wild mane.

Madda's back is to him, but he'd wager his sword she knows he's there. Stille may be his kingdom, but in this room, he is only a boy and she the ruler. Madda was born here, the Sight passing to her from her mother, along with the role of reading the royal palms of Stille, a task of fading importance in a world where all lived long lives and peace went unquestioned.

Donil and Dara mocked Vincent often as a child, their own lives with deep roots in a past they could view clearly at whim, while he peered through a haze of nilflower smoke for a glimpse of his future. Still he sought out Madda, this woman who was like a second mother, always hoping his palms had changed and that he would not find himself on the throne one day. Now he visits as the king, knowing that all Stillean lives are measured and war is on his heels.

"Whose step do I hear?" Madda calls over her shoulder from a chair by the fire. "It falls heavy as royalty, yet sounds like a boy I once knew."

"Madda," he says, preparing himself for whatever teasing she has in store.

She turns, feigning surprise at the sight of him. "So it is both I see, the boy become a king. You should wear the crown, child; it adds height."

He sits at her table, and she raises an eyebrow. "Quick to the task, is it? You'll not even bring an old woman news of the world outside before she bows her head over your hand?"

"The old woman knows more than I do of what goes on outside this room, even if she never leaves it," he tells her. Though his mother shares with him a never-ending stream of talk from her trusted servants, it is Madda who tells him how the people of Stille fare. Her position may keep her confined in the tower, but other feet than his climb her steps, and often. For the price of news and a bit of choice gossip, Madda gives them a touch of the royal treatment: a glance at their palms and a breath of the future that she sees there. Though of late she has told him of unlined skin and children born without hope of living long.

"Have there been more babes born without lifelines?" he asks, and Madda plops into the chair across from him, its legs protesting years of such abuse.

"Ask me a different question, young king," Madda says. "One with a kind answer."

"Bring it ill or good, I must know," Vincent says. "That is the way for a ruler."

She sighs, resigned to the fact that he will not spar with her today. "I can tell you only of things I have seen, not of those which I have not. My room is windowless, and that list long."

"There has been only the one, then," he says, almost to himself, wondering if the child with smooth hands is an aberration, like the three-headed or those with misplaced mouths in their chests among the Feneen.

"You mistake my words," Madda says.

"Then speak more clearly."

"I liked you better when you weren't royal," she shoots back.

"I did as well."

"Hmmm . . ." Madda eyes Vincent for a moment, tongue retrieving a wad of salium she has tucked inside her cheek. She watches him as she chews, and he waits.

"I cannot tell you what I haven't seen in palms not yet formed," she finally says. "The Stillean women who come to me of late do not show me their hands or the hands of their children. They come with little news and leave with nilflower."

"Nilflower," he repeats, thinking of Milda, the girl he released from her duties in his bed, and the nightly tea she drank to avoid growing a bastard in her belly.

"Stillean women are choosing not to bear children?"

"Some." Madda shrugs. "Word of the child with unlined palms spread, and the wave . . . Well, not all believe that the Redeemed controls the sea now, rather than it her. Much like the sea itself, word of the rising tides has not been contained in these walls, young Vincent. Stilleans talk, and the words they speak are filled with fear. Women don't wish to have babies only to see them float."

"The tides rise, yes," the king says. "But babies born in this lifetime would grow to make their own before the water wets their feet. It is a persistent fear, but a distant one."

"What of a wave?" Madda asks. "Can you promise mothers that no wall of water will tear babies from their arms?"

"Sallin thinks we should build boats," Vincent says, avoiding an answer. Madda spares him, too surprised to insist on an answer.

"Boats?" she asks. "What does a Stillean know of boats?"

"Nothing and no more," he says. "But what do we know of

warfare? Shall we face the Pietra and Feneen again, to be slaughtered as we fight for what land there is? Or do we sail in the hope of something else?"

"There is nothing else," Madda says darkly. "I feel it in the deep parts of me."

"You feel what you've been told, and the years have given it time to grow roots."

Madda shakes her head, a dried curl of nilflower falling loose as she rises from her chair. "I would not see you do this, young king. Should bodies fall on the earth, they have the chance to be returned to it. A drowned man is only a sea-spine's meal."

"Madda." Vincent lays his hands on her table. "Come and tell me what my palms say."

The Seer closes her eyes, and the young king remembers too well the last reading she gave him. She takes her seat, thumbs tracing the fine skin of his hands, well known to her since his infancy. Carefully she folds his fingers back into a fist, her aged hands covering his.

"It is as it was before," she says. "You are given to the sea."

Vincent sighs heavily, resting his head on his forearms before looking back up to her. "In that case, I'd rather go with a boat beneath me."

CHAPTER 14

Khosa

K HOSA STANDS IN THE LIBRARY AND BLOWS AWAY THE dust that has settled on the table she had claimed when she was known only as the Given.

"Scribes aren't much for cleaning," Merryl, her guard, observes. He too resumes his old place by the door, leaning against the heavy wooden frame.

Khosa sniffs the air and thinks she detects the slightest hint of decay, though she knows Cathon's body was removed from the hidden passageway soon after the wave that made her queen. She inhales deeply, relishing the smell of his death if it indeed lingers.

"No, they aren't," she agrees, eyeing the piles of books that have remained untouched since she last worked here. "But you'll find that the shelves are in order, if filthy."

The fact that no one tidied up after her search into the histories for mentions of the high tides means that she won't have to reread pages already seen. Any tale of the wandering Stillean who left on a boat would stand out in her mind, and she remembers no such story in their histories, only in the legends of her Hyllenian Keepers.

Khosa reaches for the first book on her forgotten pile to find dust resting there as well. Has it really been so long since she toiled over maps and mentions of the sea, prying through Dara's memories to find some indication of how fast it was rising?

Dara. Khosa closes her eyes against the stab of her own memories and the bright-eyed girl she'd likely never see again. That the Indiri had cared for Vincent was obvious, but Khosa's wedding to him was hastily announced and quickly performed so that Stille could find something to celebrate after losing so much. Dara had slipped away without a word to anyone save Donil, leaving Khosa with words to say and no one to speak them to.

"Tides," Khosa says when her crown slides forward as she bends to move the next book. Already a trickle of sweat traces her spine, and her fingers are smeared with dirt. Merryl is quickly by her side and the book in his hands.

"Where would you like it, my queen?" he asks.

"Merryl," Khosa says as she pushes her crown back into place, leaving a smear on her forehead. "You must call me by my name. I wear this to remind me of my role. I'd have someone to remind me of who I actually am."

"Khosa, then," he says. "Where would you like it?"

She straightens, surveying the room. "This pile here, and the one there, both can be moved over by the binding cord. I've seen every spot of ink in all of them. They hold nothing I need."

"A harsh judgment, for books long toiled over," says a voice from the door.

Khosa turns to find the Curator, his robes brushing against loose pages as he makes his way toward her.

"I count myself as one who toiled," she says, curtseying in recognition of his status. He waves it away, but she detects the faintest flush of pleasure beneath his skin.

"And your work changed the ways of this world," he says. "But those days are past. We know the sea rises and will not be stopped. What brings you back among dust and brittle pages?"

"Fear," Khosa answers honestly.

"It leads many to action," the Curator says, carefully lowering himself to sit on a tottering pile of books and resting his walking stick across his knees. "What shadows your thoughts?"

"Harta, the mapmaker," she says, carefully watching the Curator for a reaction.

"Surely you've found plenty of his work in your earlier searches?"

"I have," Khosa says. "But his maps do not interest me. At least, not the ones he made of land."

The Curator glances at Merryl, but Khosa dismisses his concern. "You can speak freely in front of my guard. I trust him in all things. He knows even that the crown I wear is unearned."

"Unearned, I think not," the Curator insists. "Whether you are the Given or the Redeemed."

"I fear that I am only Khosa, a girl who needs earth to stand on, but finds it is eroding beneath her feet."

"Harta, too, looked for earth," the Curator says. "But you'll not find anything other than his maps here. They are the least dangerous of his thoughts."

Khosa takes his meaning and crosses to be closer to him, where whispered words can travel discreetly. "And where might I look for truth?"

The Curator runs his hands along the bindings beneath him. "This room holds much, most of it true after a fashion. But there are other truths, ones that should not be left to lay where any curious hand could find them."

"And they are kept where?" Khosa asks.

The Curator smiles and rises to his feet with a wince, leaning heavily on his cane. "Somewhere it will take time for these feet to reach, and I will need some assistance." He puts an arm out to Khosa, and she steadies his elbow, the rough fabric of his robes keeping her skin from his, and the contact bearable.

"Merryl." She calls for her guard, and he takes the Curator's other arm as they wind through the castle, leaving wide halls for smaller ones and well-lit corridors for places the sconcelighters no longer travel.

"These must be dark truths indeed, to be so well hidden," Merryl observes, his breath coming somewhat heavily as they begin to climb a spiral staircase, each step the Curator takes requiring more of his assistance.

"You'll find nothing of great horror here," the Curator says as they reach a small door cut into the wall. "Only tales that, if heeded, would rewrite much of what Stille considers to be set in stone."

Khosa's heart stutters as the Curator reaches into the folds of his robe for a key and opens the door. The room she enters has neither the grandness of the library nor the light. It is small, barely more than two shoulderwidths deep, and without windows. But the walls are lined with shelves holding loose papers, some clearly torn from the ponderous histories; some only scraps, thoughts hastily scribbled. She reaches for a piece at random and sees handwriting that she recognizes from the histories.

Runnar's child by the Queen has come and gone. Born with no mouth, the Queen pinched its nostrils closed even as it lay smeared in birthblood. The child borne to Runnar's dairymaid mistress this same night wails with the strength of many and rests now in the Queen's arms, its mother dead in her chamber with the smell of barbar weed on her breath.

Khosa's hand shakes, and the paper flutters to the floor, where the Curator traps it with his foot, reading the scrawled lines. "Ah, well . . . there are some horrors here, no doubt."

"Runnar's heir was a bastard?" Khosa asks.

"Yes, and raised by a murderess," the Curator confirms. "Bandwe did not permit her children to live, as all that came from her were better suited to the Feneen. She was a cunning woman, encouraging her husband to take others to his bed as soon as she knew she bore life inside her. In this way, she kept her crown and the myth of her own bloodline intact."

"She was Feneen?" Khosa's hand flutters to her chest, aware that no small part of her shares that same dark inheritance.

"Or one of her ancestors was," the Curator says. "No one ever asked."

"For no one ever knew," Merryl adds, eyeing the shelves around them with distrust. "It is good that you tore the page away. If Stilleans knew that the line of a dairymaid had ruled them for generations—"

"They'd not cherish the fact," the Curator finishes for him. "Yet they were ruled by such as that, and ruled well."

"What else is here?" Khosa asks, scanning the shelves. "Do you remember anything of Harta?"

"I'm afraid these pages were often written in times of trouble and removed in haste. They were brought here in secret, by Scribes who felt that the truth—however harmful, should at least, continue to *be*— even if only in the dark, unread."

"You wouldn't allow them to be destroyed?" Khosa asks.

"No." The Curator shakes his head. "Deceiving the people, as you well know, is sometimes in their best interest. But it does chafe the conscience. The Curator before me handled this key, knew this room, and undoubtedly his predecessor did as well. What it holds is sometimes unpleasant, but often it is only the most mundane of tales that would rewrite history."

"I'll need light," Khosa says. "We must move them. These pages have escaped destruction; I'd not bring a flame into the room."

Merryl begins gathering sheaves. "Shall I bring them to your chamber?"

"Yes." Khosa nods. "I'd not trust them anywhere else. Unless . . ." Her eyes go to the Curator. "Is there anything here that would be disturbing to my husband?"

"Child," the Curator huffs, and eases himself onto the floor, exhausted, "the king's own deeds lie here, freshly inked. He has handled the present well; trust him to weather the past."

CHAPTER 15

Dara

I WAKE ALONE, OR ALMOST.

Kakis sleeps beside me, one leg thrown over my waist and her tail twined around my own, as if I were her littermate.

"Get off," I say, shoving her leg when I find it too heavy to lift. The big cat only yawns, her jaws snapping uncomfortably close to my face, then rolls to her other side. I brush Tangata fur from my cloak and look to what's left of the camp we made last night.

Faja is gone, Famoor as well. In a tree I spot what remains of his bridle, slashed to uselessness. I swear in Indiri and kick at the ashes of my fire. Faja is Indiri, and raised by cats. I'll find no sign to mark her path through the forest. Even if Donil were with me, I doubt he could track her.

And why should I try? I wonder, even as I make a cursory circle to be sure I haven't missed anything. Faja was no help to me, and her cat a hindrance. At the thought of Kakis, I return to what's left of last night's fire, giving the Tangata a glare that would have sent a Stillean swordsman to the privy. She licks her paw and wipes an ear, unconcerned.

"I . . ." I bite my lip and look off into the forest, feeling a fool. I clear my throat and try again. "Where did she go?"

Kakis cocks her head, looking for all the earth like she hasn't any idea who I'm talking about.

"Faja," I say. "Your . . . mistress, littermate . . . the . . ." I point to my own skin, though my spots are lighter with youth than Faja's were. "Her."

A deep purr emanates from the cat, and her paws knead the ground. Mock me she might, but I do believe the cat understands what I say to her. I switch to Stillean, a test.

"Where is your mistress?" I say, and the cat goes still, watching me warily.

"Where has Faja gone?" I use Indiri now, and Kakis crosses the space between us at her littermate's name. She reaches forward with one massive paw, delicately resting it on my knee. I bend down, for I think this is what she requests of me.

"Faja," I repeat, and Kakis stretches her neck to bring her nose to mine. It rests there, cold, wet, smelling unmistakably of Tangata.

I'd asked Faja what Kakis's name meant, and she'd told me to ask my ancestors, and so I had, diving into my memories for any recollection of the name. I'd found it and its meaning, which I remember now as I feel the cat's flesh against mine.

Loyal to only one.

"Tides," I mutter to myself, and Kakis sneezes into my face.

"Begone," I shout at the cat as I pass through the forest, but Kakis marches beside me as if I had not spoken. She's followed me since midmorning, after I covered what remained of our fire and strode for the edge of the Forest of Drennen. I am close now to the plains that stretch through the middle of our island, and in a few suns will see Dunkai, where my people were slaughtered. I have not revisited my birthplace since I crawled from the pit where my mother died, and do not intend to return with a Tangata trailing me.

Whatever Faja said to Kakis—and I shake my head to even

imagine the conversation—it has stuck. Kakis will not leave my side, even when I unhook my bow from my shoulder and swipe at her with it. She only runs ahead of me slightly, tail stuck high in the air, as if to let me know how unconcerned she is.

"I have no patience for you," I spit at her, but notice that she's found a break in the brush, one that I hadn't spotted. I follow, somewhat chastened. The cat turns to face me, and I am about to speak when she shakes her head. I fall silent and listen. I hear breathing, heavy and male. I hear horses, shifting where they stand. I hear a sword, easing quietly from a scabbard. I hear people, waiting to hear me.

Kakis slides smoothly back out from the brush, her tail bushy with alarm and ruff raised. She glances at me, and I nod that I understand. The cat's lip curls minutely and she makes a low, deep sound. I recognize it as a hunting call, one I've heard in the woods more than once.

"It's only the cats," one of the men says to the other, his voice carrying.

"Do they use words now? I heard a voice."

"Maybe it was your mother calling you home to dinner."

"Maybe it was your wife calling for something else," the other shoots back.

There are only the two of them, for if there were a third, he would have shushed them by now, their squabbling giving me plenty of time to circle around the large tree they have camped under.

Camped under for some time, I think, looking at many nights' worth of ashes between them, Pietran armor in a pile nearby. Their horses are hobbled, but even given freedom, they would not go far. They are bone thin and weary, their ears not perking when Kakis gives a call from her side of the woods. The Pietran soldiers react quickly, if somewhat stupidly, both of them giving their full attention to her distraction.

The first does not hear my step, but slaps at his neck as if expecting to find a ninpop bug there instead of the open wound I've left behind, his lifeblood leaving in a torrent. He's on the path of the dead before the second even notices, but I don't give him long to grieve.

Kakis emerges to sniff the bodies, her paws sinking deeply into the bloodsoaked ground around them. She chuffs over their corpses, then tosses dirt across them with two quick kicks of her back legs before she joins me by the horses.

They raise their heads slightly at her wild scent and spattering of their riders' blood, but only just. There is nothing left in these beasts, and I spot a crust of sea salt on the trailing end of one bridle. These animals were on the beach, then, the same night as I. They survived the wave and moonchanges of travel eating only what they could graze, and by the smell of them, have resorted to rankflower.

There is nothing of Famoor in these beasts. I unhobble them anyway, leaving them to go where they will. I will not trouble them with a rider, and they could not keep my pace. I hear Kakis fall into step behind me, her pads soft on the forest floor, a light purr in her throat. Welcome or not, I have a traveling companion.

I turn to face her, and she stops, one paw raised in midair. The forest is quiet around me, aware that death has occurred. The sun warms my back, streaming through the thinning canopy. We are near the edge of Drennen, about to leave the woods the cat knows so well.

"To Dunkai?" I ask.

And she steps forward to join me.

CHAPTER 16

Witt

Some Pietra found home before the army itself returned, running from the wave like panicked wood animals from an arrow, too frightened to regroup with their pack later. Others wander back to our shores slowly, most on foot, a few holding the slack reins of horses too tired to carry them. The Lithos before me might have punished those who ran home without searching for their brothers in arms, but I cannot afford to do so. Punishment breeds either respect or resentment, and there is already too much of the second in my army.

"The Feneen suffered little," Hadduk says. As Mason, he sits to my right, my other commanders circled around me as we toss words across a stone table. They echo in this room, bouncing back from the high ceiling and sounding even more empty than when they were spoken.

"Though we lost few fighters, it was not for lack of bravery," Ank responds in his people's defense. "It was the Lithos's own plan that sent us to the gates of Stille and Pietran feet to the beach."

He speaks truth, one that rankles even now. Though I had accepted Ank's offer of Feneen fighters, I had also sent them into the more dangerous situation, charging the freshly reinforced walls of the city, with arrows pouring down on them. I had expected his men's backs to sport more feathers than a flock of oderbirds, and the brunt of the loss to be theirs. But then the wave came, wiping the beach clean of my men. I find myself leading an army of strangers who are hard to look upon.

Yet they are still my army.

"The Feneen did as they were told," I say. "If there are harsh words to be said about what happened, they can be said to me."

My commanders glance at one another, but remain still.

"There is nothing to be gained by ill feeling among my army. We marched as one, you'll remember, our feet treading on the hands of the Feneen so that we could cross a river and set foot on land unknown by Pietra. They stood firm under our weight, holding us even as they drowned. Did they not?"

I glance around the table and see Ula nodding and Fadden watching the others to see how the wind will blow. But the Pietra know courage when they see it, and none would call the Feneen cowards.

"I know, brothers," I say, rising from my seat to circle behind them. "I know their ways are not ours. Some fight one-handed or standing on three legs. They fight with seven eyes, looking in all directions. They fight with teeth that slice, found where no mouth should be. They fight sewn to cats and ride to their deaths. They fight alongside women, each one of them a terror. No, they don't fight like us . . . but they do *fight*."

Hadduk claps a hand onto the table in solidarity, and a few others follow.

"What happened in Stille was chance gone ill. Will you have it be said that bad luck sent the Pietra back to their stones to starve?"

A round of slaps, naked palms against stone.

"Will you have it be said that the Pietra—a people who walk beneath bladed Hadundun leaves—were too afraid of the warm shores of Stille to return?"

More slaps, one of them hard enough to pop a knuckle.

"Will you have it be said that the Pietra would not fight alongside the Feneen a second time . . . perhaps because they had seen their might and could not stand on a field beside them with pride?"

All the hands strike, this time in unison, the reverberation of their agreement filling the room.

"We are Pietra," I say, eyeing my commanders in turn, and landing on Ank. "All of us."

"Nice speech," Hadduk says as we leave the chamber. "Though you said little regarding an actual plan."

"I need them as one, if we would march that way," I tell him, as we make our way to the armory. "Though we headed for Stille together last time, we did so knowing that we would not fight side by side. If we would fill holes in our ranks with Feneen, I need the man next to him to see him as a brother."

"What if the man next to him is a woman?"

"Then as whatever suits him best, if he'll fight alongside her."

Hadduk makes noise in his throat and adjusts the front of his breeches. "There's a few among the Feneen I'd not mind some swordplay with."

"Often I think you'd have made an excellent Lithos," I tell him. "And then you open your mouth."

"Oh, I would have," Hadduk agrees immediately. "Except I knew early on that I wanted women more than the distinction. Mason suits me well. Plenty of both."

I shake my head as he pulls open the armory door, and we eye what little is left of our weaponry. "You're a good reminder of why the Lithos is not to be distracted," I tell him. "I cannot speak to you of battle plans longer than a few breaths before you have a tale to share of some woman you've bedded."

"Aye, well." Hadduk hefts a spear from the wall, testing the balance. "I'm not fishing for a fight, my Lithos, but you've been doing a lot of talking, and I've not heard a battle plan yet. So I'll tell you of my conquests in the bedroom, if you've got nothing larger in mind."

It's well he's not fishing for a fight, for it's the Lithos he's luring, and I know better than any man how to quell my temper or quash a kind word. I'm of the Stone Shore, and stone I must be.

"Would you send a Pietra into battle with this?" I ask, pulling a sword that's meant only for practice from a pile in the corner.

"I wouldn't send a Lure against a fish with that," he says.

"Or a Feneen with this on their arm to protect them?" I ask, hefting a stone shield with a crack in it that widens even as I lift it.

"Which Feneen?" he asks. "The one with the hump in his back needs no shield, only to turn his arse to the enemy. That thing is hard as my skull."

"Which I'd gladly use for a battering ram," I tell him, something he seems to view as a compliment.

"I take your point," my Mason says, raising his hand to stop me. "We need to recuperate. Train the Feneen. But Stille was a clam open to us before, and we said it would take three Stilleans to face one Pietra. Now, I fear they fight with a victory behind them—unearned as it may be—and truly, there may be three of them for every one of us."

"And two Indiri," I add, remembering the girl on the beach, her mad race to fight our entire army alone cut short only by the wave.

Hadduk spits. "Those two I'll end myself, finish what was begun at Dunkai."

"You're not wrong, though," I tell him. "Stille will fight with warm bodies in their favor, and the memory of a cold sea at their backs. We came for them once, and they'll look for it again."

"And so?" Hadduk eyes me.

"We let them come to us."

CHAPTER 17

Ank

STILLE WOULD NOT CHANCE IT," I TELL THE LITHOS, MY words cold, though we are in his chambers, where the fire burns bright. "You lifted a rock and disturbed the ants; you cannot expect that they will crawl out from underneath to see if you still stand by."

Witt betrays nothing, though I know my words have taken some hope from him. I do not envy him. He leads a patched army in a dying land and would rather Stille make a move in error than relive the losses the Pietra suffered.

"Are you not bold?" I ask. "Since when do the Pietra wait for the battle to come to them?"

"Since the sea swept their legs out from under their feet," he says, eyes focused on the fire. I know what he sees there. I've led many to their deaths and yet lived to see their faces. As Lithos, he cannot stoop to asking a Feneen what should be done. And so I spare him the question.

"Did I tell you my mother is Stillean born?" I ask, my words bait on a line for him to grasp.

"Perhaps."

Though he speaks slowly, I know the Lithos is far from slow-witted.

I've seen him half answer men before, only to give them enough rope to tangle themselves in. But a knot of my own making is one I can undo at will.

"It is not common among the Feneen to keep ties with those who cast them away," I go on. "But my mother would send for me, at times. My caul kept me from seeing her face, but I knew her voice and her hands, the smell of her."

Witt watches the fire still, but his eyes are focused now. "How did you enter the city?"

"No one wishes to look upon the Feneen," I say. "We know well how to move among the hidden."

He nods as if I had answered him, but he's sharp as a Hadundun leaf, that one. I'll be sharing what I know of the tunnels within a handspan of the moon outside, and he remembering every word I say without a single stroke of a quill.

"Was it hard to be near her, knowing she'd given you for dead?"

That I did not expect. I take my own moment, as if the fire has called to me as well. I'd be wise to remember that this Lithos knows the weight of emotions, even if he hides them.

"I could not look upon her until my thirtieth Arrival Day, for my caul did not pass until then," I tell him. "By then I was a man, and many things had been buried between us. But yes," I go on, wanting to give him something of honesty, "when first I felt the touch of her hand, I did not know if I would clasp or kick."

"On which did you settle?"

"I was held," I admit. "And so I held back."

"You know Stille well?"

"The dark places."

"Dark places are what interest me," he says, leaning forward. "From them much can be overheard. We made a mistake in placing all our trust in might, knowing nothing more of Stille than their love of peace and warm tides. My army lost more than men in that wave.

Gone now is the element of surprise, and we cannot rely on brute force a second time."

I remain silent, hand at the caul around my neck, waiting for the Lithos to arrive at the conclusion I directed him toward.

"They have the advantage in numbers now," he goes on. "And the sight of living Indiri cast a pall across more of the men than I'd care to admit. We were told they were gone, an enemy long vanquished. I saw their blood stain the grass as a small boy, and have been raised learning the songs of that victory. Yet a spotted girl charged the entire army of Pietra alone, and a wave came at her heels."

"Perhaps pulling her in as well," I remind him, though I doubt it. My hand tightens on the caul as I think of the twins. "Do not be overly troubled by the Indiri, Lithos. They are only two."

"Maybe so," he concedes. "But the sight of them recalls a battle we thought finished, quickly followed by one we most definitely lost."

The Lithos rubs his hands, still stiff from pushing many into the sea this past Culling Day. The line had curved up the cliffside, many of the Pietra bringing nothing more than a chest-breadth of bark pulled from Hadundun trees to drop at their Lithos's feet, then declaring that they had made a boat. I told myself it did not matter, that those who had torn apart the trees with their bare hands had the same fate as Elders who had spent their dwindling years carving true boats. The Lusca would take them all.

Still, some who went on hastily built crafts were guided by grief that would have subsided in time; their deaths were not called for. I knew this, as did the Lithos. It was a long Culling Day, and the Lusca ate well. Witt has fallen silent, hands cupping each other, and I know he thinks of the boats that were not boats, as I do.

"What is it you would ask of me, Lithos?"

"Would your mother still welcome you, after you fought alongside Pietra and attacked your homeland?" he asks.

"Would yours welcome you, should her boat find our shores again?"

Witt's eyes close; his hands tighten. My words hit old wounds, still open.

"I'll answer first," I say, sparing him speech. "She had me at her side when she could not see my face. She'll have me again, though I stood with the enemy."

"Caul or not, you see much and know more," Witt says, his eyes now open and upon me. "Learn of Stille. Hear their plans. Know what they fear now that the sea has become an ally. For what they fear is what we must become."

I nod and make my exit. I arrived in the Lithos's chambers a Feneen advisor who fought alongside the Pietra. I leave as a Stillean who returns to his birth people to spy upon them.

And the Lithos believes it was his idea.

CHAPTER 18

Vincent

VINCENT SLIDES PAST ROOK, ONE OF THE FEW GUARDS he trusts, at the door to the bedchamber he shares with his wife. They are of an age and as boys played more than a few games of ridking together, wagering with snakeskins they had found, or ancient oderbird eggs, hard as rock. Now they are men of duty, and only nod to each other as Vincent eases the door closed behind him.

He had expected to find Khosa asleep, but their room is awash with light, Khosa propped up in bed, head bowed over a scroll. She is so lost in her reading that she doesn't notice his entrance, and Vincent takes a moment to look at this woman he married but cannot seem to reach.

Her hair is up in a simple knot, the complicated forms the castle girls torture it into abandoned for the night, the crown of Stille—one he still thinks of as his mother's—resting on her dressing table. Khosa's mouth twists as she reads, and he wonders if she is aware that the emotions she struggles to show freely at other times are amply visible on her face when she is lost in lines of ink.

A small gasp escapes her, and Khosa's hand goes to the neckline of her sleepshirt—which he can't help but notice has slipped farther downward than she would allow if she knew he was in the room.

Cursing himself for always being a gentleman, Vincent clears his throat.

"Oh, Vin." She glances up, a real smile on her face, whether from something she's read or his presence, he does not know.

"What is that?" he asks, nodding toward her reading.

"I'll explain," she says, eyes back on her scroll. "Oh, and watch your step."

She's a moment too late, and Vincent bumps into a pile of loose sheaves that splay across the floor. Khosa gasps and dives from the bed to keep them from the fireplace, her sleepshirt billowing around her and exposing more of her skin than Vincent has ever seen before.

"I'll get it, Khosa," he says. "You should . . ."

She stares at him blankly from her hands and knees, unaware of her gaping neckline as she pulls the sheaves back into order until he motions to her.

"Oh! Apologies," she says, blushing as she returns to the bed, papers crushed to her chest.

"What have you got that is so interesting?" Vincent asks, only to see Khosa turn a brighter shade of red.

"Excuse me?"

"Not your . . . the . . ." Bereft of words, the young king can only motion toward the pile of scrolls on his side of the bed while he feels a flush creep up his own neck.

"Ah . . . bits of unknown history." Khosa moves them onto her lap, making room for him in the bed. He joins her, though he is still in his dayclothes, not wanting to spurn the invitation.

"I find it hard to believe any history is unknown to you," Vincent says, grabbing a sheet at random.

It is true that his wife's knowledge of Stille's history rivals even his own, though she was raised in the bucolic village of Hyllen. Her Keepers had found it prudent to sharpen her mind as much as possible so that other shortcomings might be overlooked.

"Even I can't know what is written in books kept from my hands," Khosa remarks, trading the scroll she holds for another. Vincent is about to ask for an explanation when a hastily scribbled line on the page he has catches his eye.

Dagmar's corpulence has become so great that the attendants were required to grease the sides of his soaking bath to remove him from it today.

"Dagmar?" Vincent's brows come together in confusion. "He was my seven-times-great-grandfather, much renowned for how he sat a horse. No beast could carry such a load as they describe here."

"Perhaps his better days were in the past," Khosa says, glancing over. "Do you know how he died?"

"Wasting sickness," Vincent says, a lesson learned well, now repeated verbatim. "He secluded himself in a wing of the castle to spare his family the sight."

"Or . . ." Khosa lifts a sheet from a pile beside her, already read. "He drank himself into oblivion and destroyed whatever rooms he inhabited during fits of rage, one of which ended with him falling down the stairs of the leeward wing and breaking his neck."

Vincent takes it from her hand. "Where did you get this?"

"The Curator," Khosa tells him. "It seems that the histories of Stille exist twofold: the versions we are taught, and the truth of what actually occurred."

"This one seems recent," Vincent says, reaching for a freshly inked page before she can stop him.

The young King Vincent is a regicide, his mother a murderer, though none would call the deed badly done.

"Quite recent," Khosa says quietly. "I did not mean for you to see it."

"What harm can there be in my seeing it in writing?" Vincent asks. "I know well what I did."

And though he strives to keep his voice light, he knows his wife's ear catches the strain. There is weight in the ink at his fingertips, a dark realization at seeing his name linked with villainy. He will not be able to stand at the elbow of future Stilleans and detail the calumny of his father: the women who paraded under Dissa's nose, the unwanted advances toward Dara and his own wife, Khosa. Unless . . .

"Is there much written of my father?"

"Much and more," Khosa says, indicating a pile near the window. "Though I'd advise lighter reading."

"Such as?"

"You may appreciate this one." Khosa hands him a sheaf, edges brittle with age. The lettering is dark slashes, written in frustration.

Every Arrival Day Runnar's measurements are taken, and every Arrival Day he blots the ink and pens measurements more suited to his grandiose sense of self. I record here his actual height, weight, and various other body parts, for posterity.

"Filthy fathoms," Vincent says, eyes scanning the columns. "Runnar was shorter than I am!"

"Other body parts?" Khosa repeats.

"Yes." Vincent feels the flush that had subsided surging again. "The Scribes are very . . . thorough."

"And?" Khosa glances at the sheaf Vincent holds, quick eyes making short work of what she sees there.

"It appears that I am the bigger man."

To Vincent's surprise, Khosa giggles. He made such jests in her presence before they were husband and wife, finding her appreciative of ribald humor. But given the pristine state of their marriage bed, he has stopped, not wanting her to find some buried complaint within his words.

Perhaps he erred in this, he thinks as he watches Khosa return to her reading. The friendship they shared before marrying has stumbled beneath their careful handling of each other, politeness taking precedence over familiarity. And while he wishes Khosa could be his wife in more than name only, he regrets that their marriage has made words between them stilted, the bones of their friendship rickety.

"Tides," Khosa says, catching her tongue between her teeth as she finds something particularly interesting. "Apparently your Runnar was quite the son of a sea-spine."

"How so?" Vincent takes the page she offers him, but something other than his ancestor's actions gains his attentions.

The Given has produced an heir, though it be male. It has been left for the Feneen.

"Khosa," he says quietly, fingers brushing against her sleepshirt. She glances up, traces of their shared laughter still on her lips. Vincent watches as her mouth falls into a straight line.

"A male Given," she says to herself. "How can that be?"

Vincent only shrugs. "How is Runnar remembered as a benevolent ruler, standing tall among men?"

"Yes, but . . ." Khosa's hand goes to her mouth to gnaw upon a fingernail, a habit he remembers well from watching her work over tide calculations. "In order for the line to be unbroken, this Given would have to provide a female heir."

"Perhaps she did, at a later time," Vincent says. "Or maybe this marks the end of the blood of one of the Three Sisters?"

"It could," Khosa agrees. "The histories I know share only that the lines other than my own ended, not how. But still . . ."

She continues to stare at the parchment in her hands as if the ink there may liquefy again and change shape, taking on a form more amenable to her previous teachings. "A male Given?"

"Left to the Feneen," Vincent adds. "Could the child still live?"

"Doubtful," Khosa says. "The other lines failed long ago; the child would have passed time out of mind."

Vincent does not mention that if he had lived, the male Given could have produced heirs of his own. Khosa is quick enough to know as much without him saying, and with Ank firmly planted on the side of the Pietra, they will find no answers to questions down that path.

She blows out her bedside candle, all their shared laughter now mere echoes in the dark room. The queen slips off to a troubled sleep, but the young king allows his candle to burn as he lies motionless, still dressed, not able to unsee his own deeds set down by quill, and wondering what has yet to be written about him that may need to be hidden.

CHAPTER 19

Khosa

KHOSA WAKES TO THE SOUND OF THE SEA, WITH HER FACE pressed against the iron bars of her window, limbs smacking frantically against the stone to reach what her body desires most. In her mind, she screams for Merryl to help, to pull her away from the call of the tide and what waits for her beyond. But only her mind screams for survival; the rest of her is determined, dancing toward the sea no matter what the obstacles. Stone, iron, even the mauling of her own flesh is inconsequential once the dance has begun.

It passes, as always, and Khosa slides to the floor in exhaustion, fresh bruises blooming on her arms and legs, the tender skin of her face swelling from where she bashed her head against the bars. Blood trickles from her lip, and she sucks it away before she cries for Merryl, knowing the sight will upset him.

She calls out, but her voice is weak and inconsequential. Khosa crawls toward her bedside table, knocking aside a pile of the hidden histories she had so carefully stacked the night before. With the last of her energy, she wrenches the table covering away, bringing a pitcher of water, her bedside lamp, and a stone etching of the Stillean lands to the floor with a crash.

Merryl is through the door in an instant, his capable hands pulling her to her feet. Even though she knows he means only to help, she can feel his skin against hers, and her gorge rises. The previous night's wine comes up, along with what little dinner she'd taken before diving into the hidden histories. Her guard is unshaken, settling her still-trembling body onto the bed and covering her with blankets before tending to his sullied armor.

"So sorry," she manages to whisper, as he wipes himself clean.

The guard shrugs, tossing aside the dirty linen. "My little girl has messed me more than that, some nights. Don't worry yourself over it."

He pulls a footstool to the side of the bed. "Shall I send for the king?"

Khosa shakes her head, even the small movement draining her.

"I know you would not upset him, but he needs to be aware—"

"My husband knows I dance," she manages to say, but Merryl only eyes her sternly.

"But does he know that you do so more often, and each time more violent than the last?"

Khosa drops her eyes. No, she has not told Vincent that her fits have increased, or that the last time the strength of her dance tore the bars from their stone setting when Merryl pulled her away from the window. He'd replaced it himself, once she'd fallen into stillness, sparing her the indignity of an explanation to the ironsmith.

"Khosa . . ." Merryl sighs. "I know you would not worry him, but I'm sworn to protect you from all that would do you harm. That extends to yourself."

"I cannot help that I dance," Khosa says, too weak to swipe away the tear that escapes.

"No, but you can help being as stubborn as a hay mule . . . my queen," he adds as an afterthought, earning a smile.

"I have always been the greatest danger to myself, Merryl," she chides. "Nothing has changed in that."

"Some things have," he corrects her. "Vincent is your husband, not only the royal blood of the land you would have perished for. He carries true feeling for you and would mourn not just the loss of a ruling queen, but of a wife, should I fail in my duties."

Khosa is silent, her eyes drifting downward in the heavy lethargy that always follows a dance. "I know he cares for me," she breathes. "I care for him too, in my way."

"Aye, but you'll not be the one left behind if you go to the water," Merryl reminds her. "Your cares for him will cease, and him left to wonder what more he could have done for the woman he loves."

Too tired to respond, Khosa manages a slight nod to acknowledge the guard's point.

"I know it myself," he goes on. "This helpless love for another. If there were something amiss with my child or wife, and one in my circle knew, and kept quiet . . . well, they'd sharply regret that choice."

Khosa swallows once, the tears now sliding freely. "I hear," she says. "And I will tell him . . ."

Merryl moves to pat her hand, then thinks better of it, rising to go. The door latches behind him before she finishes speaking.

". . . when I am ready."

The girl who comes to tidy Khosa's chamber doesn't blink at the fouled bedding, instead dropping the queen a conspiratorial wink as she rests in a fireside chair. Those who tend her have grown accustomed to the queen's stone face, so Khosa is spared the need to manufacture the expression appropriate for a shared secret. Her Keepers trained her well, but only for the reactions that would be necessary in her short time as the Given: happiness, delight, joy, pointed interest. She was given no lessons on how a reigning queen should respond to a maid who believes she has discovered her sovereign is with child.

Khosa keeps her hands folded across her midsection as the girl changes the linens, removing the mess that Merryl's touch caused. The queen watches as the girl tips her a curtsy, her eyes sliding inquisitively to Khosa's lap. Once the girl tells the other servants that the queen has early-light illness, there will be no end to the fussing and hovering, when Khosa would prefer quiet solitude.

"Is there anything else you'll be needing?" the girl asks.

"No, thank you." Khosa waves the girl away, anxious to return to her reading.

She'd been enjoying herself the night before, and not only because Stille's past is more checkered than most would believe, but because she had gained knowledge that few others hold. Even before Vincent joined her, Khosa had learned of tunnels not unlike the one leading into her library—she could call it *hers* now, as queen—which had been built to serve everything from secretly moving lovers through the castle to growing a strain of igthorn that thrived on complete darkness.

"Or to hide a stray body," Khosa says aloud as she spots Cathon's writing at the top of a pile near her feet. She reaches for it, ignoring that her hand shakes as she holds it.

The Curator picks his nose.

"And lives to pick it still," she says, discarding the slip of paper for another. Her fingers fall upon a bound manuscript, cording so loose that the pages fan as she pulls it onto her lap.

"Tides," Khosa says under her breath as one breaks free, floating perilously close to the fire. She snatches it in midair and curses herself when it crumbles at her touch. Carefully, she smoothes what is left.

And so left Harta the sailor from Stillean shores, never to return.

Khosa chokes back nervous laughter at the echo from her conversation with Donil near the beach, but stops short as she reads it again.

"Harta the sailor," she says carefully. In Stille no occupation is considered lowly. The sconcelighters and trapmen alike can bring concerns to the king and queen in person and expect to be seen. But a sailor is unheard of in a country where no boats are built, and the word is written hesitantly, as if the hand that held the quill was unsure of its spelling. Khosa slips the last page back into place before moving to the door.

Merryl falls into step beside her as she exits, eyeing the book clasped to her chest, its pages nearly wider than her shoulders.

"I need to unbind these pages," Khosa says to him without preamble. "They are too brittle to be turned. Do you have a dagger on hand, by chance? Good. Also, fetch the Curator for me, please."

"If you believe I'm going to leave you alone, you are greatly mistaken," Merryl says, sidestepping a sconcelighter replacing a spent candle. "Especially with a weapon and in a room with windows."

"Send for Rook, then," Khosa says, fingers resting on the heavy latch of the library door, her breath coming quickly. "And hand over that dagger."

From a young age Harta would wander, leaving behind Stille for Hyllen, Hyllen for Sawhen, Sawhen for Hygoden. He knew the bend of the shore and the tilt of each rock, and remembered well the roads he walked. Yet he left the roads for paths, abandoned paths for brush, and reached the bases of mountains yet unclimbed to find their summit. He aged on the mountain, and came down to say that he had seen all that could be seen of land, and wished to know what lay beyond the horizon.

Few listened to his words, for the Givens had danced since a faded memory, no wave coming to tumble the flesh from our bones. Stille knew peace; it was no fault of ours that Harta had not found his. Yet he persisted, telling others that to believe we stood on the only habitable land was faulty thought.

Many and more times he came to the king asking for assistance in building a ship. Though he was always heard, the king tired of Harta's insistence, finally asking, what point would there be in agreeing to such a scheme, when no Stillean would carry the knowledge to build one? Encouraged by what he mistook for interest, Harta produced plans for a rigged ship, with sails that billowed and a mast standing tall, built to carry many.

The king was stricken at the sight, but held his composure long enough to ask how Harta had come upon knowledge of a thing so unheard of in Stille.

Harta admitted to spending many years among the Pietra, speaking with their Lures, who perch atop cliffsides and see far, into the very sun as it sinks. They spoke of things I hesitate to commit to ink, boats seen in silhouette, masses of wood and rope, sail and cloth, floating upon the sea but never coming close because of the fierce Lusca that haunt their waters.

At this the king was outraged. That such blasphemy built upon the words of an enemy should be spoken within the castle walls, to the sovereign's face, was an unthinkable thing. Harta was exiled, told that his ship looked like nothing more than another sea belly for Stilleans to rot inside of, wooden kin to the sea-spine, a Lusca built by the hands of men.

Many taunted Harta as he left the city to return to his people in Hygoden, where they had fled. Dark mutterings were heard in Stille then. What punishment is it to send away one who wanders? Can words such as these be spoken to the king and left to stand?

The king heard these rumblings, as did his advisors, and it was decided that the best course of action might indeed be to give Harta what he asked. His conviction had not waned with exile, and there were those who shared his spirit, for whom the warm beaches of Stille and waving grains of Hyllen held little interest. Those who hold our land dear took offense, and arguments erupted, leading to more than a few bloodied noses and clashes in the streets of Stille, a city that had known no violence since the wave that tore away the Three Sisters.

And so it was decided that Harta should have what he asked for: permission to cut timber in the Stillean forest, enough to build his monstrous vision. He was sent for, arriving with a handful of people who shared his proclivities, and joined by others within the city who had become incensed by his spirit. They were a mixed lot: Pietra who wished to sail with oars instead of hopelessness; Stilleans who craved adventure; Hyllenians with no interest in shepherding; Feneen, who already knew what it was to be unwanted; and a handful of Indiri, their spots shifting colors with every living thing they put their hands upon.

This last sent even more ripples of unease through Stille, and the king ordered that Harta's people would have their own outpost, a small gathering of rough homes built quickly and meant to last only the span of the shipbuilding. For the group could not be sheltered within the walls of Stille, with the speckled ones among them. The king sent messengers to report on their progress, anxious for the day when the malcontents would board their ship to sail or sink, taking their heresies with them.

But Harta would not see it hastily done, first building the ship in miniature, learning the ways of rigging and sails, teaching it to all who would crew. Years passed, and the king sent messengers less often as his interest waned. The shipbuilders stayed to themselves, and so went largely unremarked in the city until the day a rigged ship, sails full and flying, came around the cape.

Stilleans did not know if they should run to see the sight or cover their eyes. I for one, stood on the castle walls and watched, seeing the now gray-haired Harta on his ship, the mix of all this island's peoples with him, the children that had been born to them during the long wait dashing along the deck, wild with excitement.

Harta's ship passed along the shoreline once, those on board seeing the last of their homeland—the last of any land—and then turned away.

And so left Harta the sailor from Stillean shores, never to return.

CHAPTER 20

Donil

"TIDES," I SAY, ONE HAND GOING TO MY DAGGER AS IF IT could help me somehow.

Khosa rests a hand on my shoulder, and I feel the thrum of the connection between us even through my clothing.

"I did not know how you would receive this," she says gently. "To hear that you are not the last—"

"But that I *am*, in truth," I correct her, an edge in my voice. "They did not return. Indiri rest in the sea, not able to return to earth."

I have always known the rush of battle, the heat of anger, but for the first time, I understand Dara's wrath. My blood races at the thought of Indiri feet taken from land, their roots torn from the earth only to rot in the sea. I would find this Harta, tear his thumbs from his hands so he could build nothing, not lead the innocent to be a meal for those that wear scales instead of skin. But Harta is long gone, and my anger can rest nowhere but in my own heart.

"The history says only that they did not return, not that they perished."

"And which do you find more likely?" I asks. "It was a fool's errand, put into action by a madman, carried out by those too ignorant to question him."

"Do you call me ignorant, then?" Khosa takes her hand from me. "For if I had seen the boat, I would have run toward it, swimming with the sea-spines to reach its wooden belly."

"No," I concede, handing the loose pages back to her, though I wish to crush them in my hands. "You are far from that, too clever by half. Khosa, these things were hidden for a reason. Would you bring more discord to Stille?"

She carefully puts the pages back into the sheepskin bag at her shoulder. "No, I would not. I would bring them hope, the promise of something other than a battle against the Pietra for what land remains, little and less day by day. It is a fight we cannot win."

"We can win," I say stubbornly.

"At what cost?"

"What price lies on this?" I shoot back, rising to my feet. "You read the words, same as I. *Discord, malcontents, violence.* To tell Stilleans there is something other than this land will rest as well as . . . as bringing Indiri children inside their walls."

Khosa drops her gaze, but not before I see her burgeoning disappointment. She came to me hoping I would stand with her. Vincent will not be hard to sway, though he has long been taught there is no earth other than what our feet stand upon. I know my friend already doubts the old teachings. A word from his wife could easily send him on a mad quest for that which does not exist. If I lend my support as well, the deed will be considered done. Vincent will have a ship built and ready to take them away—everyone I care for—at the turn of the tide.

"I cannot go upon the sea, Khosa," I says, head down. "My sister walks this land, though she be far from me. Vincent chose you over her. Should I do the same, leave my blood behind to perish, only to be near a woman I cannot have?"

"Vincent did not choose me over her," Khosa says. "Stille made the decision for him."

"And drove her from us all," I insist. "Shall I widen that distance?"

We sit quietly together, the tide turning four revolutions, regrets and longing hanging heavy in the air.

"I hear," Khosa finally says. "And I feel your burden, though I cannot share it. For my part, I would go, and though Stilleans may balk at the idea of boarding a ship, they must be given the choice."

"I know you would go," I say, the bitterness from my stomach spiking my words with gall. "Perhaps with less thought for me than you put on."

Khosa's head snaps up. "That is unfair."

"Life is unfair!" I growl, my anger sparking hers as she comes to her feet.

"You tell *me* of unfair?" she seethes. "I am the Given, made to drown, bringer of ill news, unwitting wife, and barren queen. What will the histories say of me, or will all my pages be kept in dark places, when I ask Stille to build ships?"

"To the depths with the histories, and you too if you care more for how you appear in them than you do about the man who stands before you!"

The words are out before I can stop them, the darker part of my nature undoing all my gentleness. I can't recall them, can't gather the sounds from the air and shove them back into my throat. It is too late.

Khosa's eyes flare. "Drown then, shall I? You'd see me dead if not yours? A fine thing to say to a woman, Donil of the Indiri!"

"Khosa, I did not mean—"

But I have no chance to redeem myself. Khosa is wild-eyed with rage. She kicks sand toward me with two savage thrusts and turns her back, skirts flying in the wind and the histories she'd trusted me with beating against her side as she runs back to the castle.

Back to her husband.

I know better than to find solace in drink, as my sister did the night she nearly led Khosa to her death. Wine tends to deepen whatever emotion we feel in the moment, and I fear the results of wandering any further into self-pity. So I seek comfort elsewhere, though I knows it will only pile trouble on top of misery.

"I've missed this skin," Daisy says, rubbing a hand across my bare chest.

Though I know her body more thoroughly than any other, she never fails to get a reaction with her touch. The kitchen maid was raised in Hyllen, where women make no apologies for their desires, and Daisy is no exception.

"I've missed yours too," I answer, and it is no lie. The two of us have spent many hours with each other in her small rooms, and I know the spot on her ceiling that I stare at now better than the stars in the sky. "You still drink the nilflower brew, yes?"

She turns into my shoulder, her sigh tickling the sensitive skin of my armpit. "Yes, lover, there will be no Indiri half-breeds. Worry not."

"I wouldn't say that I worry—"

"Yes, you do," she corrects me. "Worry what your sister will say, what the Given will think."

I turn toward her, catching her tone. "My sister is gone, and the Given married to another."

"Yet I think your heart travels with both, and it is only your body that I receive in my bed." Daisy's smile is a sad one that I've not seen from her before. Our time together has always been spent in pleasure and jest, but there is a shadow upon her now.

"I do not think lightly of you," I say, twisting my fingers in her hair. "But I cannot bond with one who is not of my kind and dilute what little Indiri blood is left."

"You would for her, I think," Daisy says, stilling my lips with her fingers when I would deny it. "Hush, Donil. Your body is honest with mine. Keep your words the same."

I roll to her, covering her mouth with mine, and am quite honest with her, indeed.

CHAPTER 21

Dara

I NEEDED A REMINDER THAT THE TANGATA IS FERAL, AND IT came this morning.

Kakis has been sleeping with me every night, sharing heat and the soft touch of her fur. I've been lulled into this companionship, enjoying the way her ears twitch at my words, the small sounds she makes in her throat in agreement or annoyance. We have developed a language between us, one that has made the journey easier than when I walked alone. But I had forgotten that the soft pads of her feet carry claws, the rough tongue that sneaks meat from my hand is surrounded by teeth long as my fingers.

She has taken down a fadernal, a swift beast on four legs that only my best arrows can find. Yet Kakis raised her head, sniffed once, and broke through the undergrowth. I catch up to her some time later, gloating over prey caught but not yet killed. The fadernal, born only last season, judging by the length of its legs and knobbiness of its knees, is crushed beneath her furry belly, bleating like a goat separated from its mother.

"Kakis," I reprimand her. "Kill it and be done."

She glances at me, then pulls tufts of fadernal hair from her claws. Her body undulates as the fadernal tries to crawl from underneath her bulk. It nearly escapes, pulling itself by the front legs and freeing a third, before she casually swipes, claws going deep enough to puncture but not to kill. She pulls it back toward her, powerful jaws on slender throat, but does not crush it.

"Kakis," I say again. "Enough play."

I pull my knife and approach, ready to slice the fadernal's throat if she won't. But the cat growls the deep warning of one predator to another. This is her kill, and she'll deliver the finishing blow in her own time.

I know better than to cross a Tangata, whether it shares my fire at night or not. I give her a dark look and my own growl, leaving her to the fadernal, and it to her. There is a clearing nearby where I see a flock of oderbirds watching quietly from the treetops, eyes wide, heavy heads bobbing on stalky necks. They have eyes only for Kakis, and I could pull my bow, take down dinner for this night and the next. But I do not. I have no appetite.

The fadernal has brought out a memory, this one my own. The Tangata have never been loved, and with good reason. In my twelfth year, a clowder took up residence on the road to Stille after discovering that Hyllenian travelers made good meals and were slower prey than their flocks of sheep. The cats developed a taste for our meat, and it being Stille, no one knew how to deal with them.

Gammal had called for Donil and me, though we were only children. Our Indiri memories had given us the skills of our ancestors. Donil could track animals that leave no prints, and I could kill anything with blood that spilled. The king set us upon the clowder, leaving instructions that none should remain. I had no qualms about killing cats, though I knew Donil balked. Yet, if succeeding could win us some respect in Stille, Donil would do it. I knew well that the stares from the nobles and words spoken beneath discreetly cupped hands did not sit well with him.

We left Stille, his heart heavy at the thought of killing so many beasts, mine light at being upon the road, no more walls around us. Even leaving Vincent behind bothered me little, and my heart clenches tight now at the remembrance, Vin standing at the parapets to watch us go, Dissa beside him.

I take a deep breath, willing my chest to unbind, the raging knot there to untangle itself. Both the son and mother are dear to me, now and in my memory, and I cannot look upon their faces without feeling as if a spear has passed through me. An oderbird clucks at me, his clipped beak snapping a question.

"I'll not die down here, to be your meal," I say to it, and fling a rock into the trees, scattering the flock. They are not convinced and resume their positions moments later, eyes bright and curious as I relive that moment, Vincent's disappointment at being left behind clearly visible as we rode away, and Dissa's worry the most vibrant thing she had inside of her.

The Hylleneans offered us food in plenty, but no beds. We were to deliver them from being meals for cats, but were expected to sleep with their goats. As always, the rejection filled me with rage, while Donil would only shrug and steer me to the barn, one hand on my shoulder to prevent me from drawing my blade and putting an end to their impertinence.

"We're here to help," he reminded me as we settled into the hay, where a trio of kids nestled up to Donil instantly.

"I'll help them," I said. "Into an early grave."

"And what good that?" Donil scolded me. "Stille will not love you more for shearing heads from those who shear the sheep."

"Will they love us ever?" I asked. "We came here with bloody footprints following behind and have never become clean in their eyes. Gammal sends us to clear a Tangata clowder today. We are their tame killers, sent in to do what they cannot. What shall we be put upon next, I wonder? All of Pietra?"

"Perhaps they'll fashion us fins and ask for the head of a Lusca,"

Donil jested. I shiver now at the memory. For all of our knowledge of the past, we could not know that we *would* be sent for a Lusca, and come home to find the Given sharing a plate with Vincent, our lives altered forever by her arrival.

The next day one of the Hyllenean women had come to us with tears in her eyes and the tale of her young boy, sent out to retrieve a herd three suns before, never returned. We found his small body in the woods, and though he had been missing for some time, the death wound on his throat bled red and his skin still held heat.

There were older wounds on his legs and heels, a long scrape on his arm where he had been dragged. Donil had wrapped the boy in his own cloak, but not before I read the story there.

A story of time passed with cats who would not let him go, yet not kill him either. The tears that had dried on his face had done so not long before, and when we found the clowder, I made many die, allowing none of them to go quickly.

"Kakis!" I find my feet, the memory of the Hyllenean boy striking too deep to let me sit still. I will kill the fadernal or release it from the cat's claws. Either way, it will be over.

The Tangata slinks toward me, brought on by my call. Red is smeared across her whiskers, a spray none could shed and yet live. We eye each other cautiously, and the cat approaches, head pushing into my palm.

"Rough beast," I say to her. "I know you well."

And though it is true, I remember also the deep pain I felt at the sight of that Hyllenean child, the instinct of all the mothers gone before me raging in my own veins as I brought righteous vengeance to the cats that had harmed him.

I know hate, yes. I know it well.

But there is a part of me that loves with equal heat.

CHAPTER 22

Ank

I TAKE LITTLE WITH ME, AWARE THAT WHAT SERVES ME BEST hangs in the pouch around my neck. But the Lithos argues for a weapon made of steel, so I accept, sliding a knife into my boot. He does not know of my real force, the faded caul, the remnants of my own skin that lets me see past his. His and others.

After a tight nod, I leave him behind, the night air of Pietra cold and carrying a tinge of blood. I think one who braved the Culling Day may have found release through the sharp edge of a Hadundun leaf. Witt has kept from me the stories of Pietra gone to self-death, found bloodless and empty on the forest floor, the roots of the dark trees swollen with what they spilled. Hope is spilling from these people, and their Lithos would not have me know that those my soldiers fight beside may wield weapons with something less than conviction.

Still, I hear things. The Feneen know well how to live in a world that hates us. Keeping our heads down and mouths quiet makes it easy for others to forget we are here, and for us to hear all manner of tales. The horse underneath me snorts at the smell of freshly spilled blood, but it fades quickly, and from the corner of my eye, I see a Hadundun stretch with new strength, growing a few handspans as it drains whatever poor Pietra sought death at its base.

"On, then," I say to my horse. I've had enough of the Pietra and their stones, the trees that drink death and boats not made to sail.

"Where to?" comes a response, and I have a brief moment of confusion. A light laugh comes from my stoneward, one I know well.

"Nilana," I say, not surprised that she has caught me in a leavetaking meant to be seen by none.

"Did you suppose it was your horse that questioned you?" she asks, and I follow her voice, breaking through some low brush to find a small fire and a low cave, her dark eyes tight upon me as I rein in.

"Which is more likely?" I counter. "That my horse should speak to me or that a woman with no arms and legs should find her way into the woods and build a fire?"

"This woman has many arms and legs to do her bidding, though they be not her own."

I grunt in response. There are many Feneen men—and some women—who jump to do Nilana's bidding. A gaze from under her full, hooded eyelids has added more than a few Pietra to her circle, I don't doubt. A glint of steel from deep in the cave catches my eye, where one such set of arms and legs rests now.

"What brings Ank of the Feneen to the road in the dark?" Nilana pushes. "He goes with steel in his boot and a grim face. I think it bodes poorly for those he rides to meet."

"And perhaps for those I leave behind," I tell her, dismounting. There is no other among us whom I trust to guide the Feneen, should I not return, though in truth I had hoped to keep the arrangement between myself and the Lithos. Many minds knowing a thing leads to tongues spreading it to more. I settle beside her, soaking a bit of warmth from the fire.

"You return home," Nilana says, glancing at me.

"Why ask if you know the answer?"

"Why bother questioning a man who answers with questions?"

she says, and I can't help but smile. Nilana won't let me leave until she has what she wants, and no amount of misdirection will lure her from that point.

"I go to Stille," I confirm. "To see what can be learned."

Nilana nods. "Hadduk said as much."

"Hadduk should not know," I say, irritated that the Lithos shared our plan with one I do not trust. "And neither should you, if that's how you came about the knowing of it."

Nilana shrugs. "I have Hadduk's ear."

"Is that all?"

She only smiles at me, but I have my answer.

"You were to be for the Lithos," I remind her.

"A Lithos is not to be distracted," she tells me. "And this one has unblinking focus. I know how to bring a man to me, and that one won't come."

"How then shall we bind ourselves to the Pietra, once the killing is done?" I ask. "Bringing you together with him would hold him to his word, yourself a formidable Feneen alongside the Lithos, blending us as one."

"That was the idea, yes," Nilana admits. "I don't recall our plans including you on a horse pointed toward Stille, with your mother on your mind. Yet here we are."

Once again, she has me. I can only grunt.

"Odd how plans change," she adds.

"I hear," I say. "Yet I know where I go and what I do, and you cannot say how the Lithos's heart will feel toward the Feneen once we are no longer of use to him."

"I do not know that the Lithos has a heart."

"He does," I assure her, remembering the flash of pain I felt when I touched him. "He hurts, the same as any man. Maybe more."

"Still, I am not to his liking, and fit Hadduk's hand nicely."

"I thought you despised him?" I say, aware that I will not win her over to the side of the Lithos and so choose to pester her.

"If I cannot warm the bed of a cold Lithos, why not find some distraction with the Mason?"

I nod but hold her gaze, knowing there is more. Nilana has traded barbs with Hadduk often, and while being at his side would surely gain us knowledge, she would never go there solely out of guile.

"He knows his way around a woman," she finally admits. Though the fire burns bright, I think she may be blushing.

I laugh, the sound too often unheard among these stones. "Nilana of the Feneen, I think you may have met your match."

"Only under a blanket, perhaps," she says. "My mind could best his any day."

"There are times it tests mine," I admit.

"And times it does more than test," she says archly. "But who then shall be for the Lithos?"

"As you said, plans change," I say, rising to my feet. "It will be clear, in time."

"Ride safe," Nilana says as I mount my horse, the heat of the fire already leaving my body. "And beware those leaves."

"Mind your own self," I tell her, and ride into the night. I glance back once, to see that Hadduk has joined her, his face different when he looks upon her in the firelight, their heads close together over its flames. I spur my horse and leave them behind, knowing that if the Mason can be softened, so too can the Lithos.

CHAPTER 23

Dara

THE PLAINS OF DUNKAI ARE BEHIND US. THE DEAD SWATH of land where the Indiri died—and where I was born—still bears witness to what happened there. I stopped for a moment, laid my hand upon the dirt that used to be my people, and told them where I am headed, and what I will do there. Kakis stood at a distance, tail twitching in the sun, the blood of another hunt on her whiskers.

The sun on the plains is as merciless as my Tangata, and when the first stands of trees appeared, I greeted them in Indiri to thank them for the shade, but there was nothing in them to answer me. These trees do not know my tongue, as my eyes do not know their leaves. Kakis skirted widely around one, as a cat will, trying to appear unconcerned, though I saw her muscles were bunched to run from an enemy yet undiscovered. I do not care for the trees either, and we keep our distance, preferring to sweat in the sun than to seek shade beneath them.

We are nearing the Stone Shore. Though I have not been there in my wanderings, I have asked my ancestors about it, and they have shown me some of what I see now. Grass fading into rock, the oddly menacing trees, and the slightest tilt of the land that makes my legs burn, bringing a dull ache in the morning. Even Kakis shows stiffness when she wakes, and I hear creaks from her old bones as she goes about her morning stretch, each claw extended, every tooth exposed.

Though I told the Indiri who were given to the earth at Dunkai what my aims are, I have not thought on how to accomplish them. In truth, I left Stille only to see it behind me, with a half vision of finding the Lithos of Pietra and ending his days. Yet now I question how an Indiri will come near the Stone Shore without notice, my speckled skin marking me. Behind me, I hear Kakis let loose a massive sneeze.

An Indiri trailing a tame Tangata, no less.

"Depths, cat," I say to her. "Have you no head for stealth?"

She pauses to clean her paws, which is as good an answer as any, for there are still oderbird feathers nestled there. Kakis pulled one from its nest yesterday, the bird knowing nothing before his world changed from blue sky to the inside of a Tangata's mouth.

I sit for a moment myself, cautiously leaning back against one of the Pietran trees to check the fletching of my arrows. Kakis's meal was only half finished when I found her, and my newly made arrows sport fine feathers, though I question how true they will fly, since I made them by firelight.

"You aren't such a terrible companion," I tell her, running a finger over the black and white tips. Kakis doesn't answer, and when I look up, she is as still as the stone these shores are named for, one leg still stretched high to clean, toes spread apart. But her eyes are pinned above my shoulder, a deep growl beginning in her throat.

I unhook my bow from my shoulder and peek around the edge of the tree, but I don't need eyes to know what's coming. The smell hits me as the breeze changes, a scent I've come across only once before and am not anxious to experience again.

It's a Lusca, a monster of the sea come to hunt on land. Webbed feet better made for the surf leave odd tracks in its wake, scales casting colors in the light, first green that fades to blue, then a weak shade of purple. It may look soft as a fish belly, but these creatures have curved claws that leave anything living well hooked, once caught, and teeth that are best avoided entirely, as there are no second chances.

I slide back behind the tree, and my eyes meet Kakis's. The cat is no fool. Crouching, she makes her way to me, ruff raised, low growl still simmering. I jab upward with my bow. She doesn't hesitate, leaping onto the lowest limbs so lightly that the tree barely shudders. Kakis passes into the shadows above, leaving me to wait.

I nock an arrow and slip to the side.

The Lusca has paused, tiny eyes meant for water and darkness swiveling to and fro in its massive skull. It does not belong here, and yet it is a predator still, and one I dare not underestimate. I slide back out of sight, pressed against the tree, bow to my chest, thinking.

Donil and I hunted one as a favor to the Hyllenians whose herds it had torn into, Vincent's grandfather, Gammal, asking us to settle the nerves of Stille's frightened shepherds. Its path had been littered not only with the leavings of sheep it had fed on, but the bodies of Tangata—many and more—who had challenged it. I took down that beast with one arrow while Donil slept beside me. We took its head and two feet to Gammal to prove our kill, barely able to see each other over the humped back of the dead animal as we cut away the pieces . . . and this one is larger.

I take aim, but hope it will pass me by.

What I saw in a glance showed me muscle and claw attuned to each other, and I fear that my earlier kill was heavy and slow after much feasting, whereas this creature has an air of hunger. It may not see well in the sun, but a chuff of air tells me I've been scented. Above, I hear Kakis settling onto a branch. I imagine her preparing to pounce, balanced on lean haunches. Behind, there is a slow, ponderous footfall, heavy as a boulder falling to the sea. Followed by another.

I let out a breath of air, spin into the open, and take my shot.

As always when I fire an arrow, I know the moment I release what path it will take, and this one has not found its mark. The tip buries into the fleshy thigh of the Lusca, who bellows with pain. It turns not to the injury, but what caused it.

The beast I killed before fell with one shot, and so I do not know how to face this enemy. All I can say in truth is that I have angered it, though I am nocking another arrow even as it charges for me, the very ground beneath my feet shivering at its footfall.

"Tides," I yell, knowing the moment I release it that this one has gone wide, burrowing into the bulge of its shoulder but causing no more damage than a pinprick. And though a pin cannot hurt deeply, it *can* hurt badly.

The Lusca grinds to a halt in front of me as I draw my sword, raging at me and the new flare of pain. It bellows, mouth open wide, mere handspans from my face, and I am hit with the stench of the deep: wet and rot, foul and dark things that have no place walking on earth as I do.

I rage back at it, yelling my own wordless cry as I swipe behind an ear, the back of a knee. My blade is keen, but it comes away not with blood, but scales, a slick armor with no chinks. I take jabs and do nothing more than litter the ground with scales. I've spun to its backside, and the spiked tail swings for me. I hit the ground, rolling underneath it, but come up to catch a charge directly in the side, the Lusca's skull making short work of my ribs.

I know pain almost as well as hate. Every scar I carry has a story, and each one is remembered well, so that when the burn of blade or crush of rock comes again, I will bow under it, but not break, having survived it once before. But this agony is new to me, the feel of my chest caving into itself, the air I gasp for not filling me but burning a path deep inside.

I still clutch my blade and turn in time to parry another swipe from the tail. I take off the tip, and an arc of blood sprays across us both. I wipe my face clean with my blade arm, the other wrapped tightly around my chest. I desperately wish to draw my second blade, fight the beast from the lee and the stoneward as I prefer, but my bones feel like small stones where the Lusca hit me, and I fear that if I pull my hand away, they will scatter to the ground, my skin following in a puddle.

The beast is more wary now that I've taken some of its tail and put two arrows in its hide. We circle each other, its massive head nodding back and forth as it tries to trick me into feinting, stubbed tail whipping in and out of my vision. We've turned a half circle, and the Lusca's back is to the tree when I see the leaves parting above it.

Kakis lunges, claws stretched, eyes wide for the kill. But I see them change midpounce, slipping from the tight focus of a hunter to a questioning gleam. Leaves explode around her as she clears the canopy, but tufts of Tangata fur fly on the wind as well, and dark drops of her blood.

The cat hits the Lusca's back, but in midroll, her balance thrown. She slips off the scales, grabbing purchase with one arm only, her hindquarters dragging in the dirt as the Lusca spins, trying to dislodge her. Lusca and Tangata blood mix so that the air is heavy with wildness, the dark musk of fear and the nearness of death coming close behind.

I do the only thing I can think of. I drop my blade and run for the tree.

My bones grind against each other like glass as I say the words, hands tight on its trunk, drawing the life of it inside me. When I open a living thing with my words, I open myself too, become a gaping mouth into which power flows, and I draw until I can hold no more, every part of my skin and the unlit depths of me bursting with strength.

It is not to be taken lightly, and I open myself now, knowing I'm a filthy, witless fool to drain this tree to save a Tangata. I open myself angry that the last female Indiri may die beneath a tree she can't name, killed by a beast from a distant sea. I open myself thinking of the first time I did so, to save Donil and Vincent—to the depths with Stille.

I open myself and take, to find that it is not life I draw from this tree, but death.

It flows into me like a river, every crevice of my body coated in the blood of others, long congealed, dark and black. Roots do not untangle at my feet but instead burst with blood, turning the dirt around me to mud, sending the leaves shuddering from where they rest and falling around me like blades.

Kakis flees as far as she can, a steady trail of blood following her. But the Lusca makes the mistake of turning to look as I pull free of the trunk, now withered and dying. It cracks cleanly and falls, each leaf slicing through the Lusca and every branch crushing what the leaves do not tear. The beast heaves upward once, the remains of the tree shuddering along with it, a mix of old and new blood spreading in a pool.

Then it is still.

It is still, and I am dying. Everything I have inside of me is filth, drenched in whatever this tree held dear, all of it meant for darkness. I fall to my hands and knees to retch. Old blood and not my own comes pouring out of me, from my mouth and nose, eyes and ears. I would push all there is inside of me outward to be free of it. My gut flattens and I am sick again, the push of uncountable arrows in my veins as death tries to leave me by any means.

Kakis crawls to me, her own blood fresh and new, fur hanging in strips from her side where the strange leaves skinned her as she jumped. She pushes her head against mine in question, rough tongue trying to clean me of the mess.

"No," I say, not wanting her to foul herself with whatever I have pulled from the tree. It burns through me, my broken side a whisper in comparison. I cannot even find words, Indiri or otherwise, as Kakis takes my cloak in her mouth and pulls me like a kitten, clear of my own mess and the death we dealt out together.

"Kakis." I manage to speak her name just as the sound of hooves reaches my ears, and sunlight flashes off armored men as they clear the horizon.

"Go," I say to her. My cloak is still in her mouth and so the growl that she gives is muffled and weak. But the cat knows she is hurt and that we are outnumbered.

"Go," I repeat. There is the briefest touch of her nose, cold and wet, against my cheek. And then she is gone.

"*Now* you listen," I say, my breath sending up a puff of dirt to meet with the cloud that the Pietra bring as they come to a halt in front of me.

The Lusca is dead, the horses in front of me still.

And the ground shudders as all I have inside of me pours out.

CHAPTER 24

⚬◦◯◦⚬

Witt

I AM WITH A LURE, STANDING ON THE CLIFFSIDE WHEN THE Stone Shore begins to fall apart.

It starts with a stream of pebbles at my feet. They roll between my boots and over the edge, lost to sight long before they find water. The Lure ceases to speak of the Lusca he saw crawl onto land only the day before, his eyes on the flow of stones.

"What—" He begins a question, but does not end it. For the small stones have held larger ones for generations, and without them, the boulders tremble. The first one catches him cleanly, taking him over the side to the sea. There is a heavy sound, not unlike those I've heard from the kitchens when the Lures bring large fish in, tossing them onto stone tables to be butchered.

It's the sound of meat hitting rock, and that realization sends me back from the edge before I am fed to the sea as well. My back is pressed against the cliff, so that I can feel it shudder, each movement sending more rock falling from above. Rocks and men, for I see another Lure, and part of a third, sail past, bound for the sea.

I close my eyes, waiting for the one that will come for me.

Always I have seen our world ending in water.

I do not know what to do when the very rocks turn against the Pietra.

CHAPTER 25

Vincent

THE ARMY OF STILLE STANDS BEFORE HIM, AND VINCENT fervently wishes it were a more impressive sight. Sallin insisted on bringing every able-bodied man before the king, armed with the best weapons they own. As Vincent's gaze sweeps the gathering, he wonders if Sallin's point was not a show of power, but further argument for building ships.

"All are mustered, sir," Sallin says, inclining his head just enough to show respect.

Vincent nods back, feet pacing the training field as he takes a quick tally of the Stilleans before him. Given the number of Pietran spears that had bristled the sea after the wave cleaned the beach, he has no doubt that Stilleans outnumber their enemy. But each Pietra was raised on tales of battle and grew up on shores made of sharp rock. The Stilleans have walked on soft sands their whole lives.

"Sir—"

Vincent closes his eyes against Sallin's voice, one that has grated on his nerves much and more as the advisor presses the need to leave Stille behind and find other lands.

"There is nothing else," Vincent has reminded Sallin, again and again. He opens his mouth to do the same now, in anticipation of another argument. But his words stop as Sallin's did, and their eyes meet, asking the same question.

A sound rises from the men, the clank of armor against sword and spear, every hand unable to hold its weapon still. They look to each other as the sound grows and knees give way, the earth beneath them no longer the solid thing they've always believed it to be.

Sallin falls as well, and Vincent shortly thereafter.

All he can think of as the tremors creep into his very body, teeth rattling against one another, is that Khosa is in danger, and once again, he is not at her side.

CHAPTER 26

Khosa

THE PAPER MOVES BENEATH HER QUILL, AND KHOSA regards it quizzically as a wayward line forms, only to be blotted out by a river of ink as the pot spills.

"Khosa!"

Merryl pulls her from her stool as a bookshelf comes away from the library wall, cracked spines and torn papers sliding across the floor, the wooden shelves splitting against the table where her head had been bent over her work only moments before.

"Tides," Khosa says, only to have Merryl yank her yet again as the stacked firewood beside the large hearth tumbles. Her guard clutches her to him, and the queen is too surprised to object, as books fall from the walls and the maps above their heads wave as wildly as if the wind has joined them.

There is no breeze on her face, yet her skirts whirl around her legs, and her hair is pulled from its pins. Khosa slides to the floor to feel the stones vibrating as Merryl draws his sword to defend her from an unseen force.

The queen falls among the folds of the coral dress her attendants had brought that morning, the brush of the fabric against her face and the stones pressing against her shoulder blades reminding her of the one moment she and Donil had explored each other's bodies, hungry hands and mouths roaming.

As the first archstone falls from the ceiling, Khosa swears to herself that if she leaves this room, she will not return to it with regrets.

Regrets of things left undone.

CHAPTER 27

Ank

MY HORSE DOESN'T CARE FOR ME, NOR I HIM, BUT IT IS still a surprise when he throws me on the road to Stille. I am not a born horseman, but I've not lost my saddle since I was a small boy. I rise with wounded pride, only to find that rising at all is a challenge, the earth beneath me behaving as if it were the sea. I go back to my knees, watching as my panicked horse runs in circles, tossing his reins, unable to find a spot of earth that acts as it should.

"Something of the sea takes to the earth," I say, thinking of the cave in Stille littered with Luscan scales. "And the earth—"

I cannot finish, for the trembling has set my teeth against my tongue.

I lie against the ground, feeling it shake as if in fear.

And I, too, am deeply afraid.

CHAPTER 28

⚬◯⚬

Donil

THEY COME TO ME WITH LARGE EYES, A TANGATA KIT too small to be alone, a fadernal too frightened of something unseen to mind the cat. An oderbird lands at my feet, wings spread wide, raising the call of alarm. I draw my sword and spin on my heel, but see nothing, only the trees swaying in the wind.

But there is no breeze, and the trees do not move gently. Cracks fill the air, and I understand the animals' fear as they gather to me, and I open my arms that I may shelter them as best I can, an Indiri body against the wrath of whatever we have enraged.

I have no memory of this feeling, earth as tremulous as a sea-spine in a riptide. I close my eyes and ask my ancestors, but there is nothing. As I go to the earth, animals held tight against me so that they may have comfort, I know without remembering that something in our world has gone terribly wrong. The dirt beneath my hands cries as if in pain, and I fear that it is mourning one of its own.

One of the last.

"Dara," I say.

And the earth stills.

CHAPTER 29

Dara

I DRAW ONE BREATH, THEN ANOTHER.

A bubble of dark blood forms at my mouth, breaks, splatters against my cheeks.

The Pietran soldiers that face me are unhorsed, their mounts running wild. I draw a blade while they are distracted, opening one throat and bursting a heart with a quick upward thrust from behind before the others see that I have gained my feet.

I do not hold them long. Each step feels as if the earth itself throws daggers, and I drop, the dark blood of things long dead still coursing in me.

"Filthy fathoms, she smells like a corpse," one of the Pietran says, yanking my arms behind me to be bound.

"I am Indiri. I do not make a corpse," I tell them, spitting out another dark surge that comes from my gut. "My people are given to the earth, and when we cease to walk, that is what we become."

"Eventually," one of the soldiers says, as he yanks me to my feet. "But first you go to the Lithos."

CHAPTER 30

Vincent

THE EARTH SHOOK, AND WITH IT WHAT REMAINED OF Vincent's faith.

Always he had believed that the throne he sat on, though he had never desired it, had been eternally warmed by the sun and rooted in peace. Now he knew that darker deeds had been hidden in shadow, and those who came before him were not all he had thought them to be, the knowledge he had always depended upon greatly lacking in a time of need.

"Never have I seen such as what happened today," Sallin says, eyes coasting from one noble to the next, all the gathered advisors who sit at the table that doubles as a map.

There is a murmured agreement, one that Vincent can add to, but only weakly. The gathered years around him are many and more than his own. If any of them had felt the earth tremble under their feet as it had today, it would be one of the Elders. And yet they look to each other with tight lips and eyes clouded with worry. Vincent glances at the Curator, who shakes his head.

"There is no mention of such a thing in the histories."

"In any of them?" Vincent asks, raising his eyebrow so that the Curator takes his meaning. He and Khosa had found many things in the hidden histories, and she had shared with him the most star-tling—her discovery of Harta and his forgotten ship. If such a secret as that could be lost to memory, perhaps too the land had tossed as the sea before.

"No, my lord. No quill has ever inked such as what we witnessed today. It is a thing unheard of, and one of which there would have been many lines written, had it happened before. Of the great wave we have pages upon pages, many and more. Yet this . . ." He spreads his hands in helplessness, and Vincent sees that they are shaking.

He went through the city, after the trembling had ceased and the stable horses were calm enough to sit astride. The king met his people in the streets, wearing a smile he did not feel and speaking words of assurance that he knew to be empty. In the square, a man had been killed by a collapsed tower, and his blood flowed into the brick dust, creating a sticky clay on the ridge of Vincent's riding boots that he runs his fingers along now, thinking. Of all the lined faces and noble names that surround him, the person whose advice he wants most is his wife's.

She is safe. Khosa was the last thing he thought of as he fell to the ground, and her well-being the first thing he assured himself of upon rising. Sallin went with him, old legs keeping pace with young, the corridors of the castle an endless tunnel until he knew his wife was safe. He found her in the library, already righting fallen shelves with Merryl's help, draping torn maps and unwound scrolls across tables to be mended at a later date.

Vincent knew his face was as readable to her as any of the books at her fingertips, and that if she did not know before how he felt, she surely did after today. As for her, after leaning into him for a brief moment, Khosa brushed away the stone dust that rested on her shoul-ders, still unable to hide the way her mouth twitched when their skin touched.

He is thinking of her still as he faces a table of lined faces, all of their years weighing heavy against his few. Yet they are the ones who seem helpless, while a seed planted by Sallin and watered by Khosa grows roots that feel more solid than the earth of the kingdom he's inherited. Vincent rises slowly, the mix of blood and mud on his boots crumbling onto the floor as he does. The other men fall silent, eyes on their king.

"Today brought fear," he says, and they nod in agreement. "Fear in the face of something unknown to us. And we stood—though some of us longer than others." He drops a wink to the nobleman who lost his feet first, and some of the others chuckle.

"One life was lost, and will be mourned," Vincent goes on. "That a single building fell, and only one man beneath it, was a stroke of luck for Stille. Yet I wonder . . . what comes next?"

"I have already spoken with a bricklayer," one of the noblemen says. "The building that fell can be rebuilt, the merchant who made business there housed elsewhere until it is finished."

"And when the earth shakes again, and it falls again?" Vincent asks.

"We do not know it will," the nobleman says.

"We do not know it won't," Sallin interrupts. "The king has the right of it, to wonder what comes next. Shall we build on land that shudders, that we know is eaten by the sea, even should it rest easy? Why dig deeper roots in a place we know is dying?"

"*Dying* is a strong word—" an advisor says.

"It is not," Vincent says sharply. "*Crushed*—as that man was today—is a strong word. *Killed*—as I saw Stilleans fall by Feneen hands—is a strong word. Dying is a slow, torturous process, and I find it only too apt for this land. The only thing we do quickly in Stille is dismiss new ideas."

Sallin nods his agreement. Vincent looks to the Curator, who chews his lip.

"There is much we do not speak of here, things that are known and yet unknown. I've come to learn how much false knowledge is called true." Vincent presses his thumb against the edge of the table, and a splinter slides deeply beneath his nail. He pulls it loose, fingers trailing the edge of the known world.

"Shall I be the first to raise the question? Shall I be the king who asks if there is somewhere else I may take my people?"

He expected an uprising, outraged shouts, certainly the oft-repeated *there is nowhere else* coming from mouths aged with saying so, smooth spots on their teeth where the words have passed so often. Instead there is a lengthy silence, guarded glances, and finally, a protracted fart from an Elder who has fallen asleep.

"This is not, perhaps, the shock I had thought it would be?" Vincent asks.

"I am shocked, my lord," one of the nobles says. "But too old to show it. Outrage is for the young, change for the strong of heart. You ascended the throne of Stille long before your face was lined with age, and while there were many who questioned how our kingdom would fare in a time of such unrest with you at the helm, I now think . . ." He glances at the other Elders, who look to him to finish.

"I think it is as it should be. The old have reigned long, but now the waves—once our greatest enemy—have defended us, and the Given sits on a throne. Much has changed. And more is called for. If it is new land you seek, young hands will build the ship to take you there, strong backs row the oars. The old will be only ballast, yet I think I would like to see such a thing, even if it should be sailing away without me."

"I had not . . ." Vincent clears his throat, where it feels his heart has taken up residence. "I had not thought to leave you behind."

"Then you must resolve yourself to it." Another Elder speaks up. "For there are many who will not join you. I for one, agree with the will of the council that to remain in a land full of our enemies—where we can no longer trust even the earth beneath us—is folly. Yet I cannot give over a lifetime fearing the sea to sail upon it. There are many who will choose to stay, my king, both old and young."

"And so passes Stille," the Curator says, eyes wandering among the council. "Those who remain behind fall to the Pietra. Those who go to sea will linger upon it in search of what may not exist."

"A quick death or a slow one," a noble says. "Are these truly our choices?"

"The ships will sail toward hope, not doom," Vincent says.

But the only eyes that meet his are Sallin's, and Vincent finds his first victory as king of Stille hollow, won over a battlefield no bigger than the trunk of a tree, against an aged enemy too tired to fight. Vincent's injured hand curls into a fist, a thin trail of blood tracing the curve of his knuckle.

"Stille has not passed yet."

CHAPTER 31

⎯⎯⎯◦⎯○⎯◦⎯⎯⎯

Vincent

I WISH TO GO, OF COURSE," KHOSA SAYS.

"I thought as much," he says with a smile. Just as he hopes never to be his father, he wants Khosa never to feel as his mother did, as if permission were necessary. Given that her knapsack was already out when he arrived in their room, hands sorting through clothes for the journey to Hygoden, it was clear she felt the same.

"I would go with you," he says, sitting on their bed. "But the council thought it prudent to continue training the men. Should Stille truly be split, I cannot stand on a ship's deck knowing those I leave behind are helpless to defend themselves."

"Many will stay," Khosa says quietly, folding a sleepshirt and tucking it into her sack. "I know what it is to fear the sea, more than most. But the council underestimates your people, Vincent. The same country that can take a girl meant to die and make her their queen will listen to stories of land elsewhere, and some will wish to see it."

Vincent nods, for once more, his wife's mind has followed his own. "Training the men is only part of why I remain when you go in search of Harta's people. I will spread such stories over Stille's dinner tables, move among my people, palm pressed to palm. Someone must bring them hope beyond the promise of battle. That falls to me."

Khosa smiles absently and pulls a cloak from a trunk. "You make a good king, friend."

He watches her work, calm and relaxed as she moves without the gaze of the public upon her. She is not the only one who can read a face, and Vincent has learned hers well in their time together. Though she is mostly inscrutable, tiny deviations have made themselves clear to him over time. And he knows in this moment, she is happy.

"And you a good queen, Khosa," he says, to see the smile quirk a little wider. "We rule well together."

"Yes," she says, raising her eyes to meet his. "We do."

All else that he needs of her boils inside, the depths of his want to touch her, skin to skin, to feel her breath in his ear, the soft corner of her neck against his face as they lie together as husband and wife should. But he cannot linger too long on such thoughts with the bed beneath him and Khosa close enough to touch.

They do rule well together, side by side without one leading the other. No word the council spoke was not repeated to her, nothing she overheard from the servants was kept from him. And though their bed has so far been used only to confer with each other, how can he ask his council to hope while seated around a map of their collapsing kingdom when he cannot find promise in the friendship of a beautiful wife?

"I cannot say that I will rest easy without you beside me," he confesses.

"Truly?" She raises an eyebrow. "I believe only two moons ago, you woke me with a complaint of my snores."

"It is amazing that a girl of your size—"

She tosses a shift at him, which he grabs in midflight, the air around him filled with the smell of her in its wake.

"It is your safety that will leave me sleepless, not your snores."

"Sallin travels with me," Khosa says, surveying what she has set out for the journey to Hygoden.

"But he does not know you dance. I would have Merryl by your side."

"And his wife would have him by hers, with their second child soon to be borne. He has chanced much for my part already. I cannot ask that he leave a woman he cares for to be with one who claims only his duty."

"You mislead yourself if you think Merryl sees you only as a task," Vincent says. "If you asked, he would go."

"Which is why I will not ask." Khosa avoids his eyes, tucking the last of her clothes into the shoulder sack. "I had thought that Donil should come."

"Ah . . ." Vincent's breath hitches in his throat at the thought of the long distance that would be between his wife and himself, while the Indiri shared her fires, her meals. Khosa has been nothing but honest with him about her feelings for his friend. If he should deny her request, the trust they have built will come down as surely as the tower in the square, the blood of their bond spilling as the trades-man's did.

Can he even think of it as a request, at that? Only moments ago, he prided himself on the differences between his marriage and his parents', that his wife need not have his blessing to make her own deci-sions. And Donil is one of the few people aware that the queen of Stille is still Given to the Sea, her spasms as uncontrollable as ever.

But Khosa wishes to be a queen in truth, and not the girl who was cloistered inside walls, kept safe from even the splash of the surf upon her feet. She moves among his people—their people—and to cage her again would be to lose her as surely as if she had drowned in the depths.

"If that is as you wish," he says carefully, his voice guarded, though his anxious hands toy with the loose blankets on their bed, only now realizing that the servants haven't tended to their room.

"Khosa, why has the bed not been done up? Or the pitchers taken away?" He cannot imagine the servants would disrespect his wife;

some days he thinks the people love their new royal more than the one they already knew.

His wife slings her satchel over one shoulder before answering, pulling her hair free of the strap. "I have not felt well of late, and they believe that I . . . am with child. So they leave me to my mornings in peace."

"Oh . . . I . . ." Vincent finds that the bedclothes are not sufficient distraction and runs his hands through his hair.

"It is nothing to be concerned with." She shrugs off his gaze. "A twist in my belly that has not settled. No reason that I should not go to Hygoden, surely."

"Surely," he repeats, coming to his feet to join her now that her preparations are finished.

Vincent rests his hands on his wife's slender shoulders, able to feel the heat coming from her skin even if he cannot touch it directly. To his surprise, she raises her hands to his arms, sliding them down past his elbows, following the curve of his wrist to lace her fingers with his. He can see the effort it takes, the concentration in her brow as she rubs her thumb alongside his.

"I will miss you, Vincent," she says. "Truly."

"And I you," he says.

Neither one is lying.

CHAPTER 32

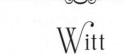

Witt

I KNOW THE SMELL OF DEATH. IT HAS RIDDEN ON THE WIND before me, and I have left much in my wake, but the stench that envelops the hall as my men drag a prisoner between them is of such strength that even Hadduk covers his nose.

"Depths, what have you—"

I break off as they bring the Indiri girl before us, dropping her unceremoniously to the floor. Her skin is slick with blood, some clotted and dark, other smears viciously red. She lifts her head enough to fix her gaze upon me, the bright flash of an eye cold as the sea buffeted by the chaos of her hair, matted and stiff.

She growls at me; there is no other word for it. The Indiri language, harsh no matter how gently spoken, churns from her. The words have no meaning, but I know what it is to be hated and need no translator. The girl spasms as if choking, and the guards take a few steps back from her as a geyser of blood erupts from her mouth.

"Son of a Lusca," Hadduk says, drawn by the sight, though it has brought with it a deep smell of rot. The Mason bends next to her, lifts her head by a handful of hair. Another litany of snarls comes from her, but the depth of her weakness is evident when Hadduk lets go, and her head meets the stones with a smack.

"The girl from the Stillean beach," he confirms, rising as he wipes the hand that touched her on his breeches. "Take her outside and slit her throat. Downwind, if you will."

"Or you can wait to hear the Lithos's wishes," I say to the men.

Hadduk glances my way. "Apologies, my Lithos. The sight of speckled skin brought me back to the plains of Dunkai, where I gave commands."

"But we are not there," I say, stepping toward the girl to gain myself a few moments of thought. Dispatching her would be Hadduk's first instinct, one of the two final blows necessary to end a campaign he began a generation before. But I've seen the guards exchange a glance at his hasty orders and would hear their thoughts.

"Where did you find her?"

"On patrol, my Lithos." The younger one, not much older than myself, speaks up. "Near the edge of the forest. She . . ." He looks to his partner, who stares resolutely ahead. "She brought down a Lusca."

"An Indiri swam in the sea?" Hadduk snorts, returning to the table where we had been conferring, Nilana alongside us. "Nonsense."

"No, my Mason. The Lusca was on land," the soldier corrects Hadduk, eyes cutting to me to gauge my reaction.

I nod, and he relaxes slightly. "A Lure told me he saw a Lusca pass from water to land. And you say the Indiri killed it. How?"

"With . . ." He pauses, looking again to his friend, who stands as still as the rocks. "With a tree, my Lithos."

"She killed a Lusca with a tree?" Hadduk repeats.

"And a Tangata."

"She killed a Lusca *and* a Tangata with a tree?" Hadduk's eyebrows fly up.

"No, my Mason," the soldier says. "The Tangata beside her against the Lusca."

"Both of them wielding trees?" Hadduk asks, what little patience the man has slipping as the story progresses.

"Perhaps the boy should sit," Nilana says. The sound of her voice releases another string of faltering Indiri from the floor, and a stream of blood spat in the Feneen's direction.

The story from another's mouth would be too fantastical to believe, but I have seen men lie, and this one is too shaken to do so. I look from him to Nilana, trusting her opinion in many ways more than Hadduk's. I know his counsel, saw his sneer the moment the girl was brought in. And while death is an instrument of war and one we know well, it is final once wielded.

Nilana listens, hearing each word and weighing it against the next while the boy speaks, telling us of webbed feet on land, Tangata claws unsheathed in defense of an Indiri, and the Hadundun tree's collapse.

"She did something similar when the Feneen faced her at the walls of Stille," Nilana says. "Although not to the same effect." She turns to look where the girl still lies on the flagstones. A trail of blood shows the Indiri has tried to make her way toward us, but it cost her. Her chest rises and falls, but only just.

"I spoke quickly when I counseled for death, my Lithos," Hadduk says. "But I do not think I spoke wrongly. If she could, that girl would have all our throats open."

"I see that," I tell him. "And I know that while she lives, you feel a duty of yours undone." His color rises, and Nilana tilts her head so that the fall of her hair hides her smile as I goad him.

"Yet this Pietran soldier has brought us something more than one of the last Indiri," I say, nodding to the boy. "He has brought us a girl who fought beside the king of Stille on the beach and charged my entire army wielding only two blades for his safety."

"At the walls of Stille, she did the same," Nilana agrees. "I saw her fight with the strength of many men, but her eyes are a woman's, and they always returned to the young king."

"He'd take an Indiri to his bed?" Hadduk cries.

"He'd take the woman he wants and who wants in return, be she

Indiri or Feneen, with spots on her skin or no legs and arms," Nilana counters, and Hadduk makes a *hmmph* noise.

"That's different," he says, and it is my turn to hide a smile.

"What shall be done with her, then?" he goes on. "I'll not sleep well with an Indiri in the same walls."

"You'll sleep fine," Nilana says. By the purr in her voice and the rise of his color, I'm guessing sleep is far from both their minds. The Lithos is not to be distracted, but I am not ignorant.

"Take her to the dungeons," I say to the soldier who remained with us. "Have Gaul find an empty cell." He complies, lifting the girl over one shoulder. Nilana's gaze follows the drops of blood that trail them from the room.

"If you would use the girl to draw out the Stillean king, we'll need her alive," she says.

"More than alive," I tell her. "I need her healthy."

"Because?"

"Because I'm going to skin her."

CHAPTER 33

Dara

THERE IS WET EARTH BENEATH ME, BUT FOR ONCE IT I's no consolation. Though I be a creature of the land, this soil reeks of years spent inside and the leakage of bodies that have gone before me. Even if this cell smelled of sun and sky, I would be desolate. I was dropped at the feet of my enemies—all of them—and could not raise a finger.

I heard the Lithos's voice, saw the Feneen woman who killed Gammal, and bore the touch of the man who rode against my people, driving them to the ground until their blood made mud. My wrath in that room could have brought down walls, yet I could not even lift my head from the floor.

I listened as they spoke of Vincent, the beach, the tree I took down on the battlefield of Stille, and of Kakis, whose tufts of fur floated on the wind as she dove to protect me, her skin opened in my defense. Thoughts of Kakis and Vincent made a fire in me, that enemies should speak of friends while in my hearing and I unable to strike. I tried, crawling, blood slicking my way. Had I reached them, I would have chewed through the Lithos's skin with my teeth, bearing no other weapon.

I swear in Indiri, my hands going to my side to feel the bones there, or what is left of them.

"None of that talk," comes a gravelly voice from outside my cell door. The jailer, a man who had lit up with happiness at his first sight of me, his hand lifting the fall of my hair for a closer look at my face. "An Indiri," he had said, hawking deep in his throat for spit to fling at me.

But he is an old man, all his juices spent years ago. He lurks now, outside the heavy wood of my door. I see him through the small grate in the door, a shadow that passes, then returns, a curious eye pressed against the bars as he tries to spot me in the dark cell.

I pull myself to the wall and sag against it, feeling as if the stones are all that keep my broken bones inside the sack of my skin.

"Depths," I say in Indiri, the single word all I can manage.

"Enough of that," comes the jailer's voice. "There's enough filth down here without your speech."

"Go and build yourself a boat, old man," I yell in the common tongue, biting down on the pain that it takes for me to do so. I hear a key in the lock and brace myself for the beating that's sure to come, and one that will cause much suffering, be he old or not. There is little left in me. I could not even curl against a kick. Light from the corridor cuts into my cell, but it is a woman's shape that passes through the door.

"His boat has not been made, for he is the only Pietran who would bide beneath rocks rather than above, and the Pietra make more bodies than prisoners. An old jailer is all they need, when there is little to guard."

Her speech is Hyllenian, and I turn my head toward her as her eyes adjust to the dark. "They send a shepherdess?" I ask, and she follows the sound of my voice.

Her hands are cool upon me, but probing. I hiss when she finds what is left of my side. "A Keeper," she corrects. "You've done yourself some harm."

"The Lusca did the harm," I tell her. "And paid for it."

"So I heard," she says.

"A Keeper," I repeat. "And what do you keep?"

"The Given," she says, and I flinch, though her fingers have found no wound.

"I see that you know of her," she says, pulling a flask from her pocket. "I am not surprised. Khosa showed deep interest in the Indiri and would have sought you out when she arrived in Stille."

"She sought my brother, certainly," I say through clenched teeth as she pours something cool over a spot on my skin where a Luscan claw caught, leaving behind a tear. "Though she could not have him."

"Does it matter who the Given beds as long as she should bear a child?"

"It matters when Indiri blood goes to the sea," I say. "And any child she bears now will wear the crown of Stille, should the land last that long."

The Keeper's movements cease. "The crown of Stille?"

"Did you not know? She was married to the king, as a savior instead of a sacrifice once a wave swept the Pietra from the beach."

"Khosa called no wave," the Keeper says, sorting through her pockets for a new flask. "I have kept many Givens and can tell you they do not hold command over the sea, but the other way around."

"You know that, and I know that," I tell her. "And we're both buried under rock."

The Keeper makes a sound in her throat, and takes the cork from the bottle. "Drink," she says.

It's not wine, or medicine, but cool water that I find. I gulp deeply, the lightness of it gliding over the rotted blood that coats my throat.

"You're poisoned," the Keeper says. "Like the sheep gone to the high meadow unfortunate enough to find an igthorn bush."

"No igthorn," I tell her. "I took a tree into myself, with leaves like daggers."

"A Hadundun?" she asks, taking the bottle from me.

"If that's what you call it, though I'd sooner call it firewood," I say.

"If you drew the life of a Hadundun into yourself, it's not poison in your body, but death itself," she says. "The trees drink blood and hold each drop close."

"That one doesn't anymore," I tell her, and she chuckles.

"I'd say not, though it nearly got the best of you."

I don't answer, the fact that I live proof enough that I overcame.

"It can be driven from you, like any poison," she goes on. "I'll bring more water. Cry, Indiri. Sweat. Retch. Piss your cell full. Death must pass through you so that you may live."

"Death has passed through me many times," I assure her. "I have not followed yet."

"That is good to hear," the Keeper says. "For you and I have much to say to each other."

CHAPTER 34

Khosa

KHOSA HAD SPENT HER LIFE IN HYLLEN AS PROTECTED AS the sheep, if not more so. The only journey she had ever undergone was from Stille as an infant, still sticky with her mother's blood, only to return years later on foot, dancing. The trees had torn her clothes from her as she went, senseless, with the surf welcoming her and the sounds of the Pietra destroying her homeland at her heels.

Though she has seen none of what the road shows her now, it is familiar. Maps and words have brought these places alive to her in ink. The road to Hygoden is a long one, for which she is thankful. It will take much travel to mend the tear between her and Donil, and many shared words to cover the echoes of anger that passed between them last.

She pulls her horse alongside his, and they nuzzle noses in greeting. "I had not thought you would be keen to join us," Khosa says, dropping her voice low so that it is lost to Sallin, riding some paces ahead.

"Keen is not how I would phrase it," Donil says. "I belong on the field alongside Vincent, training the men who would defend the place I call home."

Khosa's heart dips at his words, any thought she'd had of bringing his affections back to her gone with the breeze that pulls her hair free.

"But I could not . . ." Donil clears his throat, casts his eyes to the distance between them and Sallin. "I could not let you believe the last words I said to you were true."

"That I could go to the depths if I cared more for what the histories said of my rule as queen than I do for the man in front of me," Khosa repeats, her usual dead tones more lifeless than ever.

"Whatever our end is to be, Khosa, I would not see you go to the depths. I nearly killed Dara with my bare hands for leading you there."

"Yes," Khosa agrees cautiously. "But much has happened since then."

"You married Vincent," Donil says. "And it was Vincent who asked me to keep you safe on this journey, but a trapman could have bade me come, and I would have. I'm not here at the king's bidding. I'm here because the queen needs me, and I am unable to go against her will."

"And if I were to tell you that I do not care overly for being queen?"

Khosa says the words she practiced, running variations of the same message over and over in her head, desperate to find the one that conveyed her need without being too brazen. She has mouthed them so often since they mounted their horses that morning that she wonders if she has, in fact, spoken them at last, for Donil only stares forward.

A tremor passes through her, not one that will take her to the sea, and nothing like the one that shook Stille, bringing maps and books down around her head as she thought her life was about to end before she had lived it. It is true fear that has her in its grip now, the giving over of herself to another, and the passage of the moment as she waits for his response.

"You wear the crown often, for one who cares not," Donil says, eyes still on Sallin.

"I wear the crown to remind me of my duties," she says.

"And remind me as well," Donil adds.

"I thought it best . . ." Khosa lets her voice fade, unable to find words to explain what she had thought best. To be a queen, an honest wife, a living girl: these were all gifts that had been given to her when the only thing she'd been promised was a watery death. And she had vowed to fill these new roles as she had the part of the Given, dutifully.

"It *was* best, Khosa," Donil hisses. "You have done nothing wrong by taking Vincent as a husband."

"Done nothing wrong," Khosa parrots, his word choice following her own thoughts. "That is only too true. I would have walked into the sea, should Stille have told me to, but instead they sent me to be wed. And I went, the good sheep raised in Hyllen doing as she was told.

"Stille's past is littered with royals doing exactly as they pleased," she goes on. "Deeds that would make your hair curl, if they were known. And yet I have done what is best for others, always, to my own misery and nearly to my death. What has it brought me? A dying kingdom and a chaste marriage—"

Khosa's hand flies to her mouth, but the words have already been spilled. Donil reins his horse and reaches for hers, pulling them off the path into a copse of trees.

"A chaste marriage?" he repeats.

"Yes," Khosa says, head up, gaze meeting his. "Vincent is gentleman enough to wait until I—I . . ."

"A gentleman," Donil says. "A bit of a fool, too."

"A fool!" Khosa's eyes flare. "You think he should demand his rightful—"

"Because if he's not bedded you, then you're not married," Donil interrupts, quelling her anger.

"Our bond is written in the histories," Khosa says, her breath tight in her chest. "We are husband and wife."

"In ink, maybe," Donil shakes his head. "But a marriage isn't true until the two have become one. That's a detail perhaps a squeamish Scribe didn't see fit to write."

"You'd be surprised what Scribes write, and with glee," she tells him, her thoughts racing.

Donil spurs his horse onward, drawing hers back onto the path alongside him. "Dissa does not know, I assume?"

Khosa shakes her head. "No one knows."

Her clothes have been chosen to protect their identities as they travel, for the queen, accompanied by only two guards, would make a nice target for thieves. Khosa is dressed as a Hyllenian girl, simply, with a strand of coilweed holding her hair at the nape of her neck. Her head feels light without the crown, her limbs free from layers of clothing she puts on at rising only to have stripped off at night, a process that takes some time.

Always she has felt more like a Hyllenian girl than the queen of Stille.

Because she isn't.

CHAPTER 35

Donil

I DO NOT KNOW WHETHER TO LAUGH OR TO CRY, THOUGH I feel perhaps there is a scream deep inside me as well, one that will tear my throat out upon release.

Khosa is not married to my friend, though it is only the act that keeps them from being so. In his mind and heart, I am sure, Vincent looks on her as his wife, and *that* is what I would betray if I should make her mine, not the trivialities that claim she remains unwed. And yet, the fact that she has not lain with him fills me with a joy tinged with bitter edges, for if she remains virtuous, it is because Vincent is a kind and patient man.

Each way I look lies a betrayal. To myself and Khosa if I do not fulfill what we both want, to Vincent and Dara if I do. Yet every step of our mounts takes us farther from Stille, and it is so much easier to see her as only a girl, and me only a boy, each of us wanting the other so badly our horses have become edgy from the heavy air between us by the time we make camp for the night.

Sallin sets a fire as Khosa wanders to gather sticks. I am not far from her side, an arrow nocked that I may find us some supper. I do, and easily, pulling an oderbird from the air as Khosa goes to the spot where it fell. We are laughing children, words flowing easily between us, the night air carrying our voices.

The three of us make a quick dinner, and Khosa sleeps almost immediately, her body worn from unaccustomed travel. I watch her in the fire's light, more lost than ever in the thought that we are only two lovers, not the queen of Stille and the last male Indiri.

I'm passing water in the dark when Sallin comes upon me, much lighter on his feet than I had given him credit for. His hand falls on my shoulder, but my own is nowhere near my sword, so I'm left with little more to do than parry with words.

"It's not well to surprise a man while he's taking a piss," I say. "You'll end up with wet feet."

"Is that some old Indiri wisdom, friend?" he asks, undoing the front of his own trousers to join me.

"No, but this is: two men making water shouldn't cross streams."

Sallin laughs, his piss trail jumping with the motion. "That's old wisdom anywhere," he says. "So is this: the young will do as they must."

"While the elderly speak in riddles?" I ask, tucking myself away.

"I may be old, Indiri. But I was young once, and never blind. All I'll say to you is that you wouldn't be the first man in a queen's bed who wasn't the king, and I not the first advisor to turn his head."

Part of me wants to do that exactly: turn his head, and keep turning it until bones pop and his tongue never speaks ill of Khosa again. Another part wants to ask what he has seen between us, so that it may not be so visible to others.

"I care not what you—or she—do with our time here," he finishes, buttoning his clothing. "The sheep can lie with the goats and the oder-birds mate with the Tangata for all it matters. If we can't find Harta's people, or if they know nothing of ships, then I doubt you'll live long enough to grow a gray hair."

I clutch on to the only thing he's said that I can refute. "Indiri are of the earth," I say. "I'll not go on any ship."

"You will if she's on it."

Hygoden lies far, and though the next few days of travel are hard on Khosa's body, her spirit remains high. I see her grab at falling leaves, rest her head against her mount's neck with a small smile, even watch the whitecaps with awe, once the path takes us next to the sea. I put myself between her and it, but she only shakes her head at me, loose hair flying in the wind. She is in good spirits, and her body under her power—for now.

Travelers are uncommon in the far reaches, and the road is ours alone in the fading moments of light that mark our last day on horseback. Spirals of smoke greet us from the small village at the foot of the mountains, and I hear Sallin's bones creak as he dismounts in the square.

We attract a group of children immediately. Or rather—I do. A sea of small heads bobs around me, many fingers brushing against the skin of my arms. I squat on my heels, letting them touch my face and hair. One little girl even sticks her fingers inside my ears, blocking for a moment their continuous questions, like a nest full of unfed young oderbirds.

"Can you make it rain if you want?"

"Do trees really move out of your path?"

"Are you sad to be the last?"

"Have you got spots on your pecker, then?"

That comes from an older boy who holds himself apart from the others, arms crossed. Like all of the children, his clothes are worn, knees and elbows poking through the fabric. But the ones around me are bright eyed, curious. This one has a look I know well—wariness.

"I do," I confirm. "Do you greet all strangers this way?"

The children around me giggle, and the boy's mouth quirks ever so slightly. "No stranger," he says. "An Indiri, a girl of small build and light hair, and an Elder with soft hands? Take a knee, my friends, for the queen has come to Hygoden."

They all gasp and do as told, except for one small girl who instead rushes to cling to Khosa's skirts. She reaches down reflexively, taking the small hand in her own gloved one. My heart clenches, and I turn away.

"You're no dullard," I say to the boy. "We traveled here without our names being guessed, and me with only a cloak hood over my head."

"Hygoden breeds no idiots," he says. "We may live beyond your reckoning, but we hear of what goes on in Stille, and mark it well."

"And the doings of Hygoden are of interest to Stille," Khosa says, coming to my side, the child perched on her hip. "To me especially."

We've gathered a crowd, adults leaving their suppers behind to let chilly evening air into their homes. Doors stay open behind them as they take in the scene, an Indiri and the queen of Stille sharing words with a child of their village.

"And what would you have of us?" a woman asks, leaving the doorway of her house to collect her children to her side, an arm draped protectively around each of them. "We paid our tithe and have no men to spare for the fighting."

"We come in search of knowledge only," Sallin intervenes, casting me a sideways look of irritation. Undoubtedly he had hoped to share words in secret with the village elders, not have our business brought to the light by a kid with half his supper still on his face.

"We seek the descendants of Harta," Khosa says, clarifying when Sallin's words bring only guarded glances and more mothers retrieving their children. "I would speak with them."

"You already have," the boy says, chin jutted out with pride.

CHAPTER 36

Ank

THE EARTH ITSELF TRIED TO KEEP ME FROM STILLE, AND yet I return. Always my home has called to me. I sat in the great hall across from Gammal, he thinking I should be awed by the splendor, not knowing that I had seen those walls for many years, though always shrouded by the darkness of night.

The tunnels beneath the castle are known to few. The route leading to the beaches should the royals need an escape is the only one kept clear. In others I have found bodies, some dragged there by Tangata to be fed upon at leisure, some clearly left behind by another's hands. Stille has its skeletons, but even the Curator doesn't know that the city is built upon them.

I take a different route each visit, pilfering small things from the bodies that the Feneen may find useful. A pair of knitting needles from a woman who had perhaps been too free with advice, a dagger from a man who died with it between his ribs, a fine quill from the pocket of a Scribe who may have written something best left uninked. I do not know why they died, but the hows of it are usually clear. Skulls are fragile things that carry their damages past the grave, and a broken neck is easily spotted. I take a last turn, pocketing a hair clip from a noblewoman who once needed it, then slip out of the tunnels and into the castle halls, leaving my torch behind.

The sconcelighters are better guards than the men whose duty it is to patrol the halls, I have often thought. The women travel with fire, lighting corners that I could use if they would remain in shadow. This night I ease from behind a tapestry to find the hall yet unlit, the glow of an approaching sconceligther far around the corner. I make my way, the stones beneath my bare feet well known to me, ascending the steps with one hand on the wall to keep my balance as I travel ever upward.

My hand falls upon the door, delivering our knock. The latch slides back, and the scent of nilflower greets me moments before her embrace.

"Hello, Mother," I say to the Seer.

CHAPTER 37

Khosa

KHOSA IS TAKEN TO A SMALL CABIN AT THE EDGE OF THE village, the child's small fist clutched around one of her gloved fingers. Her heart twists at the pull of the tiny hand, quivering at the thought that any child of hers would have been taken from her the moment it left her body, and she sent toward the sea.

"Momma will be excited to have visitors," the girl says now, bare feet sliding over the stone path that leads to her doorstep.

"Papa will not," her brother says. He wishes to appear sullen, but she notices him watching every move Donil makes, then mimicking them himself.

Khosa turns her head away, not wanting the boy to see her smile. The Indiri skin is not the only fascination that Donil holds for others. The very life inside him is kind and gentle, drawing to him animals and children alike. And as their innocence fades, their interest in him changes. The girls, given a few years, learn to look at him aslant, with hooded, inviting eyes. The boys—like Pand—watch his movements, learning to do as he does, so that they too may make good men.

Pand pushes open the door to their small home, announcing who we are before his little sister, Unda, gets the chance.

"Pa! The queen has come to ask us things, and with her an Indiri.

Also, him." He points to Sallin last, who, for a man of rather large importance, makes a good job of being found the least interesting of the group.

"Sir, madam," Sallin says, nodding.

"The queen, my goodness," the lady says, coming to her feet to help Khosa out of her riding cloak. "I'll put a few more plates on . . ."

Khosa sees her eyes dart to the kettle that hangs over the fireplace, and she doesn't doubt there's more steam than food inside it. The plates already set are chipped and hold little.

"We had a good midmeal," Khosa says quickly, hoping the lie covers the rumble of her stomach at the mention of food. "We don't want to trouble you."

"No trouble," the man answers, rising as he does, and Khosa's breath stops in her throat. He has to tilt his head to keep it from hitting the rafters, and while she knows that Donil cuts a fine figure, she finds it hard to belive that Pand would imitate the Indiri when he has such a formidable father at home.

"Winlan," the man says, extended his hand to Sallin, who takes it without the slightest hesitation. Years spent maneuvering through Stillean Elder meetings have taught him well how to hide his thoughts; even Khosa can read no reaction in Sallin's face at the appearance of the man. Donil, on the other hand, has unconsciously raised his chin a bit and puffed his chest slightly. Khosa bites the inside of her cheek at the sight.

Winlan's hand comes to her next, and she takes it as a man would, thinking what a sight it would be if he were to attempt to bow to her. Even should he bend cleanly in half, his head would still be a handspan above hers.

"Khosa," she says as introduction, her title having slipped away from her entirely this far from the city she reigns in.

"And what do an Elder of the city, the queen, and an Indiri require of me?" Winlan asks, taking his seat again as he scrapes the last bites of supper from the plate in front of him.

"I think you know," she says. Winlan grunts in response. His wife looks nervously at her visitors as Unda claims Khosa's lap now that they are all seated at the table.

"Is it the papers?" Unda asks, one fist buried in Khosa's hair. "Papa says we musn't talk about them, so I don't." She promptly pops her hand over her mouth, eyes bulging, cheeks puffed full of air to illustrate how well she can keep a secret.

"Except you did," Pand says, cuffing his sister and eliciting a shriek. She burrows more deeply into Khosa, who folds her arms around the girl and latches eyes with Winlan. The big man heaves a sigh and crosses his arms, a behavior his son most definitely learned from him.

"Papers?" Khosa prompts.

Winlan's wife lays a hand on one of his arms, the length of her hand barely spanning his forearm.

"Aye, well, if you came here with Harta's name on your lips, I suppose what's written on them will be no great shock to you." Winlan rises, goes to the stacked beds in the corner, and pulls a trunk from underneath it. From his neck hangs a key knotted in leather, which he uses to open the chest. A handful of scrolls, small and musty, are placed on the table. Sallin and Donil crowd closer to Khosa as she opens them.

Intricately inked ships meet her eyes, billowing sails so lifelike that Khosa feels if she were to blow upon them, they would travel from the page. The second scroll holds columns and numbers, and small sections of the larger whole brought into focus. The third is a series of notes, detailed instructions on how to maneuver sails, steer the ship, and navigate. Khosa reminds herself to breathe as she looks upon the first lines she's ever seen that tell her how to follow where her dance wishes to take her, instead of documenting the death it will lead to.

Though when she unrolls the page farther, there are many accounts of things gone wrong. Hulls crashed upon rocks. Sailors lost to the sea. Lusca attacking the boats that did not bring passengers willing to become a meal.

"This is Harta's hand?" Khosa asks, raising her eyes to Winlan.

"Aye, and some that came after. Our ancestor took what he built with him, but left these behind so that we might follow if we wished."

"Have others gone in his path?" Sallin asks.

Winlan shakes his head. "None, as of yet."

"As of yet?" Khosa repeats, pushing for more.

Winlan shifts in his chair uncomfortably. "There was no reason to go, was there? Harta and those who went with him were never heard from again. They were either brave or very foolish, and none in Hygoden have seen fit to put their skin on the wager of which. But of late . . ."

"Of late war has come," Khosa finishes for him. "And the earth shakes."

Sallin reaches for a scroll, unrolling it fully. He is quiet for a moment as his eyes dart across it, reading. "As you say, we came here knowing of Harta, though his story was one kept in the shadows. What is written here could save all of Stille, at least those who could be persuaded upon a deck. The queen has a fair hand. Would you allow her to copy these, so that we may build ships such as your ancestors did?"

Winlan face twists into a wry smile, the first she's seen from him. "I knew well what's in the scrolls would be no shock to you, but Hygoden holds something you've not seen, for sure."

"And what is that?" asks Donil, his brow creased as he speaks for the first time since entering Winlan's home.

The big man shrugs, his nonchalance belying his words. "I've already built a ship."

CHAPTER 38

Witt

THE PLATE IN FRONT OF ME IS EMPTY, MY BELLY FULL. The glass I drink from is refilled the moment I empty it, and wine flows freely to all who sit around me at the table. The capture of the Indiri has raised the spirits of everyone who shares my evening meal, and their mood is high. Once the king of Stille knows she is ours, his army will come—and be crushed.

"What little training they have will do them no good," Hadduk says, spearing a bite of fish on his plate. "They are poor soldiers to begin with, who will be drawn out from their own lands and tired from travel. We'll make quick work of them."

There's a murmur of agreement among those gathered, the Pietran Elders and a small group of Feneen, one of whom has three eyes and avails himself of all of them while eating, two rolling in their sockets to take in whoever is speaking, and one with an eye on his food. I look away, remembering Pravin's advice about taking a Feneen wife to secure our bond with the outcasts. My former Mason had argued for Nilana as a mate, saying that even if I chose not to bed her, I'd at least have a wife I could sit across from at table and still stomach a meal.

I can't help but think that Pravin had a point, as my eyes drift to another Feneen, whose mouth is in his chest and not his face. The man eats cleanly, with no mess down his front. But seeing food and drink disappear into the tooth-lined hole makes the wine I drank shift uncomfortably, so my gaze wanders to a nicer sight.

Nilana laughs at something Hadduk whispers into her ear, tossing her head back so that the servant who feeds her has to sidestep out of the way. Not for the first time, I feel a twinge of regret that I did not take Nilana up on her straightforward offer to warm my bed. I reach for another drink, to wash away the weaknesses that make me an unfit Lithos.

"There is no doubt that our soldiers can best them, be they Pietra or Feneen," an Elder says, raising a glass to the trio of Feneen who share the table. "But what of their queen? Shall we draw them from their beaches only to have her bring our own waters down upon our heads?"

The question prompts renewed muttering, side conversations born all around the table that create a hum in the air, one that doesn't rest well on my ears. Pravin—or even Ank—would have stopped the talk with a strong word, but my tongue is heavy with wine and my Mason more interested in Nilana than the proceedings of the room.

The Keeper leans over my shoulder to refill my cup. It is full before I think to cover it with a hand to stop her.

"This queen," a Feneen asks. "What do we know of her? Who is she that she can command water?"

A fresh wave of voices crests, and I close my eyes against the arguments that meet in midair: that she is a Seer of particular strength, a Feneen raised in the walls of Stille as a weapon, an unspotted Indiri.

"The Indiri have only earth magic. They hold no power over the sea," says a loud voice that stops all others. I open my eyes to discover I am the one who spoke, and all have turned to me.

"Paid a visit to the dungeon, have you?" Hadduk asks, wiggling his eyebrows in a way I do not like.

"No," I say curtly. "I opened a history. You might try it sometime, as opposed to a woman's thighs."

Raucous laughter bursts out, Hadduk's among them.

"Ah, but there's much to be learned in both places," the Mason rejoins, to renewed laughter.

"What has the Indiri said?" an Elder asks.

"Nothing in the common tongue," I answer.

"If she is close to the king, surely she speaks it," the Elder continues. "And knows much that could be of use to us."

"Surely," I agree. "Yet as she came to us nearly dead, I thought it wise to allow the girl time to heal. I cannot entice the Stillean king to march his army into a losing battle only to recover a corpse."

"Truth," agrees the three-eyed Feneen, tipping the last of his wine into his mouth.

"There are ways to make her talk and yet live," another Elder says.

"Who do you think you speak to?" Hadduk's voice rises along with his color, his temper closer to the surface the more wine he drinks. "The Lithos can make the girl not only talk but sing, and in tongues none of you have heard before, should he choose."

"Bide, Mason," I say calmly, and Hadduk glowers into his cup.

"I don't doubt the Lithos can create songs of pain," says the three-eyed Feneen. "But I have met the Indiri, and I do not think her voice will join his choir."

Silence settles at this, and all look to me. Many thoughts are at odds in my head, wild horses that bump against one another to careen off cliffs.

"I could make the Indiri talk, should I choose," I say carefully. "But there is little to be gained from that. What do we need to know of Stille? That they are poor soldiers, and we stronger? That dragging them from their city will be like pulling a lazy worm from a hole, to chop into bits at our leisure? We know this. I'll take skin from her to send to Stille, and if she chooses to say a thing or two while my knife works, I'll listen."

"She won't," the Feneen says. "And I'd keep a steady hand on that knife."

"The Lithos knows how to wield a blade, Feneen," Hadduk growls, and Nilana catches my eye.

"Enough talk of the Indiri," I say, taking another drink to settle my nerves. "Is this a gathering of Pietra, that one girl raises strife between us?"

"It is not only Pietra here," an Elder says. "What world is this that a Feneen has set eyes upon a weapon my Lithos would wield, and yet I have not?"

Many cups rise at the comment, all of them held by Elder hands. Hadduk grips his fork so that his knuckles whiten, wine making anyone a target for his anger, be they Pietra or Feneen. I lift my palm for silence and tilt my head back toward the Keeper, the motion making it feel as if the horses in my head had all fallen into a tangle of legs and teeth.

"The girl could be brought up," the Keeper says quietly into my ear. "The poison is mostly leeched from her, but her bones are not yet mended."

"See to it," I say to her, and she is gone in a rustle of skirts.

"The Indiri will come among you," I tell the people gathered at my table, and I can't help but notice that the three-eyed Feneen pulls his dagger from its sheath in preparation.

CHAPTER 39

Dara

I'VE SLIPPED INTO A SMALL SLEEP, ALL THAT I'VE ALLOWED myself for however long I've been here. Under the rocks, there is no sun or moon to gauge time. A fever had tugged at the edges of my thought in the beginning, melding my ancestors' memories with my own, so that I did not know if I was myself or my mother, a woman long dead or one only about to be so. I awoke in darkness, slick with the sweat of a broken fever, and not knowing where I was until my hand fell upon cold rock.

There is a lantern in the hall, its solid glow steadier than Gaul's torch. I hear the light step of the Hyllenian woman and let my fists unclench. She exchanges a quick word with the jailer, their tones too low for my ears to hear. My door is unlocked, and the Keeper enters, Gaul on her heels. She lifts the lantern as if to see me better, but I think Hyllen does not make fools and she would have the fire out of my reach.

"Have you mended, Indiri?"

"Somewhat," I tell her. The word is full in my mouth, for I have not spoken since she left me last, however long ago it was. The sound of my own voice is harsh on my ears, and I curl against it, jarring the bones in my side.

The Keeper sees, and frowns. "Can you stand?"

"Is there reason to?" I ask.

"You're called before the Lithos," Gaul says. "Whether you go crawling as before or on your feet is your choice."

Though I would tear the jailer limb from limb if I could, there is no denying that I did indeed crawl before the Lithos upon our first meeting. I will not do so again. I lean heavily against the wall, but get my feet under me, though it takes everything I have not to cry out as I straighten, the mending bones in my side straining against the bind the Keeper placed there.

She leans closer to see my face, having to bend. Which means that I do not stand straight as of yet. I grit my teeth and straighten my spine. Fresh agony shoots through me, but I see the hint of a smile on the Keeper's face.

"I'll stand before the Lithos," I say.

We leave Gaul behind, in the darkness that suits him best. The stairs almost pull a cry from me as I ascend, each step a fresh stab in my side. The Keeper takes my elbow, and I lean on her, short of breath by the time we reach a lit corridor.

"Listen now," she says, voice low as she pushes hair back from my face. "The Lithos is at last meal with his Mason, the Elders, and a handful of Feneen. All have had a bit to drink, and tempers are frayed. The Pietra who have never seen an Indiri demanded you be brought forth."

"Am I so entertaining?" I ask, as she licks the edge of her wide sleeve and uses it to clean my face.

"The sight of you is enough," she says. "You need not make a spectacle."

"A sleeping Tangata is only a cat until it is poked," I tell her. "Then it becomes something else."

"Maybe," she says. "But you'll become dead if you don't heed me."

I grunt my understanding as she leads me down the hall. I can smell fish on the air, and hot bread with sea salt. I've been fed, but what's made it into my cell is first pawed over by Gaul, and I had to balance hunger against disgust when I saw my last crust of bread had a thin line of spittle down the middle. My mouth waters as she takes me into the hall, but hunger is soon forgotten, along with pain, when I see the assembly.

They sit at a table like a horseshoe, the Lithos at the crest and myself in the opening. I face him squarely, but take in those on both sides of him. The Mason—a new one, I note—sits next to the Lithos, Nilana beside him. My lip curls at the sight of her, remembering how she laughed when the Feneen left the field of battle before Stille, Gammal dying in her wake. She eyes me now as well, one brow lifting as if she were still amused.

Beside her are more Feneen, one of whom I recognize. I nod to the three-eyed man who shared my fire while I made myself scarce from the city. "Filj," I say, when my mind lights upon his name.

"Indiri." He nods in return, pleased that I remember him.

The other arm of the table holds the Pietran Elders, though what passes for an Elder here would be in the prime of youth in Stille. I see few gray hairs, and no bent backs. I have stood too long, and my bones feel as if they slip past my skin, growing like plants toward daylight.

"Now you've seen me," I say, pushing strength into my voice that I do not feel. "Is the last of the Indiri to be paraded for curious eyes? Or am I brought forth for a reason?"

"The Lithos can bring you forth and put you back at his will, Indiri," says the Mason, his face flush with drink.

"You've not been Mason long," I say. "Nor will you be, should I come close."

"Oh, come close, Indiri maiden, do," the Mason says, rising to his feet and beckoning me. "Though have a wash first."

Laughter comes at me from all sides, and what little blood I have in me rises to my face, that I should be mocked in this company. Filj does not join, I notice. Oddly, neither does Nilana.

"A wash and a blade," I say to the Mason. "Give me both, that I may end your jests cleanly."

I mimic a blade swipe, though it hurts, and am rewarded with laughs from more than a few, the Elders among them.

"You have the common tongue," one of them says.

"I do."

"And the ear of the king of Stille?"

I hesitate, eyeing each in turn. I saw the Lithos on the Stillean beach and remember him well. My gaze lands on his, and I see that he knows me too. No sense denying Vincent, since I fought by his side in full view.

"I know the king, yes," I say, returning my eyes to the Elder who spoke.

"How thoroughly?" the Mason asks, mimicking a rutting animal with his hips.

My hand goes for the crossed swords on my back, though I know they are not there, and the Mason laughs more loudly than before.

"Enough!" A voice that demands heed cuts through the air, silencing the growing chorus of laughter. The Lithos rises in his seat, somewhat unsteadily.

"The Indiri is a prisoner, yes. But you forget she is a warrior too, one who would have cut through many a Pietra had she met our ranks on the beach. The Pietra honor nothing more than courage on the field of battle, which she has shown. Speak to her as you would a soldier, Hadduk, or do not speak to her at all."

The Mason inclines his head to the Lithos, and an Elder clears his throat.

"The men who captured you said you killed a Lusca?"

"I was not captured," I tell him, watching as the Lithos eases back into his chair, one hand on the table to steady himself. "Your men came upon me sick unto death. If they had met me in my health, they would not have known me long."

"Were you badly injured?"

I turn toward Nilana's voice, and she has the gall to smile at me.

"Come down from the table and find out," I tell her.

"A woman with no legs against one with no weapons," she says, turning to Hadduk. "How do you wager?"

His answer is lost as a Feneen speaks, his voice coming deep from his chest. "We are told you fight like a man."

"I fight like an Indiri," I say. "No man among you can face me and stand."

"And no Pietra can hear a challenge while seated," a young Elder erupts, throwing his cup to the table. Wine splashes, drenching the plates of those around him. I crouch, ready, arm against my injured side. I'll call the drunken lot of them to me one by one, until it is only the Lithos and myself in a room of dead bodies, with me ready to make one more. The Elder has one foot on the table, ready to leap at me, while another man hangs from his side to stop him.

"Is this Pietra, Lithos?" I hear Filj's voice behind me. "Where an injured girl is dragged to fight a man unarmed, while others look on in drunkenness? Is this whom the Feneen allied themselves with?"

"I was not dragged," I say through clenched teeth. "As for where your allegiance lies, that choice is made. Do not take my side in this, for I am not on yours."

A few Elders slap their hands against the table in agreement.

"You'd be wise to take friends where you can find them, in a room full of enemies." The Lithos's voice is distinctive, though I do not turn my back on the Elder who stands ready to fight me.

"I'd set Nylos against you if I thought you were up to the task," he goes on. "But as it stands—"

"I stand," I interrupt him.

"What?" There's a slur in his voice, a disbelief that I will not accept the opening he left for me, the chance to avoid a fight with the Elder who fairly quivers at the chance to lunge for me.

"I stand," I repeat. "Any Indiri on their feet can best a Pietra. Especially this one." I sniff at Nylos, who by all appearances may be a good fighter indeed. But I took each man's measure when I came in the room, and this one won't take an insult. Neither will the Lithos let me fight unarmed.

"Give me a blade," I say. "And I'll show you what an Indiri can do."

Many rise to fill my hand. They are Pietra, and though I could say much against them, they know the rush of blood in a fight and wish to see one now. I choose the man nearest me, an Elder who holds a fine blade. I balance it in my hand, take a few moments to adjust to the heft of a Pietran sword, the reach of it longer than my own, the pommel a touch heavier, the grip long melded with this man's hand. I swipe at the air with my good arm, ignoring the sear of pain across my body.

This blade has known blood. And it likes me.

"Come on, then." I open both arms to Nylos, those around me fading in my vision until I see only him, this man who would open my throat over dinner.

He clears the table and lands lightly, drawing as he does. The blade swings in a wide arc meant for show, and I bounce it off my own with a smirk.

"Whom do you playact for?" I ask. "There are none here but you and I. Unless you think your mother watches from her boat?"

His attack is swift and unforgiving, thrusts and jabs that would skewer me if I allowed them to. But the Elder's blade is a solid one, and small shifts send the tip of his sword just to my lee and stoneward, one such tearing away what's left of my sleeve to show the rip in my skin from the Lusca, bleeding again.

I parry him easily, refusing to attack, letting his anger lead the fight while I keep my injured arm close to my side. Three times I could have ended it if I had my double blades, his shoulder dipping low and showing me his spine. My fingers itch to drive iron there; I feel them twitch each time a killing blow could be delivered, and an Indiri curse slips from me on the last.

"Getting tired?" Nylos asks.

"Only bored," I say, when I feel my heels hit the wall. I've allowed him to force me into a corner, a bad place for any fighter.

But not an Indiri.

An opponent who thinks he has won will make lazy mistakes, and Nylos is no different. He draws back to put force behind his final blow, watching my blade for a thrust.

So I ram my injured arm upward, ignoring the pain in my side, the snap of my cloak. All the world is the flat of my palm and the fine bone between his nostrils, which breaks easily. The impact jars me to my elbow, leaving behind a deep ache that I'll feel long into tomorrow. But I will have a tomorrow in which to feel pain.

Nylos has only a few moments left, and those are spent in confusion as I slide underneath his sword arm. He spins to follow me, unsteady on his heel, and those seated at the table gasp at the sight. His nose is gone, smashed upward into his skull, eyes on either side bulging with the pressure.

Nylos takes one step, then two. He drops his sword, and his hands go to his face as if they might undo the damage, pull the bone from his brain and make it right again. A single drop of blood drips from the crevice where his nose had been, and then he falls before me. Dead.

I make my way to the table, bare feet loud against the stones, for the room is suddenly silent, full of openmouthed fools who thought they played a game with me. I spot the Elder whose sword I hold, and face him across the table.

"Thank you," I say, handing it to him pommel first. "It is a fine sword, though I had no use for it, in the end."

CHAPTER 40

No words will keep her from being torn to pieces by my men. I'm up and over the table in a breath, the wine I've taken pounding through my veins along with my blood. I grab her by the shoulders, but she shifts away at the sound of my approach, the Elder's blade left behind in his hands. She's gone from under my touch, the faint suggestion of flesh and bone fading to thin air as she circles me.

"Careful, my Lithos," Hadduk calls from the table. "She did in Nylos with her bare hands, and hardly a drop of blood spilt."

I show her my palms, my own lack of weapons, and the girl smiles. "You can kill with those, same as I," she says. "Neither one of us is ever unarmed."

I nod my agreement, not trusting my tongue. Or my feet, for that matter. The Indiri can see my inebriation and keeps moving in circles around me, forcing me to spin to keep our gazes locked. Her eyes are bright, vibrantly blue against her skin, flickering with a look I know well: unabated joy in the heat of battle, the odd burn of respect one feels for a worthy opponent.

But there is pain there too, and as we circle each other, my heel slips in blood that didn't come from Nylos. The Indiri's wound has reopened, the careful stitching of the Keeper torn loose during her fight. I take a step toward her, breaking the circle she forces me to move in. She crouches, ready for me to lunge.

"You're hurt, Indiri," I say.

"You're not . . . yet," she tosses back at me.

I don't dare look away from her face, but I can sense subtle shifts in the room around me. No Pietra will attack the girl from behind, not after I chided Hadduk for not treating her as a warrior. Filj the Feneen has shown respect for her as well, but I cannot speak for the others of his tribe. And none will allow the Lithos to be harmed. Rules of single combat will go to the depths before they see me done to death by an Indiri at my own table.

So I'm left staring, half drunk, at this girl, wondering how to keep her from harm and save my own skin as well.

"Indiri," Nilana calls from her seat, "come away from the Lithos."

"I will not," the girl says, not breaking her eyes from mine.

"Even for your own blades?"

Indecision flickers, something that doesn't sit well on her face. The Indiri backsteps, putting some space between us before she glances at Nilana.

The Feneen woman's servant holds the Indiri's double blades, which catch all the light in the room, reflecting back onto the girl's face. They have heft and gracefulness, well honed and much cared for. I see the Indiri's fingers twitch at the sight of them, and I silently bless Nilana as the servant sets them on the table before her.

"These carry a fine edge," Nilana says. "But a Hadudun leaf can gouge stone. I'll send my man to the forest with your swords, have him go at a tree with your warrior's weapons as if they were nothing more than a crude ax."

"Those were my grandmother's," the Indiri seethes. "They belong in my hands and only mine."

"Oh, I'll give them back to you," Nilana says. "But they'll be pitted and broken, and only as deadly as a child's toy."

"Clearly you've never met an Indiri child," the girl says.

"How could she, when I killed them all?" Hadduk says, opening his mouth at the wrong time to say the wrong thing.

Nilana's eyes close against his stupidity as the Indiri breathes with fresh rage. But her attention is scattered, and it gives me the chance to move behind her and thread my arms through hers, jerking them upward.

Her breath leaves in a rush and an exclamation of pain so quiet I know I'm the only one to hear it, a small, high noise like a Tangata kitten's last mewl. The force of the pain sends her back against me, and I can smell the death that moved through her so recently, the funk of rot in her hair and the tang of fresh blood that drips from her arm.

"You're hurt," I say, quietly enough for only the two of us to hear. "And you've killed a man most here called friend. This only ends well for you if you do as I say."

"Nothing in Pietra ends well for an Indiri," she says, but her voice is fading, the pain rising in her to take wakefulness away.

"Guards," I call, and the two soldiers near the hall doors come to my side. "Take the Indiri back to her cell. And mind what you saw here," I say, nodding toward where Nylos lies cooling on the stones.

They take her from me, none too gently, and I watch her go, holding on to consciousness by sheer will, hurling a stream of what are undoubtedly Indiri curses at me until she is out of sight.

I knock on Nilana's door, ignoring the Pietran guard, who is struggling to keep a straight face. Her Feneen servant opens it, nods to me with a face much more inscrutable than my own man's, then turns for instructions to his mistress. Nilana is already abed, hair loose around her shoulders, but she does not look surprised to see me in her chambers.

"Come in, Lithos," she says, then has her servant leave us.

"Will you sit?" Nilana asks, voice quivering with amusement, as the only place to do so would be on the bed with her.

"I'll stand," I say.

"I thought as much." She nods, leaning back into her pillows. "So why do you come to my rooms, young Lithos, if not in search of what most men desire from a woman in her sleepshirt?"

In truth, I do not believe she is wearing even that. As her hair shifts away from her bare shoulders, I focus my eyes on her own.

"I wished to thank you for interfering with the Indiri tonight at dinner. It was well done."

She inclines her head. "And necessary," she adds. "The girl killed one of your Elders in full sight of the others. Pietran pride would not let her stand long, and you were wise to shield her with your body instead of words."

"I did not shield her," I say too quickly.

"My mistake." Nilana shrugs.

"I need her healthy and whole in order to draw the king and his Stillean army from their shores. Otherwise we are outnumbered and they ensconced in a fortified city with a queen who can call the sea to fight alongside them."

"So you threw yourself drunkenly to the side of a girl who had just killed your advisor, though you held no weapon?"

"I did what was necessary," I say.

"You did," Nilana agrees. "But, Lithos, you did it with a certain . . . passion."

I flush, remembering. How must it have looked as I jumped to the Indiri's aid? And it was to aid her, I know. The root of all Pietran pride lies in the strength of our bodies, the fierceness in our blood that fades with age. Once that fire is banked, we build our boats and leave the heat of battle for our youth.

Yet tonight I saw that same strength and ferocity bound in freckled skin and burning in bright eyes that denied pain, injury, and the odds so that she might do as she wished—kill me.

And I cannot say that I desire the same.

Nilana is waiting for an answer, and I straighten, searching for words that will capture how I felt when I knew the room would come crashing down on that burning flame, extinguish it with stone and leave only a tendril of smoke behind.

"I respect her," I say.

"Ah, Lithos." Nilana smiles. "That's the most romantic thing a man can say about a woman." She leans forward, the sheet around her chest gaping.

"Careful you're not distracted."

CHAPTER 41

Dara

FOREST ANIMALS WILL SEEK OUT A DARK PLACE TO DIE. Donil always said it was so that they can defend themselves, spine against stone, ready to fight until the last moment. I would see my brother again if only to tell him that here in my cell I have found the reason why they seek darkness when mortally injured: so that they may die with dignity, no eyes upon them as their bodies bend in a rictus of pain, as their mouths cry silently, each breath an agony.

I was rash, no surprise. But I could not stand before enemies and be mocked. Once already I had lain helpless in that room. I had vowed it wouldn't happen again, and it had not, though the price is somewhat high.

The stitches that held my skin together now trail from my arm, drying stiff with blood from the newly torn wound. My side feels as if someone has made a fire in it, and my wrist is swollen because of the killing blow I dealt Nylos. I'm a fine mess, and not likely to improve any time soon. Any help the Keeper may give would come to me as the Lithos wished it.

I'm slipping somewhere between sleep and exhaustion when I hear steps outside my door. Gaul's torch passes nearby, then the key in the lock. I manage to crouch, ready to take him out at the knees, but aware I can do little else. The jailer has whispered things to me when we are alone, pleasures both small and large that he'd like to visit upon my Indiri skin. Up to now, he would not dare touch me without the Lithos's permission. That may have been granted now that I've killed an Elder.

It is not Gaul but the Lithos himself who enters my cell, perching his torch in a sconce and closing the door behind him. The jailer lingers, eyes peering through the slits of my window to see whatever fate awaits his only prisoner. The Lithos follows my gaze and clears his throat. There's a grunt of dissatisfaction, and then Gaul is gone.

We watch each other carefully, both of us fighters with our backs to walls.

"You fought well tonight," he says.

"You drank well," I answer, and he is the first to drop his gaze.

"You have yet to see me at my best," he says coolly. "Only at the head of an army about to be enveloped by a wave, and now as a drunken fool presiding over a meal where you were pulled from comfort to be displayed for others' amusement."

I settle back onto my haunches, resting my head against the stones. "This is hardly comfort, and I don't believe many were amused, in the end."

"No," he agrees, crouching so that we are on the same level. "You are a surprise, Indiri."

"And you are exactly as I remember, Lithos," I say. "For I have seen you at your best, or rather my mother did. You sat, unmoved, and watched Indiri being slaughtered. Your face was the last thing my mother saw before her head was taken from her shoulders."

While the second part of what I say is true, I cannot say the Lithos is unchanged from what my mother's memories have shown me. Then he was a child, small, unquestioning, eyes bright at the glory of battle for which he had been raised. The man before me seems whole, but I know the dark gaps that fill a person who has killed, and the Lithos of Pietra has more than his share.

I've seen men fill that void with women and drink, even try to feed it with more killing, only to learn that it makes the space wider, the depths darker. I was made for death and learned early the only way to deal with it was reason, the pure logic that it was them or me, a wider purpose that opened their throats and left mine closed each day. Whatever the Pietra have taught the Lithos to close the gap has not taken root.

"I remember that day," he says, settling onto the floor across from me. "Your women and children fought as fiercely as any man."

I nod and let the silence stretch between us.

"Would you let me see to your arm?" he asks.

The offer of help is more alarming than any threat, and I am unable to mask my reaction. He raises his hands, showing me his palms for the second time this night.

"I am unarmed," he says. "And as for any other harm . . ." He trails off, suddenly an awkward boy.

"Yes, I know," I tell him. "The Lithos is not to be distracted."

"You'll let me see to it, then?"

My sleeve has grown wet against my side, and I would be foolish to refuse him. I pull away my cloak to have a look at the wound myself, now that the light of his torch is in the room. He mistakes it for permission and moves close, peeling away what's left of my sleeve with a deft touch.

"Not quite to the bone," he says, turning my arm in the light. "Do you have movement in all your fingers?"

I make a gesture that's known across all languages, and he smiles. "You'll live to wield a sword, then," he says.

"Will I?" I challenge.

He doesn't answer, but produces a pouch that holds a needle and thread, which he bites off with his teeth.

"Does the Lithos also knit?"

"I do not," he answers evenly, turning my wrist so that the light is better. "But I know how to mend skin and set a bone, knowledge any warrior needs should they find themselves without a healer."

He glances up at me. "This may hurt."

I laugh. I cannot help it. From outside my cell I hear Gaul snort in surprise, and the Lithos gives me his own small smile, one I think very few have seen.

"Lithos, since I left my own land, I've been slashed by your leaves, done battle with a sea creature on dry land, and had my veins filled with the blood of your own dead. Tell me, is there nothing here in Pietra that does not hurt?"

He thinks for a moment, then carefully sets the needle and thread on a crevice in the wall before extending his hand to me.

"My name is Witt," he says.

"Dara," I answer reflexively, and take his hand in my own. We shake, skin to skin, and I feel the thread of life that is within me tremble.

"Hopefully that was not too painful," he says, retrieving the needle and thread.

"We'll see," I say.

And he mends me.

CHAPTER 42

Ank

I HAVE PASSED DAYS WITH MY MOTHER. THE NILFLOWER SMOKE will linger on me long after I leave her, and as always, I will search the folds of my clothes for the last remnants until they are gone. I have learned much in my time with her, but little that would be of interest to the Lithos. The things we have spoken of are nearer to the heart than the mind, as we find threads of conversations ended long ago, pick them up again, and bind ourselves together with them.

Here in her tower it is as if we are the only people in the world, and I have found solace in her room many times in my life. My caul was of no consequence to her, and once it was gone, my face a found treasure. In this round room I am once again a Stillean and a son. No longer am I Ank of the Feneen, who must weigh words and share only that which needs to be seen for my own purposes. But time does pass, and I must speak to her of things unpleasant before my leavetaking.

"Did the earth move as the sea here as well?" I ask, eyeing a fissure in the wall that is new to me.

"It did." Madda yawns, and I spot a cracked tooth in the back of her mouth. My mother ages, and not well here in this room with only smoke and the occasional housecat for company.

"Were you not alarmed?"

"Bah." Madda waves her hand at the air as if the earth moving beneath her feet is of no consequence. "I have seen much, and all of it the same as I grow older. To feel something new is a gift."

I watch her move awkwardly this morning, her joints popping as she stretches old bones. "You don't seem afraid," I say.

"What does a Seer have to hide from?" she asks. "I've watched many shy from the fate I find in their palms, but you can't outrun your own skin."

"No," I agree.

My mother picks up a flagon of water, peers through a small slit of a window, the morning sun drawing more lines on her face. "I do not fear the earth moving, for it's not the earth that shall have me."

"How does the young king fare?" I ask, taking the pitcher from her hands to pour us both a drink.

"He is young and in love," Madda says, joining me at the table. "And fortunate enough to call his love his wife as well."

I have moved through halls and listened well, in the times that my mother slept in her tower. That the Given should become the queen was a surprise to me, but one that settled in and grew roots, a truth that once accepted made a kind of sense. That a girl of Feneen blood should sit on the throne of Stille was not something I could have anticipated, yet it galls. For all my cunning, I did not see this possibility and have allied my people against the country that shelters my own mother and a royal who may have taken pity upon us.

"Too much to hope that love for his wife would cloud his vision and addle his battle acumen?" I ask.

"Too much," Madda agrees. "The queen can hardly cloud his vision when she is not in sight. As for battle, I think you'll find my Vincent would sooner shelter his people than send them into harm."

"Would he?" I ask, and Madda only raises her brows.

The words that move between us are often wearing cloaks that they may pass as something other than what they are. My mother settles into her chair, elbows on the table before her, chin resting in her palm as she eyes me. I lean back, watching her as well, aware we have entered the stage of my visit where little is said, but much is shared.

"I will not allow him to be harmed," I say.

"Perhaps he will not be around for any to harm him," she counters.

I cock my head, listening to the oderbirds that nest in a crevice outside her window. The sconcelighters are as full of talk as they, and one good hiding place has brought me an earful.

"Hygoden is not so far that the Pietra cannot reach," I tell her, but Madda only smiles.

"Can the Pietra march to the horizon? Do their boots float upon water?"

"Nothing floats upon water, old woman," I tell her. "Even Pietran boats are made to sink."

"Ah yes." Madda nods as if she has only just remembered something. "Boats are for the dead." She takes a sip of water and twines a loop of gray tresses through her fingers, braiding skin with hair.

"Or so they say," she adds.

Outside, the oderbird nestlings have ceased their squawking, as if listening as well. I watch my mother, her eyes heavily hooded with the skin of age, but still shining bright. Life burns there, an enjoyment of days that I've also seen in the face of the young Stillean king. If he loves his queen, and treasures any life they would have together, he would not risk meeting the Pietra and Feneen in open battle. As a man, he may value his life, but as a king he would lead his men in battle, endangering it for their sake.

"It is a difficult thing, to be both a good man and a good king," I say.

"On this earth, anyway," Madda agrees, her tone leading me to follow.

I have the response on my lips—*there is nothing else*—but I bite down on it as Madda's eyes rest on mine, knowing where my thoughts would go. My mother speaks to me of boats and the horizon, a king who would take risks for love of his wife, and a battle that will not be fought.

Filthy fathoms.

I readjust my position, knees creaking along with my chair. "I would have liked to see the Indiri again," I say.

"Pity," is all my mother offers me.

I grunt, well aware from the sconcelighter's talk that the male has gone with the queen and an advisor to Hygoden, although for what purpose I do not know. Of the female I have heard no whispers and seen no sign, and this does not rest well with me.

"She is a fierce thing, and I would know her true nature," I tell Mother.

"You already do, to use such words," Madda says. "She may be Indiri, but there is a heart in that spotted chest, and it burns for the good and ill alike."

I nod, having seen the fire in the girl's eyes. She will love and hate with equal heat, and I feel a streak of pity for the man who is the recipient of either. But the girl does not walk these halls, for wherever she passes there is an energy, one that echoes here no longer.

"I worry for her," I admit.

I expect Mother to scoff, tell me that the Indiri female has little care for my concerns and would end them with a flick of her blade, given half the chance. But Madda's brow darkens, and her eyes go to the cup her hands curl around.

"Mother?" I prod. "Fear passed through you just now, fear on the face of a woman who would claim she has aged past such a thing."

Madda doesn't argue, but speaks into her drink. "The girl passed from here, and I fear her pride outstrips her power. The Indiri magic weakens with the land, and for my part, I would not see those people gone from the earth."

I rise from my seat, fingers resting for a moment on the Seer's bowed head. She is smoke and mirrors, as always, even her true nature shrouded in a life spent reading lines that shift and speaking words cloaked in shadow.

"I will look for her as I go," I say to my mother, resting my cheek against her hair for a moment.

"Use your ways to help us all, my son," Madda says, her words so soft they are nearly lost. "Protect Vincent, for the sake of an old woman who loves him."

CHAPTER 43

Dara

T HE KEEPER RAISES MY ARMS, RUNNING HER HAND DOWN my side. I feel each finger slide past bones that have reknit, each rib whole once more. In the light of her lantern, I see her mouth twitch at the sight of my stitches.

"The Lithos mended you well," she says.

"He did," I answer, leaving it for her to say more if she wishes a conversation to grow of it. More than once, the Hyllenian has tried to draw me with words, laying little paths she wishes me to follow as she speaks of the Given. But I did not grow to womanhood within the walls of Stille for nothing, and while my ancestors' memories showed me how to guard my body, it was Dissa who taught me to guard my thoughts.

"He has asked after your welfare," the Keeper says, resting my arms back at my sides. "And has told Gaul to treat you with respect, as you are a warrior."

"And as I am a warrior, I will not be coddled long," I say to her, pulling what's left of my cloak around me as I settle in the corner. "The respect the Lithos shows me does not translate into kindness, and the stitches he put in me are to ensure that I live, but not that I do so happily."

She steps back from me, arms crossed. "Have you ever been happy, Indiri?"

It is a question unlooked for, and I have no quick answer. The Keeper makes a noise in her throat and gathers her things, the pitcher of clean water, the comb she had offered me, that I refused.

"If you do not know, then you have not been," she says. "And I feel sorry for you, not here in this dungeon, but for all the years you spent before it, building up gall in your gut and spitting harsh words with your mouth."

"And how was your life spent, Keeper?" I snap at her. "How much happiness did you reap, raising small Givens for the sea?"

She stops, facing the door, the double slices of her shoulder blades rising and falling beneath her thin shirt.

"More than you could guess at," she says quietly. "I have lived a life. Yours is barely begun, and yet you would toss it away in the name of pride."

"Slip me a blade and leave the door open when you go," I say. "See what I toss away then."

She only shakes her head, tendrils of hair swaying across her shoulders as she leaves. I do not know what game the Keeper plays at. Though she has drawn words from me, they were only in concern of Khosa, never the Stillean army or Vincent. If the Lithos sends her thinking I will open my mouth for another woman, he is mistaken. He may as well have stitched my lips together as my arm, for he'll have nothing from me.

I run my fingers over the healing skin of my arm, counting the threads that hold me together there. The Lithos knows of my connection to Stille and wants me healthy. This does not bode well, for all the Keeper may go on about his concern for my welfare and respect for my skills. This means only that I have become a pawn in a game, an Indiri to be flouted by the Pietra in order to draw out Vincent and his army.

"Well-being indeed," I snort.

As for respect, if the Lithos holds that for me, then it will bring him only greater pride to break me when Vincent does not fall for the ploy. The king of Stille made his choice already, and it was not me. He will not endanger his kingdom and his wife for the sake of an Indiri girl. So the Lithos will put me to another use, one that I would almost prefer. For there is greater honor in dying under the knife with no words in my mouth than there would be in returning to Stille to speak only apologies.

My fingers dig through the soft dirt floor of my cell, tracing the furrow I have been digging in the dark, long after Gaul's torch has ceased sputtering outside my window and his voice has stopped whispering foul acts in my ear.

I am no Pietran trophy, and no Stillean's weakness.

I am an Indiri. And I have a few ideas of my own.

My ancestors have never been in this place, so I cannot ask them how it came to be that my hands have found a weapon, crude as it is. But I can imagine Pietra long dead, pacing how wide they want the cells to be, placing sticks on the ground, a shadow of the stones that would be laid modeled in Hadundun branches, the skeleton of a prison.

Probably it was the job of one man to gather these as the walls rose, who passed the duty to another, who asked his friend to see to it. Or maybe the branch was nudged aside by one foot, to be stepped upon by another, driving it into the ground where they worked. It has waited for me here, encased in filth from other prisoners, age hardening it, until my fingers, lazy with the press of unused time, found it as I traced the sides of my cell.

Ugly things have a habit of rising to my hand; weapons find me as the forest animals find Donil. Though perhaps it is only innocent things that lie in my palm, while my mind finds dark deeds to do with them. This is the most likely, I decide, as I curl my hand around the branch, easing it to and fro as it frees itself from the ground. It is grim work, and the soft skin under my fingernails screams as it is pushed back, far and farther, dirt filling the spaces it leaves behind.

The branch eases free of the earth, and I learn its shape in the dark, my hands tracing a smooth edge, nearly straight, and each end rounded with age. Torchlight has not reached me in a while; Gaul's voice has not interrupted my thoughts, either. I stand, ears straining against the silence, to hear nothing.

I bring my foot down sharply, the snap echoing around me but bringing no one, and reach again in the dark to feel the new end I have made, sharp and angry. I rest my weapon next to me against the wall. It is nearly as long as I am, and I slide into sleep, happy to have it hovering over me.

I have made a stick into a spear.

Now to make a jailer into a corpse.

CHAPTER 44

Khosa

FILTHY FATHOMS," SALLIN BREATHES BESIDE HER, THE wind off the sea whipping what little hair he has into a storm of its own around his brow. Donil only stares, the sullen quiet that he has adopted since arriving in Hygoden deepening, the set of his brow darker than it was even that morning. For her part, Khosa's heart leaps in her chest at the sight of Winlan's ship, nestled in a cove at the point.

"How many know?" she asks.

Winlan makes a face as if he were doing a calculation, then shrugs. "That would be everyone, my queen."

"Just Khosa, please," she reminds him. "How does an entire village keep a secret such as this?"

"A better question would be, how would one keep a secret such as this from an entire village?" Winlan says. "Hygoden is small. When my wife had little Unda, half the people knew it was a girl before I did, and I was right outside the door."

Khosa nods. "Hyllen is not much different. If a maiden goes for a walk on the high meadow with a shepherd, word reaches her mother and a binding quilt is nearly finished before she returns home."

"Begging your pardon, Khosa," Winlan says. "Hyllen is altogether a different place than Hygoden. Stille needs your grain and wool; nobles go there for a lark to playact at being shepherds and shepherdesses. The only people Hygoden sees from Stille are the tithe collectors, and it is not a pleasant visit for anyone."

"Hygoden is an outpost under Stille's protection and pays for that service as any Stillean land does," Sallin says, overhearing the conversation.

"Protection from what?" Winlan asks. "The wind and snow? These are what plague us most, and Stille has yet to change the weather on our behalf."

Sallin opens his mouth to continue the argument, but Khosa raises a hand to stop him.

"All of Hygoden feels this way toward Stille?"

Winlan nods.

"And so you've built a ship and would have put all your people upon it to follow in the path of your ancestor."

"If it came to that, yes," Winlan says. "We know well that should the Pietra take it in their heads to do to Hygoden as they did Hyllen, no help from Stille would arrive in time, should it be sent at all."

"Help would come," Khosa says, but her voice doesn't carry the conviction she meant for it to. Winlan clearly thinks otherwise but chooses not to contradict the queen.

"You've sailed it?" Donil asks, eyes still on the ship as it rises and falls with the swell.

"Many times," Winlan says. "Together with friends, I built it in my youth, and we've taken it out, learning first from Harta's notes but then from our own hands how to move upon the water."

"How far have you gone?" Donil asks.

"Once we had the confidence, we took it around the entire land," Winlan answers, a hint of pride in his voice. "Far enough out that we could see the shore, but none would spot us."

Donil makes a noise in his throat, but holds his peace.

"How many can sail?" Sallin asks.

"Any man in Hygoden was taught, and the boys have their duties too," Winlan says. "Sailing a ship is no small thing, and we've lost men to the sea, hulls to rocks, a few hands to a sail that whipped the wrong way of a sudden. But we've always known that Hygoden sees to itself, and a lost life or limb was looked upon as a lesson learned, so we'd be that much wiser when the day came to sail and not look back."

"That day may be here," Sallin says.

"It may," Winlan agrees. "And what makes you think I'll allow a single Stillean onboard my ship?"

Evening falls and the voices from inside Winlan's home continue, sometimes raised, occasionally angry, but always the low hum of many heads together. Khosa can pick out Sallin's voice as a continuous thread, cajoling and bargaining, but never pleading. The Stillean is an old master at managing men, and he will have what he wants out of Hygoden in the end, undoubtedly with Winlan and the other Hygodeans thinking they got the better end of the deal.

Khosa smiles to herself as she braids Unda's hair, the little girl humming as she builds a ninpop home out of sticks and moss.

"Is it fun to be a queen?" Unda asks.

"Fun doesn't come into it," Khosa answers her, tying off the last bit of hair. "There is always work to be done and people to please, and it's a rare thing to find one action that will make everyone happy."

"Not like my work, though. Not like bringing the goats down from the mountain or moving stones out of the path," Unda says, and Khosa looks down at the girl's hands, blistered and chapped, even at her young age.

"No," Khosa admits. "A queen's work is not like that. But your goats do not hold a grudge against you from one evening to the next, and are easily won over with a handful of grain. People are not so simple."

"No, but people don't knock you on your rear with their horns, either," Unda argues.

"Fair enough," Khosa says, pulling the girl to her feet and hurrying her along with a light push on the backside. "Go and find your mother, so that she is not worrying over you."

Unda nods, but glances around. "Should you be left alone?"

"I am not alone," Khosa says.

Donil has never been far from her in Hygoden. Even if others cannot see him, she knows he is near, always ready to intervene should her body make a mad dash for the sea. In truth, the only tremor she has felt of late has been the need for him, and the strength of it overwhelms any call the sea can make.

She leaves behind the flow of voices from Winlan's cabin, picking her way down the stony beach to an overhang Pand had shown her the day before. It shelters a small cave that overlooks the inlet where the ship rests, water breaking white against its hull in the moonlight. Khosa settles back against the cave wall and waits for Donil to join her. He's there in moments, lighter on his feet than she was, not even a pebble trickling down the cliffside to the water below.

"You've been quiet today," Khosa says as he settles next to her.

"I have much to think over," he says. "Sallin will bring Winlan around, and then what will be done?"

"He plans to bring Winlan and any others who wish to come back with us to Stille, so that they may show us how to build a fleet, teach Stilleans the ways of the sail and how to float upon the sea."

"A fleet," Donil breathes, somehow making the word sound poisonous to her ears. "How many?"

"As many as Stilleans wish to fill," Khosa says. "As well as Hyllenians, and any from Hygoden and Sawhen as well. None will be left behind who wish to go to the new land."

Though Khosa has been queen only a short time, she has learned much from her position. Her voice rings with authority and conviction in this cave, and she drops her head, ashamed that she has spoken to Donil as if she were the queen in truth. She would be only Khosa to him, and her hand slides across the cave floor to find his and squeeze an apology. He returns it, and their hands stay clasped.

"Khosa," Donil says quietly, "have you not thought that perhaps the ship the Pietran Lures spotted in the histories was Winlan himself?"

"I . . ." Her voice catches on this bit of logic, a question she cannot explain away. "I had not," she says eventually. "But even if it were, I would still go aboard and follow where my instincts lead."

"Even if it leads to a horizon of endless sea?" He turns to her, eyes glaringly bright in the dark of the cave.

"I have ignored my instincts too long and avoided many risks," Khosa says, lifting her hand to his face. She traces his lips, the fullness of them warm beneath her finger.

"I'm done living that way," she says, and puts her mouth to his.

Once before they had allowed themselves to touch each other freely, in the walls of Stille and with the spines of the histories looking down upon them. There, Donil had put an end to it before it had gone too far. Here, with the sea wind carrying the tang of salt and the darkness of the cave promising secrecy, there is nothing to stop them.

And neither desires it.

Khosa wished to be only a girl, and Donil only a boy, all trappings of who they are lost in those words. And that is how it goes as their hands find each other's bodies, mouths gasping for breath and for each other, clothes shed in a frenzy to become as close as possible and then, finally, to be one.

She cries out into his shoulder, her skin singing with his touch, a wave of her own building inside her body. Nothing is stronger than this, not the sea, not the call of a land far in the distance. In this moment her body wants only Donil, and she has him, to the very end.

CHAPTER 45

Dara

GAUL IS UP, HIS TRUDGE ECHOING THROUGH THE CHAMBER outside my door. I hear it, one boot falling harder than the other, a misalignment of the hips that makes him favor one leg, a glaring weakness if I should fight him. I lean against the far wall, both hands on my spear. The killing end of it rests lightly on the small barred window, an incongruity to catch Gaul's eye if he's sharp enough to spot it. But he blinds himself with the torch instead, raising it in the hopes of catching a glimpse of my skin.

"How'd the night go with you, girlie?" he calls. "Getting cold, a bit."

I give no response, as expected. His own solutions for warming me come soon after.

"I could slip you a blanket, if you'd like. We both get underneath it, and you'll be warm within and without."

I tighten my grip on the spear, brace my spine against the wall. Gaul leans closer, face pressed against the bars, eyes rolling in their sockets to find me.

"I don't mind your spots, girlie," he calls. "In the dark you could be anyone, as could I. You be the queen of Stille, and I'll be the ki—"

I ram him, feeling the soft give of his eyeball and the light resistance of his skull as the spear tears through his head, breaking out the other side to scrape against the wall of the corridor. He hangs, suspended, jaw open in surprise as one hand flutters to the spear, questioning.

I don't give him time to find the answers, hauling his body back toward me, hand over hand, until his face is against the window again . . . but he'll speak no words to me now. The keys around his neck are within reach, the one that fits my cell easy to spot, shining with recent use. I twist my arm through the bars of my window, my newly healed bones crushed against the door. It is a bright pain, but a short one, as the door opens under my hand. The spear comes free from the jailer's head with a tug, his body left behind in my cell.

"You'll be cooling in here alone," I tell him. "Blanket or not."

My palms itch for my double blades, and I find them resting in a corner of Gaul's room. It's a surprisingly clean place, inkpot and quill aligned on the desk, stool pushed in underneath. He even made his bed before he came to pester me, the corners pulled tight, a slight depression in the middle where he sat, putting his boots on. My blades are out of place here, their Indiri nature speaking of trees that grow limbs in all directions and wild bursts of air tamed for only a moment, when pulled into lungs.

I ease the harness onto my back, welcoming the weight of the blades against my shoulders. I draw and spin, slicing the air of the jailer's room to test the mend of my bones. They protest, but not loudly. My boots and bow are nowhere to be found; Gaul probably traded them, holding on to my blades for a larger favor, maybe to delay the building of his boat or getting someone else to do it.

I sit, resting on Gaul's bed in the same spot he did moments before I killed him. It still holds a bit of his warmth, and I absorb it, pondering my options. In Stille my spots were tolerated, but here in Pietra I'll be killed the moment I am seen. Before the Lusca nearly did me in, I had a chance to kill the Lithos with speed and cunning, or perhaps from a distance with my bow. None even need know it was an Indiri who loosed the arrow.

Now the Pietra know an Indiri is among them. They know my rotting *name*, I'm reminded, cursing myself to the depths for the moment where I forgot the boy who held my arm was not just a boy, but the Lithos. Any chance I had of surprise is lost, and the longer I tarry, the more chance favors the Pietra. I should leave, return to Stille, where at least I can be counted as a strength and not a weakness to be bartered against.

I rise, but hesitate. Though my mind is made up, my heart wants vengeance. I came into this place of stone broken and beaten. Their floors have drunk my blood, and to leave without doing what I came for goes against my nature. I draw my blades again, punishing the air in front of me for being empty. If the Lithos only stood there, I'd open him all over and be done with it. I sheathe my blades and swear in Indiri, but even my own language isn't harsh enough to put words to what burns inside me.

There are torches in the corridor sconces, but I ignore them, pulling the ragged hood of my cloak to cover my face. One glance would tell anyone I don't belong here, and so the shadows will serve me best. I pad barefoot up a stone stair and ascend another. The early sun has barely set the sky to gray when I come to the first window and a side door, set low. There are small sounds above me, people moving to rise with the morning, when I put my hand to the latch and walk free.

Speed will attract attention, and so I keep my pace slow, head bowed toward the ground. The handles of my blades brush the backs of my ears, reminding me that none in Pietra carry weapons such as these. I draw them and tuck them close against my side. I smell the earthy mulch of the stables and adjust my course, following my nose to the warm bodies of horses.

They nicker at me as I enter, thinking I come to feed them. Which means they are accustomed to a morning meal and the groom will be here shortly. I pass each stall, drawing in deep the smell of the animals, the hay, their grain, even what they leave behind them in their bedding. Pietra or Stille, all stables are the same, and the quiet here soothes me after the funk of the dungeons and the whispered threats from Gaul. In the corner I find a fine animal, gray like the morning and tall as the cliffs. I smile at him, and he shows me his teeth. I pull my blades out, to show him mine.

"I like you," I say in Indiri, and he snorts as if it means little to him, and I sheathe them across my back once more.

There is not time for tack and bridle, so I swing onto his back, and he starts underneath me, unaccustomed to a bare rider. But the walls have been around him too long and he wants air, so he argues little when I squeeze him with my knees and point his head toward the sun. We're gone in a breath, stones behind me and trees ahead.

The horse is well trained and knows his own country, shying from Hadundun trees and saving my neck more than once with a quick sidestep. His rider may be a stranger, but the earth beneath him is not, and he runs as if afraid I'll turn him back to the stables and a life of contentment.

I know his fear, have felt it myself, as the walls of Stille eased me into warm meals and soft beds, teaching me things no Indiri has ever learned. I'll set this horse loose well short of the city, and if he returns to the stables of Pietra, it will surprise me greatly. We're free of the forest, headed for open ground and what I'm sure will be a pace that will break my neck should I go over his head, when my stallion balks. I slip heavily to the side, my hair grazing the ground before I'm able to pull myself astride, hands buried in his mane.

The stallion's ears are pricked, his sides heaving. Something has caught his attention, and I reach back with one hand, ready to draw against whatever forest horror Pietra has to offer me when I hear it too.

It's the Lithos, calling his horse.

CHAPTER 46

Witt

SLEEP TEASES ME, CALLING IN LOW TONES THAT SOUND LIKE
my mother's voice rolling back against the waves. I wake tangled in my bed coverings, the sound of the surf nearly covering the light knock at my door. Hadduk tends to burst in, hoping to catch me at some sport he can mock me for, unable to believe that I take no woman. The knock comes again, a light touch, and I erase any tones of fear from my voice before calling out.

"Come in."

It is the Keeper, a lantern burning low in her hand. "Apologies, Lithos, a soldier came asking for you, and though the Mason would turn him away, I thought his words worth hearing."

As a steady mind goes, I value hers over his, and so motion for the soldier to enter. It's an older man, one I remember rallying troops to his side after his commander was swept up in the wave. He wears a band on his finger; he is a solid Pietran of good stock who has been allowed to take a wife and breed. If something has pestered this man to come to his Lithos in the dead of dark, it is worthwhile indeed.

"Speak," I say, already pulling on my breeches and signaling for the Keeper to find me a shirt.

"My Lithos, I would not have—"

"Your Lithos calls for you to speak, not explain yourself," I say. The man, a true soldier, responds by clicking his heels together and reporting.

"A clowder of cats has gathered in the forest."

My fingers pause on my bootlaces as I question my judgment. "And? The Tangata wander here from time to time. Why is that remarkable?"

"They wander, yes," the man admits. "But these cats seem to have purpose. Or rather, to be in search of some. They . . ." He breaks off, looking at the Keeper as if he would not voice horrors in her presence.

"Out with it," I say, fingers back on my laces. "This woman has seen much and done more. You will not find her easily shocked."

"Children pulled from a wagon, my Lithos. One dead before she could cry out. The other . . . she had the chance to scream, at least."

"You know more of the cats than we do," I say to the Keeper as I take a clean shirt from her. "Do they often act as such?"

"If restless," she says. "Not so long ago, Stille sent the Indiri to us, after the cats became bold and stole some of our children."

"And what did the Indiri do?"

The Keeper shrugs. "They were bolder."

"I'll ride out," I say to the soldier, almost expecting him to tell me my presence is not necessary. I will argue that sleep evades me, and what better purpose for the Lithos than to see to his people? But the soldier does not contradict me, instead moving aside to let me pass by him to the door.

"You have men?" I ask him. He's a lower commander, and not one who will have many to call to him, but enough that I will not fear for my safety against the cats.

As my door swings shut behind me, I hear an echo from my dream, my mother's voice above the surf, and I wonder if I care so much for my own well-being this night, or any other. Should my life cease, so then would my dreams of her and my small brothers, in their boat with no oars. Then I think of Dara the Indiri, sleeping beneath my feet, and what would become of her at Hadduk's hands.

I square my shoulders and sheathe my sword.

Cavallo is battle trained, but has never been tested against a Tangata. He wouldn't be the first horse to panic in the presence of a cat, so I ask my groom to bring me a horse who has been, one that won't shy at the sound of a hiss, or buck a rider to avoid a swipe. He gives me a mare, which I raise my brows at, but he hands me the reins with a confident nod.

"She's seen the cats, my Lithos, and was not impressed."

Rantoon, the soldier who woke me, is already mounted, as are his men. I'll not delay them longer in an argument over horseflesh with a groom who is undoubtedly better informed than I am. I'm saddled and by their side in a moment, the heavy fog of the night breaking around us as we ride off, my groom rubbing his eyes as he returns to his bed.

We pass by a Hadundun tree with deep claw marks, filling in red where they cut to its lifesap. Tufts of hair in all colors litter the ground around it, handfuls of orange, black, white, and gray. I swing off the mare, holding one such clump in my hand. It's soft and smooth, a misleading beauty that I know hides claws that catch and teeth that crush.

"They're confused by the trees," Rantoon says, reining in his own mount. "I've seen it on the edge of the forest. When the cats wander too close to a Hadundun they know only that they are hurt, and lash out at the source of the pain. The trees will heal themselves, and the cats move on."

"Scarred," I add, as the wind stirs the fur around my feet.

"Injured," he corrects. "And angry."

Rantoon makes a point, and one all the men who ride with us must heed well. We are tracking dangerous animals, some of whom are in pain and looking for a victim to give as they were given. I run my fingers underneath the mare's nose, so that she is aware of what I ride her toward. She snorts, unconcerned, scattering the hairs I hold into the wind.

"Clever girl," I say, scratching her neck as I climb back into the saddle.

The other horses are not so calm; a ripple of anxiety passes through them. Muscles flick, ears turn, heads rise, and nostrils flare against this strange smell on a cold wind.

"Easy," Rantoon says to his own mount, as a crashing sound comes from our stoneward. He's an accomplished horseman, but his horse is an animal, in the end, and harbors a deep fear of what he does not know. His fear spreads to the next horse, and the next, each man suddenly grappling with reins, speaking in low voices to calm them as they hear heavy movement in the brush.

The fog has lifted slightly, the first gray fingers of light reaching through the trees as I reach for my sword and spur the mare onward. The others may follow as they can, but I will not have it be said that the Lithos sought safety when on a steady mount, faced with cats that had taken children for their meal.

The mare pushes ahead, thorns tearing at my boots for purchase as we crest a hill and descend the other side, our party out of sight. My blade is drawn when she comes to a halt, confused, nostrils finding some scent that does not hold with what she expected. A tremor passes underneath me as she calls out, nickering.

And is answered by a voice I know.

"Cavallo?" I call, as confused as my mount.

My stallion answers me, honest and true. For him there is no reasoning to puzzle out. He is my horse and I his rider; how we both come to be here—and not together—is not his concern. I spur the mare on until the dawn light illuminates my horse, along with a rider who struggles to control him.

"Thief!" I yell, urging the mare onward. The groom was right to seat me on this girl. She senses my anger and responds as if her own were kindled, blood up, head held high and fearless.

Neither one of us is prepared for the attack that comes from behind.

A weight falls onto the mare's back just short of my own, and I turn in time to see a Tangata grasping for purchase. Claws find their home, and the mare screams, rearing. I'm unseated and roll free of her flailing hooves, only to come beneath Cavallo's.

He's bucking, wild to rid himself of his rider. I dodge again, coming up with sword in hand to defend my mare, who is down. Her screams tear my ears as the cat digs deeply into her hindquarters. Another springs from the bracken to end her cries with a decisive snap of its jaws. Two more slink forward and crouch behind her body, growling, eyes on me.

There's a crash behind me as Cavallo unseats his rider and the thief tumbles to the ground. I keep my gaze on the clowder, grown by three more as the others are drawn to the smell of fresh blood.

"If you have a weapon to fight these beasts, draw it in my defense, and I'll forgive your crime," I say over my shoulder to the fallen thief.

"I have two," a calm voice says. "And my own skin to worry about, Lithos."

Recognition sparks, and I have the space of a breath to turn my head and see the Indiri girl, blades drawn, facing down three cats of her own. Then one lunges. She smoothly takes its paw off midair, and it falls at her feet, spitting hate. I don't have time to see her end it, for a pair comes at me; one cat stays behind, content to tear into the flesh of the dead mare.

I take a cat as it leaps, a quick slash across the chest that won't kill it but will make it think twice before coming at me again. It rolls to the side as it falls, and I have the chance to yell, "Downed cat to your stoneward," and hear her grunt of acknowledgment before the other is upon me.

It gets a claw in the soft flesh of my ear as I duck underneath its pounce, and the entire thing goes, pulled away from my head with the same tearing sound as a cloak stuck on a branch in a brisk wind. Blood pours into what's left of my ear, and I shake my head like a dog to clear it, spinning to see that the cat's momentum rolled it off my shoulder and onto the Indiri's back, where it hooked her cloak before falling.

She's off balance as the cat pulls at her clothing, one sword defending against a cat in front of her, one swinging wildly behind to stop the other's attack. I hear brush rustling behind me in the subtle scurry before a leap, but slice away the tail of her cloak before I turn to strike madly upward, catching this one cleanly in the sternum. It's dead before it falls, but the eyes still burn bright with hate. The Indiri has handled her two, but more have arrived and we're encircled.

I take a step back as one taunts me by shaking its haunches in a fake leap, my shoulder striking the Indiri's. She presses back against me, her stronger sword arm shielding my empty one. We spin slowly, shoulder to shoulder, each of us assessing.

"Do they usually travel in clowders this large?" I ask.

"Does it matter how they behave at any other time than *now*?" she counters.

"Perhaps," I say, our feet still moving as we survey the cats. "If they aren't pack hunters—"

"Gray one," she says briskly, and the animal charges us, forgoing the leap that had brought its brothers down. It's a smart cat, going for my weak side so that my parry is defensive, opening up that side of my body to an attack—which an orange cat quickly makes use of. I see it coming, know that I can't come about quickly enough to stop it, when the Indiri takes its head off with a single slice.

But the strength required for such a blow sends her spinning forward, opening her back to attack, which I quickly cover, ending the life of a black cat that would have bitten clear through her spine. We're back-to-back again, but the girl, her strength flagging, doesn't press as hard against me as she did before. My ear fills with blood, and I shake my head again, spattering us both.

"Can you hear?" she calls to me over her shoulder.

"Enough," I answer.

"No more defense," she says. "You're hurt, and I'm weakening. I'll take the three striped ones. The other two are yours."

I want to tell her I'll take three, but it's been decided and she's gone from my back, chilly air filling the space where she was. I charge my enemy, and they react as cats do, pressing low to the ground, a line of hair on their backs rising to make themselves seem bigger. But I know where their spines are, and their brains and their bones. I am driven by fear, the desperation of the wounded and—I realize as I strike the last blow—the sudden, enveloping need to protect the girl behind me.

Who needs nothing of it.

A fool, I turn to her with my sword lowered, to find her standing over three dead cats, two blades drawn, ready to fight me.

CHAPTER 47

Dara

MY SIDE IS A BLAZE OF AGONY, MY WOUNDED ARM A dull throb. True strength has left me; all that keeps feet beneath me and hands on weapons is the fever of battle. The same thing is what sent me fighting alongside the Lithos as if he were my brother, his weak side the same as Donil's, our backs together an impenetrable cycle of blade that cuts to bone. We fought well together. Defended each other, even.

I am sick with the knowledge of it.

Yet we were allies for a breath, and when he turns to me with sword down and—depths—a smile on his bloodied face, my swords falter. His blade is back up the moment he sees my stance, but I see in his eyes a brief flicker of betrayal.

As if we were bonded in that moment, when we fought, blade for blade, blood for blood. Each of us taking account of the other as we circled, defending, striking, always with the other's strengths and weaknesses in mind.

"I have no weaknesses," I say, to still my own thoughts.

"I believe you," the Lithos answers, his sword edging downward as my own begins to fall, the morning light going dark in my vision. In the distance I hear shouting in the common tongue, and when my eyes go to his, I wonder if he sees the same betrayal there I spotted in his own.

"My men," he confirms, sheathing his sword. "Indiri . . ." he begins, voice tense. "Dara . . ."

My name, soft on his tongue.

"Depths take you," I whisper before my knees buckle and my hands unclench. The Lithos is down with me in a moment, blood dripping from his face onto mine. He doesn't move my swords out of reach, and if I had the strength, I could grip one, drive it upward, and end whatever this odd moment is between us.

But I don't.

Because I lack the power or the will, I don't know.

Filthy fathoms.

I don't know.

I awake in darkness, but can hear the breathing of another, so regulate my own, that they will not know I woke. The dirt beneath is familiar, as is the smell. It's my own stench, the rot of the trees that left me as I shed tears of blood and spit mouthfuls of the same. I've killed a Pietran jailer, stolen the Lithos's horse, and slaughtered a clowder of Tangata only to end up back in my cell.

I know the smell of him too, and hate myself for it. As we spun together in the forest, it filled my nose, not entirely unpleasant. The Lithos smells of the salty sea and the coldest of rocks, and he is here with me now.

"Did your horse pass through it?" I ask, knowing he will sit as long as I will, and I have no patience for waiting.

"A bruise on the foreleg," he says. "And a slap on the nose from a cat, I believe. But he'll live."

"Seems a good animal," I say. "Though he did throw me at the first sign of trouble."

"He's not seen a cat before," the Lithos goes on, as if we were not beneath earth and stone, speaking to each other in a space dark as the grave. "They don't often wander here, and rarely in numbers."

"The mare you were on, that's a loss," I say. "She knew you rode for me and would have driven your stallion to the ground, given the chance."

"Yes, a loss," he agrees. "She knew her target and went for it, not seeing other paths. It was her undoing."

"Ah," I smile, following. "So in this parable, I am the mare, and you are . . . ?"

"I remain myself."

"I would rather you were a cat dead on the forest floor, and I on my way home."

"Stille is home?"

"Stille is . . ." My hand falters at my side, finding a clod of dirt. I toss it into the dark simply to hear it break against a wall. "Stille is Stille," I finish.

The Lithos is mercifully quiet, and I regret the bitterness that edged my voice when I spoke the name of my adopted people, the place where my brother remains, as well as Dissa, and—I allow myself the bright stab of the thought—Vincent.

"I will tell you nothing," I inform him. "It is not home, but it was my shelter for a time and still harbors those I care for."

"Who is it that you care for?"

He has shifted, and I didn't hear the movement. The Lithos is crafty, not moving closer but showing me that he could without my knowing.

"The Indiri first," I answer. "Then those I call friend."

"Who are?"

There's no harm in my telling him what he already knows, so I lift my chin as I answer. "Dissa, former queen of Stille, and her son Vincent, king of Stille."

My voice is strong, pride evident. But the Lithos is quiet for only a moment.

"That's a short list."

"Let me name yours," I spit. "Hadduk—slayer of my people. Ank—betrayer of my father's-father. Nilana—murderer of the same. The Keeper—mother of drowned children. The Feneen—rejected by their own blood. And lastly, every Pietra who ever drew breath and those who rot in the sea that took them moments before I would have opened your throat. I may have few friends, Lithos, but they are worthy of that title."

"And mine very, very capable of hurting you."

He's moved again as I ranted, this time to my lee. I close my eyes against the darkness, finding the same within as without.

"Let them," I say, the cold comfort of the inevitable filling me. "You tire me with this game. If it is to end in blood, then let it be spilled. I'll chew through my own tongue before I say a word that benefits you."

There's a touch on my wrist before he goes, so quick and light I wonder if I've imagined it before I feel his breath against my face, his voice in my ear.

"I wish it were otherwise, Indiri."

CHAPTER 48

Ank

MY MOTHER ALWAYS LINGERS WITH ME AFTER I GO, NOT just the nilflower that scents the air, but her face, worn more each visit. I put my hands upon her lined cheeks when I left this time, felt the goodness of her, the true, hard kernel of pure love at her center, surrounded by playful coyness and a deep knowledge of things that are to come. My mother feels of hope in the face of despair, yet I couldn't help but think as I left this time that the despair had a sharper edge than ever before.

There are changes, small and large, as I head back to Pietra. Downed trees that fell when the ground shook, soil that clings to the roots now hard and crumbled, though the musky scent of rent earth still fills the air. Oderbirds fly, their feathers less vibrant as they grow older, and not many deep colors among the flocks. The trees that still stand bear claw tracks in their trunks, and clumps of hair in the lower branches.

The darkness that had settled in my middle swells at the sight, reminding me of what had sent me to Stille at the first, not long ago. Lusca on land, cats taking to trees, oderbirds refusing to make young. There is something deeply wrong in our world, and the animals know it. If Mother has seen what is to come, she did not share it with me, whether to shield me or in hopes of a different outcome, I do not know.

My horse tosses its head at a crevasse where there formerly was none, and I shiver at the sight of the deep earth, now open to the air. The skin of our island is breaking, its belly exposed. How long before sinews let go and bones separate?

I guide my mount in search of a different path. I had told Madda I would look for traces of the Indiri girl as I travel. But I see no people, only Tangata prints, bold in fresh earth. More than once, I feel eyes upon me, and know that some traveler has hidden at the sound of my approach, and cannot blame them. Those who walk on two legs have begun to feel whatever it is the four-legged already knew. Danger lurks.

I do not go in search of these travelers, not wanting to cause alarm. I doubt I would pass Dara without an arrow in my back, and though I would die at her hand, I'd do so knowing she still lived.

I shift on my mount, thoughts on spotted skin and bright eyes. Our world has long been weakened, the Indiri magic with it. Mother is right to worry that the girl's pride could be her undoing, for skin can part under a Tangata claw or Pietran blade, no matter what color. Unbidden, I think of the earth itself cracking, water gushing forth instead of blood. I ponder the image, wondering if the lives of the Indiri are tied to the well-being of the very land I walk on. The idea carries merit, and I send a thought to wherever the girl may be, that she be safe.

Pietra is not as I left it.

I hoped to find my way to the chamber that Witt has given me. Though I would prefer to be with my people, I also know that the Lithos having easy access to my advice is more in their service than my presence among them would be. This room, with its stone walls and plain furnishings, has become something of a solace, I'm loathe to admit. A lifetime spent under open skies has given me freedom and understanding of living things, but the simple luxury of a bed is welcome in my old age.

I have neither freedom nor luxury as soon as my arrival is noted. I'm taken directly to the meeting hall, where Nilana, Hadduk, the Lithos, and the Keeper are deep in argument. Nilana glances up when I enter the room, the briefest flash of relief at my presence telling me how high tempers are flaring.

"What's this?" I ask. "A gathering of minds while the best of them is away?"

"I'll not listen to your glib tongue." Hadduk comes at me immediately, finger raised to my face. "You can't wander into the night and come back pretending to know all. An Indiri moves among us in your absence, or is this no surprise to you?"

"Bide, Mason," the Lithos says, coming to Hadduk's side. "Ank left under my command, and you can see by his face he did not know of the Indiri."

Either Witt has become sharper at reading me, or I've not been able to hide my reaction. No matter which is true, I must step carefully.

"The girl or the boy?" I ask.

"Girl," Nilana says. "If only it were the boy. He seems more . . . malleable."

Hadduk shoots her a side glance, catching her tone, and I take the moment she's given me to measure the Lithos.

He's missing an ear, a nub of what's left sewn to his head in something resembling the other side. A steady hand—the Keeper's, no doubt—did the work, and did it well, though Witt's lucky to have long enough hair to hide most of the damage. Not that such things matter to the Lithos, I think, remembering Nilana's insistence that the boy refused to be distracted. And yet . . . there is something different about Witt beyond the wound, a change in the air around him that speaks to me in a language I haven't quite deciphered.

"An Indiri moves among us." I repeat the Mason's words. "Does she still?"

"And then some," Hadduk snorts. "Right out of her cell and into the forest, with a dead jailer behind her and a Lithos who won't—"

The Mason bites off his anger and turns his back to Witt, falling just short of treason by a word.

"The Mason believes I have been somewhat soft in my dealings with the Indiri," Witt says calmly, tilting his head as the Keeper puts some balm on the flesh of his ear, still the bright, angry red of a fresh wound.

"I'm confident the Lithos has acted as he should," I say, shooting my eyes to Nilana to judge if I am speaking truth or not. She shrugs, almost imperceptibly. "Tell me, how did the girl come to be here and is there only the one Pietran body in her wake?"

Witt explains as the Keeper covers his ear, wrapping a linen around his head, which soon spots with red where he still bleeds. The Indiri has left not only the jailer, but also a Lusca and an Elder rotting behind her as she tears through Pietra. As the Lithos comes to the tale of her escape, and their own pitched battle in the forest against Tangata, I hear something in his tone that he reserves for very few indeed. Respect.

Nilana hears it too, as does the Keeper. I can see it in their shared glances, a small twitch in Nilana's mouth and a larger one from the Hyllenian. Hadduk only fumes more, his back still turned to the rest of us, but the shaking of his head says fathoms.

"She is a fighter, my Lithos," he says. "And a good one. But a fighter who has killed Pietra, same as her forebears, and she should be as they are. Let me make it so."

Witt nods his thanks to the Keeper as she ties off his bandage. "I cannot do that, my Mason," he says, voice low and controlled. "The girl is necessary to draw Stille out to meet us in battle. She is not to be killed."

Hadduk spins to face his commander, heat in his eyes. "Killed, maybe not. But harm is warranted, I think, and there is a message to be sent. Or do you shrink from hurting a woman?"

Witt stands, cold as the stones he lives among. "Have you not seen me open slim throats beneath Hadundun trees? Were you not present at the last Culling, where I sent many women to the sea? If either of us has a weakness for females, Hadduk, it is you."

The Mason nods his assent, the proud jut of his chin somewhat lower than before. And yet, I do not think the man is a fool. That the Indiri girl is a female surely did not escape the Lithos's eye, but it is her ferocity that has gained his attention. I see the Keeper watching him closely as well, and wonder if her thoughts follow my own.

"She cannot be killed," I say, echoing Witt's thoughts. "To be used against the Stilleans or to save our own skins. Did the earth shudder here as it did under my feet on that path to Stille?"

Nilana nods curtly to me, and I see the Lithos and Mason exchange a glance.

"It did," the Keeper says. "And nothing like it have I ever known."

"And not long after the Indiri was brought to you, torn by a Lusca and sick unto death from taking down a Hadundun tree, correct?"

"She dripped blood like she'd been drained of it," Hadduk says, and spits. "Leaked out onto this very floor and would've pulled us to pieces with her hands if she'd had the strength to reach us."

"Yet she did not," I say, averting his anger. "She was nearly dead, and the earth shook at the thought. The Indiri are of the earth, Lithos," I say, turning to Witt. "To put her to death is to murder the very soil you stand on, and invite it to abandon us all."

"Of the earth, is it?" Hadduk argues. "Then why did it not shudder beneath me as I took them down in piles, and made mud with their blood?"

"How did it go, after?" I ask, leading him. "Did you pile the bodies and burn them?"

"We piled the corpses, many and more," he says. "But when we brought the torches, they had gone to dirt already."

"And so became one with the earth," I say. "And now we walk upon them, build our houses on their bones. The earth knows there are only two left, and it will mourn their passing with a vengeance."

The others are quiet, nervous moments betraying that my words have hit their target. "Do not take her death lightly, Witt," I say.

He raises his eyes to me, and I see the truth in them when he says, "I do not."

"So she lives that we may save our own skins, yes?" Hadduk says, pulling a knife. "But what harm is there in taking a bit of hers?"

CHAPTER 49

―◦◯◦―

Ank

I TRAIL DOWN THE STEPS AFTER HADDUK AND WITT, THE light of their torches barely reaching us as I exchange a few quick words with Nilana, who rides on my back.

"What should I know?" I ask her.

"The Lithos and Mason are at odds over the girl," she says. "To be fair to Hadduk, she has killed everything she's laid a hand on."

"Except the Lithos," I amend.

"Not him," she agrees. "Though I do not know she's had the chance."

"I'd say she has," I argue. "To hear him tell it, they fought side by side in the woods, blades in hand, yet she did not turn hers upon him."

"Nor he on her," she adds.

"What is at work here, Nilana?" I ask, and feel her shrug, shoulder blades moving against my own.

"Perhaps they are distracted."

I don't laugh. If there is indeed some attraction between the two, it cannot end well. Though, I think as we find our way into the dungeons, I do not know of a good ending for any of us who walk this earth.

I follow Witt's torchlight to find a small room that holds many terrors. There are only simple things here: a barrel of water, a chain attached to the wall, a stone slab of a table, a stoked fire, and a poker, but well I know that the most innocent of objects can bring about great pain when wielded by the right hands.

Hadduk has gone to fetch the Indiri from her cell, Witt's color slightly off in the torchlight. I rest Nilana on the table in the hopes that the Mason will not put it to darker uses with the Indiri, and go to the Lithos's side.

"Witt," I say, "this does not have to be."

He closes his eyes against my voice. "I must draw out Stille, you know this. She is close with the king of Stille, and proof of her being in our hands can bring his army to our doorstep, where we'll fight our way among our stones, not standing on sand when the sea comes to sweep us away."

I hear Hadduk struggling with the girl, a string of Indiri curses coming before them as they approach.

"Witt," I growl, words having deserted me this once.

He faces me, and I see a darkness in his eyes not of emptiness, but of deep despair. I rest my hand on his shoulder for a moment and feel all the goodness I knew from before, now heated from the center by the beginning of something bright and pure.

Fathoms. He does care for the girl. It's surrounded by a maelstrom of confusion and helplessness, but it's there.

"I'll do what I can," I promise him.

Hadduk bursts into the room with Dara just in front of him, her hands bound with iron circlets. She surveys us, eyes lighting on me with nothing short of contempt. It hurts to see, and I wish I could be alone with her, explain the plight of my people and where it has led me. How it has brought me here, to a place where we are enemies and I stand aside and let her be hurt at the hands of a monster.

"Dara of the Indiri," I say, keeping my voice light. "It has been some time since we last met. I hear you've not been idle."

"And you've not been far from my thoughts," she says.

"I'm flattered," I tell her. "I did not know you cared."

"Come closer, and I'll show you much," she says.

"Enough," Witt cuts in, moving between us. "Indiri, tell us of Stille and what plans they have for Pietra."

He turns to face her, once again the Lithos and no longer Witt. Behind Dara, Hadduk stands ready to stop a lunge at the Lithos or block her escape. But the Indiri does neither, instead smiling at the gathering.

"Bring your blades. Bank the fire. The only words I have for you are foul and spoken in Indiri."

"I thought as much," Witt says to her. "And so I've brought an interpreter."

He nods to Hadduk, who disappears into the corridor. I look to Nilana, who blinks at me, at a loss. The sound of jangling keys reaches us, then a trudging step. Hadduk returns, bringing after him—unbelievably—an Indiri.

The man is frail and bent, though I would not call him old. His skin has sagged with years spent in darkness, and gone gray beneath his spots. But he is Indiri, and male, and when he sets eyes upon Dara, it is as if the sun has risen inside of him. For her part, Dara's knees go for a moment, and she sags, the insolence she's depending on abandoning her.

The man straightens, gone from prisoner to noble in an instant. He speaks to her, the guttural language of the Indiri, and she answers in kind. Hadduk prods the man in the spine.

"What do you say to each other?"

"We greeted each other as Indiri do," Dara says. "Naming our mothers."

"I'll name your mother, and something you won't like if—"

"Hadduk," Witt cuts him off, then turns to Dara. "The Pietra granted mercy to one on the field that day, to be used against others, if necessary."

Dara does not turn from the Indiri male, her eyes locked upon his. "And so you will harm his flesh in place of my own, that I will speak freely to spare him."

"That is the thought," Witt agrees.

She turns to him, finally, and I'm startled to see the thin line of tension that had formed along Witt's jaw disappear when he finally has won her gaze away from the Indiri.

"He is my blood, the last of it I may breed with," she says. "And yet what is that worth, in a world where our children would live and die in a Pietran cell?"

"You would go free, both of you," Witt says, inclining his head toward the prisoner. "Your children would live beneath open sky."

"And their parents without honor," Dara says. "And without that, are we truly Indiri?"

She repeats the question in Indiri, posing it for the prisoner, who shakes his head.

"Depths, woman," I shout at her, my patience broken. "What is this pride that it would lead you to your own death and the loss of your people?"

"What is my life, if it cannot be led with pride? And what are my people, if they live by the grace of the Pietra?" she asks of me, chin lifted. "Not Indiri, I tell you that. But something less."

"There'll be one less of you, before I'm done," Hadduk says, sticking a poker into the coals of the fire.

"Hadduk . . ." I move as if to stop him, but Witt raises a hand.

"I'll remind you that the Feneen are allied with the Pietra, not the Indiri," he says.

"I allied my people with the leader who I thought was the best man, the wisest leader," I tell him, all control over my voice lost. "You show me neither of these things here."

"He's a Lithos of the Pietra," Hadduk says. "And this is how war is fought."

The Mason pulls the poker from the fire, the end red hot, and swings it between the two Indiri, a trail of smoke that binds them. "Who's first?"

"Me," the male says in the common tongue, and his hand strikes quick as a snake, stopping the poker in mid flight. Calmly, with his eyes fixed on Hadduk's, he curls his other hand around the burning tip.

A sizzling sounds fills the air, and the sweet scent of cooking meat, but the Indiri holds tight, smoke curling from between his fingers, his arm shuddering with the need to let go but his will keeping his hand clenched tight. It is Hadduk who finally wrests it away from him, breaking their painful union.

A gasp tears from the Indiri's throat as he falls to the ground, maimed hand curled to his chest. "Sharpen your knives, Hadduk of the Pietra," he says. "I have sat in darkness with my memories for a long while, and you have already done your worst to me."

"Hadduk," Nilana says, calling her to him. The stunned Mason can only backstep, the poker still in his hands, the blackened flesh of the Indiri's fingers trailing from the tip.

Dara goes to the wounded prisoner, on her knees beside him. He turns his head to hers, and they say a few words to each other in their own language. Then she holds his face in her palms, and calmly, cleanly, snaps his neck. His body shudders and slides from her grasp. Dara rises, the chains that circle her wrists clinking together with the movement.

"I have no weaknesses," she says calmly to Witt.

And the earth shakes.

Both above my head and below my feet, all is in movement, the walls themselves shuddering as dirt trickles loose, flowing like streams down the sides. Nilana yells, but Hadduk has her, his arms crossed over her head. Witt dives for Dara, I think to secure her, but then I see him cover her with his body as a last wrenching crack comes from the rock above us. Daylight streams in as part of the ceiling falls away, crushing the stone table Nilana had been upon moments before. I watch as a ray of light falls upon the dead Indiri and his body turns to a pile of earth.

Then all is still. No breath of air or rush of dirt. Hadduk pushes back Nilana's hair from her temple, touches his forehead to hers. Witt pulls Dara to her feet, to which she comes unsteadily, eyes on the mound of dirt that was the only male Indiri she's ever seen besides her brother.

"Do what we came here for, Lithos," Hadduk says. "The Indiri do not suffer games."

Witt looks to Dara with shame as he pulls a knife, the sound pulling her attention to him. She nods at the sight of the blade, as if in understanding.

"I cannot allow a Pietra to harm me," she says, and to my astonishment, Witt turns the blade, offering her the hilt.

"Depths, man." Hadduk leaps to his feet, crushing Dara into his chest from behind. "Would you arm this woman when you've seen her kill with bare hands?"

"I know what is to be done," Dara says, reaching for the knife. And with Hadduk pinning her from behind, she skins the inside of her lower arm, calmly handing the Lithos a slice of her own flesh.

CHAPTER 50

Vincent

KHOSA HAS BEEN GONE FOR SEVEN SUNS, AND WHILE her absence has been a constant ache, the time has passed quickly. Stilleans do not like change, and what their king proposes goes against every fiber of their being. Vincent has sat at meals, spoken himself hoarse, flattered, argued, and pleaded his way through all the noble households. Most only shook their heads, though some have listened, and there are the very few whose ears have perked at the idea and the consolation that there may, after all, be somewhere else.

Every night he falls into his bed exhausted, but missing his wife. It has become their habit to talk over their days, combing through each other's conversations to put together a full vision of their country and how everyone in it fares and feels. Without this, his daylight hours feel incomplete. Sleep has not come easily, and when it does, it brings visions of ships sinking to the depths and Stilleans he has led astray drawing a last, wet breath.

"It's a hard thing to unsee," he says to Dissa, his mother.

They sit together by the large fireplace in the great hall, their voices echoing off the stones around them, barely reaching the arches of the ceiling.

"I can imagine," his mother says, taking a sip of her wine. "But it is good for you to see these things, as it is one of two endings."

"Yet I do not dream of the other," Vincent admits, running a thumb along the rim of his glass. "Do you think I am mad to pursue this?"

"No." Dissa shakes her head, the strands of silver in her hair catching the firelight. "I think you are young and in love, and not only with your wife. Stille has captured you, though its very nature had to change in order to do so."

Vincent looks into the fire with a small smile. "Is it so difficult to understand? Long meetings about the quality of wool from Hyllen or fair tariffs for trapmen and shepherds do not kindle the spirit in the same way as sailing into the sunset in pursuit of legend."

"Or war," Dissa adds.

Vincent nods, remembering the ferocity that swept him as he fought in earnest for the first time, Dara and Donil at his side. But he remembers too the horror that came after, weak knees, a shaking body, blood-covered boots, and his grandfather dead on the ground, glassy eyes reflecting the sky.

"I would avoid that if I could," he tells his mother now. "There is honor to be found there, but I will never revel in it as Dara does."

Dissa's face twists at the mention of her adopted daughter. "Dara," she says, lifting her hands to her lips as she says the name, the only thing remaining of the girl that she can touch. "She left for love of you."

"I know," Vincent says, the subject enough for him to finally take a drink of his wine.

"It was for the best," Dissa says. "Your love for Khosa is plain on your face and difficult for Dara to look upon. I have been that woman, loving and not loved in return. But my crown kept me anchored. Dara's only constant was vengeance, and she went to wreak it on Pietran heads."

"May it find a target," Vincent says, raising his glass and taking a healthy swallow of wine.

"And may your constant remain your country," Dissa says, raising her own.

"It's an odd thing," Vincent admits. "I did not want this throne, as you well know. Yet when it was time to defend Stille, I fought for it, watched my ancestor die at my feet for love of it. I've stood on Stille's shores and faced a wave sure to topple me, and while my first thought was for Khosa, the second was for the kingdom at my back."

Dissa's mouth smiles in the only way it knows how, sadly. "All my life I've loved things that cannot love me back—your father, our kingdom. Being a ruler is very much like being a mother of an infant. What you care for drains your strength and requires constant attention, never able to return it. Yet when you wake in the night, it is your only concern, and you would send yourself to the depths to preserve it."

"In my case perhaps quite literally," Vincent says.

"How many will follow you, if Khosa returns with plans for a ship?" Dissa asks.

"More than I thought," he answers. "Our victory over the Pietra came only after a hard loss to the Feneen, and while we celebrate the former, the latter is not forgotten. And there is the matter of the earth shaking . . ." He trails off, both of them pushing their feet more firmly against the stones, as if to test their firmness.

"Never have I felt such a thing," Dissa says, her voice dark. "Stille itself betrayed us in that moment, our very soil a thing we could not trust."

"It helped win many over to me," Vincent reminds her. "Without it, few would follow me onto ships."

"Either way, what is beneath their feet will sway." Dissa shudders as she speaks, the wine in her cup making small ripples. Her fear is palpable, reaching for Vincent like a cool hand that chills him over the warmth of the fire.

"You will come, of course?" What was intended to be a declaration ends as a question, and Vincent feels an upheaval in his gut at his mother's hesitation, worse than the day the earth shook.

"Have I not already outlived my usefulness here, in a dying kingdom? What place would I have in a new land beside my son, the king, and a wife who rules alongside him well?"

"You have a place as my *mother*," Vincent says, his voice breaking on the word. "I may be a king, but am a child still. I would have you by my side."

Dissa takes a long drink, her eyes not meeting his. "We shall see."

Vincent has risen to go to her with a plea when the doors of the great hall burst open, a Stillean messenger running in.

"My king," he says, out of breath. "You must come."

CHAPTER 51

Donil

THERE IS ROOM IN ME FOR NOTHING OTHER THAN LOVE.
I know full well that guilt should cast a long shadow, one
that would turn my gut and send me begging to see a thing
undone, but I have not felt that cool hand yet, for all that is inside of
me calls for heat. The heat of her gaze, eyes on mine, her breath on my
shoulder, our combined sounds that make no words, and at last, the
heat of skin, melded as one.

We are fools, and I well know it, but we revel in our foolishness
as we journey back toward Stille. At every pause we find a clearing,
every drink a horse may need to take, we draw deeply from each other
as well, and if Khosa and I should delay while gathering firewood and
return with arms only half full, Sallin allows it to be so.

"We'll need to be more careful once we arrive home," I say,
pulling my shirt over my head. Khosa's hand sneaks underneath it,
her fingernails trailing down my back from where she still lies, her
hair fanned on the forest floor, caught in leaves. "Sallin may turn a
blind eye, but the sconcelighters and kitchen maids see much, and
say more."

"We have the rest of this day," she says sleepily, "and another to
follow."

"And then?" I ask, aware she did not add her own thoughts to mine about how we should meet once we are settled back in Stille.

"I do not know, Donil," she says, fingers now making a circle on my back, one that becomes smaller until they rest lightly on my spine. "How am I to be two people, Donil's lover and Vincent's wife?"

She says his name as if it did not weigh as much as a Pietran stone shield. The first mention of the man we have both betrayed falls heavily between us, and I sit beside her, my own hands drawing maps on her body that I have only just begun to discover.

"And how am I to be the queen's lover and the king's friend?" I counter. "Yet I am both these things, as are you. We need not ask these questions, when actions already done have sealed the answer."

She intercepts my hand with her own and sits up, the saddle blanket I'd brought with us to the clearing clutched to her chest. "Actions already done," she repeats, linking her fingers with mine.

Khosa leans into me, the blanket slipping from her hands. "I would not see them undone," she whispers, and I think I may have dressed in haste.

Dara once told me that when her anger gets the best of her, it is the only thing she feels. Her wrath burning red blinds her to all else, the blue of the sky, the green of the trees, the face of the unfortunate person who may stand in front of her in that moment. I've seen her in that state, a raging animal that wants only to inflict pain and punishment, drawing it from the eternal well inside of her to be poured upon others.

And now I understand, though my nature leans a different direction. I've lain with many girls—many and more, truth be told—and enjoyed every moment. But with Khosa I'm cracked open, the center of my Indiri self welling up and overflowing so that all I know is love. Fadernals, drawn by the pull of my affection, leave the deep forest to find me on the path. An oderbird rests upon my shoulder as I ride, beak riffling through my hair, curious to find the source of whatever drew him to me.

Khosa laughs at the trail of animals that forms behind us, but Sallin puts an end to it when a Tangata pushes through the brush, whiskers twitching. I shoo them all away with a word, and they go with disgruntled snorts and the swish of wings, a lazy feather trailing down from the sky that Khosa pulls from the air and tucks behind her ear. My happiness will not be contained, and even as I see the spires of Stille on the horizon, I feel only the rise of hope. For what friend could deny me this feeling? Is it not possible that Vincent will see how it is between us, and know that it cannot be broken only for the sake of propriety?

Such is how I feel as we pass through the gates, that the love inside me extends to Vincent as well. We return with good news, the hope of a new world where we shall make ourselves again, and who is to say that he will not bless Khosa and me in this place yet unseen, that we may be together? I am so lost in my own love that I do not think of ship's decks wavering beneath my feet, or the fear of an endless sea with no sight of land.

All I see is Khosa. As she is now and as she will be, old and gray, weathered with the wear of time, I at her side on the beach of some foreign land, our children staggered behind us, spotted but with light hair. I see it so clearly there is room for nothing else. I miss the tight faces of the guards that we pass, the drawn eyebrows of the nobles who gather in the courtyard.

I see nothing until I see Vincent and, in his hands, a strip of my sister's skin.

CHAPTER 52

Vincent

THE KING OF STILLE STANDS IN A ROOM BRIMMING WITH words. They cross in the air around him, glancing off one another like blades. Attacks and parries, offensive and defensive, they coalesce into a miasma he cannot ignore, though his mind wishes only to be alone with the long, soft strip of skin he holds in his hands.

Though they were close as children, Vincent and Dara touched each other little as they grew in age. She fought an urge that her Indiri blood would not allow, an internal battle that he didn't realize was happening until it was too late. Now he stands alone. Though his wife is beside him, he can feel her gaze drawn to another, her eyes bright with a light not for her husband.

The argument continues, Sallin's voice against Dissa's, Elders against nobles, the Curator validating both sides when an erudite point is made. Donil only stands, empty and staring, and Khosa's gaze does not move from the Indiri.

Vincent runs his finger along the strip of Dara's skin. It's soft and light, and he studies the pattern of speckles there, wondering if it's a part of her he's seen before, has touched before, and if this is the last time he'll feel her beneath his hand.

"We must go," he says, his first words since others have gathered here and opinions have flown. Vincent says them quietly, mostly to himself and directed to the strip of skin in his hands. But Khosa hears him, and for the first time, he has her full attention.

"We must go," he says again, slightly louder, and now Dissa hears him, her own argument for the same thing falling quiet now that he has spoken. Sallin, without an opponent to speak against, silences as well, eyes on the king.

"We must go," Vincent says a final time, his hand curling into a fist around all that remains of Dara in Stille. The silence of the others spreads, alerting the room that the king has spoken. There are mutters, shifted feet, thoughts rolling quietly about how to change the king's position. But in this moment there are only bowed heads, and the sound of the door slamming behind him as Vincent leaves, taking Dara's skin with him.

Vincent stands alone in the library, listening to the rustle of the maps hanging above him as they sway in the breeze from the open window. Evening has come, the last of the light failing. His family and advisors have left him alone, knowing better than to follow when he came here for privacy.

It is his wife's solace, the place that Khosa made her own upon her arrival in Stille as the Given, the stool he sits upon usually warmed by her body, not his. His feet came here from habit, listening to the deep place inside him that needs comfort. For Vincent, that equals his wife, and he came here knowing she would find him first.

Her soft step crosses the doorway, her hands alight upon his shoulders, followed by the weight of her head resting upon his back.

"I am so sorry, Vincent," she says. He reaches up, clasping her hand in his, and she allows it.

"I know you are, and truly," he answers. "But I also know you come to speak to me of ships and escape. How can I leave her in their hands when I see what they have done and imagine what more awaits her?"

Khosa sighs against him, her breath ruffling the hair at the nape of his neck. "I do not know, Vincent."

"What you must ask yourself is how many Stillean lives you balance against hers." Dissa's voice comes from the doorway, and Khosa straightens at her appearance.

"How can you say such a thing, Mother?" Vincent asks, still very aware of his wife's hands upon his shoulders. "She is your daughter, Indiri or not."

"She is." Dissa nods and takes a seat across from her son, claiming one of his hands in her own. "And I love her as I love you. But you cannot answer what you will do as her brother or—" She cuts her eyes to Khosa, censoring her words. "You must make this decision as the king of Stille. Not as Vincent, Dara's friend," she finishes.

"An easy thing to say when you do not hold a strip of her flesh in your hand," he says to his mother, putting Dara's skin on the table between them.

Dissa's eyes go to it, and tears well there, but her mouth remains thin. "How often has flesh weighed on my mind? That of other women your father hounded after; the dead, cold feel of your brother's hand as he lay during the Stoning, alive and also dead. Yet I was the queen of Stille, not a wife or a mother, and acted as a queen should, keeping my tears for myself and the walls of my empty chamber."

"So I should mourn in private and build ships in public?" Vincent asks, and feels Khosa's hands tighten upon him. "And what of the next piece they send me? Her spotted finger or the scalp of her wild hair? Do I wait until we have Dara back in full, and piece her together on a ship that sails for salvation?"

"You'll wait for nothing," Donil's voice fills the room as he walks in to stand behind Dissa. "Nor will I. Your mother is right, Vincent.

You are the king, and Stille your first concern. I am Indiri. Let Dara be mine."

"Donil—" Khosa begins, but he silences her with a look.

Vincent's eyes remain on the skin, which Dissa now reaches for, but pulls her hand back at the last moment.

"You would go alone?" Vincent asks Donil.

"It would be best," he says. "The only Stillean I would have by my side is you, and you are needed here."

Vincent nods, and hears Khosa's intake of breath behind him.

"What is this foolishness?" she asks. "You would send Donil on the same path Dara took? And who follows him when it's his skin we receive?"

"The skin will stay on my bones, my queen," Donil says, and Vincent feels her arms stiffen at the formal address.

He raises his eyes to his mother, sees the cold calculation in her face, and settles his into the same. They are of royal blood, trained from birth to gauge tone and decipher the flicker of muscles, the poise of a spine. There is great emotion in this room—despair and hopelessness, wrath and rage—but rising above that is a deep line of lust tinged with betrayal.

And it runs between his wife and his best friend.

CHAPTER 53

Khosa

KHOSA'S BEDROOM IS AS SHE LEFT IT. PILES OF THE FORBIDDEN histories are stacked within reach of her side of the bed; her dresses still hang in the wardrobe, the fullness of their skirts pushing the doors outward even once latched. As soon as she returned, she had to shed the comfortable Hyllenian clothes, surrender to the unique torture of having her hair done, even if it was only to appear at a briefing where they shared what they had learned from Hygoden with Vincent's advisors, the pall of Dara's capture hanging over all.

No. She shakes her head. She should not use the word *torture* to describe what happens to her as she sits in luxury, wine and water at hand, food brought by a beckon. There is pain in her routine, it is true, but she still wears her skin.

Khosa shudders now as she pulls a brush through her hair, preparing for bed. The bedroom has not changed, true, but her knowledge of what may happen within one has. Color rushes to her cheeks at the thought, memories of Donil and the journey from Hygoden sending heat into her blood. A smile plays upon her lips, but a black bloom opens in her belly, heavy as rankflower, when her eyes alight upon the crown of Stille, which lies waiting for her.

She is an adulteress now, and not only that but a traitor to the crown. Sleeping with Donil has endangered the legitimacy of the royal line, and while she could fan the pages of any history in this room and find instances—many and more—of the same, there is a reason why the histories were hidden away.

Shame.

It weighs on her now, within these walls. The freedom of the wilderness and the possibilities of the open sky are distant dreams now, silly fantasies that she allowed herself to indulge in when the sun shined on her face. Now, in her bedroom where the shadows loom, Khosa knows she has done wrong.

They had decided that they would not be deceitful, she and Donil. During a long break for the horses that had ended with them beneath a blanket, warm and content, they had vowed to be honest with Vincent soon after they returned. They would bring him their love, show him their respect, and leave the choice to him.

It had never occurred to her that her husband might have her burned as befit a traitor, her lover alongside her. But when Dissa reminded him of his duties to Stille above personal feeling, she had felt a shudder pass through her bones. He had that right, and could exercise it.

Yet she cannot see him taking such a drastic action. Instead maybe he will see the ships built that Sallin calls for, put her and Donil aboard one with a blessing, then ride off with his army to see to Dara's release.

The comb catches at a knot in her hair, breaking the spell of what she spins—yet another fantasy. Donil made it clear to her in the library that, given the choice, he would ride for Pietra and his sister—alone if necessary. Her gut turns at the thought, and the comb in her hand shakes.

She sets it aside, hoping the tremor will pass. It does not, instead trickling up her arm and into her shoulders, creeping up the muscles of her neck until her head twitches and she yearns for the sea.

CHAPTER 54

Vincent

INCENT HAS LISTENED TO SALLIN, HIS ADVISORS, THE Elders, his mother, Donil, the Curator, all with Dara's skin in his hands. He will not set it aside, that its weight and his responsibility for its separation from her body will not leave his thoughts while pondering Stille's reaction.

Sallin argues that it makes no difference to the fate of their nation, that boats should be built and Stilleans put upon them, especially in light of the second shaking of the earth, though it was less than the first. His mother argues for the same, but with a deadness in her eyes that echoes the life that has left the strip of Dara's flesh. The Curator also calls for the boats, with the Elders split upon the notion.

Donil says nothing, his path already decided.

"Do not leave without first speaking to me," Vincent found the time to say to him, a quick meeting in the halls while the Elders filed out of the meeting room, the nobles coming in. "Don't do to me what she did."

Donil's mouth was set tightly, but he nodded in agreement.

Vincent thinks on this now as he heads to his own chambers, wondering how long Donil's vow to his oldest friend can stand against the need of his only sister. He nods to Rook, who stands in Merryl's place, and enters the chamber to finds his wife tearing at the bars of the window.

He slams the door behind him before Rook can see, and pulls Khosa from the window, her hands leaving drops of blood behind her as he hauls her away. They crash to the floor, her body still spasming, sleepshirt billowing around them both.

"Khosa . . . Khosa . . ." he calls to her, cradling her head against his chest. In the past he has held her through the spasms, but this one is different from the others, strong and relentless. He watches a candle burn down, one fingerlength, two, and as his strength flags and still her body fights him, he wonders if he needs to call Rook. But Khosa has lost all control of her body: tears spill down her cheeks, inarticulate sounds tear from her throat, and she has wet herself, the sharp, acidic smell filling their chambers. As much as he trusts Rook, he does not think Khosa would want to be seen like this, queen or not.

It eases, the strength of her flailing relenting moment by moment, until Khosa is completely limp in his arms, her breath coming in small, weak gasps.

"Khosa," he says again, his mouth near her ear.

She makes a small sigh in response, and he lifts her to the bed, stripping her soiled clothes away with no thoughts of lust, only intense care in his touch as he puts her in something clean and tucks the bedthings around her. He dims the lanterns and slides into his own spot of the bed, his hands going to her hair, which he has learned he can touch without her recoiling.

"I did not know if you would return to me," he says softly.

She sighs, not having the strength for speech yet. But her eyes are on his, her hand reaching up to entwine with his.

"We both feared the dance would forever be a part of you, yet . . ." He pauses, not wanting to give credence to his thoughts by voicing them. "That was the strongest I have ever seen it."

Khosa nods her agreement, though she squeezes her eyes against the truth of it, tears escaping from beneath her eyelids. Her voice finally comes, weak and fragile.

"I have not been honest with you, husband," she says, eyes still closed.

Vincent's hand grips harder on hers in reaction, but his voice remains calm. "What is it you would tell me?"

She opens her eyes and fixes them upon his. "The dances come more often, and more violently than before. Merryl has been with me for most of them, but . . ." Her nose flares as the smell from the soiled sleepshirt she wore earlier reaches the bed. "I fear it was you who witnessed the worst," she finishes.

"There is no shame in it," he assures her. "You should have told me."

"I did not want you to concern yourself, with so much already on your shoulders," she goes on. "And yet I find myself a hapless heap of a woman on a night when you learn your friend has been harmed at the hand of the enemy. A friend who was driven from your side on my account—"

Her face twists into grief, and her body shudders again, this time racked with sobs. Vincent pulls his wife against him, shielding her as best he can.

"Dara left of her own volition," he reminds her. "I would have never sent her away, in spite of everything."

Khosa lifts her face to her husband. "You care for her?"

"I do," he answers honestly, pushing her hair from the tracks of tears on her face where it wishes to stick. "With a deep and abiding affection that is a separate thing from my feelings for you."

Khosa nods, and he feels a stab of pain, aware that she knows only too well what he means.

"You must be honest with me from now on," Vincent says. "True, the weight of Stille is always upon me, but that is inconsequential next to my concerns for your welfare. Whether it goes good or ill with you, I would know it."

Khosa nods again, then gets up from the bed to blow her nose and toss her soiled sleepshirt rather unceremoniously out the bedroom door. Vincent remains where he is, in the middle of their shared bed, and is pleased when she returns to it and claims the same spot she held before, their bodies nearly touching.

"I will be honest with you, husband," Khosa says, taking a breath as if she would continue, but he lays a finger upon her lips. It is a glancing touch, which he removes quickly to spare her, but the act of stopping her speech was to spare himself. There are some truths he cannot bear, and the day has been long.

"I wish only to sleep, wife," he says, laying his head on the pillow near hers, their faces almost touching. She smiles at him, runs a hand through his hair as he drifts off to sleep. Vincent is almost lost to the blackness of sleep when he speaks again, not entirely meaning to. "I love you, Khosa," he says.

And his wife silently cries.

CHAPTER 55

❦

Donil

I STAND AT THE CITY GATES, WATCHING FOR WINLAN AND THE other travelers from Hygoden. My horse nudges my arm, perhaps mistaking me for Dara and looking for a stray apple. Though I am undeniably the softer of the two of us, my sister made it a point to carry a little something for the horses, and I rest my forehead against the stallion's long nose, wishing that she were here as much as he does.

"She'll not be gone long," I tell him, spotting a small braid in his forelock that her fingers undoubtedly put there. He nickers in response, and is answered from up the road. I raise my head from his to see Winlan on foot, leading a wagon loaded with his family and what seems to be the entire contents of his house. Behind him streams a long line of people similarly encumbered, all of them familiar faces of Hygoden.

I ride to meet them, reining in beside Winlan and his wagon. Pand acknowledges me with a jerk of his chin, Unda by pulling up her hood, then peering at me from the folds.

"Depths, man," I say to Winlan. "You did not have to bring home and hearth."

"I think I did," he answers easily. "The earth moved a second time, and I fear may not have much left holding it together. I'll not leave my people behind to save yours."

I nod my understanding, but look down the baggage train that follows him. "Am I to take it then that this is *all* of Hygoden?"

"It is," his wife answers, daring me with a glance to send them away.

"I put good men on the ship," Winlan says, nodding his head out to sea. "It'll clear the point a bit after us. I thought it might be better if I brought word of such a thing before it arrived itself."

"Indeed," I say, wondering how Stille will react at the sight of sails on the horizon.

Not only Stille, but also Vincent. The matter of the ships has been settled, after a fashion. They will be built, Sallin and I working alongside the Hygodeans to learn what we can and aid in whatever way possible. Meanwhile, Vincent will stay with the army and rouse them to march against the Pietra.

There are no easy tasks on either side, my hands helping fell trees that they may float on water, Vincent convincing his men to march against an enemy for the sake of an Indiri girl, instead of sitting quietly behind fortified walls. I argued that I was of more use to the army, but he insisted I work with Winlan, being a familiar face to the Hygodeans and a trusted one.

"And what of Khosa?" I asked, working to keep my face and voice devoid of emotion. "She was well liked in Hygoden, and the ships in her interest."

Vincent looked away from me, his mouth tight with some feeling I could not quite interpret, be it anger or worry. "Khosa is unwell," he said. "I would not have her near the sea."

And so it is that I—someone whose gut turns at the thought of boats—find myself scanning the sea for the shadow of a ship and escorting an entire village of sailors along the road to my adopted home. My palms itch in their call for Pietran blood, my eyes always turning the direction in which my sister went. Yet my feet turn toward Khosa, my body at war with itself.

"Where is Khosa?" Unda asks, trusting me enough to poke her nose out of her hood.

"I do not know," I tell her as the city gates open for us. "How could I, when I am not with her?"

"The entire village?" Vincent goes pale beneath his tan when I find him on the training field and tell him Hygoden has arrived. All of it.

"I settled them in the courtyard for the moment," I tell him as he gives instructions to a commander, then follows in my steps. "I wasn't sure what else to do with them."

Vincent nods, regaining his color, already searching for solutions. "There would not be enough beds in the entire castle, even if I set everyone to turning out all the empty rooms. I can't very well ask them to sleep on the ground when they've come so far at my behest."

"No," I agree, motioning him forward to where the Hygodeans are sprawled, children holding the leads of their goats, mothers resting with infants in their laps.

"Depths," Vincent says, halting his steps at the sight of Winlan. "That man is two of me."

"Three," I correct him, earning an elbow in the side.

"Winlan is his name?"

I nod, and we walk forward together. Introductions are made all around, Vincent shaking Winlan's hand and waving off the awkwardness of a bow coming from a man who towers over him.

"I'll not lie to you, Winlan," Vincent says, surveying the line of Hygodeans who are still marching into the courtyard. "I was not expecting your entire village to answer my call."

"No," he agrees, scratching his beard. "But you need us more than we need you, so I thought they'd be welcome."

Vincent's eyebrow goes up, but I see his mouth twitch with humor as well. "Welcome indeed, but there is the matter of where to house you."

"No worries," Winlan says, waving away the concern. "Hygoden has always seen to itself. Harta made his own shelter when he walked in this place; we will do the same, perhaps even on the same spot."

"That is time and timber better used in making ships," Vincent says, to which Winlan shrugs.

"I'll not ask for your help in making houses or hulls, King of Stille," he says. "But I will ask you that you stay out of my way while I'm doing both."

I stifle a laugh, the first I have felt since returning to Stille. Beside me, Vincent draws himself up to his full height, but still has to tilt his head back to address the sailor.

"Very well," Vincent says. "Anything that you need. Stille is at your service."

Winlan gives him a stiff nod just as the first cries come from the castle walls. Vincent and I climb to the parapets and see the outline of a distant ship on the horizon, sails billowing and whitecaps breaking around it.

Beside me, I feel Vincent shudder, and I do the same. There are people on that floating monstrosity, hands that know how to turn a rudder and draw a line. They can save us all, or drag us to the depths, and we have no way of knowing which it will be.

"Filthy fathoms," Vincent says under his breath, watching as more of his people catch sight of the ship, fingers pointing and women pulling their children closer. Only a few cheers go up, and those laced with trepidation.

"Tell me I'm doing the right thing, brother," Vincent says, eyes on the horizon.

"Brother," I answer, feeling the word to my bones, "I no longer know what is right or wrong."

CHAPTER 56

⸻ ❦ ⸻

Ank

S HIPS?" WITT REPEATS, WIDE-EYED. "YOU ARE SURE OF THIS?"
"My mother walks a fine line, and does not speak openly—"
"A family trait, it seems," Witt mutters.

I shift in my seat, allowing my bones to creak and a hint of discomfort to cross my face as I pull it closer to the fire in his chambers. Age is not respected here, but Witt has always seemed to allow me such moments—even if they are feigned—in which to prepare my next words.

"I cannot ask her to act outright against the interests of Stille," I tell him. "She is of their blood and country, as much a part of the royal family as any full member. To push her to speak openly is to risk treason. Something I think you would not ask of your own mother."

It's a blow beneath the belt, but it strikes home—a tender spot. I think Witt does not know how open he has become with me, how his emotions flicker across his face in the firelight. In the great aching middle of him, I have felt a need for his own mother and a regret for the sacrifice on her part that made him Lithos.

"How sure are you of this?" he asks.

"As much as I can be," I tell him. "The male Indiri and the queen traveled to Hygoden to speak to a man there about the building of them. The Indiri is as a brother to the king, and the queen made so not only in name. Vincent cares for her and would not have sent the two remaining people closest to him away from his side if the idea did not carry merit."

Witt nods in agreement, and I prepare the next step in my argument, only to be set back by an unlooked-for question.

"The king took a great risk, making the Given his wife," he says. "Bringing a woman his countrymen would see dead to his side."

"Yes . . ." I draw out the word. "But the Given was always held in high esteem by Stilleans. A girl made to die, yes, but as their savior."

"Mmm . . ." is all Witt has in response to that, and I notice that the wine bottle the Keeper brought him before retiring for the night is quite low.

"Lithos," I say, changing to formal address in the hopes of bringing his mind back to duty, "what harm is there in letting the Stilleans leave their shores? Your people call not for blood, but land. It will be open for the taking with no blades crossed if only you let them board their ships and take to the sea."

"The people may not call for blood, Feneen, but Hadduk surely does, as well as half my commanders and their men under them. Already as Lithos I have brought your people to fight alongside mine, convinced my army to cross water on the hands of your Silt Walkers— and lost more than a few in that act, I'll remind you.

"I asked them to fight beside those they found repugnant, stand on unfamiliar sand, and be taken by a wave. Shall I now put forth an order to bide, while those we would have fought and conquered sail away on seas still brimming with the spears of drowned Pietra?"

His words are dark pebbles falling into the calmness of my mind, sending ripples that disturb all the way to the edges. He is not wrong. The simplicity of allowing the Stilleans to leave, the most straightforward and easiest of all solutions, depends upon something that does not come naturally in these stone lands.

Forgiveness.

"Should I give that order, I would be Lithos no more," Witt says.

"Would that be such a bad thing?" I ask.

I expect his anger to emerge, cold and smooth as a blade left unused, but always ready to be drawn. Instead he considers, fingers tight on the cup he holds.

"For my own sake, I say it would not," he decides. "But a Lithos who ceases to be that is no longer of any use to the Pietra. There would be boats built on both shores then, but mine not meant to sail far, or for very long."

"A sacrifice not unlike the Given," I say. "Sent to the sea for the sake of your people."

"And to what end? I've seen the boys training to fill my boots. They will not be kind men, and will spark with the need to prove themselves. I can give the order to let the Stilleans bide and build my boat, and then you would find yourself with a new Lithos eager to march for blood."

There is truth to his words, and I ponder them in silence, thinking it will stretch long until I break it. Instead, Witt continues, voice low as if he does not remember that I remain with him.

"And what would become of Dara of the Indiri then?"

CHAPTER 57

Witt

THIS IS WHY THE LITHOS IS NOT TO BE DISTRACTED.

Ank has left me, concern clearly visible on his face. He stopped for a moment after opening my door and turned, one hand on my shoulder. I've had too much wine tonight, and I nearly called him my Mason, a slip that Hadduk would have had my tongue out for. The Feneen's hand rested on me, and I thought he would give me some word of advice, some indication of which path to take, but his face only reflected my confusion, and he left me with nothing.

I rest above the bedclothes, the bloody knob that I now call my ear burning. The Keeper wrapped a fresh linen around my head, but the cooling balm she put there first is long absorbed. I could call for her, set her practiced hands to ease my pain, but discomfort is not why I lie here, mind reeling, yet always returning to the same thing.

I know what it is I want.

I toss to my side, facing the fresh air that comes through the small balcony of my chambers. Even the sea is at odds with me this night, calculatingly complacent as the pot of my mind boils over. By all rights, I should be with my Mason, making plans as to where to meet the Stilleans, how to descend upon them when they come to rescue Dara.

I snort at the thought.

More like rescue Pietra from her.

"Or me," I say to the wall.

"Depths!" I punch my pillow and rise, pulling on clothes. There is no sleep in my future, and I need a clear head if I would speak with Hadduk this night. Walking off the wine that slurs my tongue is the first order I give myself.

I descend stone steps, waving off the guards who offer to accompany me. I know these halls, let my bare feet wander where they will as my head clears. But there is wine in the blood that flows to my legs, and they have their own thoughts. I find myself before the door to the cells, hand upon the dark wood.

"What good can come of this, Witt?" I ask myself, the words echoing back from the door to find my damaged ear, the pain there no longer of much concern.

Because I can think of many good things that can come of it.

Though I admit, as I open the door that few of them are likely.

CHAPTER 58

Dara

I HAVE NO JAILER BUT TIME.

Gaul has not been replaced, no other Pietra willing to stay beneath stones with me and risk his brains painting them. My cell floor was dug up shortly after the jailer's body was removed, and I then returned to it. I'll find no more branches beneath the dirt, and what areas I'd smoothed for my sleep are now rough beneath me, fists of soil jammed into my spine.

I sigh, tossing in the dark. With Gaul dead, I do not even know whether it is day or night outside, cannot count the passages of his torch to know if it is midmorning or twilight. The man was set in his ways, and they gave me a measure of comfort, until I drove a spike of sharpened wood through his eye.

Whether it be night or day outside, it is surely night where I am, and sleep the only passage of time I can look for, though I do not know if moments or days have passed when I wake. The strip of bandage around my arm where I removed my own skin has been changed twice by the Keeper. The blood drying there tells me she is due again to see to it.

I rest my hand on the wound, feeling the soft pulse of life beneath it, blood and skin mending themselves. I wish them speed, and rest my head against the ground, trying to unsee the face of the spotted man whose neck I snapped.

He was a true Indiri, stronger than either my brother or I. That he could sit in this darkness for as long as I've spent my lifetime and not be a raving animal when brought out has told me fathoms about him. But I've had time, here in the dark, to ask my ancestors about him, riffle through their memories and learn what I can. My mother knew him, and thought highly of him.

What would she think, had she seen him catch a red-hot poker from the air and close his hand around it, to spare me the same? And what would she think of me, to have held his head in my hands, only to twist it so that it would never speak again?

"He asked me to," I remind myself aloud, something I've taken to here in the dark. And while true, it is little consolation that the fate of the Indiri tribe lay at my feet and I snapped it between my hands. Yet how could I not do as asked, when he leaned into me, smelling not of earth and sky but of stone and mold, long nights spent alone and his own charred flesh?

One other thing he said to me, before I sent him to the earth, has stuck in my mind like a ninpop in the sickly sweet juice of a rankflower stem.

"You are not the last," he said. "Ask your ancestors, cast back even to those whose faces you've not seen before."

Here, with no other task for my mind, it should be welcome. Others have tried before me to send their minds back to the beginning of time, when we were beneath the earth itself, tree roots in our eyes and ears, waiting for the rain that would wake us. But to dig that deep is to sink into a long trance, suns and moons passing as others care for your body and your mind roams. The Indiri whose neck I snapped had only a Pietran cell to look at and Gaul to see to his needs, no matter how roughly. He promised me I was not the last, and I saw the truth of it in his eyes before I took the light from them.

My hand finds a clod of dirt, and I make a fist, breaking it in frustration. Donil has been by my side since we left the pits of Dunkai, and Faja still walks in the forest. I need not dwell on the Indiri of the past in order to know I am not alone in the present. I toss the clod of dirt in my hand against the wall, listening to it scatter, so that I may not acknowledge the truth.

I do not want to ask my ancestors anything, even though I have time for that and little else. I've seen my mother's death, through her own eyes. Felt her pain and anguish at the thought of her children, heavy in her womb, the rage that split her head as she charged the Pietra, voicing it with a throat bloodied by its force. All this I've known, and gone back to my ancestors, seeing that first inherited memory before I can see any other.

And in that same memory I have seen the Lithos astride a horse, watching as my mother is killed. And this is what I cannot bear to look upon again, for I have looked upon him now as a man who would fight at my side against cats ready to shred our skins, and protect my body with his own when the very ceiling came down around us.

"Piss on a dead sea-spine," I say, and kick the wall.

"An odd pastime," the Lithos's voice says, and I come to my feet, wondering if my mind has wandered farther than it ought. Then I hear the sound of a key in the door and know that he is real.

What I do not know is which I prefer.

The hinges of the door creak slightly, then pause. "I'll have to request that you not kill me, should I come in."

"I'm unarmed," I tell him. "Hadduk even took the chains from my hands so I cannot strangle you."

"You could kill me, if you wish," he says. There is a strike of flint, and then the torch he carries is ablaze. He speaks truth. In that moment I could rush him, send the fire to his hair or clothes, rip what's left of his ear from his head and jam it down his throat. Yet it would be no easy battle, I think, as I watch him set the torch in a sconce, not quite turning his back to me. Faja was right to say she did not know if she could have bested this man even in her younger days.

"I could kill you," I agree, though I am not so confident of it as I once was. "You take a great risk."

I watch as he settles against the opposite wall. We stare at each other in the light, each of us sitting like a huddled child, knees drawn to chest, hands locked around ankles.

"These days I see great risks down all paths," he says. "And so I choose this one."

"Men have been begging me to kill them lately," I observe, and the Lithos laughs.

"You gave the Indiri a good, clean death," he says, nodding to me. "Better than what Hadduk would have given him. It was a deserved death, for his bravery. I would not have—" He breaks off, eyes leaving the dirt to find mine, so that I may know he speaks truth. "I would not have harmed you."

"No, you would have ordered Hadduk to."

"No." He shakes his head. "I would not."

We stare each other down, and I see nothing but honesty in him.

"You could have said as much before I took my own skin off," I say.

"That was a bold move," he answers.

"A bold move that saved you having to not harm me," I shoot back, wondering indeed what would have passed had the Lithos refused to put the blade to me.

"And I thank you for it," he says. "How do you heal?"

"Better in the daylight," I say, glancing at my bandage. I have the odd thought that mine was probably cut from the same bolt as the one that binds his head, and a smile twists my face as I fight it.

"What?" he asks.

"How did this come to be?" I share my thought. "The Lithos and an Indiri sitting in a cell, our wounds bound by the same cloth?"

His hand goes to his own wound, touching the stump of his ear through the bandage. "How did Dara and Witt come to stand side by side, fighting Tangata in the woods?"

He uses our names, and I think of that moment, our enemies falling under our swords. This is a memory that would go to my children, should I have any. My gut roils at the thought that they should know their mother fought beside the Lithos of Pietra. Yet he did not say it as such, only that he was Witt and I was Dara.

"And we fought well together," I finish, knowing it to be true, come shame or pride.

"Yes, we did," he agrees, leaning his head against the stone.

I rest my own, feeling my spine unclench, my muscles relax as they would in the company of a friend.

"Chance," I say, answering his question. "You and I here, us together there. It's all chance. Any thought we had each day, every leaf that turned in our path, they sent us that way."

"I've always thought chance rather a hard thing," he says, watching me. "Perhaps I'll revise my thought."

I raise my hands to the walls around us, the door that will close upon my cell, the torch that will go with him when he leaves.

"Perhaps you shouldn't."

CHAPTER 59

Khosa

THE QUEEN OPENS HER EYES TO THE SOUND OF AXES against trees, a dull, thudding repetition that has lulled her long past her usual waking hour. She rolls to her side to see that her husband is gone, his pillow cold with the length of his absence. Khosa's hand lingers there for a moment as she smiles to herself, imagining Vincent rising, tiptoeing around the bed, easing the door open, dressing in another room, all in the name of allowing her a few more moment's rest.

You are lucky in your husband, a Stillean noblewoman had said to her at her wedding, making no pretense as her eyes slid over Vincent, the level of wine in the glass she raised to her lips quite low. A wave of irritation that a guest would be so bold in her glances while Khosa looked on had fired in her belly, and it retraces the path as she remembers that moment.

The woman had been right, though, in more than what she meant. Khosa did not need the hidden histories piled around her to know that it is the rare husband who would spare his wife the duties of the wedding bed, let alone keep his best friend alongside him, knowing his wife harbors an attraction, and that it is returned.

Now that desire has been spurred into action, and Khosa closes her eyes against the duel in her body that comes with the thought each time: the rush of her heart for the want of Donil, and the sinking of her stomach for the deception of Vincent. She was lucky in her husband, more so than the Stillean noblewoman could ever have guessed. He should be lucky in his wife as well.

Khosa's fists clench as she stares at the ceiling above her bed. Since returning home, she has oscillated between coming to Vincent with the truth of what she has done and asking to be relieved of her station as his wife, or swearing off any further deceptions of the flesh with Donil. Though she cannot control how she feels about him, she can control what she does with him.

Twice she has settled upon the second course as the best action, and both times a glimpse of Donil from the parapets, a broken strain of his voice brought to her on the breeze, has reversed her decision. Yet lying with Vincent, having her husband near his treacherous wife, she wishes only that her affection for him should grow into love, that she may be the wife he deserves.

Khosa lets out a frustrated breath. "You are the Given," she reminds herself aloud, eyes on the bars of her window. Her body goes to Donil as hungrily as to the sea, though her mind knows the outcome of both destinations. If the confines of her room can keep her from drowning, then so can they can be counted upon to keep her from drowning in life. Decision made, Khosa sits up in bed to tell the maidservants she will be spending the rest of the day in her rooms, and possibly many more days to come.

And promptly vomits.

"You took your time coming to your Seer," Madda says, as she opens her door for the queen. "I may not have told you what you wished to hear at our first meeting, but that does not mean there isn't a good word or two here in my round room for you."

"Yes, I . . ." Khosa's words slip away, her knees still weak from the vomiting spell that gripped her upon waking.

"Have a seat, then," Madda says, pulling a stool away from the table. "I'm too old to stand, and you're too . . . ill." She chooses the last word carefully, eyes roaming over Khosa's face.

Khosa nods her thanks as she sits, hands going to her cheeks to feel the sheen of perspiration there, though a cool breeze sifts through Madda's tower. She wipes it away on her skirts, glad at least that her face can still keep a secret, and reminds herself that Madda has more ways of reading people than only their skin.

"I wished to speak with you," she says.

"The first step being that you put yourself in front of me," Madda answers.

"Quite so," Khosa says smoothly. "And my hands."

Madda leans forward, motioning for Khosa to put her palms faceup on the table. A small sigh escapes her as the Seer takes her hands, flesh to flesh, and Khosa's already rolling stomach takes another turn as Madda's thumb passes over the flat of her hand. Madda turns the queen's palm in the sunlight, following a line that extends from her palm down onto her wrist.

"You husband visits me often," Madda says, glancing up at Khosa. "But rarely with a question. Even as a boy, Vincent knew the wisdom in letting things come to him rather than pursuing, and often the purpose of his visit would make itself known through the course of our words. But you . . ."

She sets Khosa's hand back onto the table and—to Khosa's surprise—wipes her own clean as if to rid them of the queen's touch.

"You are a woman of purpose," Madda finishes, eyes clinched tight against the rays of light that find their way into her dark room. "You seek out answers, even when they are writ in ink best left in shadows. So tell me, Given, why did you come here today?"

"How many children shall I have?" Khosa blurts, hoping that words in her throat can take the place of the vomit wanting to fill it.

Madda leans back in her chair, eyes calm. "Counting the one in your belly now?"

Khosa swallows, holding the Seer's gaze. "Yes."

"Three, if the lines you have now hold true," Madda answers. "Though I think your real question is already answered, and came not from a royal to her Seer, but from a motherless girl to an older woman. Will you allow me a question of my own?"

A cat jumps into Khosa's lap, and she curls her hands around it, her fingers buried in the soft fur, the warmth of the animal soaking into her body a comfort. "Yes," she says quietly.

"Why come to me with it? It's not the children of the next days that concern you, but the one in you now. I'm a childless old woman—"

"You're not," Khosa interrupts, jerking in her chair and sending the cat into the rushes of nilflower.

The Seer sits as still as stone, even the dust in the air around her seeming to be held in place before she speaks. "What is this you say to me? Would you strike my heart quiet, with these words?"

"I found it in the histories, locked away," Khosa reassures her. "No one knows."

"Except you," Madda adds, nodding her understanding as a dark smile twists her mouth. "So the queen of Stille comes to me with knowledge I'd have remain secret, seeking confirmation of a child in her belly—a question best put to her husband's mother. But you didn't go to Dissa, did you, child?"

"No," Khosa says, eyes boring into the Seer. "I came to Vincent's mother."

Madda is shocked into silence, her mouth open and tongue moving, but no words to be found. Khosa reaches into a pocket and offers a page of the histories, blank except for one line, the ink too dark to speak of any other Seer than Madda.

The Seer has given birth to a male child, and claims the king as father.

The Seer waves it away weakly. "I remember well enough. I do not need to see it written. It should never have been."

"Was his brother yours as well?" Khosa asks.

"No." The Seer shakes her head. "Purcell was Dissa's, but the birth was a hard one and damaged her in ways no healer could see to. She knew Varrick took his pleasure with others and that Stille needed more than one heir during the long wait for the throne."

"That was wise," Khosa says. "Her own child was lost early."

"Wise, perhaps, but giving Varrick permission to do as he would made him even bolder. I was not young, or pretty, but what brought him to me was what he desired most." The Seer levels her gaze at Khosa, eyes more alive than the queen has ever seen them before.

"I hated him," she says. "He'd taken me once before by force, when he first married Dissa and came to my tower as the king. Varrick's only claim to the throne was through his marriage to Dissa; he held no real power. So he looked to gain some the ways many men do—kill it or rape it."

"I'm sorry," Khosa says, a tremor passing over her as she thinks of Cathon, long rotting.

Madda glances around the room and calls for her cat with a low clicking noise. It jumps to her lap, kneading, and she returns the favor on its back.

"He was a low man," Madda goes on. "Most of his pleasure was found in pain, and when his wife told him to get another with child, he chose me, knowing that I would hate every moment and saddle his wife with the knowledge every time she came to me when once I had been a refuge for her."

"I'm so sorry," Khosa says again, the words sorely short of all she holds inside of her as she watches Madda's eyes glaze over, lost in a painful past.

"So that's how Vincent came to be," Madda says, shrugging off the memories. "One good thing, in the end. When I knew I was with child, Dissa padded her waist along with mine, and the baby was brought to her the moment I delivered."

"And so you've watched him grow from afar," Khosa says, hands going to her belly once again.

"Not always easily, and not always with happiness. But I am a part of his life, yes." Madda nods.

Khosa runs a thumb along her still-flat waistline, knowing her own child could never be passed off as sired by another.

"I can make it cease to be, you know." Madda nods to the plants that hang above the table. "An easy path for the woman who should bear no children other than the king's."

"Yes, but . . ." Khosa raises her eyes to Madda's. "Vincent's claim to the throne passed to him through Dissa. If she is not his mother, then . . ."

Madda smiles a sad smile. "True, child. Vincent has no claim to be the king of Stille."

Khosa shakes, muscles giving way in a spasm that has nothing to do with the sea. "But if I tell him of the child . . ." She breaks off, tears running down her face.

"Then the wife he loves and the friend he cares for have deceived him. Stille is all he will have left, and it does not belong to him. Truth does not always bring illumination, girl. Sometimes it lets loose the dark."

CHAPTER 60

———◦◎◦———

Donil

I KNOW THE FEEL OF AN AX, THE SHUDDER OF A TREE
BENEATH my blow. I also know the touch of a blade, my skin opening beneath it. I feel the same in equal measure as I toil in the forest,
the woodland creatures fleeing at the sound of our work peering over
their shoulders at me as they run, betrayed. I watch them go, knowing
they are not the only ones I have wronged.

Guilt weighs on me so heavily that it hurts more than my arms
day after day, though I hoped hard labor might drive thoughts of both
Vincent and Khosa away. It doesn't, and the pain only serves to remind
me that, whatever I suffer, surely my sister bears up under the same,
much and more. The thought of Dara in pain makes me swing my ax
more savagely, though it is a tree that falls beneath the blade and not a
Pietran neck.

Winlan and the Hygodeans work at my side, Pand and many of
the children following along with hatchets, stripping away limbs with
quick movements. Work may not ease my mind, but it does make the
days pass quickly, and I rest as the sun makes its descent, the chilly air
of evening settling on my sweaty skin.

"Ah, there's a nice one to look at," Winlan says, pointing to Daisy as she moves among us, a dipper and bucket of water hanging from her elbow.

"I'll be sure to tell your wife you say so," I snap at him. Khosa may have my heart, but I don't like Daisy falling under another's eyes, nevertheless.

Winlan shrugs, his heavy shoulders moving against the bark of the tree we both rest against. "As long as you tell her my true words, I've nothing to worry about. I said the girl is a nice one to *look* at, nothing more. My wife knows that I've got eyes in my head, but my hands will always only go to her."

"Apologies," I mutter. I can hardly take Winlan to task over having eyes when my own are on Daisy as well. I spit, realizing I couldn't have taken him to task for wandering outside of the marriage bed, either, if that had been his meaning.

"Thank you, lass," Winlan says, when Daisy comes our way, offering a full dipper. He takes his drink, then hands it back, his eyes not leaving her face. She refills it and passes it to me, her fingers brushing mine.

"Haven't seen you in a while, Donil," she says pointedly, to which I nod toward the felled trees behind her.

"Been busy."

"If you feel like doing something more entertaining with wood, you know where I am." She tips me a wink as she leaves, and Winlan drives an elbow into my side as she walks away, which hurts more than I care to admit.

"Is she your girl, then?"

"Once," I admit.

"Erhmm . . . maybe twice?" he asks, as she looks back at me, swaying her hips suggestively.

I clear my throat. "How many boats has Vincent called for?"

Winlan rolls his eyes at my sudden—and obvious—redirection of the conversation, but answers regardless. "He asked for four, and if you don't mind my saying so, I think your king is being generous with himself concerning how many Stilleans have been swayed by his argument for leaving land behind."

"How so?" I ask.

"Lad," Winlan clamps a hand onto my shoulder, "I could fit all of Hygoden on my own ship—and their goats."

"Agreed," I nod. "But there are ten Stilleans for each one of you. Four ships wouldn't carry even half of them."

"I know," Winlan says solemnly. "And I doubt we'll need that many."

I find Vincent with a handful of soldiers who have stayed on the training field past dusk, valuing swordplay that could save their necks over food waiting at home for their stomachs. Vincent moves fluidly, his broadsword arcing and dipping around his body, defending here, attacking there. Everything he knows he was taught early, though the lessons of Stillean royals were more for show than combat.

That changed the first time Dara knocked him on his ass. Vincent rose from the ground, a smear of mud on his cheek, his royal blood rising to his face. Though we were only children, I had always played nicely with the young prince. Dara not so, and I stood by her side, hand on the pommel of my wooden sword, hoping that our friend didn't prove to have more of his father in him than we thought. Vincent spat onto the ground, the flat white streak of a lost baby tooth going with it.

"Show me how you did that," he said to Dara.

So we did, that day and every one thereafter, the wood traded for blades, playtime for training, his royal instructors for two Indiri orphans. Vincent is an excellent swordsman; a unique blend of Stillean and Indiri methods have come together in him to create a fighter only Dara and I could best. Perhaps only Dara, I have to admit, watching him now.

The Stilleans attempt to follow as he breaks down twists of the wrist, rotation of the body, dips, and arcs that can be the difference between life and death. He is a good teacher, and though his students stumble awkwardly in this moment, more than a few may live through whatever is coming because their king trained with them in the dying sun, cold sweat running down his face.

I hail him as I cross the field, a fresh burst of affection for this king I call brother rising inside of me. He smiles and waves in answer, and for a moment, we are but children again, well met of an evening. His soldiers share a nod with me, bid Vincent good night, and leave us to walk to the castle. We cover uneven ground together, our steps sending our shoulders into one another as we go.

"You look well with a sword, brother," I tell him.

Vincent shakes his head. "Indiri should keep to the sword and not take up statecraft. I see concern on your face now, and I doubt that it has anything to do with my blade skill."

"If Indiri have glass faces, it is because we are nothing but honest," I tell him, the words striking me as deeply untrue after they've escaped my mouth.

"Honesty will not serve you well within walls that you rule over," Vincent says. "Now, out with it."

"Winlan fears that much labor is put into boats that will carry no one," I tell him.

He nods, leaning against the walls of the castle to rest. "It's true that not all of Stille has welcomed the idea of sailing into the sunset with open arms. But I will see those ships filled."

"How many have refused?" I ask.

Vincent sighs, sliding down to the ground in his exhaustion. "I reject my earlier words; you would be an excellent inquisitioner. Half of those I've spoken to would rather take their chances with the Pietra and earth that doesn't rest easy."

"Half," I breathe. "I had not thought it would be so many."

"Yes," he admits. "And . . ." He blows himself empty of air, then seems surprised words have not come with it.

"What is it?" I press.

"I think even less than that will march with me to Pietra on Dara's behalf."

The news takes the strength out of me as well, and I ease myself to the cold ground alongside him, at a loss for words.

"I can order them to, of course," Vincent says. "But I don't know what use there is in half-trained soldiers who have no heart in the battle."

"Little and less," I agree. "You'd risk mutiny."

"I know it," Vincent says. "I'll make one last push, remind them of Dara's courage for the sake of Stille here on this very ground. She fought for people not her own. Can they not do the same?"

"She won the respect of many before the battle," I remind him. "Some asked to have her train them over either of us."

"Yes, they'll fight for her, and likely survive because of what she's taught them."

I sigh along with him, our breath fogging the air. "That is some-thing," I say.

"Not enough," Vincent says. "It won't be enough, no matter where they stand when they fight, or what their reasons are."

"No," I admit, finding a stick that I break in half over my knee in frustration. "Likely not. But if the force will be split, why not put each to a purpose? Ask those who would not march on Dara's behalf to learn their way around a boat."

"And if they do not wish to sail?"

I crack the stick again. "March them to Madda's tower and ask them if they'd rather learn to fly."

I mean it in jest, but my voice comes out fierce, the snap of the stick echoing the sound their necks would make when they failed to be fast learners. I expect a quick rebuke from Vincent, but it does not come.

"Perhaps you know something of ruling after all. Khosa . . ." Her name trails off between us, the camaraderie broken. He clears his throat. "She found some histories, deeds unknown to most, and for good reason. It seems that those who came before me did not always act with grace or kindness."

"Good attributes to be sure," I say. "Though perhaps not the most useful to the king of a country at war."

"Odd that I find myself wishing I were more like my father," he says.

"Don't wish that," I say quickly. "Ever."

"I wouldn't, no matter that I might lead Stille better because of it. I could never wish a husband like him upon my wife."

I nod in agreement and mean it, though to hear her called his wife burns my ears more than the sun at mid-sky. I feel Vincent's eyes upon me and return his gaze, hoping my face is, indeed, not glass.

"She is not well, Donil," he confides in me. "The sea calls more loudly to her than ever, and I fear she'll bash herself to death against walls to get to it."

"Then I will build boats to save your wife," I tell him. "And you will lead an army to the door of my sister's enemy."

We sit together and watch the sun set, the last rays lost in the trees as the voice of an oderbird calls from the sky.

CHAPTER 61

Vincent

THOUGH DONIL WILL BUILD THE BOATS, VINCENT IS THE one who must convince Stilleans to board them. The Elders were right in that many of the generations that came before stood too long on the land, growing roots that have twisted deeply into native soil. They would rather stand than sail, and while he tries to hear them out without imagining insult, there are those who have implied rather heavily that building boats is not so much an act of discovery as one of cowardice.

Vincent knows what lies in his own heart, and any shame found there does not stem from lack of courage. Yet his cheeks still flame with the indignity of words passed the day before as he knocks upon one door that he assumes will be open to him, and hopes the woman behind it will be receptive to his ideas.

Milda answers at a rush, a rag tossed over her shoulder, a bright burn across her forearm from the kitchen fire. Her eyes light at the sight of a former lover, but cloud when she sees he stands alone and wearing common clothes. She was never good at hiding her thoughts, bold when she spotted him on the street when they first met, eager yet apprehensive in her bed after their fathers came to an agreement. Her thoughts flow as clearly to Vincent now as they did then, and he calms her in an instant.

"I do not come to seek privileges no longer mine to claim," he tells her, then tries to cover his own disappointment when she sighs with relief.

"Oh no, my prince," she says quickly, spotting his expression. "It's not that I . . . Well . . ." She glances up and down the street, then takes his hand and pulls him inside.

"King, I should say." She corrects herself hastily, brushing loose hairs behind her ears, a blush rising. She is very pretty in the afternoon light of her own kitchen, a touch of flour on her nose and a glow about her he doesn't remember from their days together.

"Call me Vincent still," he says, sitting down at her table so that she is free to do the same. "I would prefer it."

"Me too," she says, giving him an old smile that he knows well as she plops into the chair opposite his. "To be clear," she goes on, "it's not that I wouldn't—"

"It's that you shouldn't," he finishes for her, well aware of the conundrum.

"*That,*" she agrees with a wave of her hand. "And . . ." She stands, pulling her kitchen covering tight against her waist to show him a bulge there.

"Milda!" he says, real pleasure in his voice. "Congratulations, truly." He rises to meet her, taking her hands in his. "He treats you well?"

"Very," she says, blushing a bit more. "I cannot complain." She releases her hands from his and goes back to the table, only to snap to her feet again. "I forget myself. Would you like a drink or—"

"Nonsense." He waves her back to her chair, taking his own. "I'd not have you serve me, regardless."

"Well, then . . ." Milda eyes him, clearly at a loss for the purpose of his visit if not to bed her.

"Have you heard talk of the ships?"

"As we were in bed, so in conversation?" she asks, one eyebrow raised prettily.

"Direct and honest," he agrees, trying hard not to remember too vividly those times together. Not at this moment, anyway.

"I have heard of the boats," she says, eyes dropping from his. "It frightens me."

"I understand," he says. "Yet believe me when I say I would not ask you to go on one if I did not think it the better choice."

She tilts her head, confusion as to the true nature of his visit still evident.

"You and all Stilleans," he adds, rather lamely. "But yes . . . there is something more I would ask of you. We were close once, and I believe still are, though the nature has changed. You have a way with words and a warmth about you."

"And so you would like me to speak in your stead to my friends," she says, proving herself to be quick as well. She sighs heavily, hands on her swelling belly. "I carry the next generation of Stille in me," she says. "Must I carry the responsibility for others as well?"

"No, you must not," he agrees. "That job is mine, and mine alone."

"But you wouldn't sniff at a little help," she says with a smile.

"Neither will you when your time comes," he says, pointing at her bulge.

She laughs in agreement, then leans toward him across the table. "Tell me this, King of Stille, for a girl who was once your lover and for the child who will be your subject—is this truly the best chance at life that we both have?"

"Yes," he says, voice unwavering. "I would not risk either one of you—or anyone in Stille—if I did not think it necessary. Should the Pietra come or the earth beneath us fall away before they do, the sea is our only hope."

"Ugh," she says, leaning back from him. "Bleak thoughts, all."

"I am sorry to be the one to carry them to you."

"That's that, then," Milda says lightly, waving away his words. "I'll take your boat, Vincent, and talk many into following me."

"I believe you will," he says, smiling at the girl he knew who has turned into a woman, yet is unchanged in many ways.

She smiles back. "How's your wife, then?"

"Very well," he says as he rises to go, regretting that the pleasant conversation has to end with a lie.

CHAPTER 62

Khosa

THERE IS NO HAPPINESS IN HER DAYS, AND WHAT MEMORIES she could lay claim to that spoke of that emotion are now clouded with concerns for the future. Any good things she has known in her life came from her Keepers, now dead; Vincent, now betrayed; and Donil, whose child she carries, its skin doubtless as spotted as his.

Khosa's hand drops to her belly at the thought. The sight of the child will send Stille into pandemonium, and she shivers when she thinks she may very well be on a ship when it is born, and hers and her child's end found in the sea after all. She shakes her head to clear it, aware that such thoughts will do her no good. Better to find time to speak with her husband and share the truth early.

Madda offered an alternative with her nilflower; the life of the last Indiri infant would leave Khosa's body with none the wiser. The Seer would know, but Khosa held heavier secrets than her own, and Madda would remain silent. She rolls onto her back to stare at the ceiling, aware that there are no good outcomes, no matter what her choice. She could rid herself of Donil's child without telling him, piling deceit upon betrayal. Yet taking the action and telling him it had been done would end their union, and badly. To bear the child means to ruin

Vincent, his wife lost to him, a king known by his subjects to have been cuckolded by his wife.

Lost, she lets her hands go to the histories. There are no answers for her situation, and so she has consoled herself of late with the knowledge that at least others who have come before her were equally despicable.

"Fathoms," she suddenly cries out, dropping a page to the floor as tears rush forward. "How have I come to this?"

Salt water leaks from her eyes, streaking between her fingers as she sobs. Khosa remembers a Hyllenian boy with light hair and bright eyes, a boy she could have taken to the high meadow and fulfilled her duties with, bringing none to misery through her actions. He doubtless lay dead soon after she ran from his side at the sound of Pietran drums, and has long rested in a shallow grave, if they did not burn him.

"Khosa, you have undone many," she chides herself, thinking of Dara, gone now from Stille, Vincent and his men determined to follow. In the past she has found answers in the histories, saving those around her by digging through paper and ink. Now it is her own story that will be written.

"It will not end well, it will not end well," she says into her hands, which begin to shake. The tremor slips into her wrists, wandering nearly to her shoulders before she jerks her hands from her face, making them into fists at her side.

"No," she says, one hand uncurling to cover her belly, though it still shudders. "No."

Khosa repeats one word over and over, willing the tremors to subside, as she cradles her unborn child in her hands. Her last thought before her body rises from the bed without her permission is that while she may have made her own mistakes, she will not repeat those of others. Her child will know its father, and the father that he has a child.

CHAPTER 63

Donil

MORE THAN ONCE, AN INDIRI MEMORY HAS SURFACED IN my body rather than my mind. My hands knew swordplay when they were too small to wield a blade; my feet the way of walking, though my legs were still bowed from the cramp of the womb; my mouth the language of my people. New knowledge comes from time to time, as when I traced Khosa's face in the sand with the edge of a shell and found a startling resemblance there when I finished. Some Indiri's skill, perhaps long in my past, resurfaced for me that day.

And it happens again now.

A boat is taking shape beneath my hands. I have put timbers into place before Winlan told me where they should go, have tied lines by instinct, intricate knots forming between my fingers. An Indiri did this once. The knowledge leaves me weak, but I force my muscles to move on, smoothing a board that will be a railing, perhaps my own hands resting on it as I leave Stille behind.

If Khosa stands beside me in this vision, I do not see her, for once. My mind is filled with thoughts of a fellow Indiri—maybe more than one— who worked alongside Harta as I do Winlan. Some of my blood has left this shore. If Dara returns, it will be a fight, but if I have to bind her hand and foot and carry her over my shoulders onto the decks, I will do so.

Winlan's finished ship is anchored offshore, sails stowed against the wind that blows this day. The deck I stand on is nearly complete, skeletons of two more on each side of it. Winlan has put all of Hygoden to work, and Vincent sent the Stilleans who chose not to march to the shipwright for orders. I smile, thinking of the nobles and soldiers from good homes who have never known hard labor shrinking from the tasks Winlan sets for them, then shrinking further at the thought of defying him.

Shared labor can make for quick friendships, and I've seen Hygodeans slap Stilleans on sore backs in congratulations as timbers were raised, and Stilleans share their food with Hygodeans in the shade of the sails. Winlan says the ship I stand on will be pushed from the shore in the next few suns, and every hand here needed to help set it free from the sand. I have no doubt they'll push together, while many more look on from the city walls to see if it should sink or float.

"Float," I say in Indiri. "For me." I run my hand along the smooth railing and lift it across my shoulders, easing it through the other laborers so that one more piece can find its place.

The sun is high above when I feel a small hand at my elbow and turn to find Unda.

"Hello, small one," I say, bending down to speak to her. "Have you brought me my midmeal?"

She shakes her head, mute in my presence as always. Instead she holds out a slip of paper, the familiarity of the writing sending a spike into my heart.

"Khosa gave you this?" I ask.

Unda shakes her head again, then ducks it when I look at her sternly. "Out with it, now," I say. "I can't very well do what is written here if you're leading me into a clowder of Tangata, can I?"

She giggles, pulling her shirt up above her nose as if she would hide her whole face. The mop of curly hair sticking from the top shakes again. "My cousin went to the kitchens to get some bread for our midmeal, and the queen asked her if she knew me, and if she could give me a note. It has your name on it, though . . ." She pops her head back out of the shirt. "Why would the queen write you a note and tell someone to give it to me?"

"Because she trusts you," I say, resting my hand on her curls. "Thank you, Unda."

She colors a little at my touch, then bounds off into the distance to gather her hatchet and strip the remaining timbers that lie by the edge of the shore. I glance around, then open the note.

Donil—Library

I feel a flush at the two words and quickly crush the note in my hand, letting it leave my fist in a breath of wind to be taken out to sea. That room is the only place inside the castle walls where we allowed ourselves any measure of freedom with each other, and I feel both a powerful lust for Khosa and the deep pull of loyalty for Vincent at her asking me to meet her there again.

Still, I know which one will prove stronger.

I wait until others are busy with their food, children come to pester their fathers in a few stolen moments. Then I make my way to the castle, raising my hand in greeting to those I meet upon the way. I have worked hard for each smile I get in return; an Indiri in Stille has never had the easiest path. But of late the smiles have come easier. Dara and I fighting the Feneen for our adopted city and standing on the beach to face down the Pietran army has earned me a place among them. Those smiles would turn to sneers, the hands that slap me on the shoulder would hold daggers if they knew I go to bed their queen.

And I do not go slowly.

My pace quickens once I'm in the halls, and I pull open the library door—unguarded, I note—to find Khosa alone, arms crossed, pacing. All thoughts of pleasure leave when I see the tears on her face, how she turns from me in shame when I go to her, yet leans into my strength when I open my arms. Her head rests on my chest, our bodies pressed tightly together. And I feel a flicker of life from her that has not been there before.

"Khosa," I say, pushing her to arm's length as I run my eyes over her. "You are . . ."

I cannot finish, my heart in my mouth as her eyes meet mine, the happiness there bright enough to burn away the tears. She nods, and I sweep her up in my arms, all decorum lost, a cry of pure joy escaping my throat as I think of this woman I love harboring the revival of my race. It is short-lived, for when her feet are on the ground again, I remember she is queen, and I am not king.

"What will we do?" I ask, pressing her forehead to mine.

"I will have your child, Donil," she answers, curling her hands into my hair. "Beyond that, I do not know."

"Beyond that is of no matter," I say, wrapping my arms around her and resting my chin on her hair. "I have made you a boat, Khosa, and it is for the living."

"You will come with us?" she asks.

"Yes," I say, my hands sliding down to rest on her belly. "I will go with you both."

CHAPTER 64

Ank

T HE MASON REACTS MUCH AS I HAD EXPECTED: WITH ANGER. "I'll not see them sail, not while I have blood in me," Hadduk yells, his voice thick with emotion. "Is this what you would have done, my Lithos? Let the enemies of Pietra go beyond where a spear can be thrown?"

"It's only a suggestion, Hadduk," Witt says, one hand to his Mason, palm outward, begging for calm.

"To the depths with the Feneen and his suggestions," Hadduk says, slamming the table hard enough to make Nilana jump beside him. "He says the Indiri must not be harmed and that we should let the Stilleans go. Who did you ally with, truly?" He turns on me, dark eyes burning. I sigh, looking to Nilana and Witt, but cooler heads cannot prevail when they both hang low, heavy with care.

"I am allied with Pietra," I say, for the first time fervently wishing it were not so. "And the advice I give is for your benefit. I know you wish to see the Indiri dead, but if what passed in the dungeons the other night did not convince you this is folly, I do not know what will. Depths, man, you were nearly brained by the ceiling, and yet you persist!"

"My Lithos—" Hadduk would say more, but emotion has the best of him, his throat closing beneath it.

"I hear, Mason," Witt says, a decision in his voice.

I felt the despair inside him the other night, swimming in wine, but floating above was heat and purpose, grown stronger since our last exchange. I know Hadduk must be appeased and what the Lithos is willing to sacrifice to do so, and what he is not.

"Burn their ships," he says to me.

I go alone, as before. The movement of many would attract attention and turn suspicious heads, and there are few among the Feneen who can pass as anything other than what they are. My silhouette has only as many heads, arms, and legs as any Stillean, and while my face may be known there, I intend to keep it in the dark. Witt suffers no argument, giving me a sharp blade and a fast horse. He would see their escape cut off and all of Stille fall, if Hadduk insists, to keep the Indiri alive.

The ground shakes only because of the hooves of my mount, and I cover the distance in three suns, there to fire the ships before I have quite convinced myself it is the right thing to do. To not act as the Lithos has instructed would mark me traitor, and my people guilty by association with me. I have no great power in strength or beauty, but only the quickness of my mind and might of my given word. If I betray my pledge to the Pietra, I become as low as Varrick, Stille's former king, who gave no promise he did not break, and kept faith with no one. I will not cast myself in the same mold as someone I despise. I leave the horse tethered in the forest's evening light and make my way on foot to the nearest tunnel entrance, descending once more into that tangle of death and decay.

And if I am to do it, I have not yet decided how it is to be done. Fire draws eyes, something I have noticed over my many years, whether it be a campfire or a stone flue. Fellow Feneen, Indiri, Pietra, and Stilleans, all are entranced by flame. I think the sconcelighters know this too, for I have seen the girls and women who work in the dark halls of the castle, bringing light. They have plain faces, and few would be called pretty, yet none ever lack companionship, lovestruck men (and the occasional woman) trailing behind them.

I watch one such girl at work now, the planes of her unremarkable face set alight by the fire she carries, leaving warmth behind her and spreading light as she goes. Fallen victim to that which I contemplate, I spend too long observing her, the shadows I would use to move freely banished as she works. Cursing myself for an old fool, I have to rely on my ears—still sharp—and my eyes, with their best days behind them.

Madda's tower remains unlit, as the Seer has little need to see the steps she does not use. I make my way to her rounded stairs with care, tapping out our knock on her door. There is a flutter of movement inside at my unlooked-for arrival, and then she pulls it open, the hinges protesting. My mother has aged since I saw her last, lines that were only traceable now furrows, worry taking up a residence in her brow and weighing heavily over her eyes.

Always I have felt that I came to her for comfort, though my adulthood was reached long ago and my childhood a distant memory. Yet now it is she who comes to me, folded into my arms before I have even crossed the threshold.

"All is undone," she whispers into my clothes. "The past is made clear to others as the future is to me."

"Nonsense," I say to her, pulling the door closed behind me. I squeeze the word past the lump in my throat, the panic in my chest. Never have I seen her in despair; always I have been the one to bring fear to her round table and have it assuaged. We sit, I helping her to a chair with exaggerated care.

"What has happened?" I ask.

"I ask the same," she says, waving away my question as guile surfaces even in her depths. "A mother should rejoice to see her son, yet I fear nothing good has brought you to my door."

"The ships must burn to spare the Indiri," I tell her. "The Lithos's grip on his people weakens if he does not move with strength, for it is all they respect. He allowed many shepherds of Hyllen to live, saw his army brutalized by the Stillean sea, and now shelters an Indiri by his own hand. He must strike now to retain his place, for should he lose it, then there is none to speak for Dara, and she would join the dirt with her ancestors in Dunkai before the sun set on his last day as Lithos."

"You stand by your claim that the Lithos is a good man?"

"I do." I nod. "But he is only a ruler, and the people he reigns over have been made hard over time, the man who sits at his stoneward the most unbending of all. To retain his position—and he must if my people are to find any fairness in this life—the Lithos must acquiesce in the matter of the ships."

"And you are here to see it done," Madda concludes. "Is this fairness, that a mother must watch a son thwart his homeland?"

"Is this fairness, that I must burn ships that my mother could escape upon, in order to save the people who raised me?" I shoot back, anger edging my voice. It is an old wound, deep in my body. Though I call her Mother, I know too well that Madda gave me up.

Madda turns her back to me, my bitterness blending with hers in the air between us. "No," she says quietly, hunched shoulders tight with grief. "People find little that is fair in life, be they raised in a castle or a cave. I've brought two sons into the world, given one to each, and raised neither as my own."

I watch her carefully, the truth of her despair having leaked from her mouth. She turns to me, eyes so bright that I have to shade my own against them, sinking into a chair.

"Who knows?" I ask, mind already spinning the complexities, should Vincent's parentage be discovered.

"Only the Given, may she go to the depths," Madda spits. "I have no care for her."

"Because she is as crafty as you," I say. "And it is hard to see the young relishing gifts going cold in old minds."

"Mmmphh." Madda has no argument, only pulls her shawl closer over her shoulders.

"There is no guile in her," I assure my mother. "The Given will not use this knowledge for harm."

"Harm is done by her knowing it," the Seer insists. "And an old woman finds her evenings darker than they should be."

"Then let your son light the shores for you," I say, rising. "I wanted only to warn you of my duty, that you may not be frightened when flames rise."

"It is not the fire you set that scares me, son," Madda says, voice suddenly gentle. "Your brother's fingers will strike another."

She rises, reaching to place a hand on my head. "Walk carefully, Ank, my son," she says. I hold her to me once more, feeling the frailty of the bones beneath her skin, like an oderbird cracked too early from her egg, or lying for the last nights in her nest.

The sconcelighter whose progress I had watched earlier with an admiring eye left a hall lined with weapons behind her. I take a torch from the wall with a silent apology that her good work shall be used for ill means. With a light in my hands, I cannot pass in shadow and so instead go boldly, for a man who walks with his head up and a clear eye is rarely interfered with. I pass a dairymaid, a pretty thing who tosses me an odd look, which I settle with a smile and a bid for a good evening.

Still, I feel her eyes upon me as I turn the corner, and quicken my steps.

The boats rise above me on the shore, two of them skeletons only, the third nearly finished. Out to sea I hear the sails of another snapping, but it is far beyond my reach. My eyes pass over the unfinished work, and I think again of an oderbird come too early, small bones unprotected, eyes unseeing. I cannot bring myself to burn what has not yet become, and so I leave the unfinished ships alone, casting the sconcelighter's torch high above my head and onto the deck of the nearly finished ship.

A rope catches first, and the fire travels up it almost tentatively until it becomes a vein of flame, which reaches a sail. That catches with a *whoosh* that is both beautiful and horrific. Heat dances above me, small flecks of fire falling toward my face through the night. The beauty has held me too long; I can hear voices in the distance, and scattered, panicked calls.

I run not away from them, but toward, my hands in the air, calling for help, screaming that the boats are on fire. I grab the first soldier I see by the shoulders and tell him to fetch buckets. I send another to wake the sleeping castle guard, pushing my appearance of innocence nearly so far that I am hindering my goal. Once inside the walls I find a shadowy corner to slouch in as the would-be heroes run past, others running back inside, smelling deeply of smoke.

Corner from corner, corridor to corridor, I make my way slowly until I am in the tunnels, all hint of heat lost in the dank and the dark. I move more quickly now that I am unseen, hoping that my horse has not smelled char on the wind and panicked. He is as I left him, but alert, ears pricked toward the city walls and the glow that has risen beyond. Any traitorous hope I had of the fire not catching is lost when I see billows of ash, thick as clouds, rising above the city.

I ride into the dark, hoping the wind will clean my clothes of the smoke that has taken the place of my mother's nilflower.

CHAPTER 65

Vincent

T HE FIRST CRIES REACH VINCENT AS HE SETTLES IN FOR A
meeting with Sallin to learn of progress with the ships and to
inform Sallin of the state of the army. Panicked voices carry a
tone that needs no clarity, and they both rush to the hall to stop the first
person they see, a sconcelighter, color high in her cheeks.

"What's happening?" Vincent demands.

"The ships, my king! They're afire!"

"Fire! Depths . . ." Sallin grabs Vincent's elbow, in full command
of the situation. "Go to the kitchens. Get anything that can hold water."

The king goes, shouting at everyone he passes to follow. There's a
trail of sconcelighters, dairymaids, message boys, bleary-eyed servants
in their sleepshirts, and guards in full armor behind him when he
reaches the kitchens. Daisy is there, already turning cupboards inside
out, tossing jars, bowls, mugs, and buckets into outstretched hands. She
gives him a pitcher, one that would normally rest on his nightstand to
see him through a dry evening.

"I'm sorry I don't have anything more—"

Vincent doesn't hear the rest of her apology, racing for the
beach and what has already become a conflagaration. His people—
Stilleans—stand in the sea up to their knees, filling whatever they have

in their hands and running to extinguish the burning ship. He does the same, meeting a wall of heat before he's close to the flaming boards, and the water he throws turns to steam before it has the chance to land.

Winlan joins him, adding Hygodean faces to those that rush past in a futile effort to bring the sea to land, something that would have only spelled terror for Stilleans before. The air Vincent pulls into his lungs is thick with smoke, and he gasps for breath on his third trip to the sea, saltwater running down his arms as he ducks his pitcher below the tide.

"Vincent!" Donil's voice carries, even over the tumult, but Vincent ignores his friend's call and rushes back toward the ship, though he knows all is lost. Each board is alive with light, the decks Donil and others have built with steady hands now visible as they crumble one into the next. A hand grabs his arm, dragging him back. Vincent loses the pitcher and it breaks, shards of glass and seawater spilling over his boots. Donil knocks Vincent onto the ground, and hands are suddenly all over him, tearing his clothes, dumping water over him, throwing sand in his hair.

"You're on fire!" Donil screams as Vincent swings at his attackers indiscriminately. Pain has found him, a searing scream that tears through his skin and melts his insides like candle wax. He lands a blow on a guard and is shocked to see that his fist leaves a trail of smoke behind it; his sleeve is alight with flame.

He's pinned suddenly, Donil above him, Hygodeans and Stilleans alike pouring water and sand upon his body. They mix together, bringing a third element of ash. It flows down his face and into his mouth; sea and sand and smoke flow into his throat until he fights it, drawing a deep breath and spewing it all back into the faces of his rescuers.

"I'm all right," he croaks, though he feels his lips blistering even as he speaks.

Donil reaches for his hands and pulls him to his feet, smoke still rising from his clothes.

"I'm all right," he says again, and Donil yanks him into an embrace, the impact of his affection sending a cough from his strained lungs.

"You weren't, brother," Donil says, pushing Vincent back again to arms' length as if to confirm he truly stands. One critical eye passes over his friend and a smile quirks his face. "You've lost your eyebrows."

"Good thing I don't have a beard," Vincent says.

"Not that you could grow one," Donil shoots back, and they lean into each other, laughing as they cry and the fate of both their peoples burns.

One ship is lost. Of the two that were merely outlines of what they would become, one has taken enough damage that Winlan declares it a waste of time and timber to continue the effort. It is left to stand and rot, though Vincent doubts the Stilleans who walk today will live to see the sight.

"The other can be saved," the Hygodean shipwright says, but his voice carries little of what the king would term hope.

"There is time to finish it," Vincent assures him. "With three crews working, it will go quickly." Winlan nods, unwilling to argue, but Vincent knows what words he would say even if he does not voice them.

Two ships. That is what they have to take all of Hygoden and those of Stille who would follow their king.

A healer hovers, a pot of balm balanced on one hand, the other coated in it as she dresses Vincent's hands and face. Most of his hair is gone, one of his eyes swelled nearly shut. The pain spikes as she touches him, then submits to the coolness of the balm. Tomorrow will bring more, he knows, and the concoction that the healer poured into his cup will ease it, not drive it away completely. He waves her off, already feeling dullness spread through him from the drink.

"Your bandages," she protests, unrolling a clean linen. He takes it from her hands, ignoring the blister that has risen on one palm.

"My wife will see to it," he assures her.

She leaves them to confer: Vincent, Sallin, Donil, Winlan, and Dissa.

"We must face a hard truth," Vincent says to them.

Sallin nods, mouth tight. "Many have argued against leaving these shores, my king, though I did not think they would stand in the way of those who would go."

"We don't know that they have," Winlan argues.

"Does a fire set itself?" Sallin asks.

"It does not, I can tell you from many nights spent in wet forests," Donil answers. "Nor does it spring from the sea or walk from the castle's walls without being carried."

"There was an empty sconce in the lower hall," Dissa says. "I spoke with the lighter. She knew nothing of it."

"You are sure?" Sallin presses.

"The girl hardly knew the common tongue by the time I finished," Dissa says calmly. "There was no deceit in her, only great confusion."

"Where does this leave us?" Sallin asks, eyes on Vincent.

Wondering who would refuse their fellow Stilleans a chance, he's about to say, when a guard enters, Daisy in tow.

"The girl claims she has something to share with the king," he says.

Vincent glances at Daisy, who pulls her elbow from the guard at the tone he carries, implying that a dairymaid would have little and less to say to the king.

"Leave her with us," Vincent tells him, and waits until the door has closed on his back to continue.

Daisy is the worse for wear, a smear of ash down one cheek and a gash on her arm, doubtless from something breaking as she shoved it into another's hands. But she stands straight, waiting to be asked to speak.

"What is it, Daisy?"

She turns to Vincent, eyes bright with tears.

"I am sorry, my king," she says. "You are betrayed."

CHAPTER 66

—◦◦◦◦◦—

Ank

THAT I WOULD EVER THINK OF PIETRA AS *HOME* SHOULD be laughable, but this is what I feel as I emerge from the Hadundun trees to the Stony Shore. A sigh of relief escapes me, and my mount increases his pace, knowing that clean straw and a good feeding await him. There is no pride in what I have done, but I can hope that the action has allayed any remaining fears Witt and Hadduk may have of my loyalty. Yet there is one I would speak to before I see them.

Nilana rests in her rooms, propped against pillows, hair fanned around her, eyes closed. She needs no firelight to draw notice, and I let the door close quietly behind me so as not to disturb her. She stirs slightly though, eyelashes fluttering as I settle onto the foot of the bed.

"Ank of the Feneen," she says. "Surely you don't wish to know me better."

"No," I assure her, though it would be a lie to claim the thought has never crossed my mind. She is as gifted with subterfuge as I, and while I am not the Lithos, it would be best to not be distracted in her presence.

"Do you bring news of burnt boats?"

"One, at least," I tell her. "What has happened here since my going?"

Nilana rolls her eyes. "Hadduk stomps his feet and glowers; the Lithos looks out to sea with lovesickness in his heart."

"You see it too?"

"Perhaps," she says, shrugging. "There is a great tension between them."

"Hadduk and Witt?"

Nilana shakes her head, eyeing me, and I make a noise in my throat.

"What of the Indiri?" I ask.

"She hasn't killed anyone recently."

I laugh. "An improvement over the last time I returned. Yet this is not what I ask."

"More than an improvement," Nilana corrects me. "She's been alone with the Lithos, and he still breathes. So, yes, there may be some feeling there. Enough to stop her from opening his throat."

"If not feeling, at least a mutual respect," I think aloud.

"From which can grow much," Nilana adds.

"But not quickly."

Nilana smiles, eyes closing lazily. "Men." She laughs. "You are not the only ones who have something between your legs. Women feel much and more, I think you forget."

"Surely she does not desire him?"

"Why shouldn't she?" Nilana shoots back. "They are both young and easy to look at, fighters with hot blood in their veins. On a battlefield they may face each other, but put them in a bedroom, and you'll find a different ending."

"Still facing each other?" I ask, with a smile.

"That's up to them," she answers with her own.

"You really think so?"

"I do."

I find the Lithos and the Mason deep in discussion, the Keeper just arrived to change Witt's bandage. He doesn't flinch as she peels it away, his words with Hadduk flowing as if she were not there. They have decided to place lancias along the cliffs, and I can't help but shiver, imagining spears falling from the sky when Vincent and his army arrive.

"Feneen." Hadduk sees me and promptly stops discussing battle plans, though I should be a part of them as the commander of my people.

"Mason." I nod at him, then Witt. "Lithos."

"You smell of smoke," Witt says. "This bodes well."

I sit before I answer, stretching my legs beneath the table we share. The Keeper's eyes land on mine, then bounce off, her hands cleaning what's left of Witt's ear.

"At least one ship was aflame when I left," I tell them. "Possibly two. The first caught quickly and brought a crowd. There was no time to ensure they would all burn."

It's a small lie, one I'll tell to those I've allied myself with if it gives a breath of a chance to the people I was born to.

"How many does this leave?" Hadduk, too clever by half, asks.

"There was one already out to sea," I admit. "One nearly finished—that one will never know water. Two that were left have many suns of work ahead of them before they will sail."

"So they have at most three, likely two," Witt says, tilting his head while the Keeper places the fresh bandage. "How many will they carry?"

"Not many," I tell him. "Not even one of every three in Stille would find a place."

"Too many," Hadduk insists. "We must draw them out or march upon them, my Lithos."

"With the Given as their queen and the sea at their disposal?" Witt asks.

"They will march," I say quickly, intervening before the Mason warms too much to his own ideas. "The king has said as much and is only training their men before undertaking the journey. They will come, Lithos."

"The training is ill-spent," Hadduk goes on. "A Pietran child could best a Stillean soldier."

"Which is why they train," I say.

"They come too slowly," Hadduk insists, rolling over my words. "We must bring them here before the boats are finished, strike off the hands that would build them and break the backs that would carry the timber. Sending the Indiri's skin was not enough, my Lithos. We must take a larger piece."

"Or"—I raise a finger—"the Lithos could marry her."

Witt nearly chokes on his wine, and the Keeper loses her hold on the bandage. It rolls away from her, a trail of white across the stone floor. Hadduk, for his part, can only gape. At least he is silent.

"Hear me out," I ask them. "We agreed that there would be a marriage between the Lithos and a Feneen in exchange for loyalty, did we not?"

"Yes," Witt says. "And I know you would cast Nilana in that role."

"Something I think the Mason would find disagreeable," I say, turning to Hadduk.

"Disagreeable is the least of it," he admits. "But if the Lithos does not see another among your people who would suit . . . I have my duties, and the first is to him, not my own desires."

For the first time, I see why Nilana has any respect for the man, and I nod to him. "I speak for the Feneen when I say that such a marriage is beneficial to us as a tie between our peoples, but also as an indication that the Pietra are willing to bring outsiders among them and call them their own. Who could be more of an outsider to you than an Indiri?"

Hadduk grudgingly nods, but Witt only remains still, staring at the table while the Keeper tucks the last edge of the bandage around his head.

"The Stilleans have not responded to us sending her skin," I go on. "The Indiri's brother is among them, close in the councils of the king. He would perhaps advise that to die a noble death—even a painful one—is no disgrace to Dara and their people. It would in fact bring her great honor, which she would welcome."

"But if her brother thinks the Lithos has taken her as his wife against her will, he would stop at nothing to spare her a life lived as such," Hadduk says, catching on. "I've seen the Indiri fight; they are relentless, sometimes to the point of recklessness. I have no doubt the brother would rather see her dead than living as the Lithos's wife, and would counsel the king accordingly."

"Who would march on her behalf regardless," I add, to see Witt raise his head.

"Is there something between them?"

I weigh my words, not knowing if the Lithos will be inclined to jealousy or cede the field in matters of love as he never would in matters of war. I settle for truth.

"There may have been at one time," I tell him. "But the king's heart belongs to his wife now, and he is an honorable man."

"Which would not stop him from marching to the Indiri girl's aid, regardless of how things lie between them," Hadduk says, hand pulling at his beard in thought.

"And what of her feelings for him?" Witt insists, and Hadduk shoots him a dark look, knowing as well as I do that the question—and the answer—has no bearing on whether a marriage will draw out the Stilleans.

I show him my empty palms. "That is a question for her."

"For my part, I think she has none." The Keeper speaks, placing a hand on Witt's shoulder. "I have spent some time with the girl, and though she reveals little, what does slip can be telling."

The Lithos nods, though his face remains guarded, his finger tracing the rim of his cup. Hadduk shares a glance with me, his impatience skittering just below his skin.

"As much as I dislike the idea of suffering the Indiri to live, it could work," Hadduk says, hoping to bring Witt to a decision. "Killing her means we remove the only anchor keeping the Stilleans on land, and could bring the cliffs down on our heads. Pain only increases her pride. This may be the only enemy I would rather see live in misery than die in it."

Witt's brow furrows at that, and he's moved to speech. "I would not have it be that way," he says. "The Lithos does not know a woman. To be the first and by force is distasteful to me."

"But not, perhaps, being the first?" Hadduk asks, leading him.

"I . . ." Witt sighs, on the brink of agreeing.

"I think she can be brought to it," I assure him. "Her greatest desire is to see her people restored, if in a place of power, all the better. There are no Indiri left to her. Why not a strong male with whom to blend her blood, and what better revenge than to see one of her children reigning over the Pietra?"

"A speckled Lithos?" Hadduk snorts. "I'd die before I saw it."

"Yes," I say, pointing to the grays at his temple. "You would."

The Mason grunts, as if this would be acceptable to him. "My Lithos," he says, "how do you find it?"

"Better if I knew how the girl would feel about it," Witt answers.

I rise from my place, knowing a nimble tongue will be needed. "Shall I find out?"

"No," Witt says, standing. "I think a proposal of marriage should come from the prospective groom, don't you?"

CHAPTER 67

Dara

THE MIND MAKES FACES IN THE DARK, DRAWING TOGETHER shadows to show my eyes what they will not see again: Donil, Vincent, Dissa. All others can go to the depths, and I would not notice or care. Of those three, two may come for me. I can only hope they do not.

I have never been helpless, and the experience does not suit me. Worse yet is the thought that others may risk themselves for my neck. The skin I took from myself bore many scars, and I believe that Donil will look on them and be reminded that I can bear much and more.

I do not wish to be saved.

Little is left for me once I come to that conclusion, which should send me into despair but instead opens up a well inside I did not know resided there. A deep calm fills me, along with the knowledge that I have done what I could with what little I had, and taken a Pietran jailer and Elder down with me.

"May their stinking corpses be eaten by ninpops, and their leavings pissed on by goats," I say aloud. My own voice is good company, and I have found songs long forgotten, notes that Dissa would sing to me as I slept in her arms, rhythms my mouth knows because my tongue asked my ancestors. I settle into a mix of these now, finding a measure of comfort in bringing Stille to Pietra, with Indiri words. There's a shift in the air around me, and one of the faces that forms in the dark is the Lithos. I shudder to a stop, not trusting my senses.

"Is that you, Lithos?" I ask. "Or is my own mind my enemy?"

"I am here," he answers smoothly. "And would make it that you have none."

"Order your army to march off the cliffs," I say. "Then fall on your sword."

"What if they would march on your orders, and my sword were drawn in your protection?"

"I need no protecting," I say, to which there is silence. It stretches long enough that I question whether I have imagined the exchange and the face that floats out of reach is truly there.

"If our swords were drawn together?"

"Against what foe?"

"I imagine there are enough Tangata to busy our blades for a good while," he says. "And you eager enough to wield them."

"There is one I would spare," I say, thinking of Kakis. "One worth allowing the race to continue."

"I feel the same about the Indiri," he says.

For once, I have no answer. He comes nearer to me in the dark. What little light comes through my barred window shows his hands out, empty.

"I have something to say to you, Dara of the Indiri, and I would say it in the light."

Light. The thought of it is enough to pull down the edges of my mouth, the beginnings of a solid cry. His hand touches my wrist, our skin barely grazing.

"Will you come with me?"

That he would ask instead of order makes my mouth twitch again, and I do not trust my voice to speak. Instead I answer by returning the touch, and find our hands clasping. We slip through the door, and he releases me to pass in front of him, guiding me down the corridor to the room where I killed a fellow Indiri and the roof came down on our heads.

It is open now, the moon shedding a white light onto broken stones and mangled chains. I find a flat rock and sit upon it to look up at the sky, a sight I believed lost to me. In my worst moments, I have thought the Pietra would leave me to my cell as they had the Indiri I killed, that I would grow old with no one knowing how I looked with wrinkles on my face or aware that I had grayed at the temples. I take a deep breath of fresh night air and look to the Lithos.

"What is it you would say to me?"

"I'll begin with a request that you not kill me."

I can't help but laugh, oddly welcome after the twist of my lips that would have left me in tears before the Lithos of Pietra. "For how long must I restrain myself?"

"I am going to speak for a short while and end with a question," he says. "I ask that you hear me out and answer."

"After that?"

"After that, you will either no longer wish to kill me or I shall not mind being dead. Agreed?"

There is little I can say to that, so I nod. The Lithos takes a deep breath and exhales sharply, his hands shaking at his sides.

"Dara," he says, "the Stilleans would leave these lands. They are building ships to take themselves away, no longer trusting the earth beneath their feet. My Mason would sooner douse the ground with their blood than see them floating on water, and wishes to attack before they can take their leave. I, for one, see no reason to block their going and would argue against it."

"Then do it," I say, and he closes his eyes in frustration. "I only promised not to kill you before you finished," I tell him. "I never said I wouldn't interrupt."

"Your adopted people are poor fighters, but not without honor.

The king will march on your behalf, your brother at his side. I see no reason for their blood to be shed, either."

He pauses, but I have nothing to say, this news striking all words from my tongue.

"The Feneen people fight alongside my own, as you well know," the Lithos goes on. "Their leader, Ank—"

"May his teeth fall from his face and stick into his feet," I say.

"He has argued many times on your behalf," the Lithos tells me, which once again leaves me at a loss.

"As part of our agreement with them, Ank has requested that I take an outsider as wife to strengthen our bonds and ensure a voice outside of the Pietra once Ank is no longer. The Lithos's wife would wield great power, as would her children."

"An empty promise, when the Lithos knows no woman."

"I would know her," he says, voice suddenly husky. "And she me."

"Then your children will die when I do," I say. "Be it by a blade or the slow passage of time. When I go, I take this land with me, Lithos. Once my body goes to earth, the earth itself goes. I felt the tremor when I pulled the Hadundun poison into me, and again when I snapped an Indiri neck in my hands. Do you think I am only quick in my sword arm and not in my mind? If Stille sails, I will give them time to be gone, then crush my skull upon the stones of my cell, knowing that my death brings yours, and no small comfort that."

The Lithos watches me for a moment, dark eyes glittering in the starlight. "Or you can strengthen the earth beneath both our feet and give our speckled children great power and memories that their mother was loved and respected until the end of her days—may they be far away. Dara, will you marry me?"

My belly hollows out, and my heart follows. There is nothing between us but air and starlight, yet I feel as if a cord has been drawn tight, one that would bring me nearer to him. I have known desire before, not only for Vincent, and have spent the long spans in my cell denying that I had felt this for the Lithos in the brief moment when he tended to my arm. Yet I cannot do so now, when it is most important.

I have seen despair, the acknowledgment of death arrived, in the faces of many men. Some I have killed, some I have ended only when another's arrow went astray, or blade did not swing true. But the Lithos wears the same face now, and it is my words that have the power to fell him.

And I have no answer.

Other men have desired me, said rough words or made crude suggestions. Some even were kind, and more than once my head was turned, but never did I consider diluting my blood on their account. I alone can make Indiri children and will not see them selling bread in a Stillean market stall.

"My children would wield power," I repeat. "How so?"

"However you please," the Lithos answers quickly. "Even to the point of becoming Lithos, should that be your wish."

"A speckled Lithos." I smile at the thought. "Something for the histories."

"Indeed," he says, and a silence stretches between us as I ponder.

"You would not harm the Stillean army," I say, ticking off a finger. "Vincent and Donil would walk from the field as easily as sheep from a Hyllenian pasture."

"Of course—"

"Not finished," I say, raising another finger. "One Pietran lancia and one spada aid Stille in building ships, should they still wish to go."

"They will," the Lithos says. "Ank brings news that the Stillean queen's spasms have strengthened. She will be carried to the horizon, or die."

"Vincent will go with her," I say, and the thought does not bring the expected wave of pain. "Many will follow him, perhaps my brother as well."

"If he does not go, he would be welcome here, with you," the

Lithos says, and I nod once, curtly, disbelieving the truth of what is happening.

"Sanctuary for my brother, power for myself and my children, the lives of my friends," I say aloud.

"Is there anything more you would ask?"

I shake my head, thinking only that it's a better offer than Vincent's own father made me in exchange for my maidenhood.

"Then I repeat myself," the Lithos—Witt—says. "Dara of the Indiri, will you marry me?"

"Yes," I say, and my voice does not falter, though there is a tremor in my hand as it clasps his. We shake as men do, and he releases me.

"I want you to know that I will not . . ." He breaks off, eyes sliding to the ground. "I will not take you unless I am wanted," he finishes.

Yet there is desire in his voice at odds with his words, and I only nod that I have heard, not trusting myself to speak, that he may not hear the same in my own.

CHAPTER 68

Khosa

Khosa reaches for the crumbled bread on her bedstand, takes a few bites, and chews slowly, swallowing with great care before attempting to sit up. The early-light illness can be managed in ways that her dancing cannot, and she has discovered small rituals that—if followed exactly—will allow her to be on her feet in a room that does not smell heavily of sick.

She stretches out, testing her body to see if it will be true to what she would ask of it today. Though the spasms come and go with little warning, she feels as if today she can trust her limbs enough to leave the bedroom. Khosa grimly looks toward the sea through the bars of her window, where the charred ribs of the burnt ship rest. Curious oderbirds circle, weaving through the spires of smoke that still rise from the wreck.

Vincent came to their room, one eye swollen shut, his hair reduced to cinders, bandages on his hands. She had cried out and gone to him at the sight, wrapping her arms around her husband. To her surprise, there had been no shiver in her skin when they touched, the slow practice of teaching her skin to know his having done its work. He had been in too much pain to notice, only rested his head on her shoulder for a second, held her face in his hands to explain that he would not be back for some time, and disappeared.

Only after he'd gone did she notice the tears he'd left behind on her shoulder.

The ships themselves are a loss, surely, but it is not like Vincent to weep over a thing done that cannot be undone. Khosa dresses simply and with care, slow movements that will not upset the babe inside of her or encourage her body to bolt for the sea, her mind for once on her husband and only him.

Yet she has her own actions to take. The ship that will carry them away may be a loss, but another will be built, and she will not stand idly by, dressed by girls, fed by others, while the kingdom she was born to protect and now fated to help lead slides into the sea.

Merryl snaps to attention when she opens the door, clearing the sleep from his eyes.

"The baby not sleeping well?" she asks.

"Not sleeping at all," Merryl answers as they make their way to the library. "I spell my wife when I can, but when a new one wants its mother, no one else will suit."

"Yes," Khosa says, her hands dipping to her waist. "I'm sure that is true."

Merryl pushes the heavy doors open for her to pass through, and Khosa critically eyes the progress they have already made together. Fallen bookshelves have been pushed aside, damaged scrolls mended, torn pages pieced together. Some bound spines lie open on tables to dry; a large crack in the ceiling caused by the earth shaking had allowed rain in from a stray storm. The maps that had hung from the ceiling and drifted over Khosa's head while she muddled over Stille's past now sit rolled in a corner, waiting for her to decide their future.

She chews her lip for a moment, thinking. The maps are large, but if she asks Winlan to secure hooks on the roof of a lower deck, they will not take up space that could otherwise be filled by Stilleans.

"The maps go," she decides. "Take them to the loading room while I sort, please."

"Is it wise to leave you alone?" Merryl asks.

"No," Khosa concedes. "Perhaps we should call Rook and some others to make the trip?"

Merryl nods and heads for the corridor to find a messenger boy, or another guard, to carry the queen's request while she surveys the room, wondering what step comes next. The Curator showed her the summaries, large compendiums that draw together pertinent facts from all the histories, leaving anecdotal stories and smaller details behind. The summaries will go, of course, and she will see that they are loaded first. But she cannot bring herself to leave behind the histories themselves, with mentions of fiverberries and waterleaf rue, descriptions of sunsets that happened only once.

Merryl and Rook work alongside her as she binds stacks of histories with cord, books that have not been touched since they were inked now brushed off and worried over. The shafts of sunlight from the window overhead move across the room. A girl brings Khosa a tray of food when she finds herself ravenous.

"Should you take a rest, my lady?" Merryl asks, but Khosa only shakes her head, pushing the tray away when she is finished. A sense of urgency has gripped her, and she cannot shake it, though the breeze that slips in through the window is uncommonly warm and the sea at rest.

"I will work through the day," she tells him. "Though you must return home at shift's end. There's a wife and baby who need you."

He nods his agreement and turns away, but not before she notices his gaze slide to her midsection. Khosa turns to a stack of histories grimly, tying a knot with more force than necessary. Instinct has driven her hands to her belly protectively at any mention of danger, something she will have to amend. A bitter smile twists her face at the thought that her body has found yet another way to betray her.

Khosa shakes her head at the thought of betrayal, knowing that she is the bearer of that wrongdoing more so than any other. Dara's capture and the burning of the ships has left no time for her to speak with Vincent, no gentle way to bring a hard truth to him. Yet she will, no matter what punishment lands on her head for it. He deserves to hear it from her own mouth, and she to bear the consequences.

She is lost to her work as her hands bind stacks of histories together for the guards to move, her mind on the hidden histories that rest in her chamber. They hold truths, but as Madda said, also darkness. Should it be known forever that Dagmar grew corpulent with age, or that Runnar's children were born out of wedlock, and in her own time, that the man she married has no blood claim to the throne?

It is in her power to erase this from the record, leaving behind the parchment that links Vincent to Madda, no one the wiser except for herself and Dissa. Yet truth and faded ink have saved Stille from the wet death of a rising tide, and the ships that she can even now hear being rebuilt would never sail if not for shameful secrets that have been uncovered. Her mouth twists as severely as the bindings she ties, balancing loyalty and duty. She is so lost in these thoughts that she does not hear Vincent arrive and dismiss the guards, is not aware he is with her until he says her name.

"Khosa."

It is quiet and sweet, as if her husband holds her as sacred as the common people, calling her the Redeemed and no longer the Given. She turns to him and finds not the man she married—confused and trepidatious, yes, but also hopeful and determined. What she sees now is desolation, the utter loss that paints his features destroying any conviction she had in truth when she sees what the world has done to him in a short time.

She goes to him, hands on his burnt face, her forehead touching his. "What has happened, husband?"

"I am betrayed," he says, voice tight and still tinged with smoke.

Khosa goes still beneath his hands, the depth of her guilt rising up inside. What should bring her to her knees buoys her, allowing her to stand as he judges her, which he surely will.

"Vincent . . ." she begins, until he collapses into her, exhaustion driving him into her arms.

"Madda," he manages to choke out, as Khosa pulls a stool over for her own support, her husband still propped against her.

"She did not carry the flame herself," Vincent says, straightening. "But she knew the ships would burn and allowed them to."

"I do not . . ." Words fail her, and confusion abounds. The guilt that had infused her spine leaves her, replaced by relief and weakness. She sags onto the stool, face lifted to his.

"I do not understand."

"Neither do I," Vincent shakes his head. "Daisy saw Ank in the corridor—"

"Ank the Feneen?"

"Yes, it was he who fired the ships, but Madda played a part in allowing it. It seems . . ." He heaves a sigh, disbelief weighing his words. "It seems she's been aiding the Feneen and, therefore, Pietra."

"Why would the royal Seer do such a thing?" Khosa, typically as expressive as the stone surrounding them, nearly scoffs. "She has nothing to gain from the downfall of Stille, no loyalty to the Feneen, and certainly none to the Pietra."

"Ank is her son," Vincent says blankly.

"I . . ." Khosa's tongue moves as her mind rolls, but no words come, only disbelief. "Who has told you these things, Vincent? Surely they are lies."

"Madda said as much to the guards when she was questioned," he says, resting his forehead in his hands. "I have yet to speak to her myself."

"You must." Khosa puts her hands on his knees. "Urge her to recant these words, claim she has the roving mind of a Seer lived past her prime. Do not let her cling to these words, Vincent. For if she does—"

"If she does, she is a traitor to Stille," Vincent says.

"But traitors—"

"Yes." He raises his eyes to hers. "Traitors burn."

CHAPTER 69

Vincent

MADDA SITS IN THE GREAT HALL, HUDDLED IN BLANKETS. Vincent has looked upon her face his whole life, always in her tower room, the rounded walls echoing her shoulders, leaves of drying nilflower reaching for her hair as she sat, leaning over his palms. Here the ceiling is high above her, and this woman who had loomed large in his life seems very small. He seats himself across from her, eyeing the Scribe who has come to record her words and the guards who flank the door.

"She is no threat," he says, dismissing them with a flick of his fingers.

They exchange a glance, one of them clearing his throat. "My king, the Seer is accused of—"

"Do you think I don't know that?" Vincent snaps, the flare of anger inherited from his father igniting.

The guards exit, but the Scribe's pen remains poised, his eyebrow raised.

"I would speak to her in private," Vincent says.

"With respect, no," the Scribe contradicts him. "My duty is to the histories, not to my king."

"And where do you think those histories will end, if your king is displeased? I can send them to water or flame if I choose."

The Scribe's eyes are stony, reminding him of Khosa's when lost in pages. "Histories do not end."

To Vincent's shock, Madda erupts into laughter. "He has a point," she says. "As long as time passes, there will be histories. Though perhaps we will find it difficult when there is no one left to record them."

"You would have your words written?" Vincent looks to her, for the first time seeing Madda without shadows to darken her eyes or nilflower smoke to soften her features. She is old and frail, an oderbird fallen from the nest not at birth but at death.

"Why should I not?" Madda answers, unconcerned. "How many have I said to you in confidence, to your mother, to your wife, to your father? Why should Madda the Seer's words always be lost or wreathed in mystery?"

"Is that why?" Vincent asks, ignoring the Scribe's pen as it scratches. "Did you need to know something you set in motion had come to pass?"

"As opposed to guessing in the dark, looking to changing lines in hands sometimes cruel to me? No." Madda shakes her head. "I need no great fame aligned with me, inked forever. I acted only as a mother."

Vincent nods. "You told the guards Ank is your son."

"He is, indeed."

"Yet I believed you to be childless. There is no shame in motherhood, even of one born with a caul as Ank was. You could have cut it away at birth, and none the wiser."

"It was not my shame that sent him from Stille," Madda says. "It was your father's."

Vincent closes his eyes against her. "Do not write that," he instructs the Scribe.

"Write it," Madda insists, before the Scribe can protest. "Purcell was not your only brother, Vincent. It should be known."

"Half brother," Vincent says, pinching his temples against the pressure that is building there. A deep part of him recoils at her words, wanting nothing but distance between himself and the man who killed his grandfather Gammal.

Madda opens her mouth as if she would contradict him, but glances to the Scribe and keeps her peace. At that moment, the doors of the great hall open and Dissa arrives, brushing past the guards with such authority that they do not question her presence. She takes a seat on Vincent's other side, her eyes passing over the lines that the Scribe has already inked.

"What have you to say for yourself, Madda?" she asks stiffly.

The Seer shrugs. "Nothing you wouldn't want me to share."

Vincent looks from one woman to the other, measuring the tension there. "Madda has given a full confession to aiding the Feneen, along with her reasoning. Her loyalty was divided between her son and her country."

Dissa nods, facing the Seer. "You understand the penalty for treason?"

"I do," Madda says, and though her voice does not shake, her eyes slide to the fireplace, and the flames dancing there.

The pyre is built amid the charred skeleton of the ship, fresh lifesap dripping from boards newly cut to drop into the surrounding ashes. The steps are not sanded, for splinters will not matter to feet that will soon blister and burn.

Most of Stille gathers in silence, stone-faced. Some remain at home, shielding children from the sight even if there is no distance far enough from the screams that will come. The crowd parts for the Seer as she is escorted from the castle, blinking against the sun.

Vincent winces at the thought of her skin, moon white from never having known life outside her tower, now exposed to the harsh light of morning. He stands with his wife and mother at the head of the crowd, the black ribs of the burnt ship rising around him, the pyre at his back. Heat rises from the ground, baking his feet in his boots. Beside him, Khosa wipes beads of sweat from her lip with one gloved hand, the other firmly caught within his own, should the sea call her.

Vincent spent the night before alone, forgoing even the company of Khosa. There was no comfort to be had from anyone, for there was nothing that could be done. Even the Curator shook his head when the king came to him asking if there was a route other than death for Madda, as there had been for Khosa. On this, the histories were unwavering. Traitors burned. Grief had filled him, pushing all else aside. The path of his life had always ended with the throne looming over it, but never had he believed such atrocities could be hidden in the shadows it cast.

"Madda the Seer," Vincent announces in a clear voice when she reaches him, hands bound, bright eyes on his own. "You are a traitor to Stille and will burn. Have you any words?"

"I do," she says, voice filling the outdoors as it had her tower. "You're a good king, Vincent, and an even better man. This is not your doing, child, only the wheels we are caught up in together. They will move, and I will be crushed, and you will go on, for it is in a wheel's nature to turn."

Tears run down Vincent's cheeks, and he makes no move to stop them. Finally Madda reaches up, wiping them away with a fold of her cloak.

"Also, three of Unter Hoff's children are not his own," she says to the crowd. "And Baura thins her cow milk with well water."

There's a gasp at the first revelation, a smattering of laughter at the second, and Madda pulls a torch from her guard's hand at the distraction. He twists to stop her, but she is gone, mounting the steps with surprising grace and dropping the torch to her own kindling. Her cloak catches quickly, the long-loved folds falling away as the fire eats toward her skin.

The Seer clutches the pyre, a cry she cannot contain escaping her lips as her hair lights, gray strands suddenly bright with color.

Vincent goes to her instinctively, Madda's cry of pain overwhelming all else. He is stopped by Khosa's hand, tight on his, and his mother's on his elbow.

"Let her go, Vincent," Dissa says, turning his face away.

"No, Mother," he says. "I must watch."

So he does, even as her flesh catches and Madda's voice rises in agony. The king looks on as others fade away, horror overwhelming curiosity. The Scribe sent to record the deed turns his head, the Curator draws his hood over his eyes, and two nobles are lost to faints. Vincent and Khosa look on, hands clasped, as the rising heat evaporates their tears and the smoke rises, smelling of nilflower.

CHAPTER 70

Vincent

SOLITUDE IS ALL HE WISHES FOR, AND THE ONE THING he cannot have. As king, Vincent must allay the fears of the Stilleans who wish to sail and fear that the boats cannot be built before a second Pietran attack. The firing of the ships has lent heat to those who would stay and think it a bad omen that one of their own—and the Seer, at that—contributed to their destruction. And yet others push for more aggressive action toward the Pietra, and wish to march on the offensive at the first opportunity. Vincent listens to all, the smoke from Madda's pyre sticking to his clothes, his own skin still blistered and red.

He sits in the great hall with Dissa and Sallin, Khosa having made an excuse to lie down. Vincent's mother and advisor give their thoughts as each Stillean leaves, then receive Winlan's estimations on how quickly their work can resume. A messenger from Sawhen arrives, responding to their invitation to any in the village who wish to sail when the time comes. Many have accepted, and though Vincent knows their lives have been saved by this decision, he fears he cannot accommodate them all. The last to speak to them is Milda, hands twisting in her skirt with nervousness and cheeks aflame when she sees that she will be addressing Dissa as well.

"I will speak to this Stillean alone," Vincent says, rising to his feet when he sees Milda's discomfort.

Dissa sends him an odd look but takes her leave alongside Sallin, who tips Vincent a wink as he closes the doors behind him. Vincent turns to Milda, grateful for the burns that hide his own flush of embarrassment.

"I am sorry for the loss of your Seer," Milda says quickly. "I know you were close, and I . . . I'm sure what passed this morning was not easy for you to endure."

"Harder for her, I think," Vincent says. "But I thank you."

Milda nods, and he leads her to a chair. "Have you had much luck speaking with Stilleans about the ships?"

"Yes," she says. "More than expected. And no"—anticipating his next question—"I do not think the burning of one will turn the minds of many. Some, perhaps. Those who can see salvation in the sea are not softhearted or thin-skinned. Stille has sat silent for years, many and more. Young blood has been stirred of late, and obstacles only fire it in their veins—oh, I—" She clears her throat. "I apologize for my choice of words."

Vincent smiles, waving away her apology. In fact he hardly heard it, his eyes lost in searching her face. Motherhood will agree with her, and the prettiness of youth has acquired the gravity of experience. His hand finds hers, and he squeezes it.

"I thank you, Milda. You have saved lives with this work on your king's behalf, and I will not forget it."

She returns the smile, squeezing his hand as well. "It is not the king I do it for, but my friend Vincent. I saw in your eyes the depth of your belief in the ships and finding new land, and adopted it as my own."

Milda rises, releasing his hand as he does as well. "I am pleased your family will be alongside us," he tells her truly.

She pulls her cloak around her shoulders. "To think that our children may play together, and on the shores of a far land."

"Perhaps someday," Vincent agrees.

"Ah." Milda covers her mouth with her fingers, eyes sparkling over them. "The queen's handmaidens had said that the early-light illness has taken her to bed of late, and that her shift grows small at the waist. But I of all people should know better than to listen to the idle chatter from the castle."

"Yes," Vincent says, forcing the smile on his face to remain there. "Idle chatter is all it is, for the moment."

He escorts Milda to the door, willing himself not to crush her arm in his grip, or ask what else his wife's servants have said. A king should know the truth from the mouth of his queen, and Vincent intends to ask for it.

CHAPTER 71

Khosa

K HOSA HAS SPENT THE DAY SCOURING THE HIDDEN HISTORIES, finding only the one reference to Madda being Vincent's mother. It is pinched between her fingers now as she rests by the fireplace in her bedroom, thoughts racing.

Watching the Seer burn turned her stomach, and for once she would have run away from the sea rather than toward it. Yet through all of their time together, Khosa had always felt that she needed Vincent more than he did her: for protection, for friendship, for the preservation of her own life. Today he needed her, and so she stood, hand in hand with her husband, knowing that he watched his mother burn, and on his order.

Khosa rubs the piece of parchment between her fingers, the single line that would oust Vincent from the throne and mark him a matricide releasing a scent at her touch. Always the mix of pulp and ink has brought a smile to her face, but now it is laced with smoke and nilflower, stinking of death. It is not the thought of Vincent losing his crown—and she her own—but the dual brand of being the killer of both his parents that makes her unclench her hand, sending the truth to the flames. It is curling in the heat when Vincent walks in, closing the door behind him. Startled, she comes to her feet, glancing first to the fire to be sure that the parchment has burned.

"What is that?" Vincent demands, a gleam in his eyes that Khosa has not seen before on her husband.

"It is nothing," she stammers. "Only a—"

"A note from your lover?" he finishes for her, advancing a step.

"No! Vincent!" is all Khosa can say as she steps backward, falling into her chair.

"Is it Donil?" He pulls her back to her feet, but Khosa yanks her wrist from his grip, her own temper ignited.

"Do not *touch* me," she cries, cradling her arm to her chest.

"Yes, how dare I?" Vincent roars at her, answering anger with rage. "What husband would put his hand on his wife's skin? What man would know the woman he is married to? Not the king of Stille, surely. So who, then, has planted a child in the queen's womb?"

"Vincent." Khosa feels the blood run from her face to her legs, her body preparing to flee from danger, though her mind insists he will not hurt her. "Who has told you these things?"

"*You,*" he yells, his throat cracking with the force of the accusation. "Every line of your body, every expression on your face, every smile on your lips when you think I'm not looking. The queen has a lover, and her mind turns to him often, even when her body is not with his. I have *seen it*, Khosa! I have known, yet I have made myself ignorant, so that I may not feel . . . this."

His last word breaks, the wrath cresting into despair, blistered skin still victimized by fire now wet with fresh tears, eyes still red from the smoke of the morning now glistening with a new loss.

"You have done this to me, Khosa," he says weakly, sinking into a chair. "And I am no more because of it."

"Vincent . . ." Khosa's heart falls at the sight of him broken, the weight of her guilt sending it plummeting. She goes to her knees in front of him, hands reaching for his face. He turns away.

"What was it?" he asks again, eyes on the fire.

"Not a note, I assure you," she says, shaking her head. "But I will say no more."

"Is it Donil?" Vincent asks, all emotion gone from his voice.

"Yes," she says weakly, hanging her head. "I carry his child."

Her husband's hands go to his face to cover it as he cries, the shuddering that racks his body so like her own when she dances that she tries to comfort him. He shoves her hands away, her touch no longer something he can desire. Khosa's own tears flow, and she wipes her face with her sleepshirt as she settles onto the floor, her own gaze lost to the flame.

"We never wished to harm you," she says. "Please believe that."

"I do," Vincent says, pulling his hands from his face. "But it does not make the pain any less."

Khosa is silent, knowing he speaks truth.

"What will you do?" she asks.

"What can I do?" he counters. "This is not only lying outside the marriage bed with another, but—"

"You are the king, and it is treason, I know," Khosa says. "We could burn, and our child with us."

"You know I will not do that," Vincent says quickly, the scent of Madda's pyre still rising from his clothes.

"I will not rid myself of the child, Vincent."

"I would not ask it," he says. "Of either of you."

They sit together in silence, the distance between them greater than what could be measured in fingerlengths.

"When the child is born, all will know I am unfaithful, and with whom," Khosa says. "Whether you wish it or not, Donil and I may find our end in flame."

"You will not," Vincent says, rising to his feet. "By Stillean ways, you are not truly my wife, as we have not been one in our bed. I can divulge this, leaving you free, any lover you have taken being a choice you made as a maiden and not as my wife."

He walks to the door, and she rises to follow, stopping him with a light touch.

"Where are you going, husband?"

The word slips from her tongue as it has become habit of late, a compliment she can pay with her mouth if not her body. It drops now between them as a lie, and his face twists in pain.

"Somewhere I do not have to look upon your face, wife."

CHAPTER 72

Donil

THE SEER HAS BEEN A TOPIC OF JEST BETWEEN MYSELF and Vincent since we were small, I laughing at anyone who thought they could see the future, though I know the past at a glance. As the smoke of Madda's burning clears over the castle walls, I mutter an Indiri thought for her ashes, that they may settle on earth and not drown in the sea. I toss a shell from where I sit on the beach as I do, listening for the far-off sound as it falls into the water.

I have not seen Khosa since the ships burned, our escape taken from us with the toss of a torch. And though I know what role the Seer played, I cannot put blame upon her head. Not when I, too, must balance my fate against that of my child.

With only one seaworthy ship—and that one rightfully loaded with the Hygodeans who built it—and many Stilleans vying for a spot on another, the chances of an Indiri finding a place on board are slim. Khosa could be saved, though, as queen, and my child with her. It would grow without me, in a land I will never see, yet know me intimately through my memories. Or it could drown at sea, torn from Khosa's arms moments after being born, cursed for bearing spots and the indiscretion of its parents.

I shudder at the thought of a child being tossed to the sea as I did the shell, yet relish the idea that I will have a child to fear for. I've struggled with the betrayal of my friend, the love I feel for a woman I cannot be with, the absence of my sister and what fresh torture the Lithos has prepared for her, yet when I think of tiny Indiri fists, and Khosa's blue eyes in a speckled face, I can only smile.

Vincent finds me at such a moment, and I rise to meet him. His face is still burned, the hair crisped away, and one eye mostly closed, so I do not see the rage on his face until it is too late.

I taught him to fight, and the punch on the tip of my jaw is well landed. I'm thrown off my feet entirely, sand kicked into a spray that falls back onto my chest as I look up at Vincent, blood running down my chin. As boys we traded blows, sometimes in jest, but occasionally with real anger. This is not the same.

I was punched by a man, one whom I have wronged.

I say no word, and he none to me.

Slowly, he reaches down to take my hand. I hesitate only a moment before grasping it, and he pulls me to my feet.

"What now, brother?" I ask.

"Now I go to find Dara," he says.

I cannot watch my friend ride in my sister's name, knowing that I have acted against him and that he may not return. Vincent put up little resistance when I said I would go with him, already mustering the men and conferring with his commanders. For him, my going along is a matter of strength, another sword that will swing by his side. There is another for whom the battlefield is a distant thought, the child in her belly a greater concern.

I go to Khosa's rooms with no care as to decency, giving the guard outside a brusque nod as I raise my fist to knock. She calls for me to enter, standing as I do. Her face is tear streaked, eyes swollen. She cries out at the sight of me, jaw still raw and bloody. I go to her, and we nestle together for a moment, finding no small comfort in each other.

"Khosa," I say, pulling back from her, "I must go with Vincent."

She shakes her head, but I stop her with a word. "With only one ship to sail and another burned, there is no sense in my staying here while others ride for my sister's sake."

"But—"

"I *will* go with you when we sail," I say. "But it is the Pietra that worry me now. They will not let us go without a fight; that much has been made clear. We have the greater army, if not the better soldiers. I will add my might to theirs, clear the land of our enemies, then return to build a ship worthy of carrying the mother of my child and the last of my blood. I would not put you aboard something built in haste, leaving you to the same fate that would have taken you when we first met."

Her face is still in my hands, tears running freely again. She nods, eyes shining.

"Donil," she says, my name heavy in her mouth. "Vincent . . ." She closes her eyes against it, the memory too difficult.

I pull her back into me, cradling her head against my chest.

"What did he say to you?" she asks.

"Nothing at all," I tell her, pointing to my jaw. "But he said it quite forcefully."

"Oh, Donil." Her fingers trace my face, her thumb rubbing against my lower lip. "I'm so sorry to have brought this upon you."

I grip her hands in mine, press them against my mouth. "I'm so glad that you did."

CHAPTER 73

Witt

I AM TO BE MARRIED.

It is an odd thought, one that should sit poorly in any Lithos's mind, unable to balance with training and tradition. Yet it is happening, and I seem to be a very small part of what is necessary to accommodate the fact. The Keeper has taken it upon herself to manage every aspect, while I move about in the same ways, drilling with my soldiers—some of whom have given bedroom advice I deem highly questionable—and meeting with my advisors.

Hadduk is less than pleased with the agreement I reached with Dara, and I know there are many who grumble alongside him, some among my high commanders. Yet we lost many and more to the sea on the beaches of Stille, and though our pride runs strong, it alone cannot stand against an enemy that outnumbers us. It is the wiser choice to let the Stilleans sail, but courage carries more weight in Pietra than cunning, and I watch the faces of my people as I move among them.

"A scout reported that the Stillean army is on the move," Hadduk tells me at our meeting. "It seems that burning the ships turned their minds toward land instead of sea."

"What are your thoughts, Ank?" I ask the Feneen.

He shifts in his chair, looking carefully at the Mason before he speaks. "We can send a messenger, carry word that what they seek—the Indiri—no longer wishes to leave with them. Let them know they can rebuild in peace and sail at their leisure."

Nilana snorts, drawing attention to herself. "They'll not believe it. I wouldn't."

"No," Hadduk agrees. "They'll want to see the girl themselves, and hear from her own mouth that she wishes to—" He breaks off, the words distasteful to him. "To marry the Lithos."

"How far out are they?" I ask.

"Three suns," Hadduk shrugs. "Maybe four. Stilleans don't fight well, I don't expect them to march quickly, either."

"If they're that far out, she'll be welcoming them as the Lithos's wife, not as his bride," Ank says. "You are to be wed the coming night, yes?"

I glance up when I realize the question is put to me.

"Yes," I say, disbelief ringing in my voice. "The coming night."

The Keeper has my elbow the moment I leave the hall, steering me toward a room flanked by guards.

"Your bride would have a word," she says, following me inside.

I have not seen Dara since she accepted our agreement—I have yet to think of it as anything as romantic as a proposal. I know that she was moved to proper chambers, fed, cleaned, and clothed. What I did not expect was how nothing would change about her. Though she has been made civilized, it is quite clear that the woman who stands before me is very much a wild thing.

"Lithos," she greets me, and I dip my head to her, forgetting that she did not do so to me.

"Please call me Witt," I say, sneaking a glance at her. The Keeper told me that Dara refused any of the traditional Pietran dresses that were sent to her, but settled for clothes a Lure would wear while she waited for her Indiri clothing to be cleaned and mended. The trousers are belted twice around her waist and the shirtsleeves are rolled to her elbows, yet she seems at ease. The stitches I put into her arm are gone, leaving a dark scar behind, a red slash through her speckles.

"May I?" I approach her, and she puts her arm out for my inspection. I run my thumb along the scar, pressing down to feel the still-swollen skin underneath. "This will not fade, I'm afraid," I tell her.

"It is nothing to me." She lifts her arm from my hand. "Only one among many."

That Dara has seen much battle I do not doubt, yet I glimpse only a handful of scars now. That she has many, and that I may know them soon, sends a shiver through me.

"You can leave us," Dara says to the Keeper, who looks to me. I nod for her to go, and she does so with a small smile.

"You wished to speak with me?" I ask, stepping back from her so that I may clear my head.

"Yes. The Keeper informed me that the ceremony will be Pietran, which I find no fault with, as I am marrying into your land. However, I would ask that we wear traditional Indiri marriage clothes so that I may honor my own people as well."

"Of course." I nod. It's an easy acquiescence, but I do not care for how she asks it. Dara grew to womanhood in Stille, surrounded by negotiations and cunning. I can see in the stiffness of her back and the formality of her words that she learned well their ways. I liked much more the girl who stared at the stars and barely promised not to kill me.

"Dara," I say, "this will go much easier if we are plain with each other."

She sighs and turns her back to me, head dropping. "How shall I do that? By telling my groom that I have lain long nights feeling myself a traitor? That I have weighed the lives of my children not born against that of my brother?"

"Your brother will not be harmed—"

"But he will *sail*." She spins on me, eyes bright. "He may as well die in front of my eyes as be gone from me forever. I will not know the names of his children or hear his voice crack with age. I will not know when he passes or he me. We will be dead to each other when he goes, we, who were born together."

"I understand," I say. "I, too, put those I love into boats."

"You did so knowing they went to their deaths. Imagine instead that they have lived a full life elsewhere, and you ignorant of every moment."

I do, and the stab of pain that comes is familiar. My mother's face, the small trusting hands of my little brothers, these I have looked upon much and more, always believing the pain will ease with each glance. Instead I have held and nurtured it, until their loss is at my center. Now I see my mother with hair gone gray and a lined face, the boys grown to men with quick smiles. It never will and cannot be, yet the thought that it might, and I would not witness it, sends my grief cresting into something sharper.

"I ask much of you," I say to Dara, settling my hand again onto her wrist, and the curve of the scar that ends there.

"No more than others, I have decided," she says. I feel the rush of her blood under my palm as she speaks, the heat of her body in her words.

"The Stilleans would have me calm my nature, a tame Tangata roaming their halls to perhaps find shelter with a commoner who would not mind having spotted children at his table. Yet the Lithos of Pietra—"

"Witt," I remind her.

"Witt," she amends. "Has a nature like mine and would see them brought together as one."

My own breathing quickens, my thumb roaming the length of her scar.

"I do not know what world this is, where marriage with you is not something I find detestable," she says, eyes following my hand.

"This world is ours," I tell her.

And she smiles.

CHAPTER 74

Dara

I PREPARE FOR MY WEDDING AS IF I WERE GOING INTO BATTLE, hands steady, breathing even, eyes sharp. The same calmness has enveloped me, a sense of fate spinning out of my control, my mind giving way to my body, the better trained of the two. I've gone into fights I thought I might lose, and the blood in my veins rushed at the thought of something new, the assuredness of my enemies falling at my feet having grown stale.

I feel the same now, as the Keeper piles my hair onto my head, exposing my shoulders and the lines of old scars that creep upon them: one from my back and a stray Tangata claw, one curving around my neck from a nomad who got a lucky slash in on the road to Hyllen when I was small. They both fell, shortly after making their marks on me, their blood given to the ground, a gift from my Indiri blades.

I do not wear them tonight, as is Indiri custom. I have no weapon, no jewelry, only the thin wrap that ties at one shoulder. The Keeper blushed red when I told her I would wear nothing underneath it, every hard line of my body showing through the wrap—and the softer lines as well.

"It's barely decent," she said, eyes running over me.

"This is the Indiri way," I told her. "We are fighters, and to marry, we meet one another unarmed, hiding nothing. It is trust to dress as such in front of another."

"Trust and lust," she muttered while she pinned my hair.

I looked at my reflection as she worked, knowing she was not wrong.

"It is time," the Keeper says now, holding me by the elbow as I rise. The Pietra have not left me to myself, a guard or the Keeper always at my side. They expect me to bolt like a fadernal or slash at their throats like a Tangata. And while I have had many chances to do both, I have not taken them. My sleep has not been pleasant when it comes, and I have called myself traitor under my breath in the night, and though my mind condemns me for it, my body wishes to stay. More than once I have told myself to lunge for a Pietran blade, snap the Keeper's neck in my hands, and slip away.

Yet I have not, my body more curious about what awaits me as the Lithos's wife than my mind is concerned about what my ancestors might think of me. All my life I have put my blood first, the memories of people I have never known in the flesh dictating my steps. And now my own flesh is awakened, and it will have what it wants.

The hall is flanked by guards who eye me, some with distrust, some more openly, their gaze gliding over my body as I pass. The Keeper opens the doors to the hall where Witt stands at the front, wearing the same wrap as I do.

"Fathoms," the Keeper says quietly, and I silently think the same.

That the Lithos is well made can be seen even when he is layered with armor. Without it, he bristles with strength, every dip and curve of muscle evident. His gaze sweeps me once, then focuses on my face as I approach. I feel a small smile twisting there and see one echoed back from him.

I reach him, and we face each other as an Elder marries us in the Pietran way. He speaks of the unbreakable quality of stone and the lasting life of the cliffs, words I can find no fault with, as I can find none in the man who faces me. Witt is made of strength and fights with honor, yet I felt a great gentleness in him when he touched my scar, and I am unable to deny the heat in my body that rose to his when he did.

If this man had spots, he would be as Indiri as I am, and that realization is what led me to the decision that I can take him as my own and be no traitor. For to me he is no longer the Lithos but a man, and I am a woman.

And I will have him.

The words are at an end and we trade rocks, I giving him a gray one that has become warm in my palm while I held it, he handing me a white pebble washed smooth by the sea. The Elder gives me a look, and I realize as the bride I am supposed to do something now, but I do not know what.

Ank leans into me, his voice in my ear. "You swallow it," he whispers.

I do so, and it glides down easily, helped along by the wine I'd taken while the Keeper managed my hair. Everyone then turns to Witt, who holds a stone half the size of his palm, and I feel a sudden horror.

"Surely you don't have to . . ." I say.

"I didn't realize when I chose it," the Keeper says, twisting her skirts. "Can I get another?"

The Elder shakes his head. "This is the stone the bride has put her skin against; her heat is inside it. The Lithos—" He closes his eyes as if it's painful for him to continue, and I mark his face well, that I will remember this Elder as our country moves forward. "If the Lithos truly wishes to marry this woman—"

Witt pops it into his mouth, throat working, eyes on mine. The hall is quiet, and my hands find his in solidarity, squeezing as I watch the lump pass down his throat. Finally he breathes, and I with him. I feel Ank's hand on my shoulder as a smattering of applause ripples through the hall—not much, I notice—and then the Elder sighs.

"I suppose you're married."

"Yes," I say, gaze fixed upon my husband. "I suppose we are."

There is a brief meal, one that I do not partake heavily of. The room is tense, very few of those in it actually celebrating my marriage. I memorize faces, making note of who will look upon me and who will not. Nilana is one who not only returns my gaze but also smiles, then, seeing the food still left on my plate, whispers something to Hadduk. The Mason rises, makes a small speech that I hear no a word of, aware only of the man next to me.

"I believe this groom is perhaps more anxious than most to see his bride in privacy," Hadduk goes on, and a wave of red washes over my husband's face. But he does not deny it. Instead, Witt offers me his hand, and we go, exiting the hall to a few barks of a laughter and some bawdy jests that can't quite pierce the tension of the moment.

For the Lithos is taking an Indiri to bed.

I shiver in the shadowed hall, and his hands go to my bare arms as he guides me to his rooms. They are sparse, with a good fire in the hearth and a jug of wine on the table.

"I thought we might . . ." Witt points to the wine without finishing, and I go to a chair, pouring myself a drink. He sits as well, taking a long pull of his own. I watch his neck muscles work as he drains it and gets another.

"I'm sorry about the stone," I say. "The Keeper chose it, not knowing the Pietra custom of—"

"Eating it?" he finishes for me. "Yes, I suppose I should have warned you."

"I managed," I say, holding his eyes. "As did you."

"I did," he agrees. "I would've chewed through a boulder to have you."

I pull pins from my hair and let it fall around my shoulders as I stand in front of him, the fire warm on my back through the thinness of my wrap. "Pity," I say, pulling him to his feet. "Then you'd have no teeth."

"Will I need them?" he asks, no longer pretending to look only at my face.

"Perhaps," I say, trailing my hand along the line of his jaw. He feels alive beneath my touch, quivering with need and barely contained energy. My skin answers his, equal to equal.

"Dara," he whispers, hands roaming over my shoulders. "I have seen husbands and wives who have nothing more between them than the title. I would not have it be so with us."

My hands find the knot at his shoulder that holds his wrap together, and I undo it with a practiced twist. He does the same, and my covering falls from me, the heat from the fire now against my bare back.

"I have read the great love stories," I tell him. "And if I look to them, I cannot call this love, but my ancestors have shown me what else can move between a man and a woman, and I do feel that."

"I feel it too," he says, eyes closing as my hands roam.

"Then show me," I say.

And he does.

CHAPTER 75

Witt

I UNDERSTAND NOW WHY THE LITHOS IS NOT TO BE DISTRACTED. I am more than that; I am lost. The only thing that exists is this bed and the woman in it, and I will stay here and die with her beside me and call my life well lived.

"Thirsty?" Dara asks.

I am, but I don't wish to leave the bed or for her to, either. She does, though, padding across the floor in nothing but her skin. There is no modesty in Dara, and I adore her for it. She finds water, for which I am thankful. My head spins already, and I don't know what to attribute to wine and what to elation. Dara comes back, pulling the bedcovers around her as she drinks, then hands me the glass.

"Do you like being married?" she asks.

"I do," I say. "How do you find it?"

"Oddly comfortable," she says. "Though I can't deny it's a cunning match as well."

"It is," I agree cautiously. "Our binding fulfills my oath to the Feneen to take an outsider as a wife, and your will allows the Stilleans to sail unassaulted."

"Yes, it does," Dara says, some of the light leaving her eyes. My heart sinks at the sight.

"Do you feel something for him, their king?" I ask.

My wife's hands find her own hair, and she begins to make small braids in it as she speaks. "Maybe once," she admits. "Though I think my heart knew him as a childhood friend, and when we grew to man and woman, it clung to him out of habit."

"And now?"

"Now I have felt something else," she says, hands leaving her hair to find me. "And it is much more powerful."

"It is," I breathe, stopping her hands for the moment. She looks at me questioningly.

"The Stilleans march on us, looking to take you back to their homeland. They'll arrive within a few suns and doubtless will not take word from a messenger as truth that you wish to remain."

"I will tell them myself," she says, nestling into a pillow, her dark hair flowing.

"And I hope your words will be well met," I say, trailing my hand along her back. "But I cannot have the entire Stillean army at my door with no Pietra in armor."

"I understand." She nods. "Prepare the spada and lancia that will return to Stille to assist in shipbuilding. They will be a force enough behind you to ease Hadduk's concerns, yet not so large that Vincent will be unsettled at the sight."

I reach for her. "I enjoy your mind."

"And . . . ?" she asks, eyebrows raised.

"And that's really all," I say, faking a yawn.

My wife shoves me lightly, and I pull her to me as we laugh, rolling together in the bed.

And we are very, very distracted.

CHAPTER 76

⋯⊶⊙⊷⋯

Vincent

THE ARMY MARCHES, AND VINCENT WITH THEM, SAVING his horse's strength. The act of putting one foot in front of another is all he can focus on, for he is pain both within and without. The burns on his face have settled into a low hum, like a gathering of ninpops under his skin. His knuckles are swollen, the skin cracked widely from where he hit Donil, yet it is only a low ache that swings at the end of his arm. It's the pain inside that he cannot endure, overwhelming emotion that flows from his stomach and past his heart, filling his throat and threatening to send him retching, though he is not ill.

His friend lay with his wife. He still thinks of Khosa as such, though he knows that by Stillean tradition she is not. She is the wife of his heart if not his body, and that she does not feel the same for him on either count is a wound gone deep, to be reopened again and again, every time he looks at Donil.

Vincent has not spoken of it to him in the time since the army set out from Stille, for he has no words. Everything he would say was neatly encompassed when he struck Donil, the Indiri's response in not fighting back the only one Vincent would accept. His wife and friend have done him wrong, and both know it. Speaking of it will only fire tempers when Dara should be first in everyone's minds. So when Donil finds Vincent's fire on the last night before they arrive in Pietra, Vincent turns his head from him.

"Vin, I would speak to you of it, though I know it is distasteful."

"What is there to say?" he asks. "I am thrice duped—by my wife and my friend, but also myself, for I knew what lay between you and trusted you to act rightly."

"You did trust us," Donil says. "You thought better of us than we deserved."

"Do you think I don't know what it's like to *want*?" Vincent spits, anger getting the best of him. "I lay by her, in my own marriage bed, night after night, burning with a need that is no less than yours, Donil. And yet I did not act on it—out of respect for her. The two of you could not do the same for me, though there be stone walls separating you and every speck of decency telling you not to."

Donil stares at the ground, head hung low. "You are not wrong, brother."

"But I have been wronged and cannot see past it," Vincent says, tossing the rest of his drink into the fire and sending sparks into the air. "When we return to Stille, you and Khosa shall board one ship, I another. She will no longer be my wife and will be free to become yours."

"Brother—" Donil chokes on his own words, eyes wet with tears.

"Once we discover land, you will find a place that suits you, and I will find one that suits Stille. May they not be near one another."

"Vincent—" Donil tries again, only to be cut off.

"What more can you want from me?" Vincent asks. "I've given you my home, my friendship for all of our years, even my very wife and places on ships that sail to a new world, though I should rightfully burn you both to ash. What else would you have? My blessing?"

Donil shakes his head. "Forgiveness."

"That I do not know I can give," Vincent says, his own eyes bright. "Maybe in the future, when I have my own wife and our youthful hearts have settled. Maybe then our children can meet and start new friendships, while you and I mend an old one."

Donil raises his cup. "To the future, then. May it come quickly."

CHAPTER 77

Donil

I HAVE LOST MY BEST AND ONLY FRIEND, THE ONLY MAN THAT I call a brother. It's created an emptiness inside of me, but deep within that fires a spark struck by his own words. Khosa and I can be together, our child born and more to follow. And yes, I cannot ask Vincent to see us together now and revel in our happiness, but once he has found his own, then perhaps it can be as he said. I imagine a day when we are not yet old men, who can look upon each other and remember our youth and affection for each other.

I ride with a commander who trained with Dara, one of the first to volunteer his men to march on her behalf. Though more left Stille with us than I expected, many remained behind with Winlan, rebuilding the ship that burned. Less than half the Stillean army is at my back, and I do not trust that they will all stand when faced with a Pietran lancia, whose spears fly true and far. I spur my mount to join Vincent at the head of the column.

"How do you think our soldiers will fare when faced with the enemy?"

"Some will surprise us—and themselves," he says. "Enough will stand. They have not trained for nothing, and those who march with us do so not only for your sister's sake. They were cheated of a chance at glory when the sea won the day for us."

There is truth to what he says, but though they may thirst for blood, they remain unbloodied. A soldier who has not fought cannot know what a fight will do to him, and even the stoutest man may lose his gumption when the one next to him falls.

"Let me ride ahead alone," I urge Vincent. "We do not know where Dara is held or if—"

Vincent stops me, raising a hand. "I have failed her, Donil. Often and again. This once I would like to say truly that I did everything I could for Dara of the Indiri. I will lead this army and see her back on Stillean land."

I want to argue, tell him that we may not be outnumbered but will certainly be outfought, when a scout crests the rise and spots us, pushing his horse to its limits until he is at our side.

"My king," he gasps, nearly out of breath, his horse heaving as well. "The Pietra are gathered not far from here."

"The entire army?" I ask, though I was not addressed.

"No." He shakes his head. "Not by half. The Lithos is with them, as well as the Mason. The Indiri is with them too."

"How is she? How does she look? Is she well? How does she seem?" Vincent asks quickly, grabbing onto the scout's arm as his horse shies away from mine.

"She . . ." He looks from Vincent to me, eyes wide.

"Out with it," Vincent says.

"She was laughing, my king."

CHAPTER 78

Witt

THE STILLEAN SCOUT'S HORSE KICKS UP DIRT AS IT retreats, the animal clearly as stunned as his rider at finding us. We rode to the edge of the Hadundun forest, past the rotting carcass of the Lusca that Dara killed. The tree was not entirely severed from the earth, and it found life in the Lusca, drawing its blood for new shoots that rooted in death, sharp green leaves bursting through the dead scales. There was an eerie beauty to the sight, and no small pride in knowing my wife brought down this behemoth. Even Hadduk was impressed, a feeling utterly lacking as he watches the Stillean scout ride away.

"There'd be almost no pride in killing them," he says, spitting on the ground.

"Which we are not," I remind Hadduk. "Bring the men into formation," I tell him. "But stay well back."

He nods and rides off, already shouting orders as I swing onto my horse. Dara and Ank spot my movement from the camp and do the same, riding to join me, my wife's dark braid bouncing between the crossed blades she again wears on her back. Hadduk grumbled at this, warning that sheathing my sword in her didn't guarantee she wouldn't do the same to me. Yet Ank argued that seeing Dara armed and beside me would be the first indication to the Stilleans that she was there by choice, and would stop them from attacking on sight.

"Witt." Ank nods to me, reining in. "Shall I do the speaking?"

I nod in agreement, knowing that any word from me directly to the Stilleans would be met with only disbelief, and Ank's way with words can smooth paths before tempers flare.

"Your brother won't kill me outright?" I ask my wife, who shrugs.

"I'm the rash one, and also the quicker," she says. "If he draws, I'll protect you."

"Very kind," I tell her, and she gives me a smile.

I heave a sigh, watching as the men form up behind Hadduk, perfect lines in the distance that I've looked upon countless times, but never with the intention of negotiating peace.

"Nervous?" Ank asks.

"A bit," I admit. "All I've ever known is death."

The Feneen follows my gaze to where Dara has ridden off a pace, checking her mount's hooves and feeding him an apple she's hidden in her cloak, returned to her along with her other clothes.

"Learned something, have you?" he asks.

"A thing or two," I admit, blushing.

"Lithos!" The call comes from the camp, a woman's voice, and I turn expecting to find a Pietran wife approaching with her husband's helmet, left behind in the rush. Instead it is the Keeper, hair astir, leading a horse better suited to a meadow than a battlefield.

"What are you about?" I ask her, urging my mount to her side, Ank following. "You're better off in camp, should something go awry."

"As if I've not seen that with my own eyes," she scoffs, and I remember the ashes rising from Hyllen, her husband dead at my command.

"Seeing and having it done to you are two different things," I tell her. "I'd not have you harmed."

"Not even Hadduk thinks blood will fall today," the Keeper insists. "And he's likely to open throats when a game of ridking goes against him."

She's not wrong, and I can only hope my Mason's confidence holds true. "What is it, then?" I ask her.

"I'd like to ride alongside you and the Indiri, if I may," she says, eyes bold upon me. "This is a day for the histories: the Stillean King, a Feneen, the Lithos of Pietra, and his Indiri wife gathering together. I would see it and perhaps have it written that the Keeper of Hyllen was there, too."

I study her for a moment, hands shaking on the reins of her horse, eyes bright with hope. Of all the things I have taken from her, surely this is a small thing to grant.

"You may come," I say.

CHAPTER 79

———◦◦◦◦———

Donil

VINCENT AND I CREST THE RISE, TWO OF HIS COMMANDERS alongside us, to find a party waiting to meet us, a small contingent of the Pietran army behind them. Vincent raises his hand against the sun.

"The Lithos, the Mason, Ank the Feneen," he lists. "A woman I can't name, and . . ." He trails off, and I find myself sharing his confusion.

I don't know that I've ever seen my sister happy. We were born among the dead, the weight of our ancestors upon our blood, the fear of failing them on our shoulders, the constant worry of the sight of our skin sparking outrage in someone who would kill us for it. A life lived as such leaves room for only contentment, drawn in small measures and celebrated only in stolen moments of safety.

Yet before me I see Dara, blades upon her back and a smile on her face.

And at her side, the Lithos of Pietra.

CHAPTER 80

Ank

THE STILLEANS RIDE TOWARD US, AND WE SPUR OUR own horses to meet them, the growing space between us and Hadduk's soldiers raising an unease that travels the length of my spine. Much could be made this day, and more could go wrong. We pull our mounts to a stop as they do, the length of a drawn blade between us.

Though my time spent among these people has taught me they know much of life, I have forgotten that they are yet children, and greet each other as such, with the simple joy found in each other's company.

"Vincent?" Dara says. "You've nearly burnt your face off."

"Would've lost more than that, if I'd not doused his breeches," Donil says.

And they're laughing, shoulders that were tense only moments before rising and falling with mirth. The very horses underneath us feel the shift and begin to crop grass, battle readiness set aside.

"You look well," Vincent says, and if I'm not mistaken, there's a blush beneath his burns, one that Dara misses as she turns to her husband with a smile.

"I am," she says.

I clear my throat before anything can go amiss. "Vincent, King of

Stille," I say formally, inclining my head toward him. "You know me as Ank of the Feneen, and I speak on behalf of the Lithos of Pietra, that we may make terms."

"Very well," Vincent says, settling back into his role. "I bring with me Donil of the Indiri."

"You of course know Dara," I raise my hand where she sits to my stoneward. She nods, and I look to the Keeper on Dara's other side, who sees my confusion.

"I am the Keeper of Hyllen," she says. "Mother of drowned children, caregiver of the Lithos, wife of Horus."

Vincent dips his head to her. "You have many names."

"And one more, given to me by my mother," she says, voice suddenly hard. "I am Gronwen. I would have the Lithos know that name and keep it well. For I now take back from him what he first took from me."

She draws a dagger and stabs Dara in the chest.

CHAPTER 81

Witt

THERE IS A SOUND, FIST UPON FLESH, AND THE KEEPER has driven a blade so deep into my wife that her hand touches skin, pale upon speckled. There is the breath of a moment as Dara looks down, confused, the hilt brushing against her chin. The Keeper has never done violence and does not know this point in between the action and the realization of it, when all is still. The Keeper herself is frozen, stunned.

Yet Dara knows these moments, has lived inside them all her life, and recovers first. She draws her blades, and they chime together as one drives downward through the Keeper's back, the other upward through her gut so that they meet in between loudly enough to be heard, steel upon spine. Blood sprays in an arc as the Keeper falls, and Dara does too, blades in hand, the ground rising to meet her as her horse bolts.

I know nothing of battle, nothing of blood. I am not the Lithos of Pietra as I jump from my horse. I am only a husband, rushing to his wife's side.

CHAPTER 82

Donil

I SEE MY SISTER FALL.

Moments ago she was light and happiness, a face I knew well but had somehow never seen before. Now I see the Dara from my memories, hurt and pain, disappointment and resentment, wrath and rage trapped inside of speckled skin. My sister is death, and she has brought one down with her even as she falls, the Keeper's body cut in half.

"Dara!" I yell, my horse rearing. I'm thrown, nearly trampled by the Keeper's horse as it bolts, terrified by the smell of its rider's insides. It barrels into Vincent's mount, knocking him aside and tearing past the two commanders who rode behind us. Panicked and poorly trained, they do they only thing they know.

They signal for our army to attack.

CHAPTER 83

Ank

I AM SCREAMING, MY HORSE GONE FROM UNDERNEATH ME, my feet too small to take me far. I yell, I wave, I plead, but having lost all words from my once intelligent tongue, I do not know what I say. It is gibberish, sounds of grief, a mourning for the peace that should have been and now is surely lost.

The Stilleans rush us, though I stand before them weaponless, my arms out to both sides. Untrained and half mad, they flow past me, swords better suited for children in their clenched fists. I turn to the Pietra, to see Hadduk bring his men to a march with a grim face. They move forward, dark blocks of armor and stone shields that meet the Stillean force with a crash.

I am yelling, I am crying, I am screaming. I make noises none can hear.

I am an old man standing amid the carnage of two armies, useless and unseen.

CHAPTER 84

Witt

I FIND MY WIFE WHILE SHE STILL LIVES.

Dara lies on the ground, one hand on the dagger buried inside her. I crawl to her side, a mounted Stillean soldier clearing my head, his horse's hooves grazing my hair. He rides into our lancia, his mount run through by a spear, the rider tossed over his head and into a fray of Pietra who will end him if he's not already finished.

My sword stays in its scabbard, my hand knows only her.

"Dara," I say, and she opens her eyes, bright upon mine. She smiles, blood darker than wine slicking her tongue.

"All my life, all I wanted was to hurt you," she says.

I cover her hand on the dagger that is killing her, our fingers entwined.

"You have," I assure her.

Then I'm hit from the side, rolling into dirt, torn from the only sight I wish to see.

CHAPTER 85

Vincent

VINCENT PULLS HIS HORSE UNDER CONTROL TOO LATE, his army already attacking in a melee, everything he ever taught them gone in the instant that blood fell and horses bolted. The commanders have run into the fray themselves, one already gone, skull crushed by a Pietran shield, the other fighting alongside his men. The Stilleans are breaking against the Pietra, and though they fight bravely, they stand atop their own countrymen's bodies to do so.

"Donil," Vincent says, turning to the Indiri to take control of the first commander's men, while he goes to the aid of the one still standing. But his friend is gone, no longer a Stillean but an Indiri who will see his people avenged.

CHAPTER 86

Witt

I RISE TO FACE THE INDIRI, DRAWING MY BLADE AS HE DOES the same. There are no words between us, only a lifetime's teaching of hate. And so we continue.

He comes at me with a practiced hand, one that I turn away with effort, striking his exposed side quickly with the flat of my fist, taking away his breath. I spin as he circles me, our blades speaking to each other with a song written in blood. We know how to kill and have both longed to see the other on the sharp edge of our sword. Yet as I lunge, I hear Ank's voice, a call rising above the chaos, a reminder of something I once knew.

There's a pause in this dance between the Indiri and me, the breath when I remember.

I've failed my people in so many ways, asked them to set aside swords for shepherding, brought the Feneen among them and called it wise, opened their throats with leaves for treachery when I have taken a wife myself, going against all they have known. I led them to a far shore, to be swept away by the sea.

And still they follow me, only because I am the Lithos, a boy who should be made of stone yet cries for his mother and small brothers in the night. I have given these people nothing, and shall take no more.

Boats are for the dead; the least I can do is leave them with the ground beneath their feet.

The Indiri strikes again, and I let my blade be knocked from my hand. He stops, questioning, when I lift my hands.

"I cannot kill you," I tell him.

"I do not feel the same," he says.

And runs me though.

CHAPTER 87

Dara

I KNOW BATTLE, KNOW DEATH, KNOW THE SMELLS OF FEAR and pain. Yet I have never known them like this, a cold blade borrowing my heat as it rests inside me, a slow death as I simply grow tired on the cold ground.

I turn my head, my cheek coming to rest against a rock. It is warm from my body like my marriage stone, still new to me, nestled in my belly. I feel it there and would tell Witt, but he is gone from my side.

Yet I hear his voice rising above all and my brother's as well. I hear Vincent too, far off but traveling to my ear, these boys grown to men alongside me. That I should hear them now is right, and I close my eyes, aware that new voices have joined them, a chorus of Indiri that swells from the ground.

Calling me.

CHAPTER 88

Donil

My Indiri blade punches through the Lithos's armor like a nail through timber. He is unarmed and emptying of life, yet smiling. I was born to kill this man, but find no end in it, only a deep confusion as he drops to his knees and says my sister's name. I step back, eyes locked with his.

So I do not see the Pietra who spears me through the side.

Another follows from the front, a well-trained soldier who finds the chink in my Stillean armor with the tip of his weapon. It has ended me, and I know it, backing away from the dying Lithos, my sword still embedded in his chest. I stumble to my sister to find her hand held out to mine. I fall by her side, our shoulders touching as the ground below us swells with the voices of our ancestors, answering us for all the times we have asked.

CHAPTER 89

———— ·⊶◯⊷· ————

Dara & Donil

A S WE WERE BORN TOGETHER, SO WE DIE.
We are given to the earth.

CHAPTER 90

——◦◦◯◦◦——

Vincent

VINCENT SPURS HIS HORSE, SLAYING PIETRA TO HIS LEE and stoneward with vicious swipes as he rides to Donil, screaming. His friend is twice run through, spears that know their work bristling from his body.

The Pietra who ended Donil meet their own deaths by Vincent's sword, quick work made even more deadly by his wrath. He would cut down even a Stillean who stood between him and the man he calls his brother.

"Donil!" Vincent screams for him, dismounting at a run and barreling into a Pietra whose bloodied arm hangs limp at his side, no weapon to be had. Vincent ducks beneath a clumsy blow from the soldier, then drives a dagger into the pit of his arm, leaving him to live or die as he will.

There are only the Indiri left for Vincent, this girl and boy who have been brother and sister to him, his life entwined with theirs as deftly as one of Dara's braids. He falls to his knees beside them, their names on his lips, rushes to put his hands on bodies already cooling.

But finds only dirt. For the Indiri have gone.

CHAPTER 91

·◦◦○◦◦·

Ank

IT BEGINS AS A TREMOR, THE SOLDIERS THAT SURROUND ME losing their footing as the swipe of a blade or the throw of a spear is adjusted, balance a new skill to be learned. The earth beneath everyone sighs, as if a great beast just below the surface is waking and now stretches, now shudders after a long sleep.

All around me arms about to deal a killing blow are stopped, men about to die at attackers' hands clutch each other to keep their feet. A tree to my stoneward falls drunkenly, knocking into another, and the very mountains behind what remains of the Pietran army shed stones, as if they would cast off a heavy coat.

Hadduk, wild-eyed, finds me. "Depths, man, what is happening?"

We hold on to each other as a fissure opens on the battlefield, men on either side running from its gaping maw, pulling one another back, regardless of whether they wear Stillean armor or Pietran.

"The Indiri have fallen," I tell Hadduk. "And so we have a common enemy—the very earth that we stand upon, though we will not stand for long."

A last great shudder knocks us, every man, down on the field, flattening each tree in sight and sending great boulders rolling from the mountains to gouge the very earth that sent them there. Beside me,

Hadduk pulls himself onto an elbow, surveying the field where all soldiers have become only frightened men, and a great silence has taken the place of sword upon shield.

"I know well enough what an enemy is," Hadduk says, spitting onto the ground. "I suppose it's time I learned how to make friends."

CHAPTER 92

———— ⋅⊙⊙⊙⋅ ————

Vincent

THEY GATHER IN A HASTILY ERECTED TENT: VINCENT, King of Stille; Ank of the Feneen; Hadduk the Mason; and Witt, the Lithos of the Pietra, Donil's weapon still in his chest. It is a deep wound and one that Vincent knows will be fatal as soon as the sword is removed. Yet somehow the Lithos found his feet before the ground ceased shaking and, with a weak voice that still carried an air of command, put an end to the fighting. Even as he dies, the Lithos has the attention of those around him, whatever country they call home.

"Vincent, King of Stille," the Lithos says. "I came to you today in peace, looking for nothing less. That it did not end so is no fault of mine, and not of yours either, but the vengeance of a woman who long harbored a wrath against me that was well earned, and better hidden."

He stops to draw breath, and Vincent hears the gurgle of blood deep inside welling forth.

"No fault lies with you," Vincent says quickly, to spare the Lithos the pain of speaking. "And though many have fallen, perhaps some peace may still be gained."

The Lithos smiles slowly, his eyes sliding shut. "You build boats, and I give you freely my people to work alongside you, that they may have their own place when it is time to sail."

"That time may have passed," Hadduk mutters to Vincent, as another small shudder passes through the earth, sending the torchbearers who light the tent into a carefully controlled tilt to keep their flames from the cloth.

"Not yet," Ank says quietly. "Too much has been lost, and there is little to be saved, yet we will see it done."

"Little," the Lithos says, eyes opening again. "Hadduk . . . see to it that the little ones who would train as Lithos have the choice to go by sea."

"Yes, my Lithos," the Mason says. "And who of them shall lead?"

"None," Witt says. "Let them be children." The Lithos locks eyes with Vincent, his will the only thing keeping him from dying. "Hadduk shall lead what remains of Pietra."

"I am not fit," Hadduk protests.

"No," Witt agrees. "But Nilana is."

A small laugh passes through the group, and Vincent crouches before Witt, sensing that he has not much longer.

"Is there anything else you would ask for your people? Say the word, and I will see it done. So much blood has spilled that the earth itself breaks beneath it. No harm shall come to any Pietra by my command, as long as I live."

Witt shakes his head, life leaving him. "Only that you make haste, for the sake of all. Do not bury the dead who lie here, for there is no time. Boats are for the dead, but yours will take them to new life. Go to it now. Do not look back."

Vincent reaches out, his hand brushing the hilt of Donil's blade. Witt nods to him, and Vincent jerks it free, Witt's blood leaving him along with a sigh of a life lived as it was called to, but never for itself.

And so passes the last Lithos of the Pietra.

CHAPTER 93

―∘⦾∘―

Vincent

VINCENT RIDES FOR HOME, THE REMNANT OF HIS ARMY traveling with him. They navigate a changed landscape, hills that previously stood now gone, new ones where they do not belong. The path they traveled is broken in places, blocked in others. One unfortunate Stillean climbed the trunk of a fallen Hadundun to glimpse the path ahead, only to lose his footing and fall through the low branches, cut to the bone in more places than could be counted. His blood pooled, spent for nothing, as the tree itself was past drinking.

There is little talk among them, their voices lost in horrors witnessed for the first time—some of them having killed and others having seen the killing. Vincent pushes them on, the camp not complaining when they do not stop for a meal on the first day and only for cold rations on the second. The earth continues to roll beneath them, like a stomach whose meal sits unsteady, but no more tremors come that drive people and animals alike to their knees.

A wretched cold night is spent among wet trees that hang limply but do not take lives. Vincent visits each fire in the Forest of Drennen, learning every face and speaking with each man in his army. Sleep does not come for him, and his horse is saddled before his men awake, cropping gently at grass and nickering to his rider, who leans against him for warmth in the low light of morning.

Stille is on the horizon when a rider approaches from the castle, grim faced. Vincent can think only that news of their losses and the death of the Indiri have preceded them, but the messenger brings his own ill words.

"Your mother, my king," he says, head low. "She wishes to see you straightaway."

Vincent finds Dissa in the great hall, a fire burning there, though the hearth is cracked through, more stones from the walls littering the shadows. A flat section of the ceiling has fallen, shattering the dining table and sending splinters the length of Vincent's arm to each end of the room.

"Mother?" he calls, when she does not turn at his footsteps.

"I have news, Vincent," she says calmly. "I would rather you hear it from my mouth than the wandering tongue of a sconcelighter or dairymaid."

The heart he had thought stopped on the battlefield accelerates with fear, and Vincent goes to Dissa's side. "Khosa? Is she well?"

His mother reaches for him, hand clasped in his. "After the earth moved, I went to her chambers to see to her safety and found her crouched against the wall, curled like an infant in its mother. She can barely speak, Vincent, so great is her pain."

He would go to his wife straightaway, her deception aside. Though she has caused him misery, he would not wish the same upon her, yet his mother's hand stops him.

"Dara?" she asks hopefully.

"No," Vincent says, his voice closing over the simple word. "Nor Donil."

Dissa's hands go to her temples, the loss of her adopted children a fresh wound to bear up under. But she has suffered much, and endured more.

"Go to her." She waves away Vincent. "Go to your wife."

He leaves too quickly to correct her.

CHAPTER 94

Khosa

KHOSA COULD ONLY WISH THAT A WALL STONE HAD STRUCK her in the temple when the earth shook, her pain was so great. To pass unaware of time and torture was what she would have asked, and it was too much. Since the quake, all of her spasms have left her body, traveling instead to her center, then rising to her head where they congregate in a sharp point of pain, as if one of Dissa's needles had found its way inside her skull and would force itself out. It does not crest or come at random as the dance did, but remains insistent, terrible, and inescapable.

When Dissa tried to pull her to her feet and toward the door, the pain showed her that there was something beyond torture—agony. Writhing and feral, Khosa had spit and clawed at Vincent's mother. The only relief that shaved down the misery to something bearable was to be found when she pressed herself against the wall of her room, her ear to the sea.

Her husband finds her there, past a place where tears can follow.

"Khosa," he says gently, approaching as if she were a cornered Tangata. "What is it, wife?"

The one word sends a fresh grief through her, eyes barely dried now pricked with new weeping.

"Vincent," she manages to say, pitching forward. He grabs her midfall, her pulsing head against his burnt face. She cries for the pain, both what she suffers and what she has caused, and because Khosa knows that for Vincent to come to her first means that Donil will never follow.

"Where are you hurt?" he asks, hand cupping her chin.

"It's in my head, Vincent," she says, resting her temple against their bedroom wall. "Every dance I've ever done waits there now, each step pressing on my skull."

"What can I do?"

Khosa shakes her head, both in denial that he can still care to help her and in the knowledge that it is futile to offer. "There is nothing. To go toward the sea brings some relief, but to move away . . ." She shudders, aware that to increase her suffering could easily bring madness. She rests against him for a moment, curling into the blanket he pulls from the bed to wrap around her.

"It's the land that calls me, Vincent," she says. "Whatever hope was still here . . ."

"I know," he finishes for her. "It left with the Indiri."

They hold each other as the sun sets, both of them aware it is the first time they have done so with no roil of Khosa's stomach or crawling of her skin, but neither hopeful enough to believe it is not the last.

CHAPTER 95

Vincent

"I won't leave Bessie, and that's all there is to it," Daisy says, chin jutting proudly for a moment before she remembers to add, "My king."

Vincent sighs, scratching the stubble of three suns that covers his cheeks, while he casts a leery eye upon the dairy cow Daisy stands beside, lead in hand. Bessie appears unimpressed with him, her cud of higher importance.

"Daisy," Vincent tries again, his patience wearing thin, "I cannot give space on a ship that could go to Stilleans to a cow."

"Why not, when the cow will make milk for the Stilleans?" she shoots back.

"Only if she is properly fed, which means taking along grain and hay—more space where people could be put."

"And what if they don't want to come?" she asks. "Winlan's boat will carry the Hygodeans and their goats. Surely if there's room for a whole village on one, I can put my cow on the ship meant to carry Stilleans."

It's not a bad argument, and he tells her he'll consider it—not adding that Bessie might be called upon as meat for Stilleans as well as milk if land isn't spotted before their stores run low.

Packing the ships has fallen to Dissa, her Scribes following her skirts like baby oderbirds with their mother. Lists have been made, provisions weighed against passengers—still too few, by far—and what can be moved to the beach taken there. One ship sits in its dock nearly finished, lacking only the deck. Sallin wanted to run a gangplank and load the lower decks, but Winlan warned that weighing it down before it found deeper waters was unwise. Small boats have been built, manned by oars, waiting to ferry provisions back and forth once the ship sails freely. Looking upon that makes Vincent think of the Lithos, and the fear he saw in him, that Vincent would abandon his word and leave the Pietran people as soon as his sails filled with wind.

Vincent looks in the direction of the Stone Shore, even the horizon there changed from the earth ripples that arrive each sun without fail. No Pietra have come, and time grows short. He closes his eyes against the sun and listens to the sounds of trees being made into timber, and timber into ships. If he must choose between leaving the Pietra behind and the sanity of his wife, he knows what he will do.

"Make haste," Vincent says, his words meant both for those who stand near to hear, and for those cannot.

CHAPTER 96

─◦◦◯◦◦─

Ank

THOUGH I NEVER LIVED THERE, I ALWAYS THOUGHT OF Stille as home, and it fills my heart when we crest the ridge to see it.

"Lost a spire," Hadduk says moodily when he reaches me.

"As have you of late," Nilana adds, from her harness on his back.

I ignore the pair, my eyes caught upon two ships at sea, sails bright against the water.

"Depths," Hadduk says, spotting them as well. "They've done it."

"And a third to join," Nilana says, tilting her head to the frame of a ship that rests in a dock, stones waiting to be pulled away from the mouth so that the tide may take it out to sea.

"Call the men," I tell Hadduk. "They should see what awaits, if they put their backs into the work Stille sets for them. I know they are not wainwrights or farmers, but they'll set their hands to both if they want to ever be soldiers again."

Hadduk sighs, closing his eyes against the truth. "What a world we live in."

"Yes," I agree, my eyes going to what trees remain standing and the Tangata huddled there among the high branches. "A dying one."

CHAPTER 97

⋯⋯⋯⋯

Vincent

A BOAT OVERTURNED TODAY, TAKING FLOUR TO THE Hyllenian ship," Vincent tells his wife, hand on one side of her face while she presses the other against the wall, her face a rictus of pain. She nods slightly, and he continues.

"We lost an oarsman," Vincent says, wishing he had not begun the tale. "And when he did not resurface, three more Stilleans asked Mother to take their names from the passenger list. I've lost five this week, added only two."

He scratches at the side of his face, where the last of his burns heals, though the skin there will be forever smooth and pink. Khosa reaches for him to offer comfort, though she grinds her teeth against the pain of her head.

"Oh, and one cow," he adds.

CHAPTER 98

Ank

T HAS FALLEN TO ME TO MONITOR THE SMALL BOATS AS THEY go out, carrying passengers and what few belongings are deemed necessary. Vincent has chosen poorly in setting me to this task. Perhaps purposely, I think, as a Stillean child passes by me, a housekitten tucked under her chin. She looks as if she'll take my eyes out if I tell her to leave it, and so I wave her on, whispering in her ear that she might at least tuck it under her cloak so that I appear to be doing my duty.

I earn a smile, and then the next problem slides under my nose, a Hyllenian shepherd whose trousers are lined with short staffs, his gait as awkward as any Feneen. I bid him a good day as he tries to sit down before the oarsmen push away. My own people line the shore, Silt Walkers wading in to their chests, welcoming the touch of water. The Stilleans watch them warily, and I decide that I will take Hadduk up on his offer to join the Pietra on the third ship. They, at least, know the value of my people.

Each sail snaps in the wind, white breakers wetting new wood as the bows sink closer to the waterline, each rowboat adding people and things—a cat here, a cane there—and still they will leave these shores with empty space on their decks.

My Feneen have known pain and rejection, death and suffering, the long looks of those who would not have them come near. Almost to the last, they have elected to go, only the oldest among us choosing to die on the land they've known rather than on water strange to them. Nilana gave me a dark look and a thorough tongue-lashing after our last council, letting me know in no uncertain terms that I am not old, and she'll drag me on board herself if she has to. I did not ask how she would do this with no arms and no legs, for I know she would find a way.

"What's this?" I ask a young Pietra, his face still hard and heavy with the Lithos training he will never finish.

"A piece of the Stone Shore, sir," he says, answering with a straight spine, his eye fixed on a point at the horizon. "I would take it with me."

"All right, then." I wave him on, allowing also the Hygodean who sneaks a braid of waterleaf rue long enough that it trails well past her cloak.

"I've a chair back home I'm rather fond of," Hadduk says, joining me. "Might I run and get it? The desk too?"

"As if you've written a line in your life," I say, waving on a Hyllenian girl who pushes a wheelbarrow full of pots.

"Fiverberry, coilweed, waterleaf rue, nilflower"—the Scribe attending the passenger line counts off her plants, pinching his nose at the last—"and rankflower."

"The king said these was necessary," the girl says, nerves getting the best of her as the Scribe runs his finger down the list of allowed possessions.

"They are," I say, waving her into the boat and signaling for the oarsmen to shove off before the Scribe has finished checking.

"I think . . ." His voice fades in thought as he runs his finger down a column. "A moment please, I think we may have reached the limit for nil—"

I take his quill and throw it into the sea, the feather sinking in the wake of the rowboat.

CHAPTER 99

Khosa

S HE CAN HEAR HER HUSBAND BUT MAKE OUT NO WORDS, the low drone of his voice familiar enough that she knows when he rejoices and—more likely—despairs. The practiced thud of hammers outside the window has continued whether the sun hangs in the sky or the moon, each one driving a nail through her skull as well as the hull of a ship.

Khosa feels as if there is nothing left of her teeth, that surely she has ground them to a fine powder that only coats her lips. Yet she presses her tongue against them, still there. The pounding work from outdoors has ceased, but she hardly notices, for the one inside her head continues. There is nothing left in her world but the bright point in her mind and the pressure of answering it, and if she cannot go to the sea soon, the wall she plasters herself against for comfort may wear her brains for decoration.

Finally she hears Vincent's voice, the only words she has heard in a while also being the only ones she wished for.

"Khosa," he says. "It is time."

CHAPTER 100

Vincent

VINCENT KNOWS WELL THE STRENGTH IN HIS WIFE, HAS held her against a dance and had the bruises to show for it. So when it is time to take her to the sea, both Merryl and Rook accompany him. It takes both of them to tear her away from the wall, the only way to reach the hall and head for the outdoors. Khosa fights, screaming in senseless agony, hands to her head, fingers digging bloody furrows into her skin. Vincent leads them, holding the chamber door open as they rush her toward the turn, where her lashing ceases, her screams now whimpers.

"Khosa," Vincent says, forehead against hers, her skin slick with sweat. "We're putting you in a rowboat to take you to a ship. Can you walk?"

She nods and they escort her down the corridor, one guard on each side of the queen, gloved hands on her elbows. Vincent leads them only to find that his wife's steps soon clip the back of his feet, though her legs could barely hold her moments ago. He turns to warn Merryl and Rook to keep a good grip on her, should a dance be taking hold, but finds instead that his Khosa's eyes are clear, her body under her control. She smiles, reaching for him, and he nods for Merryl to release her.

Khosa grabs his hand and breaks into a run, their feet kicking up sand and her hair streaming behind her as she runs for the boat, cracking her shin on the side as she jumps in. Vincent barely clears it himself in his haste to stop her, for Khosa is crawling to the fore of the boat, stopping just short of the water's edge.

"Row!" she screams at the oarsmen, hands in her hair again, fingers digging for the pain. Vincent himself grabs an oar as they push away from land, his back straining. He can feel Khosa against him, relaxing with every stroke.

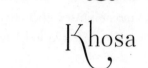

CHAPTER 101

Khosa

THE HYLLENIAN CREW AND STILLEAN PASSENGERS ARE on deck to welcome the queen of Stille, not the maddened thing that climbs the ladder from the rowboat and emerges to run past them, hair damp with sea spray flowing behind her. Khosa runs the length of the deck, knocking aside a young Hyllenian who sits coiling a rope, not pausing when Vincent yells for her and the deck sharpens into the bowsprit.

Each step lessens the pressure in her head, the needle boring its way from her skull pulling back with every stride. She lost her shoes in the sand of the beach, and as she edges her way onto the bowsprit, she can feel the wood on her bare feet and see the water below. It does not call to her as she feared, but the horizon has not lost its pull, and she slides toward it, arms out for balance as she answers.

"Khosa!"

She turns not at his voice, but the desperation she hears there, as if her pain has burrowed into him.

"I'm fine, Vincent," she manages to say, voice hoarse with disuse. The faces of everyone gathered to watch tell her they think otherwise, but Khosa is past caring. She eases herself to sit on the prow, legs dangling, the drop to the water far enough that she would regret it before she hit. Her husband edges toward her, though his feet are unsteady and his hands shaking.

"Stay back," she tells him, gently. "You have no reason to be out here."

"But I do," he insists, eyes on her. He slides his way toward her, carefully bringing himself to sit, their legs touching. "Winlan did build a cabin for us, you know," he says.

She laughs, for the first time in so long that it takes them both by surprise. Vincent's smile—something also unseen for a while— answers her, lips stretching the burnt side of his face.

"I can't." She shakes her head, an action that would have been unthinkable on land only moments before. "I must go toward it, or . . ."

"All right," Vincent says immediately, eyeing the bloodied tracks her fingernails have made in her temples, the bald spots of scalp where she tore her hair away. "I'll see if Winlan can build some sort of—"

"There will be no more delays on my account." Khosa cuts him off. "Vincent, we must go."

He searches her face and sees nothing but determination. "You can't very well sail lashed to the prow without everyone thinking you've lost your mind."

"And I can't take one step back toward Stille without them knowing for sure I have, because it will have left my skull," she shoots back at him.

Vincent sits, legs kicking alongside hers as those watching lose interest and begin to file back to their own beds. If they can be called that, Khosa thinks, remembering the braided hammocks hanging three high in the ship's belly.

Her hand finds her husband's, and she squeezes. "I have an idea."

CHAPTER 102

Ank

I DOUBT ANY QUEEN HAS EVER ARRIVED IN HER LAND HANGING from the front of a ship, but Khosa has said it must be, and so it will be. Pand and Unda have feet as sure as any of their Hygodean goats, and they skip back and forth across the bowsprit, eager to please and glad to help. Khosa's netting is hung before the sun is high, the woman who will be our compass resting easily for the first time in days, swayed into sleep by the rocking of the ship and a light breeze.

"She's fine, Vincent," I tell him, resting a hand on his shoulder as he peers over the railing. "What else is left to do?"

I look to our stoneward, where the Pietra and Feneen line their ship, Hadduk and Nilana among them. To our lee, the Hygodean ship that carries their village, though Winlan and his family have chosen to remain with the Stilleans. I can understand why, as shoulders brush together on both the others. Though ours carries the Hyllenians who survived the Pietran attack and all of Sawhen that chose to come, there is space enough for Unda to spin on the deck, her little skirts floating around her.

"What else?" Vincent asks, repeating my question. "The Scribes have brought all the histories aboard; the larder is well stocked, I'm assured. All the passengers are here, and . . ." He fades away, as if searching for one more thing to do.

"Vincent," I say, "it's time to go."

"Not yet," he says to me, headed for the ladder. I follow, helping him row. We reach the shore and head for the great hall, where Dissa and the Curator look over the last scroll left on shore.

"Mother," Vincent says, and Dissa looks up, a small line forming between her eyebrows. "Khosa is on board safely, the last of the guards as well."

"Very well," she says, going to him. Her arms close around his neck, and he leans into her shoulder. Only then do I realize.

"You're not coming," I say, disbelief ringing in my voice.

"No," she confirms. "The queen of Stille is on board her ship, and someone must remain for those who choose to stay."

"Mother," Vincent says weakly, pulling away from her, "there is room yet. Do not make me walk away from you."

"Vincent," Dissa replies calmly, palm against his burnt face, "the young and the bold will find their place in this new land. I am neither, and would only fade slowly."

He nods briskly, squeezes her once, and turns on his heel, not looking back to see if I follow.

"You may not be young," I say to her. "But you are bold, much and more so than any who stand on that deck."

"I am," Dissa agrees, her chin rising as she speaks to me. "And what will the people of Stille say as their king grows into manhood, his face never resembling mine? Better for it to be only a faded memory to them."

"I will shadow his steps and keep care of him as a brother should," I tell her.

Dissa sighs, eyes on Vincent's retreating back. "He has watched his father die, burned one mother, and abandoned another, all for the sake of a kingdom he never wanted to lead."

"He will be remembered among the best of the kings," I say.

"Yes," she says. "He certainly will."

CHAPTER 103

Vincent

THE SHIPS ARE UNANCHORED AS THE SUN RISES, A BREEZE filling the sails. The Stillean ship leads, Khosa pointing the way. Pand delicately balances on the prow and watches her, shouting directions to the rest of the Hygodean crew. The other two ships follow in their course, each one lined with nervous passengers, some of them already retching into the sea.

Vincent looks to Stille, its once strong walls now crumbled, pristine beaches littered with burnt remnants of a failed ship and deserted belongings for which there was no room on the rowboats. Some who chose to stay have come to stand on the sand, silver hair and bald heads shining in the morning sun. High on the wall, a flash catches his eye and he sees his mother, the crown of Stille once more perched on her head.

She raises a hand to him, and he does so in return, putting it down only when he can no longer see her through his tears.

CHAPTER 104

The Forest of Drennen

AN OLD WOMAN LIES DOWN, HER SPECKLED SKIN BLENDING with the ground. The trees have all fallen, their roots dried and dead. A Tangata, ancient skin lined with new scars torn by Hadundun leaves, curls next to her, as they give the last of their body heat to each other.

Deep in the Forest of Drennen, the last Indiri dies.

CHAPTER 105

The Stone Shore

THE CLIFFS GO FIRST, SHEARING AWAY FROM THE EARTH as if cut by a blade, the sea finally swallowing what it has lapped at for time out of mind. Lure lines fall like a web in a strong wind, and Witt's castle crumbles as if it were made of sand. A crevasse opens, salt water flowing into it and soaking Hadundun roots filled with old blood. The earth tears like paper all the way to the Plains of Dunkai, which shudder and sink. The fingers of water go deeper, until they have covered all.

CHAPTER 106

—◦◦◯◦◦—

Stille

DISSA IS IN THE GREAT HALL WHEN THE CASTLE COLLAPSES, her crown buried in her skull for eternity by the crash of a ceiling tile. Madda's turret falls, and the scent of nilflower fills the air for a moment, until all smells of salt.

CHAPTER 107

K HOSA RESTS IN HER HAMMOCK, THE SPRAY OF THE SEA
coating her skin, for once a comfort and not a curse. The sun
shines, and she smiles up at Pand as he passes her a handful
of bread.

"Feeling well this morning?" he asks.

"I am," she says, the words ringing true. Four suns of good sailing
have brought her much relief. Though the pain is still present, it is now
only an insistent pressure that tells her which way to point the ship.
Her early-light illness even seems calmer under the sway of the sea,
something that most of the other Stilleans cannot claim. The rocking
of the water has sent most of them to their hammocks with buckets, or
to hang over the railing.

The Pietran ship has fared no better, and Khosa has a fine view of
its side streaked with whatever food its passengers have lost, much to
the amusement of the Hygodeans who prowl their ship with the confidence of Tangata in treetops.

"Khosa," calls a small voice from the deck, and she lifts her head
to see Unda, dress billowing around her small ankles. "Will you come
inside for the storm?"

"Storm?" she asks, and Unda points to the horizon where a gray line can be seen. The bread Pand is holding falls from his hand to land on Khosa's face. She brushes it away, and a type of bird she's never seen before swoops to snatch it from the air before it lands in the sea.

"That's not a storm, sister," Pand says. "That's land."

CHAPTER 108

Vincent

THE CRY GOES UP, BRINGING EVERYONE TO THE DECK and hope to their faces. All three ships are full of people, hands lining the railing as they lean into one another for a better look as the sun climbs higher.

Vincent never doubted his wife and her conviction that the dance would lead them here, but to see it with his own eyes brings a relief that fills his throat, bringing tears. Ank claps a hand on his shoulder, squeezing.

"You've done it, Vincent," he says. "You've brought your people to safety."

"Not quite yet," Winlan warns. "We'll need to send a scouting party ahead, make sure there is nothing that would take a child for its meal."

"Or a large man," Ank adds. "We don't know what might call this place home."

"Or who," Winlan agrees, eyeing the shore for signs of life.

Suddenly Unda screams Khosa's name, and Vincent hears a splash.

CHAPTER 109

Khosa

K HOSA HITS THE WATER, HER DRESS BILLOWING AROUND her head. Yet she feels no fear, for the sea exists not to pull her under but to push her forward, where she is being led. The land calls her and she goes, the tide carrying her to the shore where she emerges, dripping. She gets to her feet, the pull not receding.

Khosa is drawn, sprinting into the woods, strange trees slapping against her arms and marking her face, her limbs awkward with the roll of the sea now that they are on land. She tumbles to her knees, the pain once again a piercing, clawing thing that will find its way out.

She screams, as it feels like something inside of her breaks, and she retches. A tide of seawater flows from her nose and mouth, her very eyes leak brine. It streaks from her ears, staining her hair as the last Given loses what has passed to her from Medalli, one of the Three Sisters. It leaves her body, taking with it the pain, the tense set of her muscles as she prepares to fight her dance at any given moment. It leaves her, flowing into the ground that it was meant to return to.

Khosa falls over, a complete calm taking her. Never in her life as she known such stillness, and she revels in it, her own heart slowing with the release, the need to move finally gone. And then, as she would give herself over to the feeling, deep in her womb, she feels a tiny kick.

She cries out, this time for joy, wrapping her arms around her belly. Tears flow, cleaning the last of her curse from her face just as a foot settles next to her.

Khosa looks up, gasping as the sun cuts into her vision. "Dara?"

"No," the Indiri woman says, bending low to help Khosa to her feet. "I am Oppwa, daughter of Yur."

Khosa wipes her hand on her skirts as Vincent breaks through the trees to find her, losing his feet from underneath him at the sight of the Indiri.

"I am Khosa, daughter of Sona," she says, and Oppwa's brow furrows.

"I do not know your mother."

"You wouldn't," Vincent says, wiping dirt from his arms as he extends his hand. "We come from Stille."

"Stille," Oppwa repeats, a smile spreading. "Finally."

CHAPTER 110

◦⦿◦

Ank

THE BEACH IS LITTERED WITH PIETRA AND STILLEAN, Feneen and Hygodean, and the descendants of Harta, who found this place long ago, along with the Indiri who traveled with him. From my perch I cannot tell who is who, all of them only people at this height.

At high tide I watched three Tangata ride in, clinging to a stripped log. They came on land, shook seawater from their coats, and stalked off, unconcerned. I should have called for Hadduk, had one of his spada soldiers take them down before they can make many and more, the children of the people that stand on the beach below frightened by tales of cats in the night.

Yet I cannot, and I watch as the tide erases their prints, and wish them safety. An oderbird flew in shortly after, long neck wobbly in exhaustion, a few more coming in its wake. I uncork the bottle in my pocket, releasing the ninpops I had caught on the beach before abandoning Stille.

It will be different.

But this will be home.

Epilogue

KHOSA SITS ON THE BEACH, HER BELLY HEAVY WITH child, the tip of a quill on her tongue. The scroll she labors over is unrolled at her feet, an emerging map of her home being cast in dark lines of her making.

"Mother!" The small voice brings her to her feet in alarm, but her face lights when she sees her small son, speckled and sure-footed, picking his way through the rocks to her side.

"What is it, Darrill?"

"I've found a . . . a . . ."

"Breathe," she reminds him, laughing at the sight of his freckles bunched together in confusion as he tries to find the word.

"It's a . . . Tangata cat."

"A Tangata? Surely not." Khosa pulls her son to her skirts and a dagger from the folds of her dress.

"It is," he insists. "I asked my ancestors, and that's what Da said."

"He would know," Khosa says grimly, pulling their belongings into a bundle.

"That's what he called it," Darrill goes on. "Aunt Dara said it's a filthy bit of blood and fluff, made to rot and piss on."

Khosa eyes her son over the scroll in her arms. "What other words have you learned from your Aunt Dara?"

Darrill's eyes go wide. "We should be getting back, I suppose."

"Changing the subject," Khosa notes. "That you learned from Ank."

"He's a wise man," Darrill says, taking her hand as they walk along the shore. "Though I think not as wise as the Burnt King, who is also good and brave."

Khosa smiles down at Darrill, pleased that Vincent has made such an impression on her son. "He is," she agrees. "That is why I married him."

The sun is setting as they get close to the village, a few lines of smoke rising from the homes of those who want to take the edge off the newly chilled evenings.

"When can we go into the sea, Mother?" Darrill asks, swinging Khosa's arm along with his.

"Once I've brought your little sister or brother into this world," she promises, hand rounding her belly. "And once I've learned to swim, so that I may show you."

Darrill stops his mother, closing his eyes in the last light of dusk. His lips move as he soars through his ancestors' memories, Khosa's quick mind combined with Donil's blood to give him the ability to delve deeply into his ancestors in the breath of a moment. His eyes open, bright as his hair against the darkness of his spots.

"You don't need to show me, Mother. I already know how."

Khosa leans into him, her forehead against his.

"Then, my son, you shall teach me."

ACKNOWLEDGMENTS

This book was the most difficult I've written, by far. With a large supporting cast and deeply structured world, I had a reference sheet beside me at all times for people, places, plants, and animals—to say nothing of the many twisting motivations and changing emotional landscapes.

Many thanks to my editor, Ari Lewin, for helping make sure that nothing and no one slipped through any cracks. As always, thanks is due to my agent, Adriann Ranta Zurhellen, who rolls rather amicably with whatever I throw at her next, even if it does sometimes come with something resembling a glossary attached.

Critique partners are priceless in my world, and for this one I've got to thank the indefatigable R. C. Lewis, who turns around even the most unwieldy manuscripts almost overnight, with excellent insight.

Lastly, humblest thanks to my friends and family, who fend off all the questions about what really goes on inside my head. They don't have a better idea than anyone else, but they're much more game about putting up with it.